Cards of Power

Helen Lawrence

Helen Lawrence—Bruce Mines, ON
Paperback ISBN: 978-1-7381274-1-2
eBook ISBN: 978-1-7381274-0-5
Library of Congress Control Number: 2023919759
Title: *Cards of Power*
Author: Helen Lawrence
Digital distribution | 2023
Paperback | 2023

Dedication

To my eighth-grade English teacher, Mrs. Moss, who told me "Never stop writing!"

Acknowledgements

First, I thank God for giving me my ability to write and my passion for it, and for blessing me with a supportive family. To my parents and siblings, thanks for always letting me talk about my book ideas and plot points, for reading my writing, and for letting my projects take up so much of my brain space. To my Dad for letting me randomly ask specific questions that I don't want to research (and for just somehow knowing the answers). To my Mom, thanks for letting me ask grammar questions, and for all the advice you've given me over the years to improve my writing. To my Grandpa, for providing writing opportunities with him, and for all the chats about writing (whether mine or his). To Michelle, who copyedited my book, made that process so easy, and made the book that much better. And all of my grandparents, aunts, uncles, and cousins- any mention of wanting to be an author or my writing, was always met with encouragement. To my amazing friends for being so supportive and encouraging, and letting me talk about my ideas (a lot), thank you SO MUCH! Nora, Elizabeth, Erin, Malia, Daniela, Temille, Kayla, Armita, John, and Jersey, you're all the best! To those who read the book in the early stages, thank you, and I'm sorry. It's much better now. To Pastor Adrian, who said the phrase "holding all the cards of power" in a sermon. I thought it would make a great book title and jotted it down in the margins of my sermon notes. To my middle and high school English teachers, for their amazing teaching. And to anyone who ever responded positively when I told them I wanted to be an author. Thanks!

Chapter One

Layla's Wednesday started like any other. She woke up to a text from Karsyn that read: *ITS WEDNESDAY MY DUDES!!* It all went downhill from there.

Once she read the text, Layla took the required minutes to contemplate how Karsyn did this *every* Wednesday without fail, and nothing Layla said or did ever convinced him to stop. It would be time to start seriously considering Operation Kill Wednesday if she didn't secretly find it so funny. Not that she'd ever tell Karsyn that. This contemplation time ended as it always did: Layla replying with her favourite emoji, the one she'd dubbed "the vaguely disapproving frowny face."

Finished, she headed out into the hallway and meandered down to the kitchen. All was quiet. Strange. Her mom *never* slept in.

A sticky note on the fridge caught her eye.

Don't worry! I'm gone for groceries. Text me if you need anything. I hope to be back before lunch, but there are a few leftovers in the fridge if you get hungry. Karsyn, don't forget that— At that point, Layla stopped reading. It was amazing how many words her mom could fit on a single sticky note.

The pickings for breakfast were scarce, so Layla semi-enjoyed a bowl of raisin bran for breakfast. That cereal was in plentiful supply since only her mom ate it regularly. She was just reaching the end when—

"I have work!" she exclaimed around a mouthful of cereal.

Layla rushed through the rest of the raisin bran, dropped the bowl and spoon in the sink, and sprinted for her room. After a whirlwind of changing that did nothing to improve the state of her room, she grabbed her phone and ran back into the hall. She almost ran into Karsyn. He was standing just outside her room, holding a container of food for some reason.

"Karsyn! What're you doing?" She rushed past him.

"Layla, could you..."

She entered the kitchen and yanked open the fridge. Nothing caught her eye.

"I'll buy lunch," she decided, closing the door.

She turned, and there was Karsyn.

He shook his dark hair out of his eyes. "I thought you said you didn't work—"

"I swapped with Chloe. She's got a thing today."

Layla sidestepped Karsyn and went to leave, but he shouted, "Wait!"

"What? I'm gonna be late!"

His ears turned red, and he held out the container. "Can you microwave this for me? Mom's not home."

"Karsyn, c'mon, can't you...?"

His face was pleading.

"Fine."

Layla took the container and removed the lid. She assessed its contents, then threw it into the microwave for one minute and thirty seconds.

"That'll do it!" she shouted over her shoulder, leaving the kitchen. One day Karsyn was going to have to learn to not be afraid of the microwave.

"You're not going to wait?" He scrambled out after her.

"Honestly, Karsyn," Layla grunted, struggling with her shoes. Note to self: *Always* undo the laces, no matter how much of a rush you're in. "It'll be done heating up before I have a chance to leave the house."

He cast a glance at the kitchen, then edged further into the entryway. The microwave timer beeped.

"See?" Layla grabbed her purse, not bothering to check if her paycheque was inside. "I can make it for ten," she muttered. Then she was out the door.

Wait.

Mom had taken the car. No!

Layla broke into the fastest speed walk she could muster. How long did it normally take to get to the bus stop? Only five minutes, but the bus was due in two. She broke into a jog-walk, worried if she went too fast, she'd sweat in the uniform. And red was not a great colour for that sort of thing.

The bus was a few minutes behind schedule, thank goodness. She wouldn't have made it otherwise. Of course, this also meant she'd be even later to work.

When the bus arrived, Layla raced on. She tapped her card, then plunked down on a seat, focusing on breathing steadily to get her heart rate back to normal. Now that she had a chance, she retrieved her emergency claw clip from her purse and used it to put her hair up. A few wavy red strands fell down and framed her face, which was unintentional but nice.

Her phone pinged. It was a text from Chloe: *Youre good*

Typical Chloe clarity. Layla's heart sank.

(Layla) *What are you saying?*

(Chloe) *It was cancelled. I'm at work*

(Layla) *And you thought texting me only three minutes before I'm supposed to be there was a good idea?!*

(Chloe) *Youre not here*

Layla tugged at her left earring. No point in getting angry at Chloe. Give it a few minutes, and she might text saying "it" was back on and could Layla please still come in. "It" was probably a date.

"This is the last time I offer to cover for you," Layla muttered.

For the remainder of her time on the bus, she tried and failed to come up with a positive spin on the day's twists. The best she got was that she could now deposit the cheque, which was in her purse. But that didn't quite make up for the major adrenaline spike.

Layla got off at the bank. She'd deposit her cheque, get a doughnut or something at Aroma Mocha (to make up for breakfast), and call it a day.

There was a line for the ATM. Of course.

"I think I've reached my bad-luck quota for the day," she muttered, joining the line.

When she was second in line, honest-to-goodness robbers burst through the doors, waving their guns. So much for the day improving.

"Everybody back!" one of them shouted. He was wearing a black bandana around his neck but didn't have it up to cover his mouth or nose.

What's the point? Layla wondered.

"Into the main lobby," he ordered.

The five people in the ATM line pressed back. The three robbers followed.

Bang! One of them shot out a window.

"Everybody quiet!" roared the same guy.

A few people shrieked. One guy who had just exited a washroom swerved and went back in.

The bandana guy strode up to the till, probably to make the usual demand of money or death. As he walked, Layla noticed that his pant leg had shifted up, revealing a few centimetres of his ankle. She could just make out a dark spot, a tattoo.

She barely stifled her gasp. It was a Club symbol! One hundred percent. Okay, from this distance it was too far to tell exactly what the tattoo was, but what else would it be? These robbers were criminals, and most Clubs got tattoos in that exact spot. But that was hardly common knowledge.

Layla averted her eyes. If she met any of their gazes now, she feared they'd know she knew. And then who knows what they'd do? It was common knowledge that the Clubs were the most violent of the three Suits. She tried to take some steadying, deep breaths, but it only brought attention to the fact that she had started to tremble.

Her willpower failed, and she glanced over at the other two Clubs. They were pointing their guns at random and grinning at how people whimpered and flinched. Bandana man was being handed some money.

All in all, things were going smoothly. No violence yet. Hopefully, they would be on their way soon. *Are robberies actually way less dramatic than movies make them seem?* Layla wondered.

Then someone seized her arm. She instinctively flinched away, but the grip was tight. It was a Club, who used her gun to brush stray hair away from her face, then pointed it at Layla.

"I wouldn't struggle," she warned.

Layla opened her mouth, then closed it. Her heart felt like it was going to burst out of her chest. Her mind whirled with fears of what could happen next.

"Hey, one of you come and help me with this," the bandana guy shouted. "What're you doing with her?"

"We're taking her with us. Never mind the extra money."

"Not what we're here to do."

The third Club, who still hadn't said anything, was at the counter grabbing the rest of the money.

"You don't understand," the girl said. "This is a *golden* opportunity. Bait for the Ace of Spades."

All Layla's breath left her in a whoosh. They were going to use her as bait? For a criminal? One of the biggest criminals in the whole city of Toronto, in fact! Why would she be a good—unless...

No. No way. Not a possibility.

The other Clubs reached them, each ladened down with money.

"Let's just take her and get out of here before the cops come," the girl said.

Bandana guy took a hard look at Layla. His eyes widened, then he grinned. "Let's do it!"

"I'm not going anywhere," Layla managed to say.

"Oh, of course you're not," the girl said.

Layla felt something stab her arm. It was as if ten bees stung her in the same spot. She wanted to scream, but her throat didn't work. Everything went numb and tingly. Then she blacked out.

Chapter Two

“**I**f it isn’t my favourite janitor!” a loud, cheery voice called out.

Daniel’s head shot up and smacked into the underside of his desk.

“Ow!”

Cody’s face appeared as he leaned over the desk. “Dani, I ask this with much concern. What are you doing down there?”

Cody. Of course it was. No doubt Daniel would have a bruise on his head for several days, but he couldn’t be mad. Not at Cody.

“My computer decided it didn’t want to function, so I’m unplugging it and replugging it,” he said. “From the power source, not the charger.” His computer was so old the system needed a shock every now and then to shake the cobwebs off.

“Ah.” Cody nodded knowingly. “The next step after turning it off and on again. Wise.”

Daniel got off the floor and sat in his chair. He gingerly ran his hand over the place he’d hit his head. Yep, bruising already.

Cody grabbed the chair from the unoccupied desk, sat down on it, then rolled over to Daniel’s desk. Daniel’s officemate glared at Cody as he turned his hearing aids down.

“What’re you doing here?” Daniel asked.

“Visiting my favourite janitor,” Cody said as if it was obvious.

Daniel frowned. “I haven’t been a janitor for the GDRS in over a year.”

“Doesn’t matter, you were still my favourite,” Cody said with a grin. “Also, what’s with the long acronym? An even longer name too—Government Dedicated to the Removal of Suits? Why couldn’t they just name it ‘Bye Bye Suits’?”

“There are so many problems with that name.”

Cody shrugged, unbothered.

Cody was the happiest man Daniel knew. Which might have been annoying, but given that Daniel was prone to pessimism, it balanced out well. In fact, a lot of things about Cody were opposite to Daniel. His brown hair, constant spring in his step, and his below-average height. Not that it hindered him in terms of presence; his personality did all the work there.

Daniel checked his watch. "It's too early for you to just be visiting. What's your real purpose?"

Cody leaned forward, placing his hands on Daniel's desk. They were wrapped around a mug that read: a clean desk is the sign of a dirty desk drawer. Cody's desk was never clean.

"You're right. It's something serious." All the mirth vanished from Cody's face with startling abruptness.

Daniel's heart plummeted. Only once before had he seen Cody look so serious.

"Do you think that poutine is a salad?" Cody asked. He broke back into his signature grin.

Daniel's bones turned to water, and he slid down in his chair, almost falling off. "Cody!" he shouted. "What was that for?"

Cody had to set his mug down on the table; he was laughing too hard to hold it. "I got you!"

Daniel stared up at the ceiling. It was a wonder Cody hadn't given him any grey hairs already. Although, it would be hard to tell, given that his hair was light red. Grey hairs could probably camp out on his head for weeks without him noticing.

"In what universe would poutine *ever* be considered a salad?" Daniel asked.

"You say that now, but once I give you all the facts—"

"What's going on?" asked a voice from the doorway.

Daniel jumped and stuck his head to the side so he could look past Cody. Harley was standing in the doorway, looking most displeased. She had this annoying habit of walking silently and catching people off guard. Once Daniel had suggested she wear high heels, instead of her astoundingly unprofessional tennis shoes. If looks could kill, he would have died on the spot.

Cody jumped up. "Harley!" Though his greeting was cheerful, Daniel detected a hint of nervousness in his voice. Cody held his hand out for a high-five.

Harley ignored it, as usual.

"That conversation sounded very off-topic," she said.

"I was just getting to that; I promise!" Cody exclaimed.

That? There was more than just a whim behind Cody's visit?

"Getting to what?" Daniel asked.

Rolling her grey eyes, Harley said to him, "Mr. Greer needs to speak with you."

"The head of the Protection Unit?"

"It's called the Protection Sub-Unit," Harley corrected.

"Only when we're using acronyms," Cody muttered.

Daniel pressed his lips together so he wouldn't laugh. He was pretty sure Harley disapproved of laughter. And cheerfulness in general.

"But Mr. Greer is head of the Civilian Protection Unit now, and he needs to speak with you." Harley turned to glare at Cody. "You promised you would be quick and to the point!"

"I didn't think it was that serious," Cody protested.

"You never do," Harley huffed. She spun around and left.

"Why'd you give me the message, then?" Cody shouted after her. "Huh? You know what I'm like!"

Daniel scrambled to stand. He grabbed his phone off the desk and didn't have to do anything with his computer, as it hadn't turned back on yet.

"Don't worry, Cody. It can't be that bad," Daniel said as he hurried after Harley.

Cody followed, and they made sure to give her plenty of space in front of them.

"What *does* Mr. Greer want with me?" Daniel asked Cody in an undertone. "I've talked to him a few times when I was a janitor, sure, but nothing extraordinary."

Cody shrugged. "I don't know. I was just sent to take you to him. I'm sorry in advance, for whatever this is. But really, no one should trust me for time-sensitive missions."

That was probably the truest thing Cody had ever said.

Daniel shrugged. "It's fine." He couldn't bring himself to be worried in the slightest. Because, well, if it really *was* urgent, they really wouldn't have sent Cody, who had a tendency to have full conversations with everyone he passed. "We'll chat, I'll be back in my office before noon, and we'll all forget about it."

"I wouldn't count on it," Harley called over her shoulder, making them both jump.

"She has the ears of a bat," Cody whispered in Daniel's ear.

They reached the elevator and entered. The ride up was as short as it was awkward. Cody was uncharacteristically quiet, and Daniel couldn't think of anything noteworthy to say. He didn't dare try to engage Harley in small talk. He'd tried once before, and he was still cringing at how it'd gone.

They got out on the main floor. Besides the security guard sitting at the front desk, there was only one person in the lobby, which wasn't typical. It was a slightly older gentleman, whom Daniel was able to recognize as Mr. Greer. He'd always admired Mr. Greer, who was always dressed professionally, not a grey hair out of place, and was always composed. Impeccable posture, too.

But outside, there was quite a crowd. One PSU car and two CPU cars. Several agents and police officers stood around, talking to each other or on their walkie-talkies.

Daniel and Cody stopped short at the sight.

"For the record, those were *not* there when I came," Cody said.

When Mr. Greer spotted them, he walked over. Harley met him halfway, but Cody and Daniel were too stunned to move. So Mr. Greer walked the extra steps.

"Daniel, I have some bad news," Mr. Greer said.

With all the commotion outside, Daniel thought he'd have been more shocked if it *wasn't* bad news.

Mr. Greer continued, "Your cousin Layla has been taken. I'm giving you the option of coming with us, but I'm afraid I must insist you decide quickly."

"What..." Daniel blinked, and his head spun. Of all the things he had been expecting and preparing himself for, this was not one of them. Layla had been...taken? Was Mr. Greer trying to avoid saying "kidnapped"?

"Who?" he asked.

"We're guessing the Clubs," Mr. Greer answered. "Who else? Kidnapping isn't the Diamonds' style; we know that much about them. And the Spades, well...we don't think they would take her either. I'm afraid that's all the information I have at the moment. Are you coming?"

"What's your advice?"

"I wouldn't be offering this if I didn't think you should come."

Harley scoffed.

"Good," Daniel said, "Because, after that intro, there's no way I would stay behind."

He wasn't a trained agent, and he had no idea what he could possibly contribute. But he couldn't stay still knowing Layla was in danger.

Mr. Greer nodded. "Then let's be off."

They headed out; Daniel trailing slightly behind. His mind was at war with itself, trying both to convince himself that Layla wasn't in any danger, that she would be fine, and to prepare for the worst. The Clubs were the worst, most violent Suit. He had to be ready for anything.

Just before exiting through the doors, he remembered Cody. He turned around. Cody was standing in the same spot, his face betraying worry and guilt.

Though he usually enjoyed his friend's carefree nature, Daniel was now trying not to resent it. What if those moments of carelessness made all the difference? Daniel squashed down his rising anger and waved goodbye to Cody.

A bit of the worry washed away, replaced by relief. Cody waved back.

Before his face could betray him, Daniel turned and walked outside.

"It's a bank," Daniel said, peering out the windows. A tiny RBC in a little strip mall in the suburbs of Toronto.

"Astute observation," Harley said with an eye roll.

"They can't possibly be holding Layla here." Daniel followed Mr. Greer out and onto the sidewalk.

"This is where she was taken," Mr. Greer said. "We're here to interview witnesses and watch video evidence. We don't yet know where Layla was actually taken."

Daniel stopped walking. His cheeks burned red. *Stupid,* he thought. *Of course, we don't know yet. And if she can't be here, clearly there must be another reason! Now you look stupid.*

Mr. Greer entered the bank. Harley followed, her lips pressed together. Daniel assumed she was trying to hold back a smile at his rookie blunder.

He squared his shoulders. He would not make that mistake again! He would be the perfect example of intelligence and professionalism.

And maybe, said a tiny voice in his head, *if you don't mess up again, you'll get hired to be a part of the GDRS.*

A dream he'd had since he was young but never thought he'd actually get to achieve. With that resolve in mind, he walked into the bank.

An agent was waiting by the door. "ID, please," she said.

Daniel still had his job ID but doubted that would be accepted. "I don't have any ID," he admitted.

The agent raised an eyebrow.

"I'm Daniel Zakkar, cousin of the girl taken, and here by personal invitation of Mr. Greer. You can ask him, Harley, or any other agent that was with them when I was picked up."

"Indeed." She gestured to the bank and took a step back.

"Thank you."

Daniel looked around. There were four tellers, all talking to the police. The floor was tiled, the lights were too bright, and many people were standing in little clusters. To the right, Daniel could see a few offices between people. They looked unoccupied at the moment.

He located Mr. Greer and joined him and Harley, who were talking to a distraught lady.

"They came out of nowhere." She had tears in her eyes and was dabbing at them frequently with a tissue. "Guns blazing, and the like. The young girl, she tried to rush out of the exit. We all did. But there they were, pushing us back in." She stopped to blow her nose.

"What followed?" asked Harley. "Specifically concerning the young girl."

This brought on a fresh wave of sobbing, so heavy she couldn't get any words out.

"Ma'am, calm yourself," Mr. Greer said, not unkindly.

The lady put her tissue into her purse and brought out a fresh one. "I'm sorry! It's just so upsetting."

"Very." The word was out of Daniel's mouth before he realized he was saying it. And a sarcastic undertone, too. That was no good.

They all looked at him.

He hadn't meant to speak. But he had, so it was no use wasting an opportunity.

"Any robbery would be upsetting to witness, let alone be involved in," Daniel said. "But when paired with—"

"It was dreadful!" she interrupted. "They forced us back in while the others demanded the money. They looked at that poor young girl and decided she'd be a good hostage, I guess. Oh, it's too horrible!" She buried her face in her tissue.

"That young girl is my cousin," Daniel said, trying to balance worry with professionalism. And probably failing. "We need to find her. Please, is there anything else you can tell us?"

"Oh, of course, young man! I'm so sorry! Well...after that, they grabbed her. And left."

"Anything else?" Harley asked after a pause where they all seemed to be waiting for her to continue.

"No." She shook her head.

"Thank you," Mr. Greer said. "You may go home now, Ma'am."

"Thank you, sir!" She looked at Daniel. "I hope you find your cousin, young man."

Daniel nodded.

She walked away, still wiping her eyes.

"Now we know it was the Clubs," Mr. Greer said.

"Are you so confident that we can rule out the Diamonds?" Harley asked.

Daniel frowned. How could Harley be allowed to ask such a question to someone who outranked her so highly?

Mr. Greer didn't seem the least perturbed when he answered, "We're only confident that the Diamonds exist because of Ottawa. Otherwise, they seem to do nothing. We have never heard of them robbing anything."

"They wouldn't go about it so clumsily either," Daniel added, again without thinking.

Harley frowned. "What do you mean?"

Daniel froze. He needed to remember that he was in the presence of people who actually knew what they were talking about now. This wasn't lunchroom gossip among people who only received news about the Suits from the television.

Cautiously, he said, "Well, all the evidence from Ottawa points to the Diamonds mainly dealing in online transactions, hacking, blackmail, and the like. I think if they wanted to rob a bank, they could have done so online. Besides, rushing in here with guns and seemingly no plans seems rather cliché and old-fashioned. I think if all the Diamonds were to do it in person, it would have been streamlined and efficient." There was a pause. They were both just staring at him, so he added hastily, "Of course, those are just my thoughts. I'm not official or anything...I could be wrong."

"No," Mr. Greer said. "It is an excellent hypothesis."

Daniel couldn't believe it. The head of the Civilian Protection Unit thought *he* had given an excellent hypothesis? All Daniel knew came from dusting old files.

A bald agent walked over to them before Mr. Greer could elaborate. "Mr. Greer, only one other man was in the ATM line when it happened," he said. "He's just over here if you wish to question him."

"Yes, excellent, thank you."

The agent led them a few paces over to where a solitary man was standing, playing on his phone.

"Excuse us," Mr. Greer said.

The man looked up. "They told me you'd wanna talk," he said and pocketed his phone. He crossed his arms. "Ask away."

"I understand you were in the ATM line when this happened?" Mr. Greer said.

"Nope," he replied. "Wasn't in line. I was in the middle of using the ATM."

"Tell us all you recall," Mr. Greer said.

"Sure." The man shrugged. "Didn't notice when they came in, only when the screams started. Then another one ushered us into the lobby with the others." He frowned. "Didn't get to complete my transaction, and my card's still in the machine."

Irrelevant, Daniel wanted to say.

"We'll make sure you get your card back," Mr. Greer said. "Continue."

"Two went to grab the money; they were yelling at the bank people. The other decided to grab that girl instead. Suspicious that. Seems like they recognized her."

Daniel's pulse skyrocketed. He asked, "Recognized? What do you mean?"

The man gave him an unimpressed look. "I mean they recognized her. The one took a hard look at her and shouted at the others, something about forgetting the money and taking her instead. The dude at the counter was like, nah, that's not why we're here. She said something about bait for an ace."

Daniel felt like he'd been punched in the gut. "The Ace of Spades?" he said, his voice hoarse.

"Yeah, that was it. They had already grabbed some money, so they—"

Daniel couldn't bear to listen anymore. He walked over to the bank window and leaned his arm against the glass, staring out into the street. If his brain were making any sound right now, it'd be the static of an empty TV channel.

Mr. Greer joined him moments later.

Daniel stood up straight. "I was just hoping she was selected at random," he admitted. "A stupid hope, maybe. But they *recognized* her. They took her on purpose, above getting all the money they could. If even the lower Clubs know her face, then it was only a matter of time before they used her as bait. This whole time, my family hasn't been safe."

Mr. Greer nodded thoughtfully. "Why do you say 'lower Clubs'?"

Daniel's eyes flashed.

"Don't mistake me. I am concerned about your cousin's—and your family's—welfare. Everyone who knew about your situation hoped that your cousin's unfortunate actions would not affect the rest of your family. But why do you say lower Clubs?"

Great, more explaining to someone who probably knew ten times what Daniel knew. But then he reminded himself of the chance, slim though it was, to enter the GDRS. He had to impress Mr. Greer.

Daniel said, "We know that all the Suits use a ranking system based on the cards. There are the leaders, the face cards. Then the others, the numbers. Two through ten, increasing in rank with the increase in numbers." Daniel took a deep breath, then continued. "From what we have been able to find out, again, mostly from Ottawa, we know that small robberies are performed by 3s or 4s, depending on the suit. Judging by the, as I said earlier, clumsy nature, this was a small robbery. At most, they were 4s, which would still be considered low. That's why I said lower Clubs."

He watched Mr. Greer for his reaction. Had his answer been too detailed? Mr. Greer already knew most of that information.

"That is impressive," Mr. Greer said after a moment. "How did someone who's only been a janitor in the GDRS find out all that information? We haven't shared that much on the news."

Daniel's cheeks burned. "For living in a century that's so high-tech, the physical records kept in that building are quite meticulous. That room needed cleaning like any other. And, well ..." He looked to the side. "I was eager to learn more. Especially due to my personal connection."

"Interesting," was all Mr. Greer said.

He wasn't upset?

"I wonder if there's something else you caught?" Mr. Greer asked Daniel.

He frowned. "Something else...sir?"

"A man is demanding to talk with you," Harley said from behind Daniel.

He jumped.

"Any update from headquarters?" Mr. Greer asked as he left with her. "Feel free to join, Daniel," he called over his shoulder.

"None," Harley answered. She continued, but Daniel couldn't make out the rest.

Daniel leaned against the wall, one hand on his stomach. "Maybe if I turn it into a petition," he muttered. "Then she'll have to wear high heels. I can't be the only one getting terrified by her ninja stealth."

He felt his phone start vibrating in his pocket. He hastily dug it out, causing it to fall to the ground. It clattered and landed face up. Cody was calling. Daniel snatched it up and answered it without checking for possible scratches or cracks.

Cody started talking before Daniel had the chance to get out the second syllable of "Hello."

"Listen, Daniel, I know I'm not assigned to this case," he said in a hushed, hurried voice. "I couldn't forget your face when you heard the news and couldn't stop thinking about how I'd delayed. Over poutine! So I did some looking anyway. You know I'm one of the best underappreciated computer geniuses in Toronto, right?" This was said without any pride.

"Get to the point!" Daniel said.

Had Cody found something? Daniel didn't think he could forgive him for delaying a second time.

"Right! Sorry. Bad time to ramble. It's a horrible habit, but I'm working on it, promise."

"Cody, I'm going to hang up," Daniel warned.

"No!" he shouted. There was a pause, then a "sorry" that Daniel guessed wasn't directed at him.

Daniel glanced over to where Mr. Greer was standing with a middle-aged man, who seemed to be ranting about something. He was doing a lot of arm-waving.

"Listen, I'm at the scene of the crime, and I've got to get back to interviewing people with Mr. Greer. I don't have time for this."

"Daniel, listen."

So he did. Rather impatiently.

"I know where they're keeping your cousin."

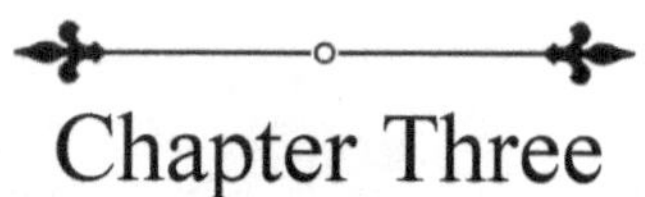

Chapter Three

Layla woke up in darkness with a pounding headache. Her senses were returning slowly but with an undercurrent of urgency, like there was a reason she should be scared right now. If only she could remember it.

She came to realize her hands were tied in front of her. The only light came from a slit at the bottom of the wall not too far from her feet. Ah, a door.

She tried to tug her hands apart. The sharp zip tie plastic bit into her wrists.

"If only I'd clicked on those articles about getting free when you're zip-tied," she muttered. That hadn't seemed like important knowledge at the time.

Layla looked around. Her eyes adjusted enough so that she could make out shelves lining the walls. What they were stocked with, she couldn't tell. A desk was to her right. All this was helpful knowledge, she was sure.

"Where am I?" Layla asked the darkness. It did not respond.

Layla wiggled into a sitting position and discovered that her legs were also tied together at the ankle. More zip ties. She brought her feet close to her body so that her legs formed a triangle. On that, she rested her head.

The last thing she remembered...the bank! Yes. Some people had broken in. No, a *Suit*. The Clubs. And they knew her.

A dart of fear shot through her. How did they recognize her? Her heart started pounding in her chest, and her breathing became uneven.

"This won't help," she told herself. "Just calm down." It helped to hear her voice out loud.

She took one deep breath. Let it out. And another one.

Now let's take stock of the situation, she thought.

She lifted her head. Yep, still dark.

"First, I don't know where I am," Layla said quietly. It felt weird to keep talking out loud, but as her thoughts were too scattered to be cohesive right now, she needed to. "Some storage room of..." She looked around some more. "A store? Why would the Clubs take me to a store? I should be at their headquarters. Unless..."

From outside the room came a burst of laughter. Layla flinched. Then she strained her ears and leaned forward to try to hear what was going on.

"Told you the King'd be pleased!" A man shouted.

More laughter.

"Say hello to a new ranking!" A female voice said. "They *have* to give us the promotion now."

"*You* don't seem pleased," the first voice said.

"I'm not," another answered. "Are you sure you covered your tracks well? If the GDRS finds us before we get picked up, we'll be imprisoned. Or tortured." His voice was one of gloomy resignation.

The woman laughed. "Hearts don't do torture. They'd probably ask us nicely to tell them what we know." Her voice was mocking. "After, of course, explaining how they don't blame us for our 'poor' choices."

"If we tell, they'll set us free—"

"And it's their fault for the society we grew up in!" rang out a fourth voice. "We wouldn't have done this if we had been raised better."

Layla shuddered. It was one thing to know that the people who took her were Clubs. It was another to hear them talking about it so casually.

And the mention of Hearts? There wasn't a fourth suit—not that Layla knew about at least. What if there was?

No, that would be something to worry about later. Right now, she needed to focus on where she was and how to escape.

The final pieces of the bank situation came back to her. The Clubs took her hostage, for bait. What were the chances they were planning to take her to their headquarters? Too high.

Let the GDRS get here first! Otherwise...

She shuddered. No, she didn't even want to think about it.

Also, if she remembered right, she had been taken as bait for...the Ace of Spades? Why?

"Think she's up yet?" one of the Clubs asked.

Layla's heart flew to her throat.

"I don't know," the girl answered. "I've never used those before."

"And how did you have them in your possession?" the gloomy voice questioned. "Last I checked, those specialized darts aren't handed out to 3s."

Layla held her breath, determined not to miss anything. Her curiosity was momentarily overriding her fear.

"What does it matter how I got them?" the girl snapped. Her footsteps pounded on the floor. "We have other things to occupy our time."

The door was shoved open before Layla had time to prepare herself. Light streamed in, blinding her. Layla blinked rapidly, trying to adjust. She wasn't quite there, but she couldn't wait. She looked up at the girl, having to squint. They locked eyes.

"Isabelle?" Layla said automatically.

Isabelle recoiled and took a step back. "How do you know me?" she hissed.

Seeing no reason to lie, Layla said, "We had calculus together." The light hurt too much, and Layla turned her gaze to give her eyes a rest. "You were obsessed with that model...Andrea Denver. Plus, you failed the class." She clamped her mouth shut. The nerves were making her ramble.

How come she hadn't recognized Isabelle at the bank? Well, she had been doing everything possible to avoid her gaze.

A guy had taken a spot beside Isabelle. He let out a shout of laughter. "I told you that would follow you everywhere! Obsessed, see?"

Isabelle glared at Layla, then at...

"Alexander?" Layla asked.

He jumped back. "That's scary. How'd you know me? We didn't go to school together."

"It's that dumb tattoo," Isabelle said. She mimicked his tone. "I told you that would follow you everywhere."

Alexander looked like he wanted to throw some punches.

Layla leaned to the side. Behind Alexander and Isabelle stood two more guys. One was leaning against the counter, arms crossed, staring at the ground.

Gloomy voice, Layla thought.

The other guy was playing with a plush toy. Looked like Mario.

We're in an EB Games! Layla realized.

She could see shelves and shelves of games, bins holding more games and merchandise. She couldn't see the tv but could faintly hear the muffled sounds of video game violence. She could just make out a gondola shelf laden with shirts.

"Hey, up here." Alexander snapped his fingers at Layla.

Reluctantly, she looked back up at him.

"So you know me because of my tattoo, great," he said. He gestured to the red sea serpent wrapped around his neck and resting in his collarbone area. "But how?"

"My brother told me," Layla said. "He knew you." They'd worked together, but thankfully her nerves had lessened, and she didn't feel the need to spill all the details.

Isabelle's eyes glittered. "Yes. And I wonder how he'll feel once he hears we've taken you."

Layla shrank back. How did they know Shayne? And why would they be trying to bait him?

The sound of breaking glass pierced the momentary silence. The front window smashed, sending glass flying into the store. Three people stepped in, guns raised.

"I can tell you," said the man in the middle. Shayne! "He'd be pissed."

Isabelle gasped.

Shayne shot his gun, which didn't look quite like a gun.

Isabelle gasped and yanked something out, the object falling to the floor. A little feathered dart. She followed the dart, falling into the storage room, missing Layla by inches.

Wide-eyed, Layla stared at Isabelle's now immobile body. When she looked back up, the other Clubs were on the floor. Two were knocked out, though it seemed like Alexander had tried to rush at the Spades. The other—Gloomy Voice—lay on his back, hands raised. One of the Spades had his foot on his chest.

"Layla, are you okay?" Shayne rushed over to her. He dropped to his knees and assessed her bonds. He turned and shouted, "J, find me a pair of scissors. Now!"

A dark-skinned man nodded, then leapt behind the counter.

Shayne turned back. "Did they hurt you?" he asked.

Layla stared at her brother. She hadn't seen him in years. Her main memory was of his bright blue eyes, which were now staring at her in concern. His black hair looked tousled but in a stylish way, of course. It was longer, too, somehow. She had many memories of their mother complaining about its length, and Shayne protesting that he liked it that way. Somehow they were siblings. People would always think she and Karsyn were the sibling pair, and Daniel and Shayne the other. Just due to the hair. She and Shayne had the same facial structure.

"Layla, did they hurt you?" Shayne repeated, interrupting her brain ramblings.

"Oh!" Her brain managed to form coherent thoughts, even though she still hadn't fully come to terms with the fact that it was him. Her brother, right in front of her. "Nothing beyond this." Layla held out her hands. "Plus knocking me out. With a dart."

Shayne rolled his eyes. "They've replicated our design, then. Typical. How are you up here, though?" Shayne tapped Layla's forehead.

She flinched. It was unintentional, and she immediately wished she hadn't, but honestly, what did he expect? They couldn't just immediately interact normally—it had been *years.*

Shayne looked like he'd been slapped. "Guess that answers my question," he mumbled.

"I'm learning lots of useful things, though," Layla said in an attempt at lightness. "Like how darts are very effective weapons, and that I should've learned how to get out of zip ties."

Shayne smiled. It looked half forced, but Layla would take it.

"Ace, here." J was standing in the doorway, holding out scissors.

Shayne grabbed them and swiftly cut Layla free. She rolled her ankles and rubbed her wrists.

"Thank you," she said.

His gaze softened. Layla was taken aback by how much pain and guilt she saw reflected in his eyes. "I'm so sorry," he said. "You've grown up so much. Changed."

Layla pressed her lips together to hold back the words that wanted to spill over.

Shayne stood. He walked over to where Gloomy Voice was still on the ground and squatted beside him.

"Now you are going to tell me exactly what your plan was," he said.

"They wanted to use her as bait for you," he answered. "To capture you. It's not difficult to understand."

"Saying 'they' doesn't make you less guilty," Shayne warned.

"It does, actually. I was minding the store when they left to rob the bank. I had no part in this."

Shayne pursed his lips.

A lady burst into the shop. "Ace, we have to go! Cop cars approaching."

Shayne muttered a foul word. He looked at Layla. "Again, I'm so sorry. I will see you later."

"You will?" Layla asked.

But they were gone.

Gloomy Voice stood. He looked around, then said to Layla, "I'm going to run now and hope they won't catch me. They probably will."

"Fair enough," Layla said. She was in no condition to try to force him to stay anyway.

He ran.

Cautiously, Layla tested the strength of her legs. They didn't tremble, so she stood up in one fluid motion. Dizziness swam over her, and she stretched out a hand to the wall to steady herself. She'd managed to push her headache to the side earlier, but now it had returned. Worse. All she wanted to do now was take a long nap.

By this point, cars were parked in front of the store. Agents and cops were streaming out, guns raised. Layla suspected these would shoot bullets, not darts.

To her surprise, Daniel leapt out of one of the cars. When he spotted her in the storage room's doorway, his face broke into a relieved grin. He ran over to her, passing everyone else.

"Lay Lay!" he exclaimed, cupping her face in his large hands. His pale blue eyes searched her face. "Are you okay? Did they hurt you?"

The words echoed in Layla's head, but it was a different voice saying them. She pushed them away.

"Yes, Daniel, I'm okay."

Of course she wasn't okay. She had been barely saved from being taken to the Clubs' *headquarters*. But Daniel was the last person she wanted to talk to about it.

"Thank goodness." He dropped his hands.

Layla blinked. That was it. No follow-up question? Did he even care?

Then, for the first time, Daniel noticed the bodies on the floor. "What is all this?"

"Precisely my question," an older gentleman said, coming up beside Daniel. Behind him, Layla could see a tanned, stern-looking agent with silver hair. "Layla, I understand you've been through a trying ordeal," he continued. "But I need you to tell us what happened."

"Layla, this is Mr. Greer," Daniel said. "Head of the Civilian Protection Unit in the GDRS"

"First you need to know that there's a fourth Club," Layla said. "He ran when he heard your cars."

Mr. Greer nodded. "We saw him and sent a car in pursuit. He was too suspicious to let pass." He turned and shouted to no one in particular, "Let the car know that they are definitely in pursuit of a Club." To Layla he said, "Now, please, enlighten us."

Layla hesitated. She looked at Daniel.

"We're not looking for all the answers, just what you know," he encouraged.

Layla brought her left hand up to fiddle with her earring. "Well, I..." she trailed off, then mentally scoffed. *Why am I hesitating?* she thought.

But it was too much, trying to still process all that happened—especially seeing Shayne—and then trying to get coherent enough thoughts to explain.

Daniel looked confused, and Mr. Greer was frowning.

"Young lady, I must insist you tell us what happened," Mr. Greer said, his voice stern.

"I'm sorry, I just..." Layla shrugged. "Shayne came. That's what happened. He broke in with a few other Spades."

Daniel took a step back. "He came to...rescue you?"

"He busted through the window." Layla gestured to the glass-littered floor. "He knocked those three out with some darts."

Daniel's expression hardened. "So now he suddenly cares," he muttered.

"I will need to question you thoroughly about this," Mr. Greer said.

"Not now," Daniel objected. "She's just been through a lot. Doubtless, she'll still remember everything tomorrow. It's a traumatic event. It's gonna be etched in her mind for a while."

Mr. Greer considered this. "Very well. But it must be tomorrow." He looked at Layla.

She nodded and wrapped her arms around herself.

"Sir!" an agent called. "We know this one!" He was standing over Alexander.

Mr. Greer left. The silver-haired lady followed.

"Are you *sure* you're all right?" Daniel asked.

"Yes, I said I'm fine," she replied, not really paying attention.

"You're sure?" He sounded like he was trying to be as careful as possible. "It was the Clubs. It's enough to shake anyone up."

Layla drew her eyebrows together. Why was he pursuing this now when he had so easily dropped it earlier?

"They only had me for a few hours at most," she said. "I didn't even make it to their headquarters. It could have been so much worse." All she wanted was to go home to her mom, watch a comfort movie, and try to forget what happened.

Daniel sighed. "You don't have to be brave, Lay Lay. Kidnapping in any form is very serious and can be quite traumatic. Perhaps we should—"

"Daniel, I'm fine!" Layla interrupted. "Seriously! Fi-ne. I'm fine, just like I was when we lost the house! Just like I was when we were on the streets!" Her voice was rising. "Just like I was fine when we could only afford two meals a day, when I had no shoes, when you wouldn't let me get a job, and when I had to go and find one anyway!"

"What...you... you worked? When did that start?"

Everyone was looking at them now.

"I'm more resourceful than you and Shayne have *ever* given me credit for. I'm fine!" She glared at Daniel, then walked off to the most agent-free corner. She sat down and buried her head in her knees. She took a few shaky breaths.

She hadn't meant to yell at Daniel like that. She tried never to yell at Daniel, no matter how frustrated she was with him, because he would only yell back and go off about how much he did for all of them. Which, admittedly, was true, but he didn't have to be such a jerk about it.

Now wasn't the time to dredge up these memories anyway. She looked up. Why didn't anyone take her home or call her mom?

She watched Mr. Greer lay a hand on Daniel's shoulder. She couldn't make out complete sentences. "Remember how you said she was upset...showing...Give her time...she needs it."

The silver-haired agent walked up to Layla. "I'm Harley," she said. "You need to come with me outside. A doctor is coming. He's going to make sure you don't have any ill effects from the dart."

"I can't wait in here?" Layla asked.

"I've been told to take you outside. Fresh air will do you good."

"It's March, and I don't have my jacket anymore," Layla said. "It's cold."

Harley looked at her.

"Fine," Layla relented.

Someone really ought to let her mom know what happened.

Chapter Four

Shayne spun around in his chair, eyes closed. Round and round he went, his knees barely missing the edge of the desk. In his right hand, he spun a pen between his fingers.

"Shayne?" It was Timothy.

He jerked in surprise, the momentum moving his chair just in time for his knees to hit the desk.

"Ow!" Shayne pulled back his knees reflexively. He opened his eyes and looked at Timothy. "Why are you disturbing me? I was—"

"Working?" Timothy said, one eyebrow raised.

"Yes, I was!" Shayne had to put a hand on his desk to stop his chair from moving. Then he lifted his chin.

"My mistake." Timothy walked forward and dropped a file onto Shayne's desk. "Naturally, spinning in chairs aimlessly is one of your most important jobs, Your Aceness."

Shayne's eyes shot sparks. "Oh, ha ha. I'm so proud of you for using any possible nickname to get out of calling me 'Ace.' I *was* working. I was thinking."

"What a nice change of pace," Timothy said, tone dry.

"I'll fire you," Shayne warned.

"You'll never find a replacement. I bring news."

Shayne looked at the folder. "What, this?" He picked it up. "What is this?"

"Complaints."

"What? *What*? We have a system for that." Shayne gestured to his open computer.

Timothy stared at him. "You had them 'temporarily disable' that system this morning. Then you decided it needed a complete system wipe and reboot. As you know, that is a lengthy process."

Shayne scratched behind his ear. "Well, it was getting rather full. Overloaded. It was going to crash if nothing happened—"

"I believe," Timothy interrupted, "that actually reading the complaints and then acting on them solves this overloading problem.

But that is not my news."

Shayne looked up. "Oh? Then what?"

"Unanimously, all 10s are demanding a meeting."

Shayne shrank back in his chair. "Did they happen to mention, uh"— he waved his hand—"why they want a meeting? Is it, like a—"

"It's blatant disapproval of your actions today."

"That's what I was afraid of," Shayne muttered.

For some reason, many of the 10s disapproved of him as a leader. Some of him as a person too, but what did they know? Going to rescue Layla without gaining their approval first had been, as most of his decisions were, a hasty and spur-of-the-moment one. But what choice did he have?

"This wouldn't have happened if they hadn't made me take away her bodyguard," Shayne said.

Timothy rolled his eyes. "She's not a Spade. We owe her no protection."

"Yeah, and see how that worked out," Shayne muttered. He flung the folder onto the desk. "I wouldn't have had to assign a bodyguard at all if our security team hadn't been so oblivious to that Club spy!"

"The spy was caught and dispatched."

"Not before he found out who my family was and sent that information to the Clubs!"

"Can we return to the matter at hand? The meeting?"

Shayne sighed and rested his head on his hand. "You know what? We can have a meeting. I will meet with them...tomorrow. Say, three o'clock?"

"They're already gathered in Conference Room B," Timothy said.

For the first time, Shayne felt something like panic flicker across his face. Sure, he didn't like the 10s anymore than they liked him. But he needed majority approval to remain the Ace. And he had to. No matter what.

"Today's incident proved just how malleable you are," Timothy continued.

"Timothy," Shayne said through gritted teeth. "I know you hate me. But I am still the Ace, and I will not tolerate insults."

Timothy smirked. "Unless they view you as incompetent and decide to choose a new Ace. I believe I heard rumours declaring—"

"Enough!" Shayne shouted, surging to his feet and slamming his fists on his desk. "Watch your tongue, or I won't care about replacements."

Timothy held his gaze.

Shayne whirled around. He stared out the window. Giant apartment buildings and office buildings filled the view. The sun had fallen behind them but had yet to set.

"I won't let them pick a new Ace," he muttered. "I won't go back to taking someone else's orders." His eyes focussed. "They can't think I'm weak. Think Layla makes me weak."

He turned and looked at Timothy, who was still watching him. "Meeting time."

"Good luck," Timothy said as Shayne passed him. His tone was anything but sincere.

Shayne glowered. He hated Timothy. Luckily, the feeling was mutual, so he didn't feel bad. He would replace him in a heartbeat if it weren't for two things. One, Timothy was one of the most organized Spades in the building, a necessary trait. Two...everyone else refused. They couldn't truly refuse, of course, if Shayne demanded it of them. But they could drag their heels every day, making Shayne's situation even worse. Open hostility with extreme efficiency was better than a constant power struggle and little work completed.

Right?

Shayne grinned at the thought of making J his secretary. Illogical. J was a field agent, not a secretary. But it would be nice to have a secretary who genuinely liked him. Of course, J liked almost everyone.

As Shayne walked through the hallway, each Spade gave a small nod of respect. He didn't look at any of them.

He reached Conference Room B faster than he would have liked. A shame they had to pick the one closest to his office. He allowed himself a quick, deep breath, then entered.

Inside, seated on either side of a long mahogany table, were a dozen 10s. The room was dimly lit, more for the aesthetic than anything else.

Shayne walked down the room to where his chair sat at the end of the table, facing the door. Everyone watched him. No one spoke. Shayne relaxed his features into a bored expression. He dropped into his chair and looked down the table.

"You called?"

For a moment, all was silent. Then one Spade leaned forward. He adjusted his glasses, then said, "Ace, we are here to discuss the events of today."

"The Clubs' foolish and direct attempt to bait me and their failure, or my rush to my sister's aid?" Shayne asked. Better to be direct about the fact that they weren't happy. You always have a one-up on people if they know you know they disapprove of you.

There was an uneasy stir down the table.

"You and Layla," the Spade said. "Your love for her makes you vulnerable. When you are vulnerable, so are we all."

"The Clubs' bait worked," Autumn pointed out, tossing her deep red hair over her shoulder. "Therefore, what's to keep them from continuing to exploit this weakness until they finally get you?"

Shayne couldn't help the tiny jump his heart made at the thought of Layla being taken again. But he didn't let them see it. He leaned back in his chair, running a hand through his hair.

Another Spade spoke up. "Your sister is not a Spade, Ace. Therefore, she is no longer your concern."

"Your wife's not a Spade either, but that didn't stop you from moving her into your quarters here," Shayne shot back.

He bristled. "That's not—that's different."

Shayne leaned forward and placed his hands on the table. "She is not a Spade. Therefore, she is no longer your concern."

Shayne stared him down, waiting for a response. The Spade's mouth opened and closed, no words coming out. He finally averted his gaze, lowering his head to stare at his hands. Shayne smirked and looked down at the others. None of them were looking at him.

This was going excellently.

"You all seem to be taking this way too seriously," Shayne said, "considering this is the only time something like this has happened. *And* it's the first contact I've had with my sister since I first joined this Suit!"

"Ace, you're missing the point," Autumn said.

"Really? Please, explain then."

"We are not concerned about the fact that you wanted to rescue your sister," she said.

Uh, really, cause that's what most of the complaining so far seemed to be about.

"Most of us, anyway," she continued. "The problem is that *you* went. Without a second thought, without a solid plan, and with only *three* other Spades."

There were murmurs of agreement.

"You should have sent a group of Spades out, after properly assessing the situation."

"You could have easily been killed or captured."

They had solid points. Shayne planned on never admitting that.

"I will...keep your concerns in mind," he said. Even that was hard to get out.

"Good!" Another Spade burst out, hitting the table. "Cause that is one of many strikes against you."

Ouch.

He continued, but Shayne wasn't paying attention anymore. His eye had been caught by Julia, who sat at the end of the table. She kept fidgeting. Her eyes would dart up to look at Shayne, then, just as quickly, dart back down.

When the Spade finished, Julia took a deep breath and said, "Ace, some of us are of the opinion that it might possibly be time to—"

Shayne rose to his feet, effectively cutting her off. Panic surged through him, and he fought desperately not to let it show. "I have a plan," he announced.

He now had their undivided attention. Great. Now he just needed a plan.

"Someone said earlier that the Clubs might try this again," he said, while his brain scrambled to come up with a point to lead to. "We can't let that happen. We have to let them know— and soon—that we are not to be trifled with. That we are the most powerful Suit."

"No thanks to you," someone muttered.

Shayne couldn't figure out who said that, so he sent a glare in the general direction.

"What exactly are you proposing?" another asked.

"A weapons raid." His eyes glinted. Ah, what an excellent idea. "A reminder of our strength."

"Only one problem," Autumn said. "We don't know where their headquarters are."

Shayne sat back down. "Yeah," he had to admit. "That's a slight problem."

"If you hadn't been in such a rush, we would have had that info right now," Autumn said.

It took a second for her meaning to fully sink in. When it did,

Shayne's ears flushed red. Under the guise of scratching behind his left ear, he made sure it was properly covered. That was one of the main reasons he had grown his hair out.

But if keeping Layla from entering the Club headquarters meant they didn't know the location, he had no regrets.

"Ace?" Julia asked, one hand playing with the bracelet around the other. "Do you perhaps have the beginnings of a plan on how to start removing this obstacle?"

Shayne briefly wondered if she'd ever offended anybody in her life.

"I don't," he admitted. Then he suddenly grinned. "Nope, I lied. I know *exactly* how we're going to find their headquarters."

Chapter Five

Layla woke up ten minutes after she was supposed to be meeting with Victoria and Jason.

Soft sunlight streamed into her room, diluted by her curtains. All was quiet, and coziness rested on the room like another blanket. Her digital clock read 11:40. She stared at it, wondering why she felt a vague sense of unease about the time. But the bed was so soft, and she was so warm. All she wanted was to return to sleep.

Late!

The word zinged through her, shattering her drowsiness. Adrenaline burst inside her like a balloon, and she leapt out of her bed. "I'm late!" she shouted.

She hastily threw on the first clothes she saw, then sat down at her vanity to brush her hair.

Her mother knocked on the door. "Layla? Are you all right in there? You sure are making an awful lot of noise."

"I'm late, Mom!" Layla shouted. Her brush snagged on a knot, and she winced, eyes watering.

"Late? Not at all. You're not scheduled to meet with Mr. Greer until late this afternoon."

Layla paused. Meet with Mr. Greer? She groaned. Right. She also had that thing!

"May I come in?" Her mother asked.

"Yes." Layla resumed brushing.

The door creaked open. "Goodness. And I thought yesterday that it couldn't get any worse in here." Her mother stooped to pick up Layla's Iron Man plushie.

"Mom, did you turn off my alarm this morning?" Layla twisted awkwardly as she tried to untangle another knot. This one was located at the back of her head and was proving more resilient than the first. She huffed.

"Of course I turned it off," her mother answered. She set Iron Man down on the bed, then took the brush from Layla's hand. "You deserved a lie-in after yesterday. Why, what's wrong?"

"I'm supposed to be meeting with Victoria and Jason right now. We were scheduled to go to the movies." She swiped at her eyes, ashamed that they were brimming with tears.

Her mother started brushing gentle strokes along the knot, coaxing it back to formation. "Honey, please remember that you are tired and emotionally spent after yesterday. Give yourself time to recover. They can hardly blame you for sleeping in. Don't get upset about it. It's not worth it." She took a step back. "Done."

Layla launched out of her chair. She found her phone charging on the kitchen counter and turned it on. Many missed calls and texts from Victoria and Jason. The latest, from Victoria, said, *Movie today cancelled due to yesterday's events. Situate yourself, then contact us.*

Layla chuckled. Just like Victoria. She went over to Jason's texts, which held considerably more capital letters and exclamation marks.

Sorry I overslept, she sent. *I still want to meet up today if it's possible.*

"I'll make you some breakfast," her mother said. "Eggs and sausage sound good?"

"I can do it, Mom, it's all right," Layla said, placing her phone down.

"Not necessary. I can do it."

Layla rested her forearms against the counter and leaned forward. She watched her mother grab two frying pans.

Her mother noticed. "What is it, honey?"

"It's just...you didn't react to this like I thought you would," Layla admitted.

"Were you expecting something more dramatic?" her mother said with a smile.

Layla nodded.

"I've been through a lot, you know," her mother said seriously. "I've found freaking out to be exhausting, even when there's a due cause. Which there certainly was yesterday. But..." She set the pans down on the stove and stood still. "Once you're done, there are still things to do. Money to make. Children to feed. Clothes to be washed. All you've done is made more work for yourself." She looked at Layla. "Isn't that sad? Don't mistake me, Layla. I don't recommend it. Don't copy me in this."

Her mother went to the fridge and got out a pack of sausages, milk, and eggs. "Will you close the door?"

"Yeah." Layla walked around the counter and closed it. "Still, I'm glad you didn't...freak out, or anything."

Her mother gave her a knowing look. "Got enough of that from Daniel?"

"He...he means well," Layla said with an effort. "It's just...a lot."

"Don't scorn help or concern, Layla. Getting them isn't a sign of weakness. So! Was that a yes to the eggs and sausage?"

"The doctor looked me over. I was fine, so I went home," Layla finished. She leaned back in the booth, weary of talking.

Victoria and Jason stared at her, wide-eyed. They hadn't said a word since she'd started talking, except for a few quiet exclamations from Jason. Their drinks sat untouched in front of them.

Feeling like a load had been lifted off her shoulders, Layla took her second sip of her caramel macchiato. She had taken a gulp before starting her story, but once she did, she couldn't find a time to pause and take another. The story had poured from her like water from a spilled cup.

"Wow," Jason said. He ran a hand through his sandy blond hair. "Are you, uh, okay?"

Layla took another sip. "I don't know how many times I've been asked that. I'm fine. Honest." She'd talked to her mother yesterday, and she didn't feel like rehashing it with Jason and Victoria.

"Lie," Victoria said.

"Excuse me?" Layla asked, her defences shooting up.

"I observe it in your eyes. You were just used as bait for your brother, a member of the most powerful Suit in Toronto. Concerning. However, he rescued you, and you want to use that to justify him. Additionally, that was the first contact you have had with him in years. You're conflicted." Victoria crossed her arms.

Layla sighed. "Can't I just have it all under control for once?" She buried her face in her hands. "Just when my life was evening out, someone had to throw a wrench in the works." Her voice came out muffled.

"At least it was, you know, over fast—quickly," Jason said. "Not that—well, you still have to go talk to Mr. Greer. So the whole—it's—

the whole thing's not over. But, like...you didn't go to the...their headquarters." He hastily took a swig of his coffee.

"True," Layla said.

In an undertone, Victoria said, "Your job demands constant social interaction, yet you're still awkward with words."

That was harsh, even for Victoria. It was anxiety related; she knew that!

"Yeah?" Jason fumbled for a moment, before spitting out, "Well, for a math major, you always sound like you've swallowed a thesaurus."

Layla suppressed a smile (not that it mattered, they couldn't see her), impressed.

"Just raised by one," Victoria answered.

There was a pause.

"You weren't, uh—your mom's a...cop."

"My father is a linguistics professor."

Layla raised her face out of her hands. "Still beats me how you developed a love for math."

"Your fault, probably," Victoria said.

Layla laughed. "Guilty."

"My question is," Victoria said, "Why would they desire to bait Shayne?"

Layla's heart skipped a beat. "What d'you mean?" She knew what Victoria meant, but that was something she hadn't told anyone yet, not even her mom.

"Why," she stressed that word, "would the Clubs want to capture someone unimportant? Shayne must be a leader in the Spades."

Layla looked down at her hands.

"Oh." The one syllable was enough. Victoria had understood.

"Wait, what?" Jason asked.

Layla looked up and said, "He's the Ace of Spades."

Jason flinched and knocked over his coffee that he had been reaching for. He grabbed a couple of napkins and started sponging at the spill, still staring at Layla.

"That is unfortunate," Victoria said.

"He must be...like...a really good criminal, since—if he's, you know, the Ace," Jason blurted out. Then he immediately, soggy napkins and all, clapped his hands over his mouth.

"No, he's not," Layla said. "He can't be a... a bad guy. Not really."

She looked at Victoria. "He *rescued* me."

"Are you trying to convince me? Or you?" Victoria said. "He rescued you. But Jason's right. He would have broken multiple laws by now, Layla. He is a criminal."

"He's my brother."

"Criminals do not deserve leniency because of shared DNA." Victoria's face hardened.

Layla shook her head. "You don't know Shayne as I do. He's not doing this because he likes breaking the law. Or wants to. He doesn't revel in criminal activity. He's a...a...good person."

"And your many years of not communicating with him have revealed this to you? You do not know how he might have changed, Layla."

"And you don't know that he has," Layla countered. "I'm glad the GDRS didn't catch him. I'm glad that he got away!"

Jason took a prolonged sip of his drink.

"Being a criminal has nothing to do with attitude and everything to do with repeated offences and willfully and continuously engaging in contraventions!" Victoria's voice rose.

Layla frowned, her hesitation in replying having nothing to do with having nothing to retaliate with. Her brain had put her on hold while it tried to figure out what contraventions meant.

"You know, you should go for, like...that is, a career in law," Jason told Victoria. "Cause you're good with, uh, words, right? Complicated words."

Victoria stared at Layla. Seeing that she wasn't about to respond, she said, "It means actions that violate rules or laws. I apologize for my outburst. It was uncalled for, especially after the events of yesterday."

"Thank you," Layla muttered. All she wanted was to put this kidnapping business behind her and never think about it again. But Shayne's rescue made that impossible. They knew where he was now, and somehow that was worse than the many years guessing.

A honk outside the shop turned all their eyes to the window. Layla's mom was outside, sitting in her car. She waved at them.

"It's that time already?" Layla said. "I've gotta go, guys. Time to give my statement to Mr. Greer." She drained the rest of her mug and stood up.

"Wait!" Jason said. He scratched the back of his neck. "If you, um...if you like, I can start teaching—giving you some self-defence lessons. As a... you know...in case this happens again. You'll be...prepared."

"That would be awesome!" Layla exclaimed. Then she frowned. "But how much would lessons cost?"

"Nothing. That is, they'd be free...for you. From a...friend to a friend."

"Thanks so much!" Layla glanced out at her mom. "I'll text you later to figure out the details. Deal?" She grabbed her mug.

"I'll be counting down the hours." As soon as the words were out of his mouth, Jason visibly cringed.

Layla smothered a laugh and quickly left the table so they wouldn't see the laughter in her eyes. As she walked over to the bin to deposit her mug, she could still hear Victoria and Jason.

"I'll be counting down the hours?" Victoria questioned. "You did not conceive of *that* on the spot. Where did you hear it?"

"Some movie—romance movie. That is, my sister was watching it." He groaned. "Don't...please, never remind me. Of that."

Layla waved to Victoria as she walked past their booth to the door. Victoria waved back. Jason had his head in his arms. She laughed to herself, then exited the coffee shop.

"Enjoy the chat?" her mother asked as Layla got into the car.

Layla shrugged, then buckled. "For the most part. Victoria and I got into an argument...about Shayne." She looked at her mother, watching carefully for her reaction.

Her mother brought the car out of the parallel park and onto the street. Once they were driving, she said, "You can't say it of many people, but Victoria is someone who is always honest. Disagreements are bound to be more common around her."

The car stopped at a red light. Layla stared at the cars passing in front of them. She took a deep breath, then asked, "Do you ever wonder what would've happened if Shayne hadn't been fired that day?"

"No."

Layla's eyebrows furrowed.

The light turned green, and they headed through the intersection.

"I do, however, wonder what would've happened if Shayne had never stolen that money," her mother continued.

"Ah." *Makes sense*, Layla thought. She did some more glancing around before saying, "If you could go back, would you stop it from happening?"

"No."

Layla whipped her head over to look at her mother, her jaw dropping.

"Don't mistake me," her mother said.

They stopped at another red light.

Her mother sighed. "I have no idea what our life would be like otherwise. Better? Worse? Three of you are stable, have jobs, and are functioning well. Karsyn, admittedly, is less independent than I'd hoped for." She looked over at Layla, who was watching her intently. "I can't risk that. I can't. No, I wouldn't go back."

The car behind them honked. The light had turned green and the cars in front of them were moving forward. Layla's mother quickly focussed back on the road, but just before she turned her head, Layla caught a glimmer of tears in her eyes.

Layla couldn't bring herself to ask any more questions on that topic, and she couldn't think of anything else to talk about, so they rode the rest of the way in silence. She wondered if she should bring up the fact that Shayne was the Ace of Spades. Now didn't seem like the right time to drop such a large information bomb on her mother. She might drive off the road. So Layla didn't mention that topic either.

When they were parked in the shadow of the GDRS building, Layla's mom turned to her.

"Now, I want you to keep two things in mind, Layla. One, they just want the facts, so answer questions honestly and to the point. Two, you're going to be thinking about these events a lot over the next couple of days because of the dramatic events of yesterday and their repercussions. That's natural. But I don't want you to..." she paused and seemed to struggle with finding the right words. "Don't let these things...weigh you down. You don't have to figure it all out today. Or tomorrow. Do you understand what I'm saying?"

"Yes."

Daniel was waiting for them in the lobby. The lobby itself was quite nice, but Layla wasn't looking at it. She was still musing over the things her mother had just told her.

Daniel walked over to them. "You nervous?" he asked Layla.

"No."

What other answer would she give him? Daniel was never nervous about anything.

"Good! All you'll have to do is answer a few questions, and then, uh—well, that'll be it. How are you, Aunt Jane?"

Layla's mom and Daniel made small talk as he led them through the lobby and into the elevator. Layla didn't participate but instead watched Daniel carefully. He had hesitated. She wanted to know why but knew he would never tell her if she asked.

They got out of the elevator on the fifth floor. Layla's eyes widened as she noticed her surroundings for the first time.

This was not the drab, office-filled space she had been picturing. There was a lobby of sorts, open-concept, and two hallways where the offices must be. The lobby had a chandelier of all things. Not extremely fancy or ornate, as chandeliers go, but a chandelier nonetheless. Everything was in different tones of blue, grey, and the occasional cream, which gave a sleek and professional effect.

People were milling about, some chatting, a few sitting and writing, one at a coffee machine. All dressed professionally.

Layla kept turning as she walked, trying to take it all in.

Daniel grabbed her shoulder and steered her to his right, her left. She turned around and realized she'd almost bumped into another agent. She smiled sheepishly.

"It's grand, huh?" Daniel said.

"Classy, I would say," Layla replied. "I'd love to work in a place like this someday."

Daniel chuckled. "I don't think that's going to happen."

She frowned.

"Come on, Layla," he said, noticing her annoyance. "You're about to go to university for *math*. That's not the best ticket into places like this." He turned and resumed walking. "Mr. Greer's office is this way."

"Who filled your head with all that hot air?" Layla muttered, following. Daniel hadn't even *gone* to college.

They reached and entered Mr. Greer's office, which Layla thought was unnecessarily spacious, especially given how little furniture Mr. Greer actually had in it. To the right sat a tiny futon couch, one that looked professional, but uncomfortable. Mr. Greer's desk was in the far left corner, two plastic chairs, which two agents were sitting in, had been placed beside it. Across from the couch sat two perfectly professional chairs that Layla hoped she never had to sit in. Was comfort a word in Mr. Greer's dictionary at all?

Through a door in the left wall, Layla could see another, smaller, office.

"Please take a seat," Mr. Greer said, rising from his desk and gesturing to the couch. "I trust you are fine with agents Suho and Janice joining us."

Janice waved, and Suho nodded.

"Yes, that is just fine," Layla's mom answered.

She and Layla sat on the couch. Mr. Greer and Daniel took the seats across from the couch.

Mr. Greer leaned forward and said, "Let me start by assuring you that all the Clubs directly involved with yesterday's incident have been apprehended and are now in custody, including the Club who was coming to pick you up, Layla."

Layla felt like she was required to say something. "Good."

"We appreciate your thoroughness," her mom added.

Mr. Greer nodded. "Now, Layla, we ask that you tell us what happened yesterday, starting where you feel is relevant. We may ask you questions once you're finished."

They all stared at her. Layla wished she had recorded the story when she told it to Victoria and Jason.

"I was at the bank, waiting to use the ATM," she started.

She relayed the story, packing it with more detail than she had subjected Victoria and Jason to. She hoped that if she told them enough, then they wouldn't ask her many questions at the end. Suho and Janice were constantly taking notes. Even Mr. Greer wrote the occasional note. It had distracted Layla at first, but after ten minutes, she got used to it. She never emphasized the word "Ace," though she figured they would still question her about it after.

"Then I fell asleep," she finished, wishing she had another caramel macchiato. Or a throat lozenge.

"Thank you," Mr. Greer said. "And you are positive in your two identifications of the Clubs?"

Layla nodded.

"The way they reacted further proves she was correct," Daniel added.

"But you don't know who the other two Clubs were?" Janice asked.

There was a condescending note in her voice that made Layla want to give a snappy retort.

"No, I don't know," Layla said, curbing that desire.

"But you are *sure* it was Shayne, your brother?" Janice said.

"Pardon?" Layla said. She had almost said "*Excuse* me?" but doubted Janice would have appreciated that.

Janice set her clipboard down on her lap and leaned forward. "Daniel has reported that the last time you had any sort of contact with Shayne was six years ago. A lot can change in that time. So how are you positive that the Ace of Spades is your *brother*?" She said this like a teacher having to go over a subject she just finished teaching.

Layla's mom flinched. "The Ace of Spades?" she asked.

"Yes, I'm certain," Layla replied. "I seriously doubt that the *Ace of Spades* would rush to a stranger's aid or tell them they've grown up so much."

Janice's eyes shot daggers. "Right. So you admit then that he is the Ace of Spades?"

"Layla?" her mother questioned.

"He is, Mom," Layla said. "They all called him 'Ace.'"

Mr. Greer nodded. "We had suspicions based on the eyewitnesses of yesterday, but your accounting confirms it."

"I can't believe it," her mother said faintly.

"I am sorry, ma'am," Mr. Greer said, sounding like he actually was. "As you are well aware, this places your family in much more danger. But I get ahead of myself—Suho, Janice, do you have any more questions to ask?"

They both shook their heads.

"Excellent. That leaves just this topic to discuss."

Daniel suddenly made it a point to be looking anywhere other than Layla.

Mr. Greer continued. "Your safety has been compromised. It has been for a long time. There has just been no opportunity for another Suit to exploit it."

"What are you saying?" Layla's mom asked.

"Daniel raised an excellent point yesterday at the bank," Mr. Greer said. "If even those lower-level Clubs knew Layla's face well enough to recognize it like that, then they *all* know your face. Shayne's actions have placed your whole family at risk, and they might try to use any of you as pawns. Again."

Layla's heart constricted at the thought of anyone using Karsyn as bait.

"Therefore, we will be assigning you all bodyguards," Mr. Greer finished.

"What?" Layla said at the same time her mother exclaimed, "Thank goodness!"

Mr. Greer looked at Layla. "Are you objecting to this safety precaution?"

"No. It's just..." Layla searched for the right words. "Are you certain that the Clubs would try again after failing?" She just wanted life to go back to normal, not get more complicated. Then again, the thought of the Clubs trying to grab her again filled her with more dread than she would have admitted.

"We don't think they view it like that," Daniel spoke up. "They were successful in getting the Ace of Spades out and vulnerable. They might try again. This time with a preconceived plan."

Layla shuddered. "Good point." It wasn't that she didn't want protection. It was just so irksome to have someone hovering over you, like an overprotective mama bird.

"We appreciate this immensely," Layla's mom said.

"It's no problem, ma'am," Mr. Greer said. "We're only doing what we should have thought to do earlier."

Her Mom waved her hand. "You had no idea Shayne was the Ace, therefore no huge cause for concern. We are not the only family in Toronto who's lost members to the Suits."

"Indeed. Would you like to meet the team that will be working to assure your safety?"

"Yes, that would be very nice." Layla's mom stood up.

"Suho, you take them down and introduce them. Janice, the agents should be gathered for the meeting now. Please go inform them that Daniel and I will be along shortly."

Layla followed Suho and her mother out of the room.

Chapter Six

"Layla seems exceedingly attached to Shayne," Mr. Greer mused, watching the doorway everyone had left through.

"She'd never admit to it if you asked, but I believe you're right," Daniel said. "She can't look past her memories and the fact that he's her brother and see he's changed."

"What about you?" Mr. Greer asked, turning to face him.

Daniel was aware of his scrutiny and made a conscious effort to choose the right words. "Two days ago, my feelings were quite different," he admitted. "I'd still hoped he might come to his senses and leave the Spades. But...he's the Ace!" He ran a hand through his hair.

"It's quite the blow," Mr. Greer said. "Much more complicated."

"Not really." Daniel sighed. "He's still a criminal, Ace or not. No grey areas. He's no longer the same cousin I grew up with."

Mr. Greer leaned forward and placed his hands on his knees. "I'm glad you're able to make up your mind so decisively. It doesn't do to have a conflicted agent."

Daniel nodded. Then he frowned. "Agent, sir?" Was Mr. Greer saying what Daniel hoped he was?

Mr. Greer cleared his throat and stood up. "I must say, I'm impressed with the way you handled yourself, Daniel, today and yesterday, and with the knowledge you've acquired despite only being a janitor in this building. I must admit, I've had my eye on you for a while, now. Even as a janitor, you stood out."

Daniel's heart was thumping so hard, he almost couldn't hear Mr. Greer over it. This was it! Any moment now, he would be offered a job in the CPU. But, he mustn't look too eager.

"I would like to offer you a conditional place in my unit," Mr. Greer declared.

Daniel's heart leapt for joy, then sank just as suddenly as he registered an out-of-place word. "Conditional? Sir?"

"You must go through a training process. In the end, should you perform well, a job will be yours. I am confident that you will pass. But first, I need you to answer these questions. Will your main objectives be to protect civilians from the threat of the Suits and discipline those who break the law?"

"Absolutely," Daniel answered, without hesitation.

"Can you follow orders without question?"

"Yes."

"Even if you disagree with them?"

Daniel kept his features as neutral as possible. "As long as they're on the side of the law."

But he only said that because he knew that's what Mr. Greer wanted to hear. If it came down to it, he wasn't sure he'd be able to follow orders he didn't think were right. He would work on that.

"Congratulations. You are officially offered a spot in the CPU." Mr. Greer held out his hand. "Will you take it?"

"I will!" Daniel shook his hand, refraining from being too enthusiastic. He didn't want Mr. Greer to think him childish. "Thank you, sir. You won't regret this."

"I'm sure I won't. Now, accompany me to this meeting. We have important information to impart." Mr. Greer headed out of his office.

Daniel followed. They went down a hallway Daniel remembered well from his janitor days. It led to several conference rooms, all the same size and design.

Agents were waiting for them, sitting at the circular table. It was an odd design. Like a donut, with a hole in the middle. Every time Daniel had to sweep the floors, he thanked the manufacturer for that hole. Made it so much easier to sweep.

Daniel estimated there were ten agents, including himself and Mr. Greer. The chatter died down when the other agents noticed Mr. Greer enter. Mr. Greer took a seat, and Daniel sat in the empty one next to him. When all was silent, a lady stood up. She was very tall, with a face that screamed "no-nonsense." Daniel didn't know who she was, but he knew immediately he wouldn't want to get on her bad side.

"As I'm sure you all know, today's meeting primarily concerns the Clubs' action yesterday," she said.

Most agents nodded.

She continued, "Normally, this would only concern the Protection Sub-Unit and the Civilian Protection Unit. However, for discussing these unsanctioned actions, I wanted the input of you all. There are more than just yesterday's events to discuss. Mr. Greer, as head of the CPU, will lead this meeting." She sat down.

Mr. Greer stood. "Thank you, Ms. Curts."

Daniel choked back a gasp. That lady was Ms. Curts? The *head* of the GDRS?

"Before we begin, I want to make sure everyone is clear as to yesterday's events." Mr. Greer looked around the table. "Are there any questions?"

"Yes," a woman said immediately. "This girl, Layla. Does she have any connection to the Suits? Or are the Clubs taking random people hostage now?"

The way she said it set Daniel's nerves on edge. She said it like she already knew there *must* be a connection, otherwise that would be stupid. If Mr. Greer said there was no connection, then *he* would be stupid. Because obviously, she knew, there *had* to be a connection. Daniel was so busy getting angry about her tone of voice that he almost missed when Mr. Greer answered.

"Excellent question," he was saying. "It also brings me to a main point I wanted to discuss." He took a deep breath. "Layla Zakkar is the sister of the Ace of Spades."

Gasps resonated along the table.

"Bodyguards have been assigned to their whole family, of course," Mr. Greer said.

Mr. Miller, the (scary) head of the PSU, interrupted. "That's correct. The finest bodyguards we have. They are meeting right now."

"Do you realize what this means?" Charlotte broke in, her voice bursting with excitement. "We know who the Ace of Spades is! We *know* who the Ace of Spades is." Daniel remembered cleaning her office. So many knick-knacks everywhere it was a miracle she could see the office around them.

"We have agents setting up cameras to search for his face," said Cody's boss and head of the CD, the Computer Department. (Daniel always mentally face-palmed whenever he remembered. They couldn't come up with any other name? Anything cooler?) "When Shayne shows his face to a public camera anywhere in Toronto, we will be alerted."

"Which means we could capture the Ace of Spades!" exclaimed Charlotte. "This is huge!"

"Don't get too excited," Mr. Greer warned. "He has to show his face first, which could take weeks.”

His warning didn’t dampen the excitement that Daniel felt brewing in the room. He knew how they felt. This was *something*. They were one step closer to removing a Suit. It would be a huge accomplishment. One down, only two to go.

Thank goodness the gangs didn’t perfectly align with the cards. Three Suits were enough. Daniel couldn’t imagine the havoc if there was a gang of Hearts. Although, he mused, it’s not like the Diamonds did much, so maybe it wouldn’t be that bad.

“On that note, we also anticipate a break-in attempt from the Clubs,” Mr. Greer said. “They will want to rescue the Clubs we have in our custody here.” He looked over at Mr. Miller.

Mr. Miller said, “We’re prepared. The cells are well guarded.”

“Fantastic. Now, as we all know, this hostage situation is one incident of several these past couple of weeks. The Clubs have always been the most active, but their level of activity has increased dramatically.”

“It’s true,” said the head of the unit dedicated to the Clubs. “About three weeks ago, with no warning, there was a 13 percent increase in their activity. That percentage has risen since then.”

“The Spades as well,” said another agent, whom Daniel assumed was the head of the Spades unit. “Their recent activity level has spiked as well. I don’t have a percent though. But we figured this was because of their annual tournament. It should be happening in the next month or so.”

“What annual tournament?” Daniel asked.

Everyone looked over at him, and he fought down the red that wanted to rise to his cheeks. He hated asking and seeming ignorant, but he hated not knowing more.

“They have a card tournament. All branches of the Spades gather in Toronto, along with their leaders, and they have a tournament of the card game Spades.”

Fitting, Daniel thought.

“They also have a meeting,” the agent continued. “It’s a prime time to capture not only the Ace but the King, Queen, and Jack.” He frowned. “Or, no. The Queen was the branch in Ottawa, and they’ve been removed. Just the others then.”

“The Clubs have no such tournament that we know of.”

Since Daniel had already spoken up (and he was eager to not look like an idiot), he said, “It could be due to the Spades activity.”

It felt like *everyone’s* head swivelled to look at him again.

Honestly, he thought. Out loud, he said, "The Clubs probably know about the Spades' tournament. Even if they don't, they've probably noticed their activity level increasing. Perhaps they're doing more themselves as a competition of sorts. Not to be outdone."

"It is a good theory," Mr. Greer said.

Daniel almost thought Mr. Greer looked proud of him. He sat up straighter.

"Except for the fact that the Spades activity level increased *after* the Clubs," the head of the Club unit said.

Daniel frowned.

"Whatever the case, we must all be more vigilant," Ms. Curts said. "They could be working up to something huge, so we must all be ready to take action."

"It could all be climaxing," Charlotte said, eyes sparkling. "Maybe this will all culminate. Maybe Toronto will be the next Ottawa!"

Her words had a rippling effect around the table.

Daniel frowned. Did Toronto really want to be the next Ottawa? In terms of no more Suits left, absolutely. But what about the violence, deaths, and displacements (both temporary and permanent)? The city had practically shut down and engaged in war with the Suits. All residents had been trying to leave. It was chaos. Ottawa eradicated the Suits months ago, and the city was still recovering.

No, Daniel was convinced there was a better way to go about removing the Suits. He would make sure Toronto wasn't the next Ottawa. That it was the better Ottawa.

Ms. Curts was frowning too. "Charlotte, I do not approve of your recent fondness of that phrase, especially in your interview. Toronto isn't anywhere *close* to being the next Ottawa, and I wish to avoid using those extreme measures. That is our goal."

Charlotte shrugged. The reprimand didn't seem to make an impact.

"Is the Diamond activity increasing?" another asked.

Mr. Greer looked over at Austin.

Austin spread his hands. "Honestly, I mean, I know our whole unit is dedicated to the Diamonds, and I'm the head of it, so I'm supposed to know stuff...but really, there's very little to know about the Diamonds. So, I don't know." He smiled sheepishly.

"Thank you for your input," Mr. Greer said, which Daniel thought was overly generous. "That reminds me, I wanted your input, Daniel. Any insight on Shayne that might help us capture him?"

Daniel thought. "He's a combination of cocky, careless, and impulsive," he said. "Which means he often won't take the proper precautions. We saw that yesterday. He only had two or three other Spades, and I assume no plan."

"How do you know this stuff about the Ace of Spades?" Austin asked.

Daniel mentally prepared himself, then said, "I'm his cousin."

The table erupted. Everyone started talking at once. Words piled over words, and Daniel could only make out a few of them. Half of the agents thought Daniel was too suspicious and should leave at once. The others were ready to take him on as an agent so he could reveal all the Spades' secrets.

Ms. Curts watched it all in amused silence. Daniel could tell she was thinking, but couldn't figure out what.

"QUIET!" Mr. Miller bellowed.

Absolute silence. Daniel was both impressed and terrified.

"Daniel, perhaps it would be helpful for you to explain some of your back story," Mr. Greer said.

Daniel cleared his throat. "Okay." He stood up. "Layla and Shayne are my cousins. We grew up together. When we—my brother and I—were really young, our parents died in a car crash."

Well, technically, only their father had died. Their mother asked Aunt Jane if they could stay with her for a while. Then she took off and never came back. But there was no need to go into detail here.

"My Aunt Jane raised us," Daniel continued. "One day, Shayne stole money from our boss. Aunt Jane told him to return it. He didn't. He joined the Spades, though we didn't know it for the first few months. Then he left. We've never had any communication since then. It's been years."

He sat back down.

"Thank you, Daniel," Mr. Greer said. "Does anyone have any questions?"

"Who's your brother?" one agent asked.

"His name is Karsyn," Daniel replied. And before anyone could ask, he said, "And he's never had any involvement with the Suits."

"You only mentioned your Aunt Jane," another said. "Have you no uncle?"

"He left," Daniel said. Again, no need to go into detail.

"Any other questions?" Mr. Greer asked after a moment of silence. "No? Very well. Then this meeting is concluded."

Chapter Seven

Layla had never been to the Miscellaneous Martial Arts Studio before (that was *such* a long name. Surely they could have come up with something better?), and she looked around, taking it all in. The lobby was filled with seats, a small coat rack, and a receptionist's desk. About seven parents sat scattered around the room. The walls held photos of past students and cheesy martial arts posters. The desk was the first piece of furniture to the right.

The receptionist didn't look up but said in a monotone, "Do you have an appointment or are you here for a class?"

Layla was struck with a sense of familiarity about the man's voice but couldn't place it. She was certain she'd never met him before.

"No—that is, don't worry, Mr. Payton," Jason said. "She's with me. That is, she's here for a lesson...with me."

"Just as well," Mr. Payton said, nodding. He slowly turned the page of the interior design magazine he was reading.

They walked through the lobby, and Jason led her to the second room on the right.

Layla looked around. The wall to her left was made up of mirrors. Mats lay curled up to the side. In front of the mirrors, there was a large blank space. To her right, in the back of the room, sat several exercise machines. Layla identified a treadmill, a rowing machine, and one she couldn't name but knew you used for doing bench presses.

"Versatile room, isn't it?" she said. "What's it usually used for?"

"Whatever it's needed for," Jason answered. "One-on-one lessons...if there's, like...an error and everywhere—that is, the other rooms end up full...It's also available by the—for rent by the hour. For people who don't like—or prefer—to work out alone. In a small gym. Or, you know, with a group—you get the idea."

"Cool. Uh, is there a room I could change in?" Layla held up her backpack. "I don't feel like exercising in skinny jeans."

"Oh, sorry!" Jason hit his forehead with the palm of his hand. "Yes, if you walk—that is, go out the door—I mean, walk back towards the lobby. You'll see it. It's...marked."

"Okay." Layla left the room. She searched all the doors as she walked. Then she came to the first one marked "Changing Room."

But when she stepped closer, she realized it said "Men's" underneath. Before she could make a hasty retreat, it opened, and a man came quickly out.

He bumped into her, and she stumbled backwards. Her backpack fell. The stranger's arm shot out and gently grabbed her shoulders, steadying her.

"Are you okay?" he asked. His deep, rich brown eyes stared into hers, and Layla forgot how to speak. And breath.

Somewhere in the back of her mind, a thought managed to form, and she started to say, "Hey, don't you work—"

"Ryden, come on! We're starting!" Another guy called from down the hall.

Ryden picked up Layla's bag and handed it to her. "I'm so sorry," he said, then took off down the hallway.

Layla turned to watch him go. Wait, she knew who he was...a cashier from Aroma Mocha! Huh, what a coincidence.

In her preoccupied state, she almost walked into the men's room again. But she caught herself and, shaking her head in embarrassment, managed to enter the right change room.

When she finally made her way back, Jason was at the end of the room, pressing some buttons on the treadmill.

"What took you—that is, that took a while," he said, hopping off the treadmill.

"Just...had trouble finding the right room is all." Her cheeks felt very red, but luckily Jason didn't seem to notice.

The next hour was the most physically demanding of Layla's life, and they didn't even do any martial arts for the first thirty minutes. Jason assessed her basic fitness to get a sense of where they should start in training. Layla was pretty pleased with herself. She was able to do two and a half push-ups. That was impressive, no? She ran what she felt was basically a marathon and was ready to quit after that, but Jason then moved on to covering some basics of self-defence.

For the basics, Layla sure had trouble performing the moves with any sort of grace. But Jason was very encouraging and generous in his assessment of her skills. And after all, it was only the first lesson. She had to get better from here, right?

Once they were done, Jason had to run to his next lesson. Layla lingered in the room, taking a couple of minutes to wipe her sweat off with a towel Jason had given her earlier and drinking some water. Then she went to get changed. Her eyes, unbidden, glanced at the door of the men's room as she passed.

Wait, why'd she do that? It wasn't like Ryden was going to come out again. And why would she want him to? She knew nothing about him.

Moving on!

The lobby held many more people than it had an hour ago. Two people caught her eye. One was a lady arguing with the receptionist, who could not be induced to raise his voice. With a start, Layla realized who he reminded her of: the sourball from *Wreck-It Ralph*. She almost laughed aloud. Their voices were practically identical!

The other person was holding a magazine so high and so close to him that no part of his face could be seen.

Layla raised her eyebrows. Countless memories surfaced of movies where people held magazines and newspapers to cover their faces. But not like *that*. She would be surprised if there was an inch of space between the guy's face and the paper. Either he was kissing the magazine, or he was practically blind. Or he was following her.

She had her answer when the lobby door had barely closed behind her before it opened again. Layla hummed to herself, trying to keep her adrenaline from rising. This was either a Club or a bodyguard from the GDRS. Either way, if she panicked, it wouldn't be good. Time to prove she wasn't as weak and defenceless as people thought she was.

Casually, Layla pulled her phone out of her coat pocket. She turned on her camera and made sure selfie mode was on. Then she raised it to eye level and used it to look behind her. She saw a man hastily dive behind a magazine stand.

Layla rolled her eyes and lowered her phone. Whomever the man was, he was clearly inexperienced. It was doubtful the Clubs would send such a clumsy person to follow her. Which didn't say much for the GDRS.

She glanced at a store window as she walked by it. In the reflection, she could see the man there, only a few paces behind her. Too close. He kept ducking behind people and other objects. Why couldn't he walk normally? Obviously, he had seen too many spy movies. The whole street must know he was following her by now.

Layla hiked her backpack up, annoyed that her bodyguard was incompetent and frustrated that she cared when she hadn't even wanted one in the first place. In an attempt to lose him, she sped up. She didn't bother to be subtle about it, assuming subtlety would be wasted on that guy.

Just before she crossed the street, the red stop hand popped up. She hastily stopped, and the lights changed. Someone bumped into her jostling her forward but not into the street. They muttered a hasty, "Sorry, sorry!"

I'm just not going to look, Layla thought.

As soon as the lights changed back, Layla took off across the street.

They promised I wouldn't know anyone was following me, Layla mentally huffed.

A loud BANG sounded behind her. She winced and instinctively turned to look. Her "bodyguard" had knocked over a trash can. His frantic gaze swivelled between her and the trash as his hands scrambled to pick it all up, his blond curls bouncing.

Layla sighed. She sat on a bench and got out her phone to call Daniel.

He answered promptly. "Hello?"

"Could you explain to me why there's an unknown man following me?" Layla asked.

"What?! Who is he? A Club?! Where's your bodyguard?"

Layla held her phone away from her ringing ear. That had been the wrong thing to lead with.

"Layla? Layla? Are you still there?"

She brought back her phone. "Yes. Sorry. I don't think you need to worry. I doubt he's a Club."

"But he's definitely tailing you? And you definitely don't recognize him?"

Layla could hear the sounds of Daniel walking quickly.

"A trained monkey could follow me with more subtlety. He's currently picking up the trash can he knocked over."

Daniel's footsteps stopped abruptly. "Nathan!" he exclaimed.

"What?"

"He's Mr. Miller's nephew," Daniel explained. "Basically incompetent, but he's got enthusiasm."

Layla looked over. Nathan was peeking around the now upright trash can. She sighed.

"Don't worry," Daniel said. "You should have another bodyguard close by. Nathan doesn't work alone. That would be disastrous."

Layla glanced around her, then stood up and resumed walking.

"I don't see anyone else," she said.

"That's the point," Daniel replied. "Seriously though, don't worry. I promise there's another bodyguard. *And,* if anything does happen, Nathan will fight to protect you with all he's got."

"That's not extremely reassuring," Layla muttered.

Daniel gave a long-suffering sigh. "Honestly, Layla, be kind. Why can't you just appreciate that he's working his hardest?"

Layla pursed her lips and frowned.

"I have to get back to work now," Daniel said. "I have important CPU stuff that has to get done." He hung up.

Layla stared at her phone for a second. "CPU? He doesn't work for them. He's a computer...programmer...person." She shook her head and pocketed her phone.

She looked around. She was nearing her house now.

A delicious aroma of cinnamon buns and coffee wafted across the breeze to meet her. Her feet stopped and her stomach rumbled. It was lunchtime, and there was the quaint cafe Aroma Mocha.

Layla grinned and headed inside. Just as before, the door barely closed behind her before the bell jingled again. Nathan slipped into a booth closest to the door.

Layla headed to the counter, and there he was! Ryden. The guy who had bumped into her. Standing behind the cash register, grinning.

Layla's cheeks turned red as she walked up to him. She realized he was significantly taller than her—but she wasn't going to hold that against him.

He winked at her. "Hello again." His face morphed into one of anxiety. "You weren't hurt from our run-in, were you? I'm sorry I ran off so quickly."

Layla waved her hand. "No, no, I'm fine. You just startled me. Although, it was my fault for heading into the men's room."

He laughed, and the whole room seemed to brighten. "True that. May I take your order...?"

Layla detected the implication and said, "Layla."

"Ah. Beautiful! May I take your order, Layla?"

Did he just say her name was beautiful? She shook her head slightly, trying to clear her clouded brain. "I will have a caramel macchiato in a medium to-stay mug." She paused while Ryden punched that in. "And...a breakfast sandwich. No tomatoes. Whole wheat bread. Toasted. Please."

"Is that all?" Ryden asked.

Layla surveyed the desserts, then felt a twinge of guilt. Shouldn't she be avoiding desserts if she wanted to improve at self-defence?

"Yes, that's all," she answered.

Ryden nodded, then frowned the tiniest of frowns.

"What is it?" Layla asked as she slung her backpack off her shoulder.

"I feel like I should pay for your meal," he said.

Layla paused in the act of unzipping her backpack. "Why?" It came out more incredulous than she meant.

"For bumping into you," he said. "Startling you, almost knocking you down."

"No, that's not necessary." Layla returned her attention to her backpack. "It was just a tiny accident." *He's almost being too chivalrous*, she thought.

"Then how about just because I want to?"

Layla's head snapped up. Ryden winked at her, and she could feel her cheeks heating up.

"Unless you feel that's too forward," he added. "I respect that."

He had a hint of an accent when he talked. Layla had never noticed that before.

"I'll pay," she managed to get out.

He grinned with one side of his mouth, then relayed the total.

She paid, then rushed over to the counter to wait for her food. Though she tried to stop, she kept glancing over at Ryden, then looking away before he could notice. When the food was ready, Layla grabbed it and went to a booth.

As she was situating herself, she noticed a strip of paper peeking out from underneath her breakfast sandwich.

She pulled it out. A phone number and a smiley face? It was Ryden. Had to be.

Layla stared at the paper. Part of her wanted to text him, but something held her back. How could *she* have snared his attention so quickly? What if something wasn't right here? She didn't want— Layla glanced around the cafe as if worried someone was watching her, reading her thoughts.

She didn't want to get her heart broken.

No guy had ever shown interest in her. Except for the one Daniel had chased away in grade ten. She hadn't even found out about that until a few months ago, when Karsyn let it slip.

She pushed those thoughts aside. She folded the slip of paper and slipped it into her pocket. She felt eyes on her, so she looked up.

It was Ryden.

For a second, Layla felt guilty, like he had caught her doing something she wasn't supposed to be doing. Then he smiled reassuringly and nodded. Somehow, Layla knew he meant it was okay. She could take her time to decide if she would text him or not.

Her heart lighter, she turned back to her food.

I'll text Victoria, she decided. *She'll have good advice about all this.*

With that encouraging thought, she tucked into her lunch, unaware of how often Ryden's eyes would roam around the room and come to linger on her.

Chapter Eight

Daniel glanced around his old office space, setting a box for his stuff on what was no longer his desk.

He had gotten a job without a degree. An apprenticeship based on how he aced all his math and computer classes in high school. He had always dreamed of going to university, but the opportunity was too good to pass up. He was the CPU's janitor at the time and continued to be until his apprenticeship was over and he was fully hired. Luckily, the two buildings were close.

Daniel chuckled. "Now I'm about to do the same thing, just in reverse," he muttered to himself.

He shook off the cobwebs of memory that were clinging to him and got to work.

The first things in the box were his two notebooks and three pens, which were all different colours. He took down the picture of him, Layla, and Karsyn that was taped to his computer. That computer. That slow bane of his existence.

"Won't miss you," he said.

"Ouch! And I thought we were friends!" Cody exclaimed from behind Daniel.

Daniel jumped, the picture fluttering from his hands into the box. "Cody!"

Cody grinned. "Did I scare you?"

"No!"

"Good! You deserve it. Saying you wouldn't miss me." Cody scoffed. "I can't believe you."

"I wasn't talking to you. I didn't even know you were there. I was talking to this ancient hunk of metal." He gestured to the computer.

"You talk to inanimate objects often?"

Daniel rubbed his forehead. "Forget about it." He started taking down the few other pictures that were taped around his desk space.

Cody watched him. "Watcha doing, Dani?"

"Packing."

Cody sat sideways on Daniel's desk and shook his head. "Dani, Dani, I possess great powers of observation—"

"That don't extend to reading social cues?" Daniel cut in, his tone light.

"I'm going to pretend I didn't hear that. Daniel, I possess great powers of observation, and I am pleased to say that these powers extend to things like noticing the basic actions another human is taking. Now, why are you packing?"

Daniel couldn't resist saying, "To move stuff." How could he say anything else after Cody had set him up so perfectly?

"My. Goodness. You irritating—"

"Sorry. Sorry. I've been offered a temporary job in the CPU."

Cody dropped his mug and jumped into the air. "Seriously?!"

"Dead serious."

Cody started laughing a laugh of pure joy and excitement, and Daniel had to join in.

"You mean I'm not going to have to haul myself all the way here every time I want to see you?" Cody asked around his laughter.

"You're gonna get lazy only having to go two floors," Daniel joked.

"I just might!"

They laughed again.

"I can't believe it," Cody kept repeating.

Somehow, they managed to stop fooling around long enough for Daniel to finish packing and Cody to pick up his mug. Somehow it hadn't broken, which was good, because Daniel figured it was the only mug Cody owned.

"I never laugh so much as when I'm around you, Cody," Daniel said.

"You need to lighten up."

"Yeah, well." Daniel closed the box and picked it up. "There's not a lot of lightness in my life. Never has been."

Cody frowned. "Things just got really serious." He tugged on the collar of his forest green shirt. "Too much seriousness in this atmosphere. It's choking me."

Daniel cracked a smile. "C'mon, let's go. Mr. Greer's probably waiting for me."

"What's he doing here?"

Daniel left his office. After a sweeping glance of the room, Cody followed.

"Mr. Greer went to talk to my boss," Daniel explained once Cody's stride matched his.

They walked through hallways that Daniel could have navigated in his sleep. He dearly hoped never to see them again. Being a computer programmer was okay. But not enough. His grip tightened on his box, and he made himself a promise. He *would* get the job. He *would* go on to be the best agent the GDRS had ever had. He would rid Toronto of the Suits, without going to the drastic measures Ottawa had had to use. He *would*.

They met Mr. Greer in the elevator. His eyes were distant. He kept adjusting and straightening his tie.

"How'd the meeting go, sir?" Daniel asked.

"Oh? Just fine. Your boss has no problem releasing you from your job and accepting you back if necessary. Though I'm not entirely sure she knew who you were."

"Hmph, figures," Daniel muttered.

Mr. Greer noticed Cody for the first time. "Cody? What are you doing here?"

"Visiting Daniel." Cody's answer lacked his usual enthusiasm.

Mr. Greer checked his watch. "This isn't a break time for your division."

Cody winced and glanced at Daniel.

Daniel had never thought about it before. Now that he did, he realized Cody's visits were never regular. At any time of the day, Cody could wander through the door.

He looked at the walls, sure that Cody was about to get into massive trouble. He had left when he should have been working!

But Mr. Greer didn't seem to care. He muttered something short under his breath that Daniel couldn't catch. Then Mr. Greer went back to adjusting his tie. This time mixing it up with some toying with the ends of his sleeves. When the elevator doors opened, Mr. Greer walked out immediately.

Daniel felt a sense of urgency, and he quickened his pace until he was walking beside Mr. Greer.

"Sir, what's going on?" he asked.

Mr. Greer glanced at him and said, "The GDRS has had a break-in."

"What?!" Cody had caught up to them. "Isn't that, like, impossible?"

"It's supposed to be," Mr. Greer answered.

"Who was it?" Daniel asked.

"We must hurry back," Mr. Greer said. He walked through the lobby's automatic doors.

Daniel raced after him and got in front of him. "Who was it?" he repeated.

Mr. Greer sighed. "The Spades. And they took the Clubs."

Shayne paced around the edges of the room, avoiding the few Spades who were gathered around the table in the middle of the room. A map of the Greater Toronto area lay on the table, and these Spades examined it.

Why they bothered, Shayne didn't know. The Clubs hadn't revealed their headquarters' location yet.

A laugh bubbled out of Shayne. The looks on those agents' faces! Did they think their little building was invincible? Sometimes, Shayne wanted to just take them out. But where's the fun in that?! If he took them out too quickly, the only real competition left would be the Diamonds, who rarely interfered with Spade work, and who were untouchable anyway.

"You're giving me a headache," Timothy said. He was leaning against a wall, arms crossed in front of him.

Shayne scowled. "Then don't watch."

He glanced at the door he was passing. He itched to go through it and see how things were going, but he held himself back. The 8s in there knew what they were doing. He'd only make things worse by interfering.

Not his typical line of thinking. But his pride was already bruised. He hadn't been allowed to participate in the break-in. Only watch through the security cameras they had hacked.

"Patience, Ace," Chhaya said. "You will have your answer soon enough." Her eyes gleamed as she regarded the map. "It will not take long to make our plan."

"Then, we attack," Shayne said, relishing the words. "When they realize what we've done, they will fear us like never before!" His words rang out in the small room.

"Are you sure this plan is wise?" Timothy asked.

"If any Spade had concerns about the plan, they would have told me," Shayne said.

"I just did," Timothy said.

The door opened. Shayne whirled around. Every nerve in his body was already buzzing with adrenaline. He couldn't wait. He wanted to be doing the robbery *now*.

Autumn stood in the doorway. "We have all the information we need," she announced. "They have revealed their location."

"Where?"

Autumn walked over to the map and pointed. "Innisfil. An hour's drive out of Toronto. Their headquarters are located in a forest, they said. Between Crescent Harbour and Glenhaven beach. 25th Side Road."

Shayne looked at where she was pointing.

"Curious choice," Chhaya murmured.

"That's why we got to Layla first," Shayne realized. "It's such a long way from their headquarters."

Autumn frowned like she'd just taken a sip of sour milk. "Yes. What's more, the Clubs told us of activity tomorrow night. Trucks will be coming to be loaded with weapons. The trucks will then drive down to the coast, where they'll be shipped to their buyers."

Shayne was practically vibrating with excitement. "Perfect!"

"Almost too perfect," Chhaya said. She looked at Autumn. "Are you sure this isn't a trick?"

Autumn pressed her lips together, which she really couldn't afford to do. Her lips were so thin this action made them disappear completely. Shayne had never worked up the courage to tell her that, though.

"I know my job," she said. "They did not lie."

Chhaya inclined her head, like a polite nod.

"Why would they pick a spot so far away from Toronto?" Shayne wondered.

"I think they have Clubs stationed all over," Autumn said. "As mini headquarters. Like these Clubs. They were 'running' an EB Games." She turned to Shayne. "One of the Clubs wants to speak with you."

Shayne stared at her. "Really?"

"He does. He was most insistent."

"Very well. Bring him out."

Autumn disappeared into the inky darkness of the interrogation room. A few minutes later, she reappeared, leading the Club named Louis. The mere sight of him caused Shayne's blood to boil.

"You have a lot of nerve wanting to speak to me after what you did," Shayne snarled.

Louis shrugged. "I already told you. I had nothing to do with that," he said slowly.

"Right. Forgive me if I still hate your guts."

"Fair enough."

Shayne stared at him for a moment. "So, what do you want?"

"To go with you and rob the headquarters."

"Out of the question," Shayne said immediately.

"No, Ace, listen," Autumn said, as though chastising him. As if she outranked him.

This did not improve Shayne's mood.

"He could be a valuable asset. He knows all the ins and outs of their headquarters. Any passcodes that get thrown our way, he can handle them. Plus—"

"He can easily betray us at any moment," Shayne interrupted. "And you, in all your wisdom, must have realized how strange it would be for any Club who recognized him. They all know he's supposed to be held captive by the GDRS. But suddenly he's part of the transportation crew? No, not suspicious at all."

Autumn's face flushed different levels of red, and her eyes shot sparks.

Louis was regarding him with some surprise. "Amazing," he said, though still in monotone. "There actually is a brain that works in there? It isn't all just play-acting?"

Shayne felt his ears burn red. He avoided looking at Autumn, whose expression changed into one of triumphant justice. His brain was so stunned by this sudden attack that he couldn't come up with a snappy retort. So he settled for a hard glare.

Louis expelled a breath of air in a manner that made Shayne think it was a laugh. "Stealing won't solve anything," he said, speaking faster. For the first time, Shayne caught a hint of a French accent. "You're only proving that we got under your skin. They'll do it again—"

"Put him back in his cell!" Shayne ordered.

Louis shrugged and allowed Autumn to lead him away.

Shayne collected himself as quickly as he could. He didn't want the others to see how much Louis's words had rattled him. But Timothy did, judging from the way his eyes glittered as he carefully watched Shayne.

"Now that we have the location, how quickly can you finalize a plan?" Shayne asked Chhaya.

"Three hours," she answered. "No more."

Despite still being rattled, Shayne began to grin. "We're doing this," he said. "They're going to get a harsh reminder of who's the most powerful Suit."

"How many do you want to send, Ace?" Chhaya asked.

"That's your jurisdiction, isn't it?" Shayne replied.

"Four." Autumn had returned.

Oh joy.

She continued. "They all said that's typically how many people there are per truck."

"Four..." Chayya mused. "Ash, for certain. J and Lamai... For the fourth..."

"Hang on," Shayne protested, suddenly realizing something. "What about me?"

They all stared at him. Nobody moved.

Then Chhaya blinked. "What do you mean, Ace? Are you saying you wish to go on this mission?"

"Yes, of course," he said.

Chhaya frowned. "With all due respect, Ace—"

"It's a terrible idea," Autumn cut in. "You may have been one of the best to send when you were a 6. But now you're the Ace, and you haven't gone on a mission in at least a year. You're rusty."

Shayne opened his mouth to argue, but Autumn raised her voice and sped up, not giving him a chance.

"Plus, sending the Ace of Spades into the Club headquarters? Terrible idea. If they recognized you, you could get captured or killed—"

"Doesn't sound so bad to me," Timothy muttered.

"—along with the other three," Autumn finished.

"Your concern would be touching if I didn't know it was completely for your sister," Shayne said. "Besides, if I get recognized and the Clubs start grabbing, Ash'll make sure they don't take me. Probably by shooting me, but there you go."

Autumn pressed her lips together. "So you're still going?"

"Yes."

They had a glaring contest. Autumn was always unwilling to back down, which Shayne would have admired if it hadn't gotten in his way so many times.

"Plus," he said, "If I die, Timothy doesn't have to deal with me anymore, and you have a shot at Ace, which is what you've always wanted, right? Win-win."

Her glare deepened, but her gaze became less hard.

"Fine."

There were lions with scowls less fierce than Autumn's.

Shayne turned back to regard the map.

Chhaya cleared her throat. "So, that will be J, Ash, Lamai, and...our Ace."

Shayne gave his best evil grin. He *would* go. The Clubs *would* feel his revenge. His own Spades would stop regarding him as just a figurehead. He would prove he still had what it took to ace missions. And the Clubs would not *dare* try to bait him again.

"You're grinning like a boy who just got a fellow student in trouble with the teacher," Timothy said.

The grin vanished. "I hope I looked more mature than that!" Shayne exclaimed.

Timothy's face clearly disagreed. Shayne looked over at Chhaya, but she wouldn't meet his eyes.

He scowled. "Fine. I guess I'll have to practice that. Chhaya, I want this plan ready by two o'clock and the other Spades gathered here for the debriefing."

Without waiting for an answer, he left.

"Prepare yourselves, Clubs," he muttered. "I'm coming."

Chapter Nine

Layla set her books down with a thump, jarring Victoria, who had been intensely perusing her textbook.

"I've been flirted with," Layla announced. She plopped into the seat across from Victoria.

Without raising her head, Victoria said, "A common experience for young ladies, believe it or not."

Oh boy, Victoria was in hard-core study mode. Her curly hair had been pulled out of her face into two buns at the back of her head. She was wearing her boyfriend's bright green sweater that had always made him look washed-out but popped against her dark skin. It was the ultimate comfy sweater, and she always wore it when she was going to study for hours.

Layla hated to interrupt, but this was more important. She said, "Not for me it's not. And not from guys like that."

"Like what? From whom?"

"A worker at Aroma Mocha. He's fairly new."

Victoria moved her finger down the page.

"His name is Ryden," Layla added.

"Him I do not know," Victoria wrote something in her notebook. "What is he like?"

Layla rested her chin on her hand. "Oh, you know...just your average fan fiction, Italian model barista."

"Perfect, then," Victoria said. She was still paying more attention to her schoolwork than Layla's story. Clearly she didn't realize the importance of the situation.

"He is," Layla answered.

"So naturally, you regard him as highly suspicious."

Layla leaned forward in her chair. "He had to have been acting, right? Why else would he flirt with me?"

"It could have been acting," Victoria admitted. "Everyone has a mode they go into when they work, however slight the difference may be. That could be his mode."

"Would his mode include giving out his number?"

Victoria's head snapped up. "He gave you his number?"

"Yes."

Victoria shut her textbook. "Details." She propped her chin on her hand.

Layla spilled her story, making it as concise as possible, while still giving all the necessary details. "Basically," she concluded, "he's the perfect flirter. And he's got the looks to go with it."

Victoria raised her eyebrows. "Is he a Greek god? I have never seen you so infatuated."

Layla was too serious to even take offence. "You know Isabelle? She was in our calculus class?"

"Yes."

"You know that model she was obsessed with?"

"Are you saying that Ryden looks like Andrea Denver?"

Layla nodded.

"And you have his number? Girl, text him! Immediately."

They both laughed.

"We're not shallow at all, are we?" Layla joked.

"Physical appearance is a perfectly acceptable reason to be initially attracted to someone. Text him."

Layla brought out the slip of paper that held his phone number. She had been keeping it in her pocket. "What should I write first?" she asked.

"Hey."

"Hey?" Layla echoed. "How's he supposed to know it's me?"

Victoria shrugged. "If he wishes to be flirty, you should respond in kind."

Layla frowned. It made sense...

"Fine. But only because I can't think of an unlame opening."

"'Unlame' is *not* a word," Victoria muttered.

Layla input Ryden's number. She hesitated, wrote out the word, hesitated some more for good measure, then hit "send." "Oh, and while I'm thinking of it," Layla leaned forward and looked at Victoria, "Did you give a reporter my number?"

Victoria slowly breathed out. "My deepest apologies. I meant to warn you."

"So you did? You just gave my number away. Without asking me."

"Yes."

Layla stared at her.

"You underestimate her powers of annoyance. They are extreme."

"She says she wants to interview me about my family and about getting kidnapped by the Clubs."

Victoria nodded. "She is part-time at Tim Hortons, alongside me, and at a newspaper company. According to her, she wishes to interview you because that is a "surefire" way to be hired full time."

"Which news company?"

"I have no idea."

"You don't remember?"

"No, I do not believe she told me."

"Hmm. I'll ask her." Layla looked down at her phone. "Oh my goodness, he texted already."

"Seriously? What did he write?"

"'Layla,'" she relayed.

She wrote back: *Yes*

(Ryden) *Thank goodness I was worried you weren't going to write at all*

(Layla) *Why wouldn't I? We just met and all I know about you is your first name & job*

(Ryden) *At least you know I have a job*

Layla snorted.

"The suspense is too much," Victoria said. "What did he write?"

"Oh, sorry," Layla said. "Here, it'll just be easier if I..." She got up and sat next to Victoria. "There." She positioned the phone so they could both see it. "Better?"

Victoria leaned forward. "Italian. That makes sense."

"Huh?" Layla refocussed her attention on the texts. Three more had popped up.

(Ryden) *But you're right*

So how about a date? Then you can get to know me better ;)

P.s My last name is Vanga

"I cannot believe he would already ask you on a date," Victoria said.

"Does this support the genuine or imposter theory?" Layla asked, unsure.

Victoria thought for a moment. "I cannot imagine a reason why he would take his acting this far. He must be genuine. Unless..." She glanced at Layla.

"Unless what?"

"He is working with the Clubs." Victoria raised her hands. "I do not think that is likely. But, if he is acting, that is the most likely reason."

Layla frowned, then said, "Let's take the blunt approach."

(Layla) *I dunno, I have to be careful. What if you are secretly working for the Clubs?*

"I don't know if that is genius or just dumb," Victoria said.

"If he is a Club, maybe it'll scare him off."

(Ryden) *C'mon, what bad guy is this handsome? ;)*

Victoria scoffed. "All of them, nowadays. He is supremely egotistical. If that was the best proof he can procure, I would be suspicious."

"I really don't know how to respond to that," Layla said. "I give up. For now." She turned off her phone. "All right, I gotta get going. I'm making supper tonight."

"What happened to our study plan?" Victoria asked. "So you could get a jump-start on next year? In addition, Casper will be here in twenty minutes. He is starting to worry that you dislike him."

"Sorry." Layla stood up. "Tell Casper not to worry. He's cool. How's his pottery shop doing?"

Victoria suppressed a smile. "He sold it and is now starting a doggy daycare. Out of his house."

"That...does not surprise me. All right, I really gotta go!" Layla gathered her books. "Sorry to waste your studying time, but...this was important." She walked off.

As she did, she could hear Victoria say dubiously, "More important than school? I disagree."

Chapter Ten

Shayne lounged against a tree as he waited in the darkness. He tapped his sports watch, illuminating the face. He sighed. Barely any time had passed.

"Aren't the trucks here yet?" he asked.

"If they were, we'd be by the road," Ash hissed. "Just wait. Quietly."

Shayne grimaced. He had thought he was prepared for going on a mission with Autumn's sister, but Ash was more abrasive and disrespectful. Although, he had noted she was like that to everyone, not just him.

"I'm just making an observation about how long we've been waiting," he said. "It's been a long time. You're welcome."

Ash sighed long and loud. Shayne couldn't see her glare, but he could feel it.

Maybe hostility ran in the family.

"The trucks will be here soon," Mai said. "J will let us know."

Chhaya was one of the only Spades that called her by her full name, Lamai. Most just called her Mai.

The walkie-talkie at Ash's belt crackled. J's voice came through clear and distinct.

"Ash, trucks are coming up the road now. Better get her quick. Don't be seen. Over."

"That goes without saying," Ash replied. "And you don't have to say *over*."

"Don't have to say what? Over."

"Ugh." Ash replaced the walkie-talkie and turned to Shayne and Mai. "Move out."

They ran through the woods, heading towards the road. They tried to make as little noise as possible, which is difficult when running through unfamiliar woods on a cloudy night. A branch slapped Shayne's cheek, but he ignored it.

J was waiting in the ditch, watching the trucks go by. Ash, Mai, and Shayne waited just inside the treeline, lest they draw any attention to themselves.

The trucks rumbled by. Each was a cross between a normal eighteen-wheeler and a large FedEx moving truck. These, however, were completely nondescript, all painted a dark, dusty red (the official colour of the Clubs, ironically enough) and no markings whatsoever.

"Do you have the bomb?" Ash hissed.

"Chill, A," J said, not turning his head. "I know what I'm doing."

"Don't call me A," she muttered threateningly.

J tightened his grip on the bomb. It was small, rectangular, and made of a sleek stainless steel. A tiny slit around the perimeter emitted a faint blue light.

The sixth truck, the last truck, was passing them. J straightened and tossed the bomb underneath the truck. What looked like blue lightning shot out. The tendrils went into the bottom of the truck. There was a sound like electricity dying. The truck lurched and stopped.

"Now!" Ash whispered.

The four of them leapt from the ditch and ran to the truck. Shayne could hear the drivers shouting and cursing. With luck they'd have at least ten minutes before the engine would run again.

Shotgun's door opened. Shayne sped up to get behind the truck, almost knocking Mai over.

Ash was analyzing the back door.

Shayne peered around the truck's edge. The door was still open, but he couldn't see anybody. They must be inspecting the engine.

"Stand back," Ash ordered.

Shayne, J, and Mai scrambled away, making sure to stay behind the truck so they wouldn't be visible.

The doors swung open, forcing Ash to duck. Two Clubs stared down at them.

"What the—"

"Don't move!" the taller one pulled out a gun.

Ash stood to her full height, grabbed his ankle, and yanked, causing him to wobble dangerously but not fall.

The other, who was bald, reached for his gun. J ran and jumped up. They wrestled for the gun.

Meanwhile, Ash leapt into the truck just as Not-Baldie reclaimed his footing. She kicked the back of his knees. His legs buckled, and Ash shoved him out of the truck. He hit the ground hard, his gun skittering away.

Shayne started towards him, but another gun came flying out of the truck and hit him on the chest. He stopped, startled, and lost his chance to fight the Club. Mai did instead.

He got ready to jump in and help her out. After all, she was only five foot two, and the Club was at least six feet. But she knocked him out with alarming swiftness.

Shayne returned his attention to the truck, but they didn't need his help there either. Under the combined forces of J and Ash, Baldie hadn't stood a chance.

"Hey, what's going on?" a gruff voice shouted.

Shayne whirled around. Who authorized this man to be a driver? If he could see anything under those bushy eyebrows, it was a miracle.

Eyebrows Man took in the situation. He lunged at Shayne, who was so startled by the abrupt attack, he exclaimed aloud, "You can see!"

And quite well, apparently. It took all of Shayne's concentration to just avoid all his advances, forget trying to fight back.

Eyebrows suddenly grunted, falling to one knee. Not about to waste the opportunity, Shayne grabbed the man's head, smashing it onto his knee. Eyebrows reeled backwards, and Shayne noticed Mai standing behind him. She used the butt of a gun against Eyebrows's head, knocking him out.

Breathing heavily, Shayne looked at Mai. "That was unnecessary. I would've handled him."

Mai gave a short nod. "Of course. But you're welcome."

She grinned. It was quite unnerving. Shayne was glad when Ash hissed, "Stop standing around you two. Get changed!"

"The other driver?" J asked.

"I'll take care of him," Ash jumped down.

"How tall is that one?" Mai asked, pointing at Baldie.

"Taller than the other two," J answered.

"You didn't even look," Mai protested.

"I fought the guy; I know how tall he is," J said. "His clothes are probably the best fit for you, Ace."

"Oh, right." Shayne jumped up into the trailer.

"Try these, Mai," Ash called as she rounded the back of the truck. "The driver was the shortest out of all of them."

Mai accepted the clothes.

Shayne did his best to undress the unconscious baldie. It was a lot harder than he'd thought it would be. Shayne grunted with the effort.

Why were unconscious bodies so heavy to move?

"Need help, Ace?" J asked.

Shayne looked over at him and frowned. How was he dressed already?

"Nope, I'm fine."

"You're struggling."

"The Ace of Spades...never...struggles."

Shayne pulled, but the material was stuck under the Club's body.

"Here, I'll lift him up. You pull." It was easy to detect the amusement in J's voice.

Shayne nodded.

Between the two of them, they got the uniform off quickly. Shayne almost tried to make an excuse about how it would've been easier if the uniform wasn't all one piece. Which it would! But he kept quiet and focussed on changing with lightning speed. It would not do for Ash to come back from wherever she was changing at and see that he wasn't finished.

Changing was easy, but, unfortunately, even he couldn't make these work uniforms look good. A muddy red-brown colour, a baggy unisex shape, and sleeves that managed to just get past his elbow, then stopped. Taken together, it was a sure recipe for disaster.

"We are way behind schedule," Ash shouted, coming into view. The uniform was no more flattering on her.

Mai's looked baggy but not comically so. Passable, except under direct scrutiny. Shayne hoped no one would pay them a second glance.

"Let's move them into the ditch," Ash ordered.

Between the four of them, it was easy to move Baldie, Eyebrows, that other guy, and the other driver. They'd probably be cold when they woke up, given they were only wearing underwear and tank tops. But the forecast didn't call for rain, so they should be fine.

"Now, move out!" Ash said. "Everyone remember the plan?"

"Of course we do," Shayne said, hopping into the truck.

She frowned, then left. She was going to drive.

Shayne sat down on the bench that jutted out from the right side of the trailer. It was just a flat slab of wood with straps on the wall to hold on to.

"How safe," he muttered.

He noticed hooks on the bottom of the bench and realized it could fold up. The straps were both for hanging on to and hooking on to the bench.

Mai took a seat to Shayne's right while J closed the door. As much as Shayne despised the Clubs, he had to be thankful to them for making their doors accessible from the inside.

Before J had a chance to sit down, the truck started moving. He stumbled and fell onto the bench.

The ride was quiet except for the noise of the engine and Mai's humming. It was hard to tell the speed, but Shayne was convinced Ash was breaking the speed limit in a major way.

Seized by a desperate need to have some conversation, Shayne said, "Don't forget, Mai, you fainted."

"I know. Don't worry." She smiled. "I'm always the fainter. Even though J is more likely than me to faint."

"Not true!" J protested. "That was one time, man!"

"One time is still one more time than me," Mai sang.

The truck slowed abruptly, causing them all to lean to the right and grip the straps tighter.

"We must have arrived!" Mai whispered, eyes shining with excitement.

She was such a bubbly extrovert all the time. Shayne briefly wondered why on earth she joined the Spades. Was it a sad story? Would she tell him if he asked?

The truck was crawling now. Shayne couldn't bear it.

Park already! Let's get to work!

The truck stopped. Shayne waited two seconds, just to be sure she was parking. Then he leapt up, racing to the doors. He pushed them open and jumped out.

Conscious of appearances, he didn't start running but walked around the corner of the truck.

He choked on air. What was this?

In short, it was a mansion. The Clubs' headquarters looked like it had jumped straight out of a textbook on the Victorian era in England. Massive. Expensive. Balconies and windows to spare. Lots of lights.

Shayne felt a stirring in his chest. Why should their location be so grand and fancy? Why did the most violent and clumsy Suit have the most elegant headquarters?

Then he noticed the warehouse. If he had been driving, it definitely would have caught his eye first, purely due to size and modern lighting. But because they were parked right at the end, and he had gone to the left, the mansion had been the first thing he saw. All he could see inside the warehouse were stacks and rows of large boxes.

He glanced over his shoulder. Mai and J were there but hadn't made it far. They were both openly gaping. He couldn't blame them. Aside from the place's presence, this was the first time any Spade saw Club headquarters.

He shook himself. They couldn't just stand here! They had to blend in, or they were screwed.

Ash was making her way towards a tall and thin man in a pinstriped suit of all things! The pants and his tie matched the suit coat. That was overkill.

The man kept adjusting his clipboard and checking his watch.

"You're exactly seventeen minutes and forty-three seconds late," he said in a tone of disapproval.

"Mai fainted," Ash said. "We stopped to give her air."

Shayne was close enough now to read the name tag: Davis Donnerman.

Davis noticed the rest of them, and his eyes narrowed. "Fine," he grumbled. "You'll have to hurry to complete your order on time. Try not to fall further behind." He shoved the clipboard at Ash.

Ash's left hand twitched as she watched Davis stalk away. She turned to look at the others. "J, drive the skid steer—"

"Can't," he interrupted. "Don't know how to drive one."

She glared. "Then take Shayne—"

"Ace," Shayne corrected.

Her glare deepened. "Ace. He can drive it. Gather one pallet of those poison darts you were talking about."

J saluted.

"Mai, pallet jack—what?"

Mai was frowning. "I'm too short." She flapped her arms. "There's not enough of me to pull one."

Ash threw her hands in the air. "Then I'll do the pallet jack, and you can be in charge of the clipboard."

Mai grinned. "Okay." She took the clipboard.

Ash stalked away, much in the same way Davis had.

Shayne and J exchanged glances, then shrugged.

"What were we supposed to do?" Shayne muttered as they walked towards the warehouse. "Let you drive? You'd crash into crates and expose the whole operation."

"Girls," J said.

They both nodded at this sage wisdom.

Ash grabbed a pallet jack. Her eyes shot daggers at them that clearly said "Hurry up!"

As they went through their entrance, Shayne glanced around as casually as he could, taking it all in. Despite the warehouse being open concept, there were six distinct entrances for trucks to park at. Every entrance had someone with a clipboard standing by it. They checked off items as they were brought to the trucks, then issued the next orders. Interesting.

Clubs were everywhere in the warehouse, all grabbing different items. Everyone had either a pallet jack or a skid steer. Theirs was waiting just inside their entrance and to the left.

"A BobCat, yes," Shayne said, hopping up into it. He lowered the harness, securing himself in the seat and making him feel like he was about to start a cheap roller coaster ride.

J leapt onto the forks. Dangerous and totally against safety regulations? Yep. But Shayne knew J could keep his balance.

For the first however long it was (he wasn't keeping track, he was busy!), everything went smoothly. The other trucks were focussed on completing their orders, and no one looked twice at them. J perched on the forks when they weren't lifting anything and on the flat space just before Shayne's seat (and a bit to the left) when they were. With his height advantage, he was able to direct Shayne around so that they weren't obviously wandering and reading every label.

Then, before Shayne fully realized it, the trucks started closing up and pulling away.

Makes sense, he thought. *We were, what? Fifteen minutes behind? Plus time lost not knowing where things are.*

He turned the skid steer and headed towards their truck. Ash was already there, and it looked like she was arguing about something with Mai. Shayne frowned. Ash waved her hand towards the truck, then at the other trucks pulling away. She stepped close to Mai and said something. Mai shook her head and gestured to her clipboard. Ash grabbed the clipboard and shook her head.

Shayne's gut sank. He drove the skid steer as fast as he dared. As soon as he stopped, J jumped down. Shayne loaded the boxes into the truck. There was no need for J to hop in and use another pallet jack to bring the boxes to the back. The trailer was almost full. Shayne reversed the skid steer carefully, then stopped it again.

Mai walked to the front of the truck and got into the driver's seat. What was going on?

Ash said something snappy to J. Shayne stopped the engine, lifted the harness, and jumped down.

"What's going on?" he asked.

"Nothing," Ash said pointedly. "We're done and ready to leave. That's all."

Shayne looked at J and crossed his arms. "Is that all?"

J frowned. "There are still items on the list we haven't gotten yet."

Shayne held out his hand. "Give me the clipboard," he ordered.

Ash clearly didn't want to, but she wasn't about to refuse a direct order from the Ace of Spades. She slowly handed it over.

He glanced at it, his jaw clenching. He looked up. "So explain to me why we're leaving."

Ash pressed her lips together. "Better we leave now with less than stay and increase our risk of being discovered."

"Everyone knows this truck was late and running behind," Shayne said. "They'll be wondering why we left so soon."

Another truck pulled away. That left only them and one other truck.

"If we are the only ones here, they will look at us more," Ash said urgently. "They could recognize us! We're just drawing more attention to ourselves!"

J left them and jumped into the back of the trailer.

"Don't be ridiculous," Shayne said. "We're finishing this load."

"We don't have time!"

"Is there a problem?" someone asked suddenly, startling both of them. Davis.

"Loading the last couple of boxes will put us majorly off schedule," Ash said.

Davis's eyes widened. "That is a dilemma." He looked past them. "Why is part of your crew in the truck already?"

Shayne pointed at Ash. "Because *she* told them we were done."

She narrowed her eyes.

Davis inspected Shayne's face. "Hmm..."

Shayne fidgeted, nervous. Ash froze. What would happen if Davis recognized him? Was it even possible?

Davis took a couple of steps away and pulled a walkie-talkie out of his pants. "I need backup at loading door six," he said into it.

"Run," Ash whispered. She whirled around and ran to the front of the truck, to the driver's seat. Was she going to kick Mai out or something?

"Stop!" Davis ordered, pulling a gun out of nowhere. He pointed it at Ash.

She froze, one hand on the door handle.

Shayne slowly took a couple steps towards the truck, whose engine, at some point, had been turned on. Mai.

"Move again and I'll shoot," Davis warned, swinging the gun to face Shayne, then back to Ash.

Shayne raised both hands in the air.

Davis's stance relaxed slightly. "Ah, could you just"—he pointed to Shayne's left hand. "It's much higher than the other."

Shayne looked up at his hands, confused. They were, in fact, not raised to the same height. His head whipped back around as he heard shouts directed towards them. Four men were running towards them, guns out.

Ash opened the door and leapt into the cab. Shayne, not wanting to be left behind, turned and jumped towards the trailer.

The truck revved, then started moving.

"Stop!" Davis ordered.

The men running towards them quickened their pace.

"Wait!" Shayne yelled. He hadn't quite made it into the trailer and was trying to lift himself up when the truck really took off.

J leapt up off the bench. He ran over, grabbed Shayne's wrists, and pinned them to the floor. Shayne's legs were dangling out of the truck. They hit the ground, the impact running up his legs and almost making him fall out.

"Get up!" J cried. "You fall out, you're dead, man!"

"Trying," Shayne grunted. He swung his legs up and managed to roll over into the truck. He lay still, panting heavily.

J flinched and fell backwards as bullets flew after them. The truck turned sharply, and Shayne rolled to the left. He quickly got himself up.

The truck lurched and shuddered. Shayne almost fell face-first out of the truck, but he managed to keep himself upright by grabbing onto a box. They had busted through the gates.

No one was chasing them anymore. They had either given up or gone to get vehicles for further pursuit.

Shayne reached into his pocket and pulled out a single card: an ace of spades. He let it fly from his fingers and watched it settle to the ground, right in front of the gates. Then, as the doors of the trailer swung towards him, he grabbed them and shut them with a loud bang.

Chapter Eleven

Victoria was already waiting in front of Aroma Mocha when Layla got there.

"You put braids in!" Layla said.

"How can you tell?" Victoria asked, her eyes widening.

Layla wasn't sure how to respond to that question without sounding condescending. "Because...your hair is now in braids? And it wasn't yesterday?"

"Oh! Right." Victoria shook her head. "Sorry. I am *exhausted*. I finished putting them in around three this morning."

"Well, they look great!"

"Thank you!" Victoria ran her hand down the black braids that she had gathered into a high ponytail.

"All right, ready for Operation Potential Date Reconnaissance?"

"Remind me. How were you sure he would be working now?"

"Uh...I asked him. Last night."

"Huh."

Layla entered the cafe. Its familiar smell washed over her, causing instant relaxation. She smiled. Then she noticed Ryden, and her heart jumped.

Victoria came up behind her. "Ryden is the cashier, yes?"

Layla nodded.

"I understand why you were freaking out yesterday."

"I was not freaking out."

"I beg your pardon? You most certainly were."

"Just, let's not make this weird, okay?"

"I shall do my best."

They got in line and made the normal small talk about what they were going to order. That included who was paying, dine in or dine out, and all the other issues that make ordering stressful and complicated.

"I can help who's next!" Ryden called.

Wait, that was them.

Victoria walked up. Layla waited. Even though she already knew what she was going to order, she continued to study all of the signs.

Once Victoria was done, Layla walked up to the register.

Ryden grinned. He looked genuinely thrilled to see her, though Layla told herself she must be imagining it.

"Did you bring your friend to inspect me before you agreed to a date?" he asked.

"What makes you think that?" she said.

"She was asking me questions like I was a suspect or something." Ryden scratched the back of his head. "I couldn't even understand half of them. She uses complicated words."

"That's Victoria all right."

Another worker was walking behind Ryden and cleared his throat. Ryden jumped.

"Oh, right, sorry. What would you like to order, Layla?"

She told him. Then, as he was inputting it, she said, "Sorry about Victoria grilling you. It's just I have to be wary of strangers."

"Strangers?" he scoffed. "I have officially been your cashier twice now. I'd say that's a big milestone in our relationship."

A laugh bubbled out of Layla. "Sorry, but you have to be my cashier at least three times for me to agree to a date."

Ryden's grin widened. "Your total comes to $12.50."

Layla handed over a ten and a five and received her change.

"Feel free to order dessert after," Ryden said with a wink.

Layla smiled, then went and joined Victoria at her table.

"You could not wait to hear my report before you launched into flirting?"

Layla grinned and shrugged sheepishly. "I do want to hear what you think, though."

Victoria held up two fingers. "Two items. One, he does indeed possess a work mode, which entails being flirtatious in manner."

Layla deflated slightly.

"And two," —Victoria lowered a finger— "He was nowhere near as flirtatious with me as he has been with you. In you, he possesses real interest."

"I just wish I knew why," Layla said.

"Who knows the reasonings behind any attractions? Love is no science."

"But you think he really likes me? Cause I just...I wanna be sure.

I've never done this before."

Victoria smiled softly. "I believe you should give him a chance. However, know that even if you have one date, there is no guarantee that he will become your boyfriend."

"I know that!"

"Your breakfast, ladies," another worker interrupted. She placed their dishes and drinks before them, and both girls said thanks.

During the meal, they made trivial small talk.

When it was over, Victoria said, "That was delicious. Shall we walk back now?"

"You go on without me. I'm going to buy Karsyn something, and I'm waiting for him to text back what he wants."

"Curious that someone who is always on their phone would delay so in responding to an offer of free food," Victoria remarked.

A faint blush curled along Layla's face. "What are you saying?"

"Nothing. Only that it is curious." Victoria stood up. "Good luck," she said with a wink. Then she left.

Layla frowned. How did she know? She looked down at the text Karsyn had sent mere seconds after she'd sent one. He was always up for food.

Luckily, the line was short, and Ryden was still the cashier.

"Well, well," he said when she walked up. "What can I get for you, random customer?"

"Medium hot chocolate and a large blueberry muffin," she replied. "I've got a hungry cousin at home."

"Ah. A convenient reason to get served again? Five-ninety is your total."

Layla paid.

"You know, this makes three times I've been your cashier," Ryden said as he handed over Layla's change.

She faked a gasp. "What? Nooo, you must be mistaken."

"You challenge my counting skills?" He stood straighter. "Well, I am pleased to report that I passed kindergarten. And grades one and two."

"What about grade three?"

"Now that one proved a challenge."

Layla laughed.

Ryden said, "All right, I'm gonna get in trouble if we talk any longer, but I'll text you, okay?"

"Okay. I'll look forward to it."

Layla moved out of the way to collect her order and let the person behind her make his.

"I should've gotten another caramel macchiato for the way home," she muttered as she exited the store.

Her eye was caught by a man leaning against the bus stop sign, watching the store. He wore sunglasses and a black jacket. Layla's pulse shot up, and she fought the instinct to take off.

Wait...

She knew that hair. Unruly and blond.

Nathan.

She sighed and walked off. She didn't have to look back to know he was following her. Hopefully, he could avoid knocking over any trash cans this time.

The rest of the way home was uneventful, aside from two minor mishaps.

First, having to loiter on a street corner because Nathan missed his chance to walk. She felt bad, okay?

Two, Nathan running to make it to the bus stop before the bus arrived and just barely making it on.

When Layla got home, she dropped the food off to a grateful but verbally unexpressive Karsyn. Then she went into her room and lay on her bed. Fingers crossed nothing else eventful happened, and she could just enjoy the rest of her day off in peace.

"Layla! Come set the table!" her mother called.

Layla rolled off the bed and onto the floor. "Coming!" She stood up and brushed herself off. "I really need to sweep my floor," she muttered to herself as she made her way into the dining room.

She picked up the plates her mother had set out on the kitchen counter and distributed them around the table.

"Mom, you set out too many plates," she said, holding up the odd one.

"No, honey, Daniel's eating with us. Remember?"

Layla groaned and set his plate down with a thump.

The front door opened, then made a sound like a gunshot. Someone had slammed it without managing to close it. Three seconds later,

Daniel appeared at the kitchen entrance, still in the process of yanking off his shoes. His messenger bag had slipped from his shoulder to his elbow. His coat was only buttoned twice, both in the wrong holes, and his hair looked like it hadn't been brushed since yesterday.

Layla stared.

Daniel managed to yank his other shoe off, and he threw it to the right, in the direction of the entryway. He stood up straight.

"I'm so sorry! Am I late?!"

The messenger bag slid down his arm and thumped to the floor. Then he actually noticed his surroundings.

"Oh, you're still setting the table. Thank goodness."

He went into the living room and plopped into a chair. He ran his fingers through his hair, doing nothing to improve its dishevelled state.

Layla was able to move again. She shot her mother a questioning look, but she shook her head and gestured to the table. Then she wiped her hands on her apron and went over to Daniel. Layla returned to her task but kept glancing over at them.

"Big day at work, honey?" her mother asked.

"You could say that," he said. "I'll explain at dinner. I just need to rest for a bit."

She frowned. "Are you wearing pyjama pants?"

He looked at her, then looked down at his pants.

"Oh, go change!" She shooed him with her hands. "Go grab some pants, maybe even a new shirt."

He got up and headed down the hall. "Are they still in the closet?"

"Yes." She started heading back to the kitchen, then stopped. "And brush your hair!"

Layla finished setting the table as quickly as she could. She wanted to hear what had happened! Never had she seen Daniel so un-Daniel-like. Something big must have happened with the Suits.

Once she finished and dealt with the messenger bag and the door, they could all sit at the table.

Her mom, closest to the kitchen and looking put together, as always. Karsyn, with paint smudges on his forehead. He always forgot he was holding a paintbrush and would sweep his hair back. Daniel, now looking presentable but with considerable bags underneath his eyes. And Layla, wearing the same outfit she had gone to the cafe in.

Layla's mother grabbed Daniel's plate for him and began scooping food onto it. He nodded his thanks and took several long sips of water. Layla stared at him, waiting for him to start talking about what had happened. Karsyn grabbed two biscuits and passed the basket to Layla. Without looking, she grabbed one and set the basket next to her mother.

Daniel took his full plate and began eating.

Layla was going to explode if he didn't start giving some explanations soon.

As Layla's mother began to get her own food, she said, "So Daniel, how have you been doing lately? I hope you're getting enough sleep with this new internship with the GDRS."

"Well—"

Layla couldn't wait any longer and burst out, "No, tell us what happened *today*! Was it the Suits?"

"Layla," her mother reprimanded.

But Daniel didn't seem to mind. He leaned forward, his eyes shining. "The Spades broke into the Club headquarters and stole equipment last night!"

Layla's mouth dropped, and her mother froze.

Karsyn nodded. "Sick," he said before shovelling more food into his mouth.

"I know!" Daniel exclaimed. "It's crazy."

"Wait, wait." Layla held her hand up. "I thought you said you guys don't know where any Suit headquarters are."

Daniel shrugged. "We don't." He took a sip of water. "We only know what happened because we caught them."

"Who?!"

"The Clubs."

"But the Clubs were the ones who got robbed!" Layla set her cutlery down hard, causing her fork to ping off her plate.

"Okay, okay, hold on. I'm sorry. I'm pretty tired." Daniel ran a hand through his hair. "Let me explain from the beginning."

Her mother interjected. "But once your story is finished, let's move on to more pleasant subjects."

"Of course, Aunt Jane, this won't take long," Daniel said reassuringly.

She pursed her lips but nodded.

"It all started last night." Daniel frowned. "Uh, this morning, actually, I guess. Close to one o'clock, and I was just getting ready for bed when I got a call from the GDRS."

Karsyn snorted. "You go to bed at midnight? Lame."

"I have to be up at six every morning," Daniel said.

"Oh dang." Karsyn looked horrified but in a mild way.

"Daniel, you really should try to go to bed earlier," Layla's mother said. "Get at least seven hours."

"ANYways," Layla interrupted, looking pointedly at Daniel.

"Right. So, I got the call. There had been a car chase, and three of the vehicles involved had been apprehended. All Clubs." Daniel paused to swallow a bite of his biscuit. "Turns out a small group of Spades stole a shipment of weapons from the Clubs. They had taken over the truck carrying it, or something."

"Were any civilians hurt in the car chase?" Layla's mother asked.

Daniel hesitated. "No, no. Everyone was fine."

She sighed and returned to her food. "Thank goodness."

Layla stared at her cousin. She knew that look. The liar.

"But yeah, that's never happened before," Daniel rushed to continue after catching Layla's look. "Pretty much everybody was called in. We worked hard to catch the Spades, but they got away." Then Daniel mumbled, "Which was good."

"What do you mean it was good?" Layla demanded.

Daniel fiddled with his fork. "I wasn't particularly looking forward to seeing Shayne again."

This time, all three of them stopped and looked at him.

He said slowly. "All the Clubs' accounts confirm it. Shayne was one of the Spades who committed the robbery."

The oven timer beeped. That would be the cake her mother had made for dessert. She jumped out of her chair and went into the kitchen to attend to it.

"But why would the Ace of Spades be there?" Layla asked. "From everything you've told me, that never happens."

Daniel's eyes flashed her a harsh no-more-questions look.

Layla gaped. She pointed to herself and mouthed, "Me? Payback?"

Daniel jerked his head in a way that said yes but stop talking about it.

Layla's head spun, and she hardly heard it when Karsyn said, "Wait, Shayne's the Ace of Spades? Since when? And no one told me?"

Still in the kitchen, Layla's mother said, "I'm sorry, honey, but I didn't think it was something you needed to know."

"Why? Cause I'm too young to handle it? I'm not! All of you were doing way more by the time you were seventeen, but I can't even know what my cousin's up to!" He slammed his fork down on the table and stalked off.

Layla rolled her eyes. "And you wonder why we don't tell you things?" she muttered.

Daniel pointed his knife at her. "Don't be so harsh on him. We're all at fault here too."

"What—"

"You complain too much, and he echoes it."

The oven door closed with a clang. "I think we've said enough on this topic," Layla's mother said. "I'm going to get Karsyn, and when I get back, we're going to talk about better things." She disappeared down the hallway.

Layla crossed her arms and stared at the floor. The sound of Daniel's knife scraping across his plate was fiercely annoying, but she resisted the urge to say so.

"Do I need to tell Aunt Jane about that cashier boy you're flirting with?" Daniel asked.

Layla brought her head back up. "Why was that phrased like a threat?"

Stupid Daniel, getting a government job and thinking he was the coolest thing since sliced bread. Ugh.

He raised an eyebrow.

"Mom doesn't need to know anything because nothing's happening," Layla answered.

"You do know I also get full reports from your bodyguards, right?"

No.

She wanted to scream: Why? Why are you being so suffocating?

"If you say a word to Mom, I'll show her the article I read about the three pedestrians killed in a freak car chase."

Daniel dropped his fork, and it clattered on his plate. He stared at her. "Aunt Jane has enough on her plate right now, and I'm simply trying to protect her. Why do you want to ruin that?"

Why are you trying to shelter all of us? She wanted to demand.

Her mother and Karsyn returned.

The rest of the night managed to be quite pleasant. Karsyn went overboard in trying to make up for his earlier outburst by trying to make them laugh about everything. But it worked, and Layla was wiping away a few tears of laughter by the time her mother started cutting the cake. The only other hiccup in the evening was when her mother said, as she passed a slice to Daniel, "Oh, and Layla has some pretty exciting news. Want to tell him?" She looked at Layla.

Normally, yes. But today had proven he was rather touchy and judgemental when sleep deprived.

"We found an apartment," she mumbled.

His brows furrowed. "You...found an apartment?"

"It's super close to the university's campus, pre-furnished. So I don't have to buy a couch and stuff." Layla rushed to explain. "And it's way cheaper than living in residence, cause it's owned by this really sweet older lady. She's moving into a retirement home, but she doesn't want to give up the apartment or any of the furniture yet. For sentimental reasons or something."

Daniel glanced at her mom, then back at Layla.

She deflated. Which was her fault, really, for expecting a positive response.

"I just...well, last time you told me you were looking for an apartment..., I didn't think you were serious," he confessed.

"Well, I was."

She needed out. A place of her own, where she could live by her own schedule and without anyone telling her what to do. Oh, shoot. She was starting to sound like Shayne had. Maybe she should work on that.

Daniel scratched his head. "I just don't see the need. Why bother paying extra for rent and groceries when you can just stay home? Plus, you'll be able to focus better on school—"

"You moved out at eighteen as soon as you found a place you could afford," Layla interjected.

Her mother cleared her throat.

Hastily, Daniel said, "That's true, that's true. Well, congratulations. I'm glad you found an affordable apartment. Toronto's prices just get crazier every year."

"The apartment is in an excellent spot," her mother said. "And we'll be moving her in at the end of this week."

Daniel's mouth dropped, but just as quickly he snapped it back up. He gave Layla a quick nod and said again, "Congratulations."

Layla dug into her cake but stayed silent. Daniel, of all people, should have understood her desire to become independent. If her mother hadn't cleared her throat, for sure Daniel would have pointed out that he'd wanted to make things easier for Aunt Jane, he didn't have university bills to worry about, and a dozen other things that made his actions a noble sacrifice and hers irresponsible.

Daniel didn't stay long after dessert was finished. He wanted to stay and chat, but once he started yawning, her mom dragged him out.

"You need to sleep. I'm driving you home."

Once they left, Karsyn and Layla stared at each other and then went to their rooms. A text from Ryden was waiting for her. It was both a welcome surprise and distraction after that event of a meal. It read, *So… I've officially served you three times now*

Layla considered for a moment, then, chuckling, wrote back, *Yes.*

His reply came swiftly, as if he had just been waiting for her to reply. *C'mon, that's not fair*

Really laughing this time, she answered, *You sent me a fact, I confirmed it. What's unfair in that?*

She threw her phone at her bed and changed into her pyjamas. She was done with the day. But when she went to retrieve her phone, it wasn't on her bed. Instead of looking for it, she stared at her bed for half a minute while her brain short-circuited. Because she distinctly remembered—

Her phone buzzed, redirecting her attention to her line of shoes on the ground at the foot of her bed. There it was, sticking out of one of her golfing shoes, like a poor imitation of a foot.

She scooped it up and read the new texts from Ryden.

Yes, but I was implying, didn't you realize

And then, a minute later:

Can I ask you out on a date?

Layla grinned so suddenly and so widely that her cheeks hurt. This was it! She was going to get asked out.

She hastily wrote back, *Definitely.*

She held her breath as she waited for a reply. She didn't want to get her hopes raised anymore in case this was some sort of awful prank.

Typing bubbles appeared.

Yeesh, how slow did he type?

Centuries later, it felt, a new text appeared.

Then, officially: will you go on a date with me, Layla Zakkar?

Layla responded: *I would love to*

Her heart burst into song. It felt unreal that a guy like Ryden could be interested in her, but she was glad for whatever it was. She planned on enjoying every minute of it.

(Ryden) *Tomorrow?*

(Layla) *I have work. I'm free all day Saturday*

(Ryden): *Too far away. Friday?*

She thought for a second. She had reserved that day for any extra moving, though it should be pretty much done by then.

(Layla) *Well, I guess I'm free after 5:30.*

(Ryden) *Perfect! Come to Aroma Mocha at 5:45. Be prepared for the best first date ever!*

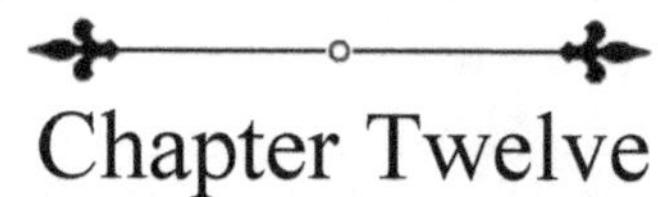

Chapter Twelve

As Layla walked into the lobby of Jason's studio, the sourball receptionist slowly lowered his magazine. So, it wasn't really "Jason's studio," but saying that in her head instead of "Miscellaneous Martial Arts Studio" was a lot easier and faster.

"Do you have a lesson or room booked, or are you here to book one?" the receptionist, Mr. Payton, asked, each word filled with the same mix of boredom and distrust.

"Um..."

She did have a lesson with Jason today, but she didn't know if it was official with the studio. She was about to tell him as much, since he was staring at her expectantly, when Jason appeared in the lobby.

"Layla!" He rushed over. "You're here—that is, I'm late to meet you. I'm sorry. It's...well, the lesson"—he waved both hands back towards the rooms— "lesson went over time—late."

"Hey, I don't mind. Paying customers come first." Layla tried to instill her words with as much reassurance as she could pack into them.

The receptionist let out a low, displeased hum.

"You—I mean...you haven't been waiting long? Here. That is, for me?"

"About thirty seconds before you came in," Layla said with a smile.

Jason relaxed.

"I'm assuming this is a 'she's with you' situation, then?" Mr. Payton interjected, already reaching for his magazine.

Jason started. "Oh! Mr. Payton...I—yes, she is...uh—that is, yes, I'm giving her a lesson."

"Have fun," he said, his words and tone complete opposites. He disappeared behind his magazine.

"You ready? For...actual self defence?" Jason asked.

"Let's do this!"

Once Layla had changed, she joined Jason in the room they had used last time. Only this time, there was a dummy as well. She assumed it was for practicing your moves on. Its arms and legs were missing. The torso was impaled on a black pole that became a round base, which was probably filled with sand or something so it wouldn't fall over.

"First things, uh, well, first!" Jason called out.

Layla whipped her head over to where his voice had come from. Ah, there he was. What was he doing over there?

No.

The treadmill!

Jason grinned. "Warm-up!"

Layla stayed where she was. "I don't really need to warm up. Do I? How important is that anyways?"

Jason's expression completely flipped. "Very. It's so important. You have to!"

He looked like he was gearing up to give her a full-on lecture about the mechanics of warming up.

"No!" Layla shouted, before he could really get started. She hurried over.

"Appreciated," Jason said. He set the treadmill speed to two, whatever that meant. "Besides, it's just a...warm-up. We're not—that is, just to get your blood moving, pumping. And your...muscles warm."

So Layla walked on the treadmill for a little bit, only really getting up to a brisk walk. Compared to last time, this was heaven.

After some dynamic stretching, they started the self-defence.

"Okay, so, real life… not like movies," Jason said. "Don't be complica—fancy. You wanna hit the, uh...sensitive spots on the body. Eyes, stomach, kidneys...also, the nose really hurts." He tapped his nose for emphasis.

"So how do I do that?" Layla asked.

Jason took her through the most effective ways to strike at those body parts. To jab at the eyes. Where to even find the kidneys on a person's body. The difference between hitting the stomach and hitting the diaphragm. Kicking the back of their knees to make them fall, even though this dummy had no knees so Layla had to stop before she kicked the pole.

She repeated the moves many, many times, to the point where it felt unnecessary. Hitting someone's stomach with your fist is not difficult to accomplish. The stomach is a big target.

As if Jason sensed her thoughts, he said, "The more you practice...the more you'll be, uh...the moves will be more natural. If you need to defend yourself, you don't want to have to think. You want instinct—reflex."

Which made sense. It didn't make the exercise any less boring, but Layla had more patience for it. Soon, Jason introduced a variation. He would call out a body part, and Layla had to attack it how he showed her. Knees, head, stomach, head again, eyes. Soon each move was coming almost automatically.

Jason would stop her at times to correct her form or offer advice. At one point, he said, "But, you know—that is, you can use your height to your advantage. Like with the kicks. Just stay balanced." His eyes were intense. "If a move, like...is gonna cost you balance, don't do it. If you're unbalanced, you can go down...boom, just like that. Stay balanced."

"I will," Layla promised.

Then she got to practice against him. They both moved slowly so no one got hurt. It was a lot trickier to hit your opponent when they were actively trying to avoid getting hit. But Layla actually enjoyed the challenge.

This hour and a half was much more physically demanding than the previous lesson. By the end, both of them were sweating. But Layla felt great. Tired, but proud of what she had accomplished so far.

Jason grabbed a towel and wiped off his face. "Good job! You're really...a fast learner."

"Thanks! It helps that you're such a great teacher."

"Oh, uh, thanks." Jason grinned. Then he hesitated and played with the edge of his towel. "Hey...um, would you like to—"

"Shoot, I have to go!" interrupted Layla, who had stopped listening after "thanks."

"I have to meet Ryden at Aroma Mocha in twenty minutes, and I am definitely showering first."

"Oh, okay. Who?" Jason's voice was infused with confusion.

"He works there, actually," Layla explained as she gathered up her stuff. "I don't know where he's taking me, but he told me to meet him there." She beamed at him. "He's taking me out on a date!"

Jason's face fell, then split into a wide smile. The change happened so quickly, Layla wondered if she imagined it. She didn't dwell on it; she was too excited about the date.

"That's awesome!" Jason said, drawing his shoulders in. "I hope...uh, have fun!"

"I hope it's a lot of fun too," Layla said. "Uh, bye. Thanks again!"

She rushed out, barely hearing his mumbled, "You're welcome."

Layla arrived a few minutes late to Aroma Mocha. There was Ryden, standing just outside the door. When he saw her, his face lit up. He rushed over to her.

"I thought you might not be coming," he said.

"I was only a few minutes late," Layla replied.

He sighed and nodded. "That's true, I just..." He stared into her eyes. "I really wanted to go on this date with you. I guess I got into my own head."

The date hadn't even officially begun and already her heart stopped. That was it. His eyes were still looking into hers, which did not help her to form coherent thoughts. Especially when she was trying to wrap her head around someone wanting to go on a date with her so much, they'd be this worried when she was late.

"Sorry," she breathed out, because she couldn't think of anything else at the moment.

Ryden placed a quick, but gentle, hand on her arm. "No, no, you don't have to be sorry. If I placed the date too quickly after something else, then I'm sorry."

"A little close, but nothing too bad," Layla said.

"Awesome. You ready for the best date ever?"

"Don't set the bar too high. Aren't you supposed to be trying to surpass my expectations?"

"You're right," Ryden said, with a sudden switch to seriousness. "This will be a terrible first date. You should probably just leave now, honestly. It might end up being *kinda* fun. Maybe."

His tone remained serious, but Layla could sense the undercurrents of humour. She played along.

"Well, if you insist," she said, turning like she was going to leave.

"Oh no!" Ryden wrapped his hand around her elbow and turned her around. "This way, m'lady."

They headed down the sidewalk.

"Can I ask where we're going?" Layla said.

"If you approve, I thought we could go minigolfing."

Layla gasped.

"But if not—" he began hastily.

"No, that's awesome! I LOVE minigolfing. We just barely go. Karsyn doesn't like it."

"Whew!" He mimed wiping sweat from his brow. "Perfect. How do you feel about Putting Edge? This bus"—he stopped at the bus stop, and Layla followed suit—"will take us there."

She thought for a second. "Is that the one that has the glow-in-the-dark course?"

"Yes."

Layla grinned. "Awesome."

Twenty minutes later, they were at the first hole. And wow was it cool! The lights were off, and their surroundings were glowing. It was like you were underwater, with sea animals and coral reefs.

Layla loved it.

Ryden was, to say it nicely, terrible.

"You're giving it too much power!" Layla barely managed to get out around her laughter, as Ryden missed the same hole for the fifth time.

"No, that one went in! It did! It just..." He muttered something under his breath as he went over to where the ball had stopped. "It just bounced out."

"Exactly, too much power. Like I said." Layla took a few steadying breaths and composed herself. "Your form is fine, so just try being a little softer when you hit the ball."

Ryden took extra time on his form, then lined up his club with the ball...adjusted his form again...gently brought his arm back...and hit the ball forward two inches. Layla pressed her lips together, doing everything possible to keep the laughter in. Ryden sank to his knees. They both stared at the ball.

When Layla trusted she could open her mouth without laughter spilling out, she said, "Maybe...a little more power?"

"Nope," Ryden shook his head, "I'm cursed!" He lifted up his club and then laid it on the ground by the ball. "Go on without me," he said dramatically.

"No, no, none of that." Layla walked over to him. "You're not cursed. You just lack skill."

He glared up at her.

"Skill that comes with practice," she continued hastily, "which you will only get if you keep going." She glanced behind him. "Plus, we're not the only ones here. That couple behind us is gonna want to use this hole once we're done."

"True," he conceded, allowing her to pull him to his feet.

Ryden managed to improve somewhat over the course of the night, avoiding any more skill-related breakdowns. Layla still won, naturally. He never stood a chance.

After minigolfing, they got dinner. After a self-defence lesson and minigolfing, Layla was hungry. Olive Garden was the perfect restaurant for that, thankfully. Although she tried to keep herself from being too excessive with the breadsticks.

Conversation with Ryden flowed easily and was always interesting. He could think of the most unique topics. He was so easy to talk to, and Layla had to stop herself twice from casually mentioning her brother.

She was having more fun than she thought she would.

They left about twenty minutes after they were through eating. Ryden had stood up and said they should go before the staff had to kick them out. From there, they hopped on a bus to Layla's apartment, as Ryden insisted on seeing her to her door. Such a gentleman.

It felt weird to be going to her apartment instead of back to her mom's. The apartment didn't feel like home yet. It didn't even feel like hers. True, it had only been two days, but it felt like she was taking over a stranger's house. Which, she figured she was, in a sense.

Then she heard Ryden mutter, "What kinda fish-mermaid tail pants are those?" and she was immediately distracted from her musings.

Ryden was looking at a photo his brother sent him, and the brother was wearing some truly odd, sequinned and shiny pants. So naturally, they spent the rest of the time judging his fashion decisions—Ryden had lots more photos. Then Layla remembered they were on a bus, which meant having to get off at some point. She looked up and gasped.

"This is my stop!"

They scrambled off, then halted on the sidewalk to catch their breath and, for Layla, to calm the spike of adrenaline.

"Wow, this really is the suburbs, isn't it?" Ryden remarked.

Layla looked around. She felt a growing sense of unease but couldn't pinpoint its cause.

"Very few people out," she noted.

Ryden shrugged. "It's just like that sometimes."

Oh! Nathan! Where was he?

She spun around, looking. Nope, he definitely wasn't here. She always knew when he was following her. Was that it? She frowned; no, couldn't be. Guaranteed, she still had that other bodyguard, the one she'd never actually seen.

Ryden was watching her, his eyebrows furrowed. "You all right?"

"I don't know, something just isn't..." she face-palmed violently, making Ryden jump. "This isn't my street." She shook her head. "This isn't my street." She turned and pointed. "We just have to backtrack a little bit, then make a left. Ugh!"

"Hey," Ryden said softly.

She looked over at him. He smiled.

"It's not a problem. Don't worry about it." He looped his arm through hers. "Plus, it means I get to spend just a little more time with you! Worth it."

Gratitude at his understanding rushed through her. Not for the first time that night, Layla found herself wondering how she'd been so lucky as to go out with a guy like Ryden.

They hadn't walked far when five men, who had been waiting at a bus stop, suddenly formed a line in front of them. No subtlety.

Layla's pulse skyrocketed. Were they Clubs again? She moved closer to Ryden. She didn't want to go through that again, no way.

But you've got Ryden with you this time, she told herself. *And a bodyguard. So just breathe.*

"Could you excuse us? We're trying to walk here," Ryden said with much more politeness than the situation warranted.

One of the men spat his gum on the ground. "Nah. I don't think so," he said.

Another man said, "Hand over your wallets and you can keep on walking."

Ryden's whole attitude shifted. Layla could feel him draw himself up taller and his body stiffened. He glared at the men. "I don't think so."

What? Layla was totally ready to hand over her wallet if that meant they would leave them alone. She had maybe ten bucks in cash and no more than three in loose change. The cards she could cancel in an instant, so they would be useless.

"Ryden, let's just do what they say," she said quietly.

"Not a chance."

The man raised an eyebrow. "You wanna get hurt?"

Ryden just stared. And yeah, sure, he was over six feet and pretty muscular, but how intimidating could one guy be when he faced five? Layla didn't like this situation one bit. And where was her bodyguard? Shouldn't he be stepping in by now?

Without warning, the tallest man stepped forward and socked Ryden on the jaw. He stumbled backwards.

"No!" Layla yelled.

Without thinking, she swung her foot up and kicked the one in front of her in the forehead. His head flew backwards, and he almost fell. The kick threw off Layla's balance, and she wobbled on one foot. Ryden's hands flew to her back to support her.

Jason's words flew through her mind: *But remember, stay balanced.*

Before Layla had time to fix her error, the other men struck. Someone punched Layla's hip, making her twist out of Ryden's grip and fall to the ground.

Ryden lunged forward, his fist barrelling into one man's face.

Layla scrambled to stand up. The man in front of her backed up slightly when she stood to her full height; she was taller than he was.

She used the heel of her hand to try to hit his nose. But she wasn't fast enough. He ducked under her arm and tried to punch her in the ribs. Tried. At that moment, Ryden backed up into her, making her fall to the ground, and the guy ended up punching Ryden in the back.

Layla twisted onto her back. She brought her legs up and thrust them forward at the shorter one. They hit him low in the stomach, and he stumbled.

Two others had already been knocked out. Ryden was simultaneously fighting the other two. Layla jumped up. She kicked the back of one's knees, making him crumple to the ground. He whirled around. He drew back his fist but suddenly halted. He stared at her face.

Layla froze as well, confused.

"Y-you're...you're..." he stuttered.

Layla's eyes widened. Were these guys more than just random muggers? She almost fell backwards in her attempt to put distance between them.

"Barry, we gotta get outa here!" he shouted, jumping to his feet.

Ryden and Barry both stopped fighting and turned to face them. Ryden's fist was drawn back, poised to punch, his other gripped the front of Barry's shirt.

"Dude, she's on the no-harm list!"

Barry jumped back, shaking off Ryden's hand. "Let's get out of here!"

They ran off into the rapidly darkening night.

Layla watched them go. Then her adrenaline evaporated. Every place she got punched blazed with pain. Her legs wobbled, and she collapsed to the ground.

Ryden rushed over. "Are you all right? Are you hurt?"

"We were just in a punchout. Of course I'm hurt!" She took several deep breaths, then shook her head. "But no, I...you know, with what we just went through, I'm fine. Just a few bruises."

"Okay." He started brushing himself off. "Thank goodness you're on the no-harm list." He looked up. His face scrunched together. "Wait, what is the no-harm list? And why are you on it?"

"Let's go inside somewhere first, please. Then I'll explain."

They headed to her apartment, which was thankfully in the opposite direction from where the men had run off. Layla wanted to run, to get off the streets as soon as possible. But her body ached and protested with each step, and she couldn't manage a pace faster than walking. Ryden was limping and winced occasionally, although he tried to stifle the sounds.

They reached her apartment building and entered, which gave Layla some relief. But she would feel better when she was in her apartment with the door locked. For a moment, they stood there, silent, in the lobby.

"All right...we're inside," Ryden said. "What's the no-harm list?"

Layla hesitated, a thousand things running through her head. "Listen...if I tell you, you have to promise you'll never tell anyone else."

"Because then you'll have to kill me?" Ryden whispered.

"What?" Layla was taken aback. "No! At least, I don't think so."

"Oh, good. You don't have to worry. I won't reveal anything. Unless it's illegal," he joked.

"Well...kinda," Layla said.

"Excuse me?"

Layla sighed. "It's complicated."

Ryden crossed his arms. "Then make it simple."

"My brother is the Ace of Spades."

This was it. The moment he would say goodbye and walk away. Because sure, tons of people knew someone who had joined a Suit, but how many had a sibling running one?

Ryden's eyes widened. "Woah." He looked at a spot in the distance for a moment, and Layla could almost see the gears turning in his head. He turned back to her. "And this has what to do with the no-harm list?"

Her eyebrows went up. That was his only question? Why was that his only question?

"Um, well, I don't know exactly, but I would assume the no-harm list is for people who aren't supposed to be harmed because they're important. Or, they have family members that'll hurt you if you hurt them. Something like that."

"Oh, right. That makes sense. So you're on it because you have a very powerful, criminal brother that'll harm anyone who harms you."

Layla cringed. "Yeah. Listen, I know it's a lot, but I don't want to discuss it tonight. I just wanna go to bed."

He nodded, his dark eyes full of concern. "Of course. I'm sorry our date had to have such a poor ending."

She smiled, just a small smile, in spite of it all. "True. But the beginning was great."

"I'm glad you think so. Listen," he reached out and put his hand on her shoulder, "just know this doesn't change how I feel about you. I still want another date. If you do, that is."

In spite of the mugging that had just happened, Layla felt her heart lifting. How could a man so perfect, so kind, fall for her? It was almost too good to be—

No.

His shirt had shifted, revealing a tattoo. Tiny, inconsequential, right below his collarbone. A black "S."

Layla couldn't keep her face from reacting, feeling it contort in shock.

Ryden took a hasty step back and raised his hands. "But not if you don't want to!"

"No, no, sorry." She looked away, her mind reeling. This was too much, too much to process. "It's just, I can't think of anything right now except sleep. And some Tylenol."

"Of course." His eyebrows furrowed in concern. "Take all the time you need. I'm here if you need me."

"Thanks, Ryden. Good night."

She watched him turn and walk out of the building.

She wanted to cry. Forget the fact that she was in the middle of the lobby. Her mind raced as she hurried to the elevator.

A Spade! A *Spade*.

What did that mean? Was it just a coincidence that a Spade wanted to date her only days after being taken by the Clubs?

Too many thoughts, too many unknowns to try to figure out for tonight. She wanted sleep. Tomorrow she could think about it. Tomorrow. What would she do tomorrow?

Chapter Thirteen

Someone knocked at her apartment door. Layla fumbled with the plate she'd just grabbed and managed to clutch it to herself and not drop it. She took a deep breath. Who would be knocking? She wasn't expecting anyone, and most of them would have called or texted before coming over.

She steadied herself, walked over, and peered through the peephole. It was Shayne!

"What are you doing here?" Layla exclaimed.

As if he heard her, Shayne grinned and stuck his hands in his pockets.

Against her better judgement, and mostly due to the fear that someone might recognize him, Layla opened the door.

As soon as there was enough space, Shayne squeezed himself into the entryway.

"Lay Lay!" he exclaimed.

Layla's heart faltered. It had been a long time since she'd heard anyone but Daniel use that nickname. Shayne swept her up into a hug, squeezing so hard Layla thought her ribs might crack. At the very least, they screamed in protest. She had acquired several bruises from the fight last night, after all, and they didn't appreciate being pressed on. The embrace was brief, and then Shayne was already moving on.

"I can't believe you finally got your own place! You've talked about it for so long, I thought you'd never do it! Wow, it's a really nice place too." He walked into the living room. He spun in a circle, taking it all in. Then he laughed and ran down the hall.

Layla followed, walking slowly. She was still trying to wrap her head around the fact that Shayne was here. In her apartment.

"That sink is so extra." Shayne exited the bathroom. "And please tell me you didn't pick out the wallpaper."

"What, are you a part-time interior designer now, too?" Layla managed to say around a frozen tongue.

"I have eyes."

"I didn't pick it. This apartment was pre-furbished."

Shayne laughed again. "How are you affording this? You're working at Staples, plus you're saving up for university."

"Mom's paying for half."

Shayne sobered. "Really? Can she afford that?"

Layla nodded.

"Great! And now that you have your own place, I can visit whenever I want!"

"You're not worried someone will recognize you?" The words came out with more bite than Layla intended.

Shayne's expression fell.

For the first time, he seemed to notice her stiffness. Layla felt her eyes were revealing too much. Shayne was staring into them.

"Do we need to talk?" he asked.

That question broke the walls Layla had thrown up the second she saw Shayne.

"No, why would we?" She threw the words at him. "You think you can just let yourself into my new place? After years of not speaking to me? And that things are just supposed to stay as they were before?"

"How was I supposed to contact you?" Shayne demanded. "I'm the Ace of Spades. I can't just knock on Mom's door. I have no idea how she or Karsyn would respond."

"And you're just taking it for granted that I won't call the police?"

Shayne looked like he'd been punched in the gut. "Lay Lay...we're siblings. I thought that you, of all people...You know, I'm not really bad. Not really."

Layla stared at him. What did he mean by that? How did being the leader of one of the biggest gangs in North America still classify him as "not really bad"? But, it had been years since she'd seen him. She wasn't going to ruin a chance at having him back in her life by arguing.

"I do know," she said at last. "But that doesn't change what you've done, Shayne."

He swept her up into another hug, just as fierce as the last but also gentler.

"Please, let's not talk about what I've done. Let's not talk about me or any of that. I just...I just want to be a normal brother, visiting his sister because he missed her."

Layla relaxed into his embrace. "I missed you too, Shayne," she admitted.

His arms tightened around her.

"But I'm also quite hungry," she said.

He released her immediately. "You haven't eaten breakfast yet?"

"My toast is waiting for me."

"Go eat!" He made shooing motions with his hands.

Layla hurried to the kitchen, and Shayne followed. The toast was significantly cooler now, so she pushed it back down and turned the setting lower. Just to heat them back up a bit.

"So...guess what I did last week?" Shayne said, voice bubbling with excitement.

"Broke into the Clubs' headquarters?" Layla said nonchalantly as she turned to face him.

He lifted a hand, then let it limply drop. "How did you know?"

Layla shrugged and grabbed jam out of the fridge. "Plenty of articles written about it. It was a pretty big car chase."

"No. No one knew the details, or what the car chase was about. The GDRS didn't tell the public anything either."

Her toast popped up. She looked briefly at Shayne before giving her attention to her breakfast. "Daniel told us."

She put the toast on her plate.

"How did Daniel know?" His voice was quiet.

"He's doing this internship thing with the GDRS to become a full-time agent," Layla answered, just as quietly.

Shayne was silent for the entire time Layla spread jam on her toast. His upbeat mood had vanished, sucking most of the life out of the kitchen.

Layla once again turned to face him and leaned against the kitchen counter.

"Daniel is..." Shayne's voice failed him. "Huh." He nodded.

"Can you blame him?" Layla said gently.

"Hard to feel like it isn't personal," Shayne mumbled.

Layla crunched on her toast. What do you say to that? What is there to say?

They both knew the implications. What this could mean for the future.

"Oh, I forgot," Layla said. "Thank you for rescuing me. I know that was a while ago, but I never got a chance to properly thank you." Also, the tension was starting to choke her, so she had to break it somehow.

Shayne brightened. "Of course! No way I was letting them hurt you. I know I haven't been the best older brother, but I still..." He hunched his shoulders. "You know."

She did know, and it warmed her heart. Now that he was here, in her apartment, the years of anger towards him for being gone slipped away. Besides, after her last couple of interactions with Daniel, she decided she preferred physical distance with love over proximity with condescension.

And then she remembered her last interaction with Daniel, and what he had implied about the break-in. She pressed her lips together. Did she want to know? Maybe not, but she had to know just the same.

"Shayne...why did you guys break into Club headquarters?"

"Cause they tried to hurt you," he said as if it was the most obvious thing in the world. "We couldn't let them get away with that, or think they could try again."

Layla froze. Somehow, the answer was both what she expected and not what she expected. On the one hand, revenge on her behalf was...a sweet (?) notion and appreciated. On the other hand...well, but it's not like the Clubs were innocent people. They're actually the worst Suit. So it was kind of a good thing. Except it has given the Spades even more violent weapons. But the thought behind it had been in the right place...right?

With a jolt, she realized Shayne was staring at her, face contorted with worry.

"Thank you," she said. Not because she finished processing what had happened but because it seemed like the right thing to say.

Plus, it was her brother. Here. The thing she'd wanted for years, and she wasn't going to let their relationship fall away again.

Shayne shrugged. "Least I could do. Helped me out too. Anyways! How's that new boyfriend?" He wiggled his eyebrows.

Layla's heart jumped, but she managed to say evenly, "We've had one date. That hardly makes him my boyfriend."

"Right, but judging from the look on your face, that's what you want to happen."

Was that what her face looked like? Good. She hadn't decided if she wanted to ask Shayne about Ryden being a Spade. But the fact that Shayne knew about Ryden somehow seemed to confirm a thought she'd been trying to avoid.

Layla ducked her head. She put her plate in the sink.

"But if you don't," Shayne said, "that's fine—"

"No, I do! It's just, um...I don't know how likely there is to be a second date anymore."

"Huh?!" Shayne's outburst held far more passion than Layla expected. "Why not?" He was looking at her intently.

She sighed. How was she supposed to explain why she never wanted to see Ryden again without mentioning that he was probably, almost definitely, a Spade?

"We were mugged," she said instead. "Well, attempted, actually—"

"You were what?! ARE YOU—wait." He held up his hands. "Firstly, not your fault, so I don't see why there can't be a second date. Secondly, attempted? So, your bodyguard from the government stepped in and stopped it, right?"

Layla gaped at him. How did he know about her bodyguard?

Her bodyguard!

"No, he didn't!" she said with indignation.

"What? What happened then?"

"Well, at first Ryden was doing a pretty good job of fighting them off."

Shayne gave a nod, as though satisfied.

"But then one of them realized I was on the no-harm list, so they ran. I guess I owe that to you?"

"Oh! Yeah, you do. Well, specifically the raid on the Clubs. It really sent out a message."

Ah. That complicated her thoughts on that.

"Were you hurt?" Shayne asked.

She stared at him. "It was a mugging. There was fighting. Of course I'm hurt."

Shayne threw his hands in the air. "Well okay, Miss Specifics. Are you in-need-of-medical-attention hurt or just bruised-and-sore hurt?"

Layla grinned in spite of herself. "Just bruises."

"Excellent. I'm upset about your bodyguard not showing up though."

"Me too. I should call Daniel. He can talk to the right people about it."

"I suppose that's a good idea," Shayne said.

He didn't seem happy about it. But honestly, what did he think *he'd* be able to do?

"I should get going then," Shayne said. "If I wait any longer, I'm gonna get a full-blown lecture from Timothy." He muttered, "But what else is new?"

She nodded. "All right. But you will...will you visit again?"

He looked at her and grinned. "As often as I can. Which probably won't be that often." He gave her a quick one-armed hug, and when he pulled away, he pointed at her and said, "Now you're gonna rest for the rest of the day, right? Ice the bruises. Or would heat be better?"

"Ice. In fact, I should avoid using heat on them for several days."

"All right, all right, you don't have to sound so unimpressed. You will rest though?"

Why was he so concerned about her resting? In spite of her desire for independence, it made her happy that he cared enough to ask again.

"I will. For most of the day. I have this meeting with a reporter at two."

Shayne narrowed his eyes. "A reporter?"

"Aspiring reporter, actually, who's hoping my story will give her a breakthrough. Or something like that."

"Okay...Well, rest as much as you can around that. And don't stress. Bye."

Layla barely had time to register that he was leaving, let alone say "bye" back, before he had left.

"Bye," she said anyway. "Hmm." She stared after him for a while, processing. Then, the realization hit her. "I'm still hungry."

She went back into the kitchen to make some more toast. While the bread was in the toaster, she called Daniel and told him what happened. His reaction was rather explosive, and she once again had to move the phone away from her ear. She should just start calling him in speaker mode.

He promised he would talk to Mr. Greer and figure out what happened, then hung up.

Once that was done, all that was left was to eat her next piece of toast and rest until the meeting, which, thankfully, was still four hours away. She took full advantage of the rest time by icing her bruises, lying on the couch, and rewatching a favourite: *House M.D.* She slipped in and out of sleep, which didn't matter much as she could practically recite any episode from memory.

At one o'clock, she had to start getting ready. They'd agreed to meet at a Tim Hortons close to Layla's apartment. But it was still about a fifteen-minute bus ride, and she had to look presentable.

At 1:57 p.m., Layla was walking into the Tim Hortons, scanning the customers for the reporter. She knew exactly what to look for, as Victoria had given her an extensive description of Neylan. As it turned out, that wasn't necessary, since Neylan popped her hand into the air and started waving it vigorously.

"Layla, Layla!" she called out.

Layla walked over to the booth Neylan was sitting in, all her reporter gear spread out across the table. Including eleven pens, all of different colours. Talk about overkill.

Neylan jumped up, grabbed Layla's hand, and shook it several times.

"Thank you so much for agreeing to meet with me!" she exclaimed. "I appreciate it so very much!"

"I—yeah, you're welcome," Layla said. She went to sit down, but Neylan exclaimed,

"Wait! Would you like to buy anything first? Coffee, a doughnut? Make you more at ease?"

"No, thank you. I actually just ate lunch." Layla sat down. She really just wanted to start this interview as soon as possible and get it over with.

"Well, I dunno, but it is your choice!" Neylan sat down across from Layla. "But you might want something sugary before this is over. Ah, but you can always get it later!" She pulled her open notebook closer to her and grabbed a pen. "So..." she swept her hair back over her shoulder.

Her earring caught Layla's eye. A small, bright red diamond that glittered when it caught the light.

"Now we can begin the interview," Neylan said.

Layla readied herself.

Neylan clicked the pen and looked at Layla with quite possibly the biggest smile in the world. She asked, "What do you know about the Diamonds?"

Layla froze. What? She had expected the first question to be something along the lines of "Tell me what happened that morning before the bank, or at the bank." Not this. Why on earth would she ask about the Diamonds?

Feeling vaguely uneasy, Layla said, "Like, the Suit?"

Still smiling, pen poised over the paper, Neylan said, "Yes. Like the Suit.”

Solidly creeped out now, Layla said, “Well, uh...nobody really knows much about them. Their branch here is led by a Queen. They mostly do hacking and blackmail...stuff. Online.”

Neylan was still staring at her. She had yet to write down anything.

“Right?” Layla asked. Maybe her information was all wrong.

“Oh yes, that is some of what we do,” Neylan said.

Layla’s stomach dropped, and she pressed back against the booth. We? Did the earrings mean... No, they couldn’t...

Neylan’s whole demeanour changed. She put the pen down, and her face took on a seriousness Layla had assumed she wasn’t capable of.

“Now, Layla, don’t be alarmed. I’m not going to harm you.”

“What...what is this all about?” Layla managed to ask.

Neylan leaned forward and put her hands together. “There are some things my Queen feels you should know. And, she has a proposition for you.”

Layla didn’t think it was possible for her stomach to drop anymore, but it did.

They looked at each other. Neylan was waiting for her to say something.

“I think I need to get a coffee first,” Layla croaked.

The corners of Neylan’s mouth barely curved upwards in a smile. What a contrast.

“Yes, I thought you might.”

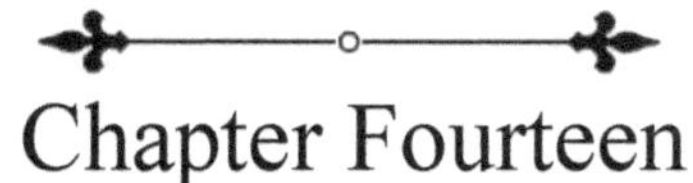

Chapter Fourteen

aniel set down his phone and looked up. Mr. Greer was watching him with calculating eyes.

"I believe I've got most of the information," he said. "But lay it all out for me."

"Layla was almost mugged last night," Daniel said. "She's fine. It was unsuccessful but no thanks to Cameron. Apparently, he never stepped in to help. Why not? That's his job. Was he even there at all?"

"Be careful of your condescending tone," Mr. Greer warned. "There may be a reasonable explanation." He frowned. "Though I can't imagine what. No bodyguard would abandon their person. But to not interfere...hmm." He pushed himself up. "We shall go find out."

"We, sir?" Daniel asked.

"Yes. It's best if we both talk to him," Mr. Greer answered.

Daniel nodded and fell in step behind Mr. Greer. His brain went into overdrive. Why would it be better if they both went? Had Mr. Greer sensed something in his earlier attitude that made him think Daniel was unfit for the task alone? He drew himself up, standing taller (even though Mr. Greer couldn't see it).

No, he would show that he had the skills necessary for a calm, rational discussion without condescension. His heart sank. Wait, what if it was a test? Was Mr. Greer only coming to see how well he performed?

They were in the elevator now, but Daniel barely noticed.

Should he take charge, then, when they got to Mr. Miller's office? But if he took charge, Mr. Greer might think he was being impertinent. Especially if he was coming because he knew best what to do and wanted to show Daniel so he could learn.

They exited the elevator.

Daniel rolled his shoulders. *Relax*, he told himself sternly. *He could be coming literally just because you don't know where Mr. Miller's office is.*

He let out a long, measured breath. He would be calm and

professional and follow Mr. Greer's lead.

Mr. Greer knocked on the door of the office, even though it was already open. Mr. Miller looked over from his computer.

"Benjamin," he said. "Come in."

They both entered. Daniel noticed that Mr. Miller was playing solitaire on his computer. At work. Without trying to hide it. Daniel didn't know if he gained or lost respect for the man.

"You were not someone I expected to see this morning," Mr. Miller said. He eyed Daniel. "What brings you here?"

"Daniel has something curious to report about someone from the bodyguard unit, and we thought you should be made aware," Mr. Greer answered.

A good answer. Clear in purpose but lacking in detail. And also not saying what Mr. Miller had to do upon hearing it. Daniel took note.

Mr. Miller gestured for Daniel to speak.

Daniel stepped forward. *Clear and without condemnation*, he reminded himself. Then he began. "Layla called me this morning because some people attempted to rob her last night. They were unsuccessful, but there was a fight. Layla is bruised and sore but otherwise unhurt. However, Cameron never appeared to help her. She found this odd, as that is his job."

"And Nathan?" Mr. Miller asked immediately, catching Daniel off guard.

"Na—oh."

That's right, Nathan was her other bodyguard. Layla hadn't mentioned him at all, but to say that would mean Daniel didn't think to ask, which would show inadequacy. His brain came to that conclusion in mere seconds.

"From what I gather, Nathan was not there either," Daniel heard himself saying.

"Now that I find extremely concerning," Mr. Miller said, sounding completely unconcerned. "Nathan would be more likely to jump in when he wasn't needed."

Daniel wasn't sure if he should say something here, but fear of saying the wrong thing kept him silent.

Luckily, Mr. Greer said, "Yes, precisely why we wanted to bring this matter to your attention."

"Would either of you like to be present when I speak to Nathan and Cameron?" Mr. Miller asked as he stood up. He looked at Daniel.

"Since you have a personal connection."

Daniel didn't allow himself time to overthink his answer. "I would greatly appreciate that."

Mr. Miller humphed and walked over to the door to the side of his office. He called for his assistant to send Cameron and Nathan to his office.

Mr. Greer nodded, then said, "I'll leave this matter to you two." He left.

Daniel looked at Mr. Miller. Mr. Miller looked at him. It occurred to Daniel that he was alone with a guy he'd only directly talked to twice, both in the last five minutes.

"You a silence or small talk kinda man?" Mr. Miller asked, his tone giving no indication of which he preferred.

"You seem to have a solitaire game up and running, and I wouldn't want you to rack up anymore time on it," Daniel answered.

Mr. Miller looked at him, and Daniel wasn't sure if he was going to laugh or get mad at him for pointing the game out.

But then he just sat down at his desk...and continued his game. It was a little awkward standing there in silence while Mr. Miller played solitaire with a tightly furrowed brow and equal silence. This, however, was preferable to trying to carry on a conversation about the weather or something. It also gave him time to mentally prepare for Nathan, who was usually intense and in-your-face cheerful. But if he was sad, he felt it just as intensely. Frankly, it was draining.

Cameron, on the other hand, didn't seem to feel anything, appearing thoroughly unbothered 100 percent of the time. His hair was shaggy, and he always wore one earring—a red diamond. Daniel thought it was supremely insensitive, given that their whole thing was getting rid of all the Suits. Yet here he was showing up to work every day wearing a symbol of one of the Suits.

But, Daniel had to admit, Cameron was quite competent and able to make fast, smart decisions under pressure. So Daniel trusted him, even if he harboured some dislike for him.

Cameron and Nathan showed up much sooner than Daniel expected.

Mr. Miller stood up. "Thank you for being prompt. I didn't catch you just before you were heading out?"

Cameron shrugged. "Nah. Lisa's in place. We head out at noon."

"Good. This is Daniel, Layla's cousin." Mr. Miller didn't bother gesturing to him. "Nathan, were you on duty last night?"

Nathan's smile vanished, replaced by a look of immeasurable guilt. "No. But—Cameron told me it was okay!"

"Cameron is not your boss. It's not his place to give you a night off." Mr. Miller's voice was gruff but not more than usual.

Was Nathan's bottom lip trembling? Daniel refrained from rolling his eyes.

"Sorry." Nathan hung his head.

Mr. Miller frowned. "You won't do it again?" he asked.

Daniel thought he might be attempting a gentler tone, but his voice just wasn't made for that.

Nathan nodded vigorously. "Yes, yes, I promise! Never again!"

"Then you may go."

Daniel's surprise must have shown on his face because, once Nathan had scurried from the room, Mr. Miller said to him, "No sense in making him more upset. Not his fault something happened the one night he wasn't there." He turned to Cameron. "Why did you tell him he could take last night off?"

Cameron blew a bubble of gum, then popped it. Daniel stiffened. How unprofessional.

"I just didn't wanna have to deal with him that night," he said. "Figured I'd give both of us a break. Layla too."

"Layla?" Mr. Miller asked.

Cameron nodded. "Yeah. She's smart, you know. Figures out where he is. Not that you have to be super smart to notice him. Anyways, figured she'd rather not have that while she was on her date."

"Date?" The word was out of Daniel's mouth before he realized he was saying it.

"Yeah." Cameron half-smirked, half-smiled. "What, you didn't know?"

Daniel shook his head. "No. She didn't tell me that when she called about the mugging." And that stung more than he thought it would. Why didn't she trust him? Was she still upset about what he had said about Ryden at the dinner? He hadn't meant to—

Cameron interrupted his thoughts. "What, you thought she just fought off five guys by herself?"

"Five?!" Daniel nearly shouted.

"Dude. Did she even call you?"

"I didn't ask for the specifics," Daniel mumbled angrily.

Cameron looked at Mr. Miller. "Is that what this is about? The mugging?"

"Yes. Layla was confused, and Daniel concerned, about why you didn't interfere."

Cameron frowned and popped another bubble. "Why would I? That Ryden dude was handling them just fine, and they clearly weren't Suits."

Daniel stared at him. "Your job is to protect Layla."

"Yeah, against the Suits. And Ryden was protecting her."

Daniel frowned, hating that his logic was actually sound. "How well did Ryden fight?" he asked.

"Quite well."

"That's curious."

"Why should it be?" Mr. Miller asked.

Maybe it wasn't odd. Maybe Daniel was just mad and looking for somewhere he could actually place it. As annoyed as he still was with Cameron, his reasoning made sense.

Mr. Miller was frowning, but he didn't look particularly upset. "Cameron, you may need to change your mindset if the family's not comfortable with it." He looked at Daniel.

Daniel opened his mouth, ready to answer, but then shut it. Maybe Layla wouldn't really appreciate him making decisions about her bodyguard. Not that she'd notice, probably. But all the same...

"Layla should decide," Daniel said.

Mr. Miller nodded once. "Great. Cameron, you may go."

"Thank you." He grinned at Daniel, then left.

Mr. Miller looked at Daniel. "Good decision."

Daniel made a noncommittal "hmm" sound.

"He annoys you, but he's an excellent bodyguard."

The words held a tone of finality, so Daniel said, "Thanks for all your help, Mr. Miller."

Mr. Miller nodded again, and Daniel left.

Layla sat back down in the booth, her coffee cup held firmly between both hands. "So, getting back to the fact that you're part of a dangerous Suit and are probably going to kill me if I don't agree to whatever it is you want.”

Neylan sighed. “Ah, Layla. So much of your brother in you. It really is too bad.”

“I’m similar to my brother? No way!” Layla muttered sarcastically. “It’s almost like we’re related or something.”

“Enough impertinence,” Neylan said, folding her hands together on the table. “You’re using humour to deflect your fear about this situation, and I don’t appreciate it. You’re currently not in any danger.”

Layla wholeheartedly disbelieved her. She also wasn’t a fan of the word “currently” that Neylan threw in there. But she steeled herself and nodded for Neylan to continue.

“This meeting has two purposes. One, to impart some information my Queen feels has been wrongfully hidden from you. And two, a proposition.”

Layla took a long drink of her coffee. When it became obvious that Neylan wasn’t going to say anything, Layla asked, “What information?”

“Ryden is a Spade, and your father was a Club.”

Layla dropped her cup onto the table, where it proceeded to create a puddle. She couldn’t give any attention to the confirmation about Ryden, although that in itself was bad enough.

“My father...?”

“What do you know about him?” Neylan asked.

“Not much. He left us when Shayne and I were really little. Mom once said something about it being her own fault for being surprised, or something. But she never elaborated on what that meant.”

Neylan nodded. “He was a Club. She knew. He left to go be fully involved.”

He was a what?

“You say, um, he was?” Layla asked.

“Yes. He is dead.”

Layla sat back and looked down at her hands.

“I will clean this coffee up. You take your time.”

Layla was barely aware of Neylan wiping the table and throwing the coffee cup away.

Her dad was—

Her mom *knew*.

Was it irrational to be angry at her mom? How do you explain all that to toddlers? Still, as they got older, she could have explained.

It's not like she had ever thought highly of her father to begin with. He had left their family, and that was bad enough. Knowing he was a Club, that was a hard pill to swallow. But knowing her mother had lied to them about why he left and who he was...

Why was everyone in her life determined to not treat her like an adult? All this "protecting." No, lying.

Shayne told Ryden to lie to her. Out of all the ways Shayne could have placed a bodyguard for her, he decided to go with *that* kind of deception?

Suddenly, she was angry.

"Ah, now that you're in the right mindset," Neylan said, "hear the proposition. Obviously, the aim of the Diamonds is to be the only Suit. To get rid of the other two. Given your proximity to the current Spade leader, we would love your assistance in his elimination."

Layla's head snapped up and her eyes widened.

"Not yet, obviously. The Spades would come after us, not that they have much ability to do us damage. But our concern is that Shayne is not in a place quite yet to give up their location. And in any case, we haven't yet amassed the needed forces to take them down once we had that information."

Layla tried to control her breathing. "So what is it you want me to do?"

"Spy on him for us. Then, when the time is right, drug him so that he becomes unconscious. Then we can take him and get the location."

"No."

"Rest assured; no harm will come to him. When we choose our time, he will be quite willing to give us the location."

"No."

Neylan's face hardened. "What do you owe him? He left your family for a life of crime. He hasn't been a part of your life for six years."

"He rescued me from the Clubs," Layla said, her voice not working properly.

Neylan scoffed. "A situation you were *only* in because of his position. If he wasn't the Ace, your family would no longer be in danger. And I'm sure you wouldn't want anything to happen to Karsyn, now would you?"

Layla's stomach dropped. Neylan said that like a warning and a threat. "Still," she stammered, "I'm not going to poison my own brother!"

"Relax, you would just be knocking him unconscious. Besides, that time is a long way off."

"No." Her tone was sounding more uncertain now, and that concerned her.

"Layla, remember when I said you currently aren't in danger? Let's keep that status the same, hmm?" Neylan stood up. "Spy on Shayne for now. We'll talk further when it comes time for the action."

She started to leave, then stopped beside Layla. "And I'm sure this goes without saying, but don't tell anyone about this. Karsyn's never been hurt by a Suit, and I'm sure you'd like to keep it that way."

Then she was gone. Her notebook and multitude of pens still on the table.

Layla wanted to cry. Neylan was right. Her whole family would be completely safe if Shayne wasn't Ace of Spades, but that didn't mean she could do that to him! Right? But did she actually owe him anything? After he left them. And told Ryden to lie to her.

And Karsyn...Karsyn couldn't be hurt!

What was she going to do?

Layla lay in bed, processing, but no closer to answering the questions that plagued her. Every answer was in a grey zone, except for the one that would get her or Karsyn hurt, which was not even a choice.

Her phone rang. She rolled onto her side to pick up her phone from the bedside table.

It was Daniel.

She groaned.

The last person she wanted to talk to right now. And yet.

She answered. "Hello?"

"Hey! I hope I called late enough for your interview to be over?"

Her interview. She frowned. "Yes, it's done." She was relieved to hear how normal her voice sounded.

"Okay, great. We talked to your bodyguards, and I wanted to update you."

Daniel went on to explain how the meeting went. Layla found Cameron's reasoning excellent and told Daniel so.

"Yes, I still want him to be my bodyguard. I never wanted one anyways. So this is perfect."

"It is your choice," Daniel said. He even sounded like he was actually okay with it. "Well, I've got to get back to work now."

"Okay. Bye."

Well, that was fast. He hadn't asked how the interview went either, thank goodness. She had no idea what she would've said about it.

She looked at her phone. A text from Ryden. She stared at it. A sweet message about enjoying the first date and inquiring about whether or not she'd like a second. She wanted to cry. She should have known he was too good to be true. And it had been *one* date. How did it hurt this much?

She'd want to disbelieve Neylan, if she hadn't seen Ryden's tattoo herself. But how could the Diamonds possibly know about him? And about her dad? Was she just going to take their word for it when they offered her no proof?

Before she could change her mind, she called Daniel back.

"Something wrong?" he asked.

"No." She was careful not to lie. "But something came up in the interview, and I've been curious about it. Do you know what really happened to my dad?"

Daniel was silent for a long, long time. Layla held her breath.

Finally, he sighed and said, "Layla, are you sure you want to know?"

Her eyes widened with dread. That was practically confirmation.

"Yes," she answered.

"He joined the Clubs. But he's dead now. He was driving a truck to load it onto a ship, but one of the weapons malfunctioned. The whole truck exploded. I read it in the GDRS's files."

All Layla could manage was a tiny "oh."

Neylan had been right.

"Does Mom know that you know?" she asked.

"No way!" Daniel answered quickly. "She probably doesn't even know he's dead. I never had the heart to tell her."

"Probably for the best," Layla managed to say.

"Are you okay? Hearing that? It can be a shock, I know."

"Yes. But I'm okay. I never knew him anyways. I'll let you get back to work now."

She waited for him to say "goodbye" before she hung up.

So.

Well.

Well, well, well.

Something in her stomach hardened.

She wrote Ryden back, saying she enjoyed the date and would love to go on a second. What was he thinking about doing? He might be a Spade, but at least she knew he was committed to protecting her. It might be smart to have another person like that around. Plus, no way was she going to alert Shayne that she knew. He would find some other way to spy on her. She just had to make sure she protected her heart.

Then she stared back up at the ceiling.

She still didn't know which path to take. She was going to forge ahead until one presented itself clearly. And then she would take that path.

Without hesitation.

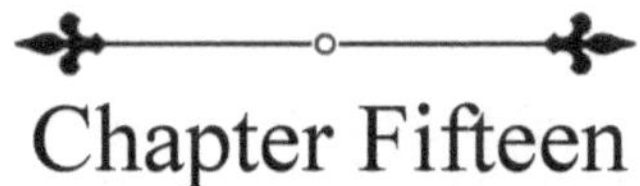

Chapter Fifteen

Nothing eventful happened in the week or so following the interview.

Work. Settling into her new apartment. Cooking all her meals. Phew, that one took some getting used to. And, of course, more thinking. Processing. Considering the same points and angles again and again, never arriving at a more definite conclusion.

Before Layla realized it, it was time for the second date. She was nervous but ready, sitting on a bench a little ways from the cinema, in the pre-arranged spot. The date was to see a movie, get some food-court food, and then go on a little walk while window shopping.

"Excuse me," a voice said timidly.

She whipped her head to the left. It was...Nathan? Sure, she'd never seen him up close before, but the curly blond hair was distinctive.

He was all scrunched in on himself, fiddling with his hands. His gaze kept flitting from her to the ground.

"I...I don't know if you know who I am, but—"

"You're Nathan," she said. "One of my bodyguards."

She didn't say it harshly, or unkindly, but he flinched all the same.

"I heard you got mugged on your date night," he mumbled. "I wanted to say I'm sorry. I took the night off, but I shouldn't have." He peeked up at her. "This was the first chance I got to apologize."

Layla looked at him. He was genuinely sorry he wasn't there to help her. As if it was troubling him. While she still preferred Cameron's philosophy, Nathan's concern was touching.

She smiled. "It's all right. No harm done."

Nathan smiled back, his face shifting. "Thank you, thank you!" he exclaimed. "Oh, I should go now! Well, I'll still be here! Watching. But you won't see me!"

Layla shook her head. No, she probably would see him.

Ryden arrived a few minutes later. "Layla!" he exclaimed.

She jumped up. "There you are! I was beginning to get worried." Shoot. Her heart had skipped a beat at seeing him. She was going to have to be careful to stay in the act. He couldn't know she knew. Her heart had to remember this was all fake now.

He grinned. "Aw. Did you miss me?"

"Actually"—she held up her phone with the time displayed—"our movie starts in ten minutes. Didn't wanna miss it."

"I'm glad you're so excited to see me," Ryden deadpanned.

"No, I am, sure," Layla assured him. "But if we wanted to get popcorn before the movie starts..."

Ryden gasped. "Popcorn! Oh no!"

He grabbed her hand and took off towards the cinema. Layla ignored the fact that his hand was around hers and focussed on keeping up with him and not tripping. She guessed he was going nowhere near as fast as he could, which she appreciated.

Ryden slowed to a walking pace once they reached the doors. They headed straight for the food counter.

"There's a line!" Ryden exclaimed. "How much time do we have?"

Layla looked at her phone. "About eight minutes—why is Mom calling me?"

"Does she know you're on the best second date of all time?"

Layla snorted. "Are you ever low on confidence?" The audacity of this man.

"Those brief five minutes where I was failing mini golf," Ryden answered. "Which shall henceforth never be mentioned again."

"Let's go get our popcorn, Mr. Overconfident," Layla said with a roll of her eyes. She got into the line, and he followed.

"You're not going to answer?" he asked.

"Nah. If she calls again, though, I—"

Her phone screen caught her eye. It was lit up with her mom's contact info. She was calling again. Layla's heart constricted. Why would she be calling again? She answered.

"Hello, Mom—"

Her mom cut her off. Layla had never heard her speak so fast or with such a worry-infused tone. It sounded like she'd been crying, too. Or still was.

Layla nearly stopped breathing. Her mother hadn't even been like this after that Club incident. What had happened? It didn't help that she couldn't understand a word her mother was saying.

"Mom, I can't...Mom." She didn't stop talking, so Layla decided to just talk over her. "Mom, I can't understand you. You've got to slow down! Mom!—"

Layla caught the word "Karsyn" amidst the fairly hysterical words. She grabbed Ryden's arm for support.

"Mom." Her own voice was considerably more panicked now. "Mom, what happened to Karsyn?"

Her Mom was definitely crying now. Layla was trying to breathe, but it seemed impossible. She couldn't make her legs work. Karsyn had to be okay. He had to. She hadn't told anyone about Neylan being a Diamond!

She barely registered that Ryden was leading her away from the line and over to the wall. She half slid down it, half fell.

If anything happened to Karsyn...

Layla paced in the waiting room, walking the same path as she had been for the past... Well, she didn't know how long it had actually been. Too long. Karsyn was still in surgery.

Daniel had left a while ago, saying something about "getting more information."

Her mom had worn herself out and had fallen asleep in a chair. Her mom would feel incredibly guilty when she woke up, but still Layla couldn't bring herself to wake her. She would only worry more. Let her escape from that for at least a little bit.

Layla was trying not to think. She kept remembering Ryden's words about not freaking out until she knew the full story. Ryden...

Without a second thought, he had abandoned their date and come with her to the hospital because he didn't want her to be alone. He was in the hospital's Tim Hortons right now, getting her some food and a drink.

Why did he have to be so nice when she was supposed to hate him?

Her feet were getting sore. But every time she sat down, a restless worry formed a pit in her stomach, and she had to get up and pace again.

Daniel entered the lobby. He quickly spotted her and headed over.

"How's Aunt Jane?" he asked.

"Sleeping." Layla gestured and came to a halt. At least, for now.

"I found out what happened," Daniel said, his voice low.

Layla stared at him. She didn't know if she wanted to know. She would only picture the possible injuries and how much pain he must be in.

"Let's sit," Daniel said.

Reluctantly, she followed him and sat down beside him.

"He was in an Uber, going home," Daniel said. "And another driver crashed headfirst into the side he was on. The Uber driver is mostly unharmed, apparently, and the other driver just drove away, his car barely damaged. Somehow. It's being investigated right now; they're looking for the driver."

Layla stared at the floor. She didn't even bother asking who "they" was. "Was it deliberate?" she whispered.

The clock ticked. A short distance away, hospital staff were talking.

"Was it the Clubs?" Layla asked.

"We don't know yet," Daniel admitted. "The GDRS has people on the case, though, if it turns out it was a Suit. Don't rule out the Diamonds."

The Diamonds. But why would they do that? She hadn't told anyone, so it couldn't be for her. They weren't the type to send that kind of warning.

"It's not the Diamonds," she said. "Not their style."

"You never know," Daniel reprimanded softly.

"I suppose," Layla admitted.

"But we must not rule out any possibilities. Including the possibility that it was just a normal hit and run."

"Nothing in our family is ever normal," Layla said darkly. Not even her father, apparently. "And now Karsyn, who's not even involved, is paying for it."

Footsteps were coming towards them, and Layla snapped her head up. It wasn't a doctor coming to tell them Karsyn was out of surgery. It was Ryden with Tim's, which wasn't unwelcome. She started to get up, but he shook his head.

"No, no, sit," he said, taking the chair next to her. "Cinnamon raisin bagel with strawberry cream cheese, as requested." He handed her the bag and dropped his voice. "That is an *awful* combination, by the way. But if you enjoy it."

"I do," Layla said, not even offended. She took a big bite and sighed. The food didn't lessen the anxiety of the situation, but it made it easier to face.

Ryden put her coffee cup by her feet. "And your medium double-

double," he said. He had gotten himself a muffin and coffee too. He looked at Daniel. "I'm sorry. If I had known, I could have gotten you something."

"That's fine," Daniel said. He was surveying Ryden as if he didn't trust him.

It occurred to Layla that Daniel had never met Ryden. Might not even know who he was. Look at that; the food was bringing up her blood sugar and improving her brain's thoughts already.

"Daniel, this is Ryden!" she exclaimed around another mouthful of her bagel.

"Nice to meet you," Ryden said automatically, holding his hand out.

Daniel cautiously shook it. "It's good to meet you, too."

Ryden smiled, at ease. He dug into his muffin.

The three of them sat in silence.

Layla was just throwing out her Tim Hortons trash when a doctor came into the lobby and told them Karsyn was out of surgery. She almost fainted with relief, which would have been embarrassing. As it was, her knees buckled, but she was able to stay upright. Ryden was by her side in a flash.

"You okay?" he asked.

She nodded. "Just relieved."

Daniel woke her mother up and explained. She was, as Layla predicted, ashamed at having fallen asleep, but they both assured her it was probably for the best.

The doctor led them to Karsyn's room and explained some of his injuries as they walked. Layla caught some of the words but most of it she couldn't understand. Broken ribs, some sort of head injury, and bruising (naturally), and his right arm was broken in two places. It sounded as if there were also some internal injuries, but Layla didn't catch the details.

She didn't pay attention to their surroundings at all. They were a blur. She just wanted to see Karsyn, to know for sure that he was all right. Out of danger.

"He's still unconscious," the doctor was saying as they approached the room. "We don't expect him to wake tonight."

They might have been saying more, but Layla didn't care to hear. She rushed into the room and then stopped short at the sight of him.

Karsyn.

He looked terrible, and Layla could only see his arms, neck, and head. His right arm was in a full cast. Bandages everywhere. His head had a cloth wrap, even. His face was bruising, mostly on his right side. The rise and fall of his chest was uneven and shallow. And, of course, he was hooked up to so many machines.

Layla wanted to cry. He must be in so much pain.

Her mother sank into the chair next to his bed. Looking considerably calmer, she reached out and put her hand over his left hand. Layla had a hard time believing she was the same person who had been in hysterics over the phone earlier. Maybe it was the unknown that had scared her. Maybe her Mom could face reality, no matter how tough, as long as she knew, but not knowing how injured Karsyn was had terrified her.

Daniel walked over and stared down at Karsyn. His jaw worked.

Layla knew that look on his face. He would find who did this and make them pay.

Where was Ryden? She looked behind her.

There he was, in the doorway, texting someone.

She looked back at Karsyn. Her poor younger cousin. If it had been the Clubs, it was an injustice. They had taken her hostage, sure, but it had been a spur-of-the-moment type thing, and she hadn't been hurt. Shaken and knocked out but nothing major.

This, on the other hand...deliberate injury. He could have—her breath caught. Karsyn could have been killed by this. And they wouldn't have cared. They just wanted to hurt Shayne.

Suddenly, she was angry. Not just at the Clubs but at Shayne. He had caused this. He had stolen weapons from the Clubs. So to retaliate they'd hurt Karsyn, knowing they couldn't get to Shayne directly so instead going after his family. Layla knew it wasn't fair to blame Shayne, but she couldn't help it. If he wasn't the Ace, Karsyn would be okay.

As long as Shayne was the Ace, they were all in danger.

Exactly what Neylan had been telling her. That knowledge now seemed much more real.

Layla became aware of Ryden's presence behind her, but she didn't say anything to him. She was caught up in her thoughts, which were starting to race ahead of her. She was beginning to get frightened by their intensity.

Someone's phone started ringing, giving a thankful interruption to her thoughts. Layla looked at Daniel as he answered it.

"Cody, this better be an emergency. You know I'm at the hospital." He sighed. "Slow down, please...Mr. Greer wants me to do what? Right now? Cody, come on—" Daniel stiffened. He licked his lips and glanced at Layla.

She tilted her head.

"Okay. No, I understand. I'm on my way. Stay on the line." He held the phone against his chest. "I have to go. Emergency, and I'm the closest one." He looked at Aunt Jane. "Are you okay if I leave?"

She nodded.

"I'll be back as soon as I can," he said. He walked towards the door but stopped beside Layla. He lightly touched her arm. "Don't worry."

"But what is it?" Layla asked. "What's going on?"

Daniel didn't answer. He put the phone back to his ear as he left the room. "I'm back. What? No, no, Cody, just give me the facts. Only the facts!"

Layla glowered at the door. "I hate it when I don't know what's going on."

Ryden looked like he was about to say something comforting when his phone buzzed in his pocket. He took it out and read something. His eyes widened, and he quickly typed something.

Layla frowned.

He looked up. "Listen, if you're fine here, then I'm gonna leave," Ryden said. "It's really late."

"I suppose so."

Something else was going on. Something Spade related.

"If you could stay, I'd really appreciate it," she said, testing the waters.

"No, no, I really couldn't," Ryden said hastily. "I have the early morning shift at work. A coworker just texted to remind me. I had forgotten all about it."

He could be telling the truth. But it was too much of a coincidence that Daniel just left and now Ryden had to leave too, so Layla didn't believe him.

"Okay. Well...thank you so much for all your help this evening. I don't know what I would have done without you."

He smiled tenderly. "It was my pleasure to be there for you, Layla."

In spite of her best efforts, her heart melted.

"I'm sorry I have to leave so suddenly. But call me if you need anything!"

And just like that, he was gone too.

"You're free to leave too, Layla," her mother said. "No shame in leaving. He's asleep. You should get some sleep too."

Layla scoffed. "Not a chance." She settled herself onto the couch. "I'll get some sleep right here." No way she was leaving Karsyn. And she didn't want to be alone and have to face her thoughts yet.

Her mother smiled at her, as if in approval.

Not long after that, Layla fell asleep.

Chapter Sixteen

Shayne stumbled out of a dark alleyway. He nearly crashed into a small clump of people, but they—more in control than he was—swerved out of his way. Unevenly, he walked along the sidewalk, probably looking like a sailor walking on land for the first time in months.

The sky was dark, but the streetlights were lit, and light from windows streamed onto the sidewalks. Too many shops were still open. Too many people were walking around. But this was Toronto after all. Even at eleven at night, it was alive.

No one paid him any extra attention, except to move farther away from him as they passed. They probably just thought he was drunk or high. But while he had been drinking, he was certainly not *drunk*.

He stumbled over nothing, almost falling.

Okay, maybe slightly drunk?

He messily wiped at the cut above his eye, smearing blood on his hand.

"Tried to stop me from leaving," he mumbled. "I'm the Ace of Spades...my cousin."

Even in his addled state, which he hoped was more distress and pain-induced than alcohol-induced, he remembered that he shouldn't say that sort of thing out loud. It was too much to hope that if some passersby heard him declare himself the Ace of Spades, they wouldn't be alarmed and possibly contact the GDRS. That wouldn't be great.

He whirled around. "Where is that hospital anyway?"

Was he even in the right part of town? He had been so focussed on getting away from those stupid Spades trying to keep him from leaving that he may not have paid close enough attention to where he was going.

He angrily rubbed at a sore spot on his leg. "Didn't have to get so violent."

The more he walked, the fewer people were on the sidewalks. That was probably a bad sign. Was he just getting farther and farther away from the hospital?

Shayne halted as he spotted a familiar store.

"That's where I am," he muttered.

He tried to hurry past it, but it was no use. Waves of the past rolled over him. It was here, in front of this electronics store, where he first got mixed up with the Spades.

He had been heading home from work. Well, what used to be his work. His boss had fired him. Then, to top the cupcake with a cherry, he and Daniel had argued over Shayne's response. But Shayne had been done taking orders from someone without a soul, and, once fired, why shouldn't he let his boss know what he really thought of him?

He had taken a different, longer path home to get space from Daniel.

Never great with directions to begin with, he had decided to let himself get a little lost. He could easily find his way home, but he wanted to delay that. Daniel was in a particularly self-righteous mood that day, and that was to be avoided at all costs.

He had just walked in front of the store when the alarm blared, making him jump. Someone was robbing it? His curiosity was sparked. He had never seen a robbery in real life. He peered inside and saw three men, one looking sheepish.

"You had to go and trip the security system!" the one closest to the window yelled at the scared-looking man. "It was going so perfectly!"

Shayne bristled. The man sounded like his boss, yelling at the people under him just because he could.

"Whatever, let's just get out of here! The cops could be here any minute," the third man commanded.

"Bloody 3's," grumbled the first man.

The other—whom Shayne assumed was the "3"—didn't say a word. What was a 3 anyways? Shayne felt a thrill run through him. This was a Suit! They used numbers like rankings. 3 was low. Was it that man's first mission?

As the men in the store gathered up their stolen goods, Shayne wondered if he should call the police or something.

You don't have a phone, idiot, *he thought.* How would you call the police?

He looked around to see if anyone else—who did have a phone— was calling the police. Nope. Most were scurrying away from the scene as fast as they could.

He stared at the men as they exited the store. They were wearing quality clothes. Good, sturdy material and fashionable too. The Ferrari waiting by the curb must have been theirs. Shayne snorted. Ridiculous. The most obvious getaway car ever; even he could tell that.

But clearly, the Spades had lots of money...

"What are you doing?" A man from somewhere behind Shayne shouted.

With the alarm blaring and the men carrying bags from the store and climbing into their car, it didn't need a genius to figure out what was going on.

The man ran up to the scene, and he pulled out his phone—to call the police, probably.

One of the criminals looked straight at Shayne. He looked calm, not at all worried. He raised his eyebrow, as if asking Shayne a question.

The other two pulled out their guns.

Shayne could never remember what had made him do it, and sometimes he wondered if he regretted it. But he had turned, grabbed the guy's phone, and threw it on the ground, shattering it.

The rest was a confused jumble of memories. He could vaguely recall being dragged by one of the Spades into their car and being interrogated at their headquarters. He was only allowed to live because he had stopped the man from calling the police, and because he promised to join the Spades. He had seen the Ace—powerful, collected, everyone respected and listened to her. He had returned to his worried family with lies on his lips and a promise to himself that he would become the most powerful Spade.

Shayne was brought out of his recollection when he stumbled and fell to the ground. The impact jolted through his bruising body, making him groan. He threw his hands out, finding the large rock that had tripped him. What the heck was a rock this size doing on a sidewalk in Toronto? Didn't matter!

Grabbing it, he surged to his feet and hurled the rock at the nearby shop window, which was no longer the electronics store.

The sound of the smash seemed to echo and grow larger up and down the streets. An alarm started blaring. The store's security.

Shayne muttered something under his breath and shook his head. The sound of the alarm cleared his head, and adrenaline pulsed through him. He took off down the street, ignoring the way his legs protested.

Some minutes later, when the sound of the alarm had faded, Shayne stopped running. He slumped to the ground and leaned against the wall of a closed stationery shop. He was alone now. No one else was on the sidewalks that he could see.

Chuckling to himself, he said, "You idiot. Why would you think you could see him in the hospital? There's no way you wouldn't have been recognized." He sighed. "And now I need a hospital too."

There were consequences to becoming a major criminal, and tonight his mind was screaming all of them at him. They were easy to ignore on the flashy days, when the thrill of the crime drowned out all other noise. But today, with Karsyn injured—

He sucked in a breath. Was that his fault? If it had been the Clubs...

Panic caused his heart to do a double-take, and doubt filled him.

"What if I've made a huge mistake?" he whispered to himself.

"You certainly have," said a voice.

Shayne jumped to his feet, coming face to face with...Daniel.

"Hello...cousin," Daniel said.

Shayne straightened his jacket, at a loss for words. "It's not my fault we're related," he managed after a moment. "Are you here to arrest me?"

"From your face and bleeding leg, it looks like someone's already tried."

"Some of the Spades didn't agree with my decision to check in on my injured cousin," Shayne said. The shock of seeing Daniel was wearing off, and he concentrated on what would get him out of this alive and uninjured. Well, no more injured than he already was. "As you can see," he said, "I prevailed."

He scanned Daniel. Sure enough, he had a gun on his belt.

Daniel scoffed. "I can't believe you actually care about him enough to visit. And if you call this"—he gestured to all of Shayne—"prevailing, I don't know how you've lasted on your own this long."

Shayne took a step closer. They were the same height. He chose to ignore Daniel's jab about prevailing and said, "Of course I care about him. Both of them. Have you forgotten all the long hours we both spent working? Being treated like dirt. All so we could make enough money for our family to get back on our feet."

"We were basically homeless, and our boss was an idiot. Did you expect to be given VIP treatment?" Daniel asked.

Shayne narrowed his eyes. "I expected to be treated like a human!"

Shayne felt Daniel's eyes scanning him and resisted rolling his eyes. He hoped he had been less obvious when he scanned Daniel. But he was confident Daniel wouldn't remember his old habit of carrying around a knife. Not that he particularly wanted to use it against Daniel, but he had to be prepared. He was not about to get taken in.

"You were never the same after that," Daniel said.

"Neither were you."

Even wounded, Shayne had quick comebacks. It was something that always irritated Daniel when they were younger, and it was irritating now.

Daniel had already scanned Shayne and found him defenceless. Defenceless and wounded. This would be easy.

So why couldn't he make the first move?

Shayne grinned. "It's hard, isn't it? Even after years, probably, of insisting that I'm a criminal, you can't believe it when you're looking at me."

"Yes, I can," Daniel said through gritted teeth.

He had never felt an affinity for Shayne, who was too careless, too cocky, too impulsive, and tried Daniel's patience every day. Shayne had always shown a disregard for rules and for proper conduct of behaviour. And now that he was a criminal, Daniel should have had no problem immediately taking him down.

"Then do it," Shayne's eyes were taunting. "Shoot me."

Daniel almost reached for his gun but stopped when he remembered what Cody had said. They wanted Shayne alive. They needed him to give up the location of the Spades' headquarters.

So he took a quiet, deep breath in and readied himself. He was always stronger, but Shayne was always faster. He hoped Shayne's wounds would change that.

He launched his fist at Shayne's face.

Shayne dodged, just like he expected him to. Unexpectedly, Shayne managed to block the other fist heading for his stomach.

Shayne grabbed his arms, and they stood frozen for a second.

"You're out of practice, *cousin*," Shayne hissed. "Working at a desk make you soft?"

He shoved Daniel away. Daniel stumbled but quickly regained his balance.

"I'm still strong enough to beat you." Daniel rushed forward and punched Shayne in the shoulder. "I always beat you." That may or may not have been true, but Daniel didn't have time to recall the past.

Shayne retaliated. Despite his injuries, he was still able to put up a fight. Better than Daniel expected. They went back and forth; both taking hits that would surely turn into bruises later.

Daniel was internally panicking. He wasn't wounded, sure, but Shayne had an extra edge—it was his life he was fighting for, after all. Daniel was trying to debate if he should use a weapon or not. Shayne didn't have any, so it would give Daniel the edge he needed to take Shayne down faster.

Daniel let himself get distracted, and the next thing he knew, he was falling backwards. He twisted and his hands fell to the ground, breaking his fall. While he was down there, he might as well. He grabbed the knife from his boots, then launched himself up towards Shayne.

He didn't want to seriously wound Shayne, just incapacitate him. Before Shayne could notice the knife, Daniel stabbed at his side. In his haste, he missed. The knife just scraped along Shayne's left side, no doubt stinging and drawing blood.

Shayne reeled backwards, surprise printed clearly on his face.

The two froze, staring at each other. Daniel brandished his knife.

"You can't win this one, *Ace*." He spat the word. "It's over."

Shayne scoffed. "Why? Because you have a knife? Remember who you picked that trick up from?"

Daniel's eyes widened, but he wasn't fast enough to stop Shayne from grabbing his own knife. How had he missed that? Worse, now they were once again evenly matched.

Except Daniel suspected Shayne had actually been trained on how to fight with a knife.

If he was nervous earlier, he was terrified now. Shayne was a hardened criminal who wouldn't have any qualms about killing him. Was he making it out of this alive?

His fear was probably written all over his face because Shayne laughed.

"You're the one who brought a knife out first," he said, then rushed him.

Daniel's only thought was to avoid the knife, but it slashed Daniel's shoulder. It burned. Daniel drew up his leg and kicked Shayne in the stomach. Shayne stumbled backwards.

Now was his only chance. If he let Shayne advance again, he could die.

Daniel whipped out his gun and pointed it at Shayne.

Shayne's knife clattered to the ground, and he gaped at the gun.

"You will come with me quietly, or I will shoot you," Daniel warned.

Would he actually? Could he? He didn't know and didn't want to find out. Why was Shayne like this? Why couldn't he just follow the rules?

A cocky grin spread across Shayne's face. "Oh, will I?"

Something hard collided into Daniel's skull, and he fell into darkness.

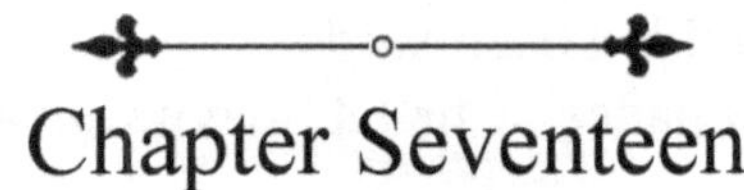

Chapter Seventeen

When Daniel woke up, he was propped against the wall of a bus stop. He was sporting a headache, the rays of the rising sun beating in full force against his body. He blinked against the hard light and brought his hand up to block his eyes.

What had happened? Someone had snuck up behind him and knocked him out. How had he not noticed them approaching? Who was it?

He scoffed. Well, obviously, it must have been a Spade.

He rubbed his head. Different parts of his body slowly came awake and were already protesting. His arms were sore, his shoulder hurt and was caked with dried blood, and everywhere Shayne had gotten a hit in was bruised.

Gingerly and carefully, he got to his feet. Oof, and there were his ribs, sore and on fire.

Guilt and shame washed over him, and he wanted to scream.

The Ace of Spades had been in his grasp! He could have brought him in! He could have—

"Argh!"

He did shout. It was too much.

"Taking in Shayne could have meant the end of the Spades!" he exclaimed. "You *idiot*." He whirled around and punched the wall of the bus stop.

He quickly realized what a stupid idea that had been.

Massaging his hand, he mumbled, "Any crime the Spades commit from this point on is my fault. Because I couldn't beat an already-beat-up Shayne."

He surveyed the area, trying to find his gun, but it was a half-hearted search. If Shayne and the mystery Spade hadn't taken it with them, then they were fools. Sure enough, the gun was nowhere to be seen.

Daniel pulled out his phone. It was 7:47 a.m., and he had several missed calls and frantic texts from Cody.

He groaned. He didn't know what was worse: his failure last night or having to tell his superiors about it today. He would be lucky if they let him keep his internship.

Not that it mattered—he would still work to take down the Suits, even if he was no longer a part of the GDRS. Whatever he could do, he would.

He sent a quick text to Cody, assuring him that he was still alive.

Cody replied instantly, with a flurry of text messages proclaiming worry, relief that he was alive, and asking him where he was so they could send a car to pick him up.

Daniel frowned. He wasn't ready to face people yet. He needed time to remember as many details from last night as possible, anything they could use. And figure out how best to frame his story so that they wouldn't kick him out. Maybe even devise a plan for taking down a Suit. If he could come up with a stellar one, they'd have to listen.

He sent one text back to Cody, saying that he would be back at the GDRS as soon as he could. Then he tucked his phone into his pocket and started walking.

When he got there, Cody was waiting for him in the lobby. Cody rushed over.

"What happened?" Cody exclaimed. "I thought you said you wouldn't have a problem! You look beat up!" He stared at his face.

"We fought. What'd you expect?" Daniel gingerly touched his cheek and felt dried blood. He couldn't remember what had caused that. "I had him, Cody. Right where I wanted him! Then another Spade snuck up behind me and knocked me out."

"How do you know it was a Spade?"

"I assume they were. Who else would have knocked me out to save the Ace?"

"Oh, shoot!" Cody shouted. "You have to report to Ms. Curts. You were supposed to go to her office the second you arrived!" He frowned. "I guess we've failed at that." He shrugged, cheerful again. "She won't know. C'mon, we'll take the elevator." He led the way.

Daniel massaged his temples as they entered the elevator. "Why am I talking to Ms. Curts? Why not Mr. Greer?"

"Probably Mr. Greer too! But, you know, you *did* fight with the Ace of Spades, Dani. No surprise that the head of the GDRS wants to hear about it."

Daniel stared at the floor. Perfect. "Does she know I failed?"

"I told her everything you told me. Which wasn't much, Daniel, honestly! I was worried sick! Just letting me know you're alive isn't much! Also, rejecting a ride back? I don't think she was pleased about that, by the way. Taking longer." He shook his head.

"Fantastic," Daniel said with a sigh.

Cody slapped Daniel on the shoulder—perhaps a bit too hard—but luckily not the one Shayne had cut. "Don't worry, my friend. I don't think anyone expected you to capture Ace. Ms. Curts just wanted to know that you *could.* A test."

"Thanks, Cody." That made him feel so much better.

"You're welcome!" Cody said, missing the sarcasm. Or ignoring it.

The elevator dinged, and Daniel stepped out.

"You coming?" he asked Cody.

"Nah. I think I won't risk it." Cody waved goodbye as the elevator doors closed.

Great.

Daniel turned around and started walking down the hallway. He stopped when he realized that he didn't know where Ms. Curts's office was. He facepalmed.

"You could have told me the way, Cody," he muttered.

It turned out it didn't matter, because there she was, walking towards him. She stopped before reaching him.

"Daniel," she called out and beckoned twice with her finger. "Follow me please." It wasn't a request.

Daniel nodded, steeled himself, and walked after her.

She led him to her office, which was a palace compared to Mr. Greer's and Mr. Miller's.

And Mr. Greer was there too, sitting on the couch. She had a couch in her office. A large, comfy one. She sat down on it next to Mr. Greer and gestured for Daniel to take a seat on the single chair across from them. In between the couch and the chair was a sturdy coffee table with absolutely nothing on it. Daniel slowly took a seat.

"So," Ms. Curts said at last. "You didn't capture the Ace of Spades and you got ambushed. How's your head?"

"Fine."

His head felt like someone was attacking it with a really sharp hammer.

Mr. Greer leaned forward. "We're not mad at you Daniel. We didn't expect you to be able to capture the Ace of Spades all by yourself. If there's anyone to be mad at, it's us. We waited too long before sending in backup."

"*You* waited too long," Ms. Curts said, steel in her voice. "Mr. Greer wanted to use this opportunity as a test of your skills, a way for further assessment. And now we've lost a far greater opportunity—one that may never come again."

Well, wasn't this a lot of information to take in at once. They had expected him to fail? He didn't have any objection to the sending of more agents, of course that should have happened. But to admit to his face that they didn't have faith in him? Ouch.

Hoping his face was staying as neutral as he wanted it to, Daniel said, "So when you sent your agents, they just completely missed me?"

"You were not their objective," Ms. Curts said simply.

"What if it had rained?"

"You would have gotten wet."

Ms. Curts met his gaze, her face and tone all business. Daniel had nothing but respect for her after that exchange.

"I'm guessing the agents didn't find Shayne or figure out where he went," Daniel said.

"No, but the CU is currently examining all the security footage we have of the event," Ms. Curts replied. "We may discover some sort of lead, but I doubt we'll figure out their location. And I will want you to look over the footage at some point to see if you recognize the Spade that ambushed you."

Daniel nodded. "Well, Shayne was heading for the hospital, but I doubt he—well, maybe he actually did! Layla would know. She probably stayed there all night!"

Mr. Greer held up a hand.

Daniel deflated. "Yeah, I know. It's a long shot."

Mr. Greer chuckled and shook his head. "No, Daniel, I admire your drive and passion."

"Thank you, sir."

"But you don't have to worry about fixing last night's error."

Daniel frowned internally. He knew he had failed, but did Mr. Greer have to word it like that?

Mr. Greer continued. "I simply needed you to prove that having a cousin so high up in the Spades wouldn't impact your ability as an agent. You have proven yourself capable in every other area. I just needed confirmation in this one."

Daniel had mixed feelings about this. On the one hand, he could tell he was about to get offered an official spot in the GDRS, which he'd work so hard for, and hearing Mr. Greer's praise was relieving. But did Mr. Greer even care that they could've had the Ace of Spades in custody right now? Could possibly be making a plan to infiltrate their headquarters?

A fire lit inside Daniel's stomach. He had been so close! He was sure once he had a spot he could bring down the Spades.

Mr. Greer smiled. "Daniel, you are now a full agent. How would you like a spot in my unit?"

"I'd like nothing better, sir."

"Excellent!" Mr. Greer nodded.

"Except I'd like to be assigned to the Spades," Daniel said.

Mr. Greer paused. Ms. Curts even raised an eyebrow.

"I can do it," Daniel insisted. "I *have* to. I have first-hand inside knowledge about Shayne. I'm the best person to be assigned to him."

"Better than seasoned GDRS agents?" Ms. Curts asked rhetorically.

"Our whole aim here is to dissolve the Suits," Daniel said. "Let me help do that in an area where I have extra knowledge."

"Well, that hadn't been my plan, but..." Mr. Greer looked at Ms. Curts.

"No," she said firmly. "I respect that you have zeal for taking down the Suits, and that you're eager to prove yourself."

Daniel wanted to object to the second half of that statement but decided that wouldn't help his case.

"But you are too connected with the Spades. I don't want your work here to turn into a personal vendetta against a cousin whom you feel has wronged you."

There were so many things Daniel wanted to say to that. But some of them might make him lose his job before he even fully had it, and he was pretty sure all of them would be seen as argumentative. The last thing he wanted to do was get on Ms. Curts's bad side.

Pick your battles, he told himself. So he said nothing.

"If you want to be directly involved in a Suit," Ms. Curts continued, "you can be assigned to the Diamond Unit."

Daniel frowned. "The Suit we know the least about and have the smallest chance of destroying." He couldn't keep himself from saying that.

Ms. Curts leaned forward. "All we do here, every day, is try to destroy the Suits and keep them from doing more damage in the meantime." Her voice had a dangerous edge to it. "It doesn't matter what unit I place you in. *You* are not going to magically make that possible."

Daniel figured he was really close to getting on her bad side. Maybe now was the time to voice the plan he had come up with on his walk.

"What if we made a deal with the Diamond Queen?" he said.

Mr. Greer gaped at him. Ms. Curts was suddenly standing.

"Absolutely not—!"

"No, wait, please let me explain!" Daniel held his hands out. Shoot, she took that way worse than he thought she would. "Please."

Ms. Curts crossed her arms but nodded. She didn't sit back down.

Daniel took a deep breath. He was walking a thin line here. "This is just something that came to me this morning," he said first, then got into his plan. "The Diamonds are the Suit that specializes in secrecy. If we can find a way to reach out to them, we can make a deal. Tell them we'll pay them if they can find a way to deliver the Ace into our hands. We'll have the Ace of Spades and more information about the Diamonds, but they'll have done all the work."

Ms. Curts let out a very long, very slow breath. "I am going to put this plan down to stress from last night and your head injury, and you will never speak of it again, understood? We do not make deals with criminals."

Daniel schooled his features to show only obedience. It didn't matter what he thought about this; he had disagreed with Ms. Curts enough for one day. "Of course," he said. "I apologize. I don't think I'm thinking straight after last night."

She looked at him with calculating eyes but said, "Naturally. Mr. Greer will take you to the Diamond unit and help get you set up with an office. Once that's done, you are to take the rest of the day off. Yesterday was taxing for you."

Daniel stood in his new office. All his. He didn't have to share it with another coworker or keep his personal effects limited to what was easily removable and fit into one tiny box. He was finally a worker at the GDRS. He could *finally* start making an actual difference.

So why wasn't he happier?

The more he thought about it, the more he became convinced that *his* plan was the best one to capture Ace. The Diamonds wouldn't fail. The government could have the Ace of Spades without doing any work, and it could be done quickly. That's what they were working towards—the Suits gone as soon as possible. The only real problem was making contact with the Diamonds, but Daniel brushed that aside.

He couldn't understand why Ms. Curts had acted so shocked. Surely he wasn't the first person here to ever think about making a deal with the Suits? And it wasn't like he was suggesting in return they stop hunting the Diamonds. Just pay them a bit. They must want the Spades gone too.

And once the GDRS had Shayne...er, no, the Ace...

Daniel flopped down in his chair and ran his hand over his face. Maybe he really wasn't thinking straight after last night. He was starting to view Shayne and the Ace as two different people.

But weren't they really? he reasoned. Shayne was a memory, a young cousin who no longer existed, and Daniel no longer knew. Ace was also someone Daniel didn't know. A high-up criminal figure who, as a government agent, Daniel was duty-bound to try to take down. But how?

All his energy drained from his body. The fire that had been lit earlier went out, as if someone had poured a massive bucket of water on it.

He slumped down in his chair.

He didn't know anything about the Diamonds except what they *didn't* do. And that this branch was led by a Queen. He had never been one of the janitors responsible for the Diamond Unit, which meant he had never gotten a chance to read their files.

So he didn't have a plan. All he had was a vague sense of the plan's components. It wasn't an outline. It wasn't even steps.

He had never felt so miserable. He couldn't do this. Could he even be an agent? What had he been thinking? He had no formal training. He was going to let everyone down. He—

Austin, head of the Diamond Unit, stuck his head into Daniel's office.

"Dude, what are you still doing here? You're supposed to go home. If Ms. Curts thinks I'm keeping you here, she'll, you know, come for my neck and what not."

Daniel sighed. "Sorry. Just got lost in my thoughts." More like he was drowning in them, but...details.

Austin shrugged and fully entered the office. "Fair enough. But seriously, you need to go home and take care of yourself. You've got blood on your shoulder. I'm guessing you haven't eaten yet either."

"Ah." He *hadn't* eaten yet. That's why he was feeling so depressed all of a sudden—low blood sugar. "Thanks, Austin. I'll head home."

"Sure thing." Austin pointed at him. "Take care of yourself now!" He left.

"I will," Daniel said quietly.

He made a plan. This one had steps:

1. Go home.
2. Eat.
3. Sleep and rest.
4. Tomorrow, get as much information about the Diamonds as possible and come up with an iron-clad plan to contact them.
5. Take down the Suits.

Easy.

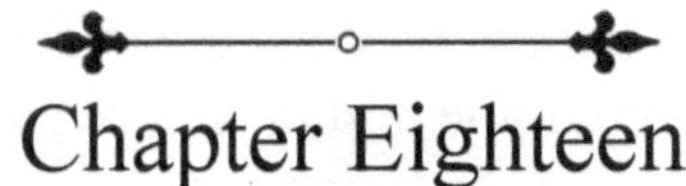

Chapter Eighteen

Daniel felt so much better than yesterday. It was amazing what food, sleep, and rest could do for the mind and soul. Plus, his head no longer felt like a drum at a rock concert so that helped.

And he was ready. Mentally prepared to take in as much information as was necessary. Physically prepared to not leave his office until he was confident in his plan. Emotionally prepared to be...burnt out. Definitely. But ready nonetheless.

To his surprise, it was Austin again who came into his office about fifteen minutes after he'd arrived. Heck, Daniel hadn't even sat down yet. He'd been walking around, drinking from his water bottle, and taking it all in.

"You ready to know everything there is to know about the Diamonds?" Austin asked. Then he spread his arms. "Welcome to the most boring unit!"

Strange thing was he didn't sound upset about it.

Daniel set his water bottle down on his desk. "Are you going to be the one explaining things to me?"

Austin crossed his arms. "Well shucks, you don't have to sound so excited about it. If you don't like m—"

"No, no, that's not it at all," Daniel hastened to say. "I just would have assumed the head of the unit would have better things to do."

Austin laughed. More than Daniel thought was necessary.

"Dude. Do you know why we're one third the size of the other two Suit units?" Without waiting for an answer, he said, "Not only is there not enough work to be done to justify more agents, the ones we do have usually end up leaving for a more exciting unit. This will probably be the most interesting part of my day."

"Guess that explains why I got my choice of offices then."

Wanting to begin, Daniel gestured for Austin to take the chair.

"Oh, no, thank you. I'm fine to stand. I won't take your chair from you."

So Daniel sat down. He opened his mouth to ask the questions that had been on his mind, but Austin snapped his fingers.

"Ah! Almost forgot." He dug around in his front pocket and brought out a crumpled sticky note. "This is your login information. You'll have full access to our network and all the information we have." He took a step closer and held out the sticky note.

Daniel took it with a "thank you," annoyed but not surprised at the unprofessional method.

"And, of course, you got your badge and access card, so you can also see the physical files if you want." Austin thought for a moment, then dipped his head to the side. "Course, I don't know why you would. It's all on the computer."

Daniel stuck the note to his desk, only half-paying attention.

"And I suppose if it is all online, you don't really need me to tell it to you."

"Actually, I have a few questions," Daniel said.

Austin brightened. "*Yes*. Ask away."

"With the branch in Ottawa dissolved, that leaves how many?"

"Three. Although our branch could soon become the lead one. That is to say, the Queen would become the Ace, and they would set up another branch in another city."

Daniel nodded. He considered asking what other two cities held Diamonds but figured that would be easy to look up.

"And no credible rumours as to their headquarters' location?"

"Ha! I wish." Austin frowned. "Nah. Best rumour we have about them is that they like to frequent casinos. We've checked out every casino at every possible time but never been able to identify a Diamond."

Daniel's pulse quickened. Here was some information! Yes, they were rumours, but all rumours had a basis in truth, even if they ended up wildly twisted.

"Do they have an identifier?" he asked, eager to know the answer. "The Clubs and the Spades have their tattoos. Do the Diamonds also—"

Austin threw his arms up, catching Daniel off guard. He huffed. "No—that is, we don't know."

Daniel got the sense Austin was tired of the question and even more frustrated with the answer.

"They should and almost definitely do, but we don't know what it is. Something that's either so subtle all of the Ottawa GDRS missed it or something easily hidden or removed. But we don't know."

Austin's mood appeared to have soured significantly.

"Okay, well, thanks." Daniel wanted him to leave now. He didn't want Austin's sourness to infect and bring down his own mood.

Austin vaguely waved his hand, gesturing to the office at large. "Well, enjoy." He mumbled, "Try not to die from boredom," as he left.

Daniel rolled his eyes. Honestly. Talk about beating a dead horse. If all Austin talked about was how boring his unit was, no wonder no one wanted to join.

But Austin had given him something solid to work on! If he could figure out what identifier the Diamonds had...game changer.

He waited until he was sure Austin was back in his office. Then he grabbed everything he'd need, which wasn't much. His access card, water bottle, notebook, and a pen. Then he headed towards the storage room that held all of the Diamond Unit's physical files. He assumed the room would also come with a table and giant corkboard, just like all the other units.

It did. Excellent.

He set his things down on the table and went to search for the files from Ottawa. Austin's words echoed back at him. Something so subtle everyone missed it. Would it be foolish to think he'd be able to catch it?

No.

Prideful, maybe. But he had time and determination. He was *not* leaving this room until he found a link. Because if he managed to, then he could identify anyone who was a Diamond. He could find them at the casinos. He could make contact with their Queen.

He plunked a box of files down on the table and went to retrieve the others.

Guilt twinged at him. His conscience raised a few points of protests as to why he would continue on with this plan when Ms. Curts was so very stern in her orders to drop it. But he brushed those aside. Once he succeeded, she wouldn't mind that he'd disregarded her orders.

They needed to eradicate the Suits. Daniel was willing to do whatever was necessary. Why wasn't Ms. Curts?

He set the last of the boxes of Ottawa files down on the table.

For the next thirty minutes, he pulled out the mug shots of all the

Diamonds arrested in Ottawa and pinned them to the corkboard. When he ran out of room there, he taped them to the wall. There were at least two hundred, and those were just the ones that got caught.

Once he was finished, Daniel took a step back and stared at the collection of photos. He mused for a moment, deciding on the most efficient course of action. He settled on picking a sort of attribute and looking at just that throughout all of the pictures to see if a pattern or similarity emerged.

Luckily, there was a full body shot for each of them in addition to the close-up of the face. So naturally, he decided to start with what was easiest: clothes.

Nothing was obvious at first glance, but then, he hadn't expected that. No similarity in types of clothing. There wasn't one colour that everyone was wearing. No colour combos such as warm colours, cool colours, or complementary colours. He even looked to see if there was a shared brand but no. That would have been really obscure, though, and probably too much work on their part.

Only once he was sure, absolutely sure, that he had exhausted every possibility when it came to clothing, did he allow himself to move on.

Shoes. No dice.

Tattoos. Nope. That was expected, as the Diamonds were much cleverer than the others, but Daniel felt he should at least check.

He briefly considered their eyes. Coloured contacts were a thing after all—but that was a quickly discovered dead end.

Then he moved on to jewellery, only to be disappointed by that idea as well. No matching necklaces, rings, bracelets, or earrings.

Just before he began to feel frustrated, the door swung open. Daniel spun around, almost dropping the pen he had been tapping his chin with.

Mr. Greer walked in and chuckled. "I thought I'd find you in here. Hard at work already, I see."

Daniel nodded and gestured at the display of mug shots, though that wasn't really necessary. "I'm trying to see if I can find their identifier."

"Ah. That is an excellent place to start."

It was clear from his tone that he didn't really expect Daniel to find it, which made any frustration Daniel had started to feel vanish, replaced by determination to prove Mr. Greer wrong.

"I don't want to interrupt you," Mr. Greer said, "But I thought you should be reminded that Ms. Curts wishes for you to look over that footage sometime today."

Daniel smacked his forehead with his palm. Thankfully, instinct kept him from using the hand that held the pen, otherwise he might have lost an eye.

"I totally forgot!" He looked at his wall of people, then back at Mr. Greer. "It's a good time for a break, too. Where do I go?"

"Anyone in the CU can call up the footage for you. Although I suspect Cody would have a few things to say if you didn't ask him." Mr. Greer's eyes were twinkling.

Daniel laughed. "That's true. I would never hear the end of it. Thanks for the reminder. I'll be sure to do that."

"Of course."

Mr. Greer seemed hesitant to leave, but after a moment's indecision, he walked out.

Maybe he had been expecting Daniel to leave right then. But Mr. Greer's appearance had brought on a fresh batch of guilt about his plan. So Daniel decided to stop by Austin's office and ask a few questions that would hopefully help. It would be no good going through the footage while distracted. Either he was clear-minded, or he wasn't going to do it at all.

Unfortunately, Austin was not in his office when Daniel checked. Oh well. He'd go review the footage first, then check again.

Cody, you'd better be in your office, he thought as he headed to the elevator.

He wasn't. He was in the elevator.

Daniel raised an eyebrow. "Cody?"

Cody struck a pose. "The one and only! Wait." His grin vanished. "Don't tell me you're coming in *here*?"

"I am, actually," Daniel said.

The doors started to close, and he scrambled in.

Cody pressed a hand to his forehead. "All that hard work for nothing!" he exclaimed. Then, when he noticed that Daniel had pressed the button for the second floor, he yelled, "I came all this way just to go straight back to my floor?"

He looked at Daniel as though this was the greatest offence.

Daniel shrugged. "Not my fault. You should've gotten off faster."

"No. Because I came to see *you*." Cody jabbed a finger towards Daniel.

"Oh. Well, I was coming to see *you*."

Cody laughed. "Evidently," he said with a dramatic flourish of his arms that accomplished nothing but forced Daniel to move out of the way.

"Hang on." Daniel checked his watch. "It's definitely not your lunch break. Do you just up and leave whenever you feel like it? You're supposed to be working."

Cody pondered this for a moment, as if the answer was complicated.

"Yes, yes I do. But," he sighed, "today it's because something was pressing on my heart." He looked off into the distance. Or, he would have, if they had been in a location that had distance. As it was, he just stared at the elevator wall.

"You tried talking to Harley, and she wouldn't let you?" Daniel guessed.

Cody smacked his fist into the palm of his other hand. "I just don't get it! We're meant to be." He squinted his eyes. "The cheerful, funny one always ends up with the serious, no-nonsense one. Every movie, that's how it happens."

"Yeah, but we're not in a movie."

The elevator dinged, and the doors slid open. They had reached the second floor. Cody jumped out, and Daniel followed in a more restrained way.

"So, you were coming to see me," Cody said. "That never happens. And it's not your lunch break either, is it? Hmmm—oh." His face fell. "Which means it's work related."

He actually looked upset, which never happened, so Daniel said quickly, "And I chose to come to you! Could have gone to anyone else, but I chose you."

"True!" Cody stood straighter. "Well, let's go get some amazing work done, shall we?"

As they walked to Cody's office area, Daniel explained what he had come to do.

"Oh, easy!" Cody said.

They entered the CU office area, and Cody went straight to his computer. Daniel looked around. It didn't look like anything had changed from his janitor days, except the retiring of a few agents and the addition of some others. A few more fake plants had been added too, and the effect, Daniel had to admit, was nice.

The CU was an open-concept room filled with cubicles. Dozens of agents just clicking away at computers all day. Many were wearing headphones right now. Some possibly watching the same footage Daniel had come to see.

"Dani, it's all called up," Cody said, waving Daniel over to his cubicle.

Daniel hurried over. The next thing he knew, he was watching that night unfold again, just from a different perspective. He couldn't help shaking his head when Shayne broke the window with the rock. Like, really? Not necessary.

"Oh, I guess I can just fast-forward," Cody said. He looked over his shoulder at Daniel. "To the part where the Spade shows up? Since that's what you're here to see?"

Daniel contemplated this for a second. But what could he gain from watching all of it? Wasted time and embarrassment. The sooner this was over, the sooner he could be back at work.

"Yeah, skip ahead," he said.

He expected Cody to just fast-forward it, but with a few quick clicks, Cody jumped the footage ahead. Right to the moment when Daniel whipped his gun out. The Spade would be there any second, though Daniel thought it was a thousand-to-one chance that he'd recognize them.

Someone called Cody's name from another cubicle to their left.

"It's happening again!" the person shouted. "Doing that split-screen thing."

"Coming!" Cody popped up, said, "I'll be right back," to Daniel, and hurried on over.

Daniel watched him go for a second, then remembered he was supposed to be doing something. So he turned his eyes back to the screen just in time to see the Spade hit Daniel over the head with the butt of a gun.

Daniel felt his breath leave him all at once. Because he did know that Spade.

He had met that Spade just earlier that very night.

His cousin was dating that Spade.

Ryden.

Daniel was tremendously glad Cody was not there to see his face, because he was sure it held all sorts of shock and horror.

Ryden was a Spade. *The* Spade, who had knocked him out. That *jerk.*

What was he supposed to do with this information? Well, tell Ms. Curts, obviously. How could he do otherwise? And yet...Something was holding him back.

If they took Ryden in for questioning, which they undoubtedly would, they had a chance at finding out where the Spades' headquarters were. But Daniel felt in his gut two things were surely true.

One, Ryden would not give up any information to the GDRS, no matter how forgiving they might promise to be about his prison time. (And wasn't that like making a deal with the Suits anyways, Ms. Curts??)

Two, that Ryden was only dating Layla because Shayne had asked him to, for some reason. Which meant as soon as Ryden was arrested, the Spades would know. Precautions would be taken. Perhaps even abandoning their headquarters!

Daniel's hand curled into a fist.

That would ruin everything. No, their only chance was to contact the Diamond Queen. If Daniel let the GDRS know the identity of this Spade, it would be a major setback. No gain, only losses.

He rearranged his features to show neutrality and maybe a twinge of disappointment. Cody could be returning to the cubicle at any moment.

Daniel briefly considered telling Layla of Ryden's identity but decided against that. The more overconfident Shayne was, the better. It would make it easier to find and arrest him.

And Layla was in no danger. If Shayne had sent Ryden, then it was for some purpose of protection. As if the bodyguards from the GDRS couldn't do the job. But Layla would be safe.

So he was just going to lie to the head of the GDRS about not recognizing Ryden?

"Any luck, Dani?" Cody's voice boomed exceptionally loud next to Daniel, and he jumped. Cody laughed and held up his hands. "My bad! You were deep in thought."

"Yeah, trying really hard to recognize the Spade, but no luck," Daniel said with a shrug.

"Shucks." Cody flopped down into his seat. "That would have really been something."

"Uh huh." Daniel wasn't really listening. He was too busy telling himself that it was fine. He could always say he had never seen Ryden before today if they somehow found out he lied. What were they going to do? Check with Layla to see when they had first met? Besides, he planned to make contact with the Diamond Queen long before that had a chance to happen, so what did it matter?

He was vaguely aware of making small talk with Cody for the next few minutes until Cody said, "All right, shoo." He made the hand motions. "You're clearly thinking about something else work-related, and, despite my best efforts, I have actual work to get done."

Daniel said some sort of goodbye, and then he was walking out of the CU. He walked as fast as he could without drawing extra attention to himself. He had one goal: get back to work and figure. Things. Out!

And then he bumped into Austin on the way back to the file room. It was both what he wanted to happen and not what he wanted. But before he could think about it, he heard himself saying,

"Hey, Austin, I have another question for you, if now works!"

Austin stopped walking. "Daniel, hey, yeah, what's up?"

"Has the GDRS ever made a deal with one of the Suits and it just...went sour?" Daniel asked. He had figured that must be the reason Ms. Curts was so against it.

Austin's eyebrows drew together, and he frowned. He glanced around, then muttered, "Man, you sure know how to ask all the wrong questions."

Daniel drew back. "Wha—"

"Come into my office."

Daniel followed Austin the short distance to his office, which was nicer than Daniel's but not extravagantly so. Austin turned to look at Daniel and crossed his arms.

"Ms. Curts told me what you said yesterday," he said. "I get that you're curious, which is why I'm gonna answer your question. But we're not gonna tell Ms. Curts about it, and you won't ask about it again, got it?"

Daniel nodded. He was mentally holding his breath, trying to prepare for whatever Austin might tell him.

Austin frowned some more, then said, "Years ago, you would've just been a kid, we made a deal with the Clubs. One of them had reached out to us. He was bringing us a truck full of weapons as evidence, and then he was going to provide us with the location of their headquarters." He took a deep breath. "Well, the Clubs found out. Another Club hid in the back, and then, when the truck was waiting at a stoplight downtown, that Club detonated a bomb. Set off a chain reaction with the other weapons in the truck." His shoulders dropped. "There was...a lot of damage."

Daniel's head spun. He shouldn't have asked. It was too much information, too soon. This story was too similar to the one he'd just told Layla the other day, only with details he hadn't known.

"Thank you for letting me know," he said. "I understand why...um—that is..." He couldn't speak for trying to process it all.

The corners of Austin's eyes crinkled. "I know. It's a lot to take in. You don't have to say anything more. I hope you do understand now, though."

Daniel nodded, then stumbled out of the office. He made his way back to the file room automatically. When he entered, he all but fell onto a chair.

The million-dollar question—that he would probably never know the answer to—was had his uncle been the driver or the saboteur? Had his uncle been trying to turn from his life of crime, or had his uncle sacrificed himself so that the GDRS wouldn't be able to take down the Clubs?

He could try to search the files, but it would be pointless. He had read them already, and they had said nothing, *nothing*, about this. They were embarrassed, so they covered it up. No wonder Ms. Curts had reacted so strongly.

Daniel felt queasy. No, ill. His eyes were staring at the mug shots on the wall without seeing them.

Ryden. His uncle. The Queen?

His brain was firing in too many directions at once, and it was threatening to tear him apart if he didn't get his thoughts under control.

Then, as he looked at the mug shots, something tugged at him. There was some nagging feeling that he was missing something, which he definitely was, but there was more to it than that. As if he'd noticed something, and he'd just failed to realize what.

He got up, moved around the table, and stood in front of the collage of photos. He looked carefully from one to the next, not focussing on anything in particular, just trying to look at the whole picture at once, taking everything in. Giving his brain the opportunity to realize what it had spotted.

His eyes were snagged by a girl who had multiple ear piercings.

Daniel had looked up the names of them earlier to see if that could provide any connection. She had an industrial piercing, a helix, a daith, an upper lobe, and a standard lobe, in both ears. But that wasn't what caught his attention this time. All of those piercings had earrings in them, except the standard lobe piercing.

Odd. But nothing exceptional.

He looked at the picture directly beside it. An older, but distinguished, gentleman. If Daniel were to meet him in person, he would half expect a British accent. The last person, at least for Daniel, that one would expect to have any piercings. And yet, he had a standard lobe piercing. Also devoid of an earring.

His pulse quickening now, Daniel looked from picture to picture. Everyone had a standard lobe piercing. Everyone. What were the chances? A quick Google search told him that around 83 percent of Americans have their ears pierced. He couldn't find a Canadian statistic but close enough.

Eighty-three percent.

So how statistically likely was it that 100 percent of the Diamonds would have a piercing?

Not only that, but they were all—Daniel's eyes moved from photo to photo—empty.

Not one single person had an earring in their standard lobe piercing. If they had more piercings, those ones had earrings. But not the standard lobe.

Daniel's heart jumped and then nearly stopped. What was the other thing Austin had said? Easily removable?

His brain leapt to a memory. The earrings he thought were so unprofessional because they were diamonds.

Diamond earrings!

His legs were wobbly. He put a hand on the table, steadying himself.

The Diamond identifier...

He had found it.

Chapter Nineteen

Layla was hurrying through the hospital, heading back to Karsyn's room. She had gone on a walk, both to find a bathroom and for the sake of moving around. Her mom had texted saying that Karsyn was awake, and now Layla was bursting into the room.

"How is he?" she shouted.

From the bed, a weak voice said, "Chill."

Layla released a long breath. In a more dignified manner, she made her way over to Karsyn's side.

"How do you feel?" she asked, trying to sound normal for his sake,

"Like I got hit by a car," he said, grinning as much as he could. "And you can look worried—I know you want to."

Layla flopped onto the chair and let her forehead crease. "Yeah, well, like you said: hit by a car."

"Sure, sure, but consider this: I am on so many painkillers right now."

Layla pursed her lips. His point didn't seem to have a point to it, but if he was on lots of painkillers, that was probably to be expected.

"I am so sorry this happened to you, Karsyn. If Shayne hadn't—" Her gaze darkened, but she decided not to continue.

Karsyn held up his left hand, pointer finger raised. "I am too high for your angsty attitude, Layla."

Layla raised an eyebrow and looked at her mother. "Is he on too many painkillers?"

Her mother was suppressing a grin. "He was in a lot of pain. This is preferable."

Layla rubbed her eyes.

"You look awful," Karsyn informed her.

"You're one to talk," she spluttered.

"Layla!" her mother tried to reprimand her, but Karsyn was laughing—as much as he was able to.

"That is funny, I'll admit," he said.

Layla couldn't help but grin. "Well, as long as you're happy."

Her mother walked over to her and said, "He does have a point, though. You slept on a couch in your clothes after all. Why don't you go back to your apartment and freshen up, honey? You can come back as soon as you've changed."

"Yeah, shoo." Karsyn made shooing motions with his left hand. "Your wrinkly clothes are ruining my vibe here."

Layla snorted and thought of a few things she could say to that. But she felt her mother's hand on her shoulder, a warning not to engage. So instead she saluted and just said, "Sounds good."

One Uber ride later, and she was walking down the hallway to her apartment, fishing around in her purse for her keys. They weren't there.

Layla groaned and sifted through her purse again. But she kept few items in her purse, and it was apparent her keys were not in there. How frustrating. She distinctly remembered putting them in there.

She was just gonna try the door and pray it had somehow unlocked itself. Even though, after the countless lectures from her mom about safety, she had never once forgotten to lock it.

She tried the door.

It opened.

She frowned and didn't go in. Not sure if she should be happy it was somehow unlocked or freaking out, she opted for being suspicious and on the alert. Cautiously, she stepped through the doorway.

"It's just me," a voice called out.

Well, that was creepy.

The voice seemed familiar, but she couldn't quite...

Then he appeared at the end of her entryway. Oh.

"Hey," she said. Because what else do you say when your brother basically breaks into your apartment looking as if he just lost a fight?

"I'm sorry," he said. "I needed a place to crash."

Layla shut the door. "Right."

"How is he?" Shayne asked.

"How'd you get into my apartment?"

Shayne's face turned pleading, but whether it was for her not to push it or to reveal how Karsyn was, she didn't know.

"I locked my door, Shayne."

Plus, Karsyn had the car crash. She'd slept on a couch. She hadn't gotten to finish her date either. Which reminded her—Ryden. That didn't improve her mood, or her feelings towards Shayne at the moment.

"And I...unlocked it."

He was trying to be casual, but the guilt was oozing out of him.

"With *my* keys? Shayne?"

He actually flinched. Layla had never heard her voice so cold either, but given the circumstances, she felt she was justified.

Just admit to it, just admit it!

"I have my ways," Shayne said.

"Ugh!" She threw her purse on the bench. "Stop. Just stop." She shouldered her way past him and into the living room area.

"What? Your keys are on the coffee table, if that's what you're mad about."

"What I'm mad about"—she whirled around—"is Ryden stealing the keys from my purse in the first place!"

All the blood drained from Shayne's face.

Layla's hands were balled into fists at her side. It had been a wild guess, but based on Shayne's reaction, that's exactly what happened.

Shayne took a limping step forward. "Layla..." he began, then trailed off.

She crossed her arms. She wasn't going to be the one who spoke first.

"I just wanted to protect you," he said at last.

"Right. And instead of getting someone a job at Staples and letting them watch me from afar most days of the week, you chose for someone to fake being my boyfriend?"

Shayne winced. "Layla, I just—"

"No!" she shouted. She was tearing up but ignored it. "You lied to me, Shayne! My first boyfriend was a lie! You let me fall in love with a lie!" Well, maybe that was being a little dramatic. They hadn't even finished the first date before Layla realized what Ryden was. But she didn't care. She had every right to be dramatic right now.

"No, no, Layla..." He looked heartbroken, but then, so was she.

"You betrayed me," she said, quieter this time. "You could've asked, but you jumped right to lying."

"You would've said no!" Shayne said, voice rising.

The anger flared up again in her. Wasn't he even sorry?

"Yes! I would have. And if you and Daniel would ever give me a chance, you'd see I don't need you to protect me all the time. And I'm going to prove it whether you give me a chance or not!" She thought of Karsyn, and before she knew it, she was saying, "In fact, we'd be better off without you! If you weren't the Ace, I wouldn't have gotten taken by those Clubs, and Karsyn wouldn't be in the hospital right now!"

She was breathing heavily now.

Shayne took a step back as though she'd slapped him. But just as quickly, it turned to anger. "None of that is my fault!" he yelled back. "It's the Clubs! Just because I'm the Ace—"

"That's just it!" Layla waved her hands around. "It's exactly your fault *because* you're the Ace! If you weren't the Ace, none of this would have happened! If you weren't a *criminal*"—she spat the word—"we would be safe."

In an instant, all the rage vanished from his countenance. Shayne suddenly looked worn and beaten down. Layla wished he would just pick a mood and stick to it. It was exhausting trying to keep up, and she was already tired to begin with.

"I'm not...really, a criminal, Layla," he said haltingly. "As Ace, I mostly oversee. I don't really, you know, commit the crimes. Anymore."

All right, she'd match his tone then. "Right. Cause you didn't just participate in breaking into the Club headquarters. And enjoy it."

Shayne frowned. "That's different—"

But she didn't let him finish. She raised her voice but kept it controlled this time. "Planning, authorizing, committing, turning a blind eye, allowing—they're the same thing, Shayne! You're just as guilty. Especially killing! Allowing and actually helping, those under you to kill—"

"And how is that any different from the government?" Shayne demanded. "You think the GDRS has never killed anybody?"

"That's...different."

Shayne scoffed. "How?"

"They're killing bad guys. Criminals. Enemies."

People like you, her mind added.

"The people we're hired to kill must have been someone's enemy. Otherwise we wouldn't have gotten hired, would we?" Shayne said, his voice soft and challenging.

Did that actually sound...sensible? No, couldn't be. Ugh, she was too tired and emotionally spent to analyze that thought.

After fumbling for a few seconds, she said, "If you start talking like that, you can justify anything."

Shayne threw his arms up. "I don't need this right now! I'm going." He started walking away but turned back. "You haven't even asked me why I'm hurt. Why I'm bleeding."

"I don't care."

She did care, very much, but just didn't have the capacity to hear it right now. Besides, whatever it was, she was sure he deserved it.

"Fine then. Sorry for trying to be a brother."

Whatever that meant.

Shayne limped out of her apartment.

All the energy sustained by her anger drained from her body, and Layla sank to the floor.

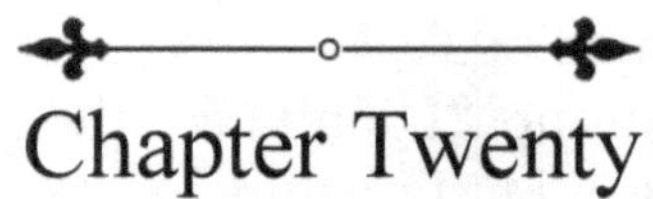

Chapter Twenty

Earrings. It had to be.

Daniel could allow for the statistical unlikelihood of all the Diamonds having their ears pierced but not for the complete lack of earrings in any standard piercing. That was too improbable.

But what were the earrings? His mind flashed to Cameron and his bright red diamond earrings. Surely, that must be too obvious, though.

He couldn't stand still any longer and started pacing.

What if they all wore the same earrings, but it was something random? Completely unrelated? That's how he'd do it, but if that was the case, he was sunk. He'd never be able to identify—well...he could just hang out at some casinos and hope to be able to spot several people all wearing the same earrings.

He scoffed. "Yeah, right. Let's assume I even could figure that out—what am I supposed to do next?"

On the other hand, if the earrings were red diamonds...

Part of him just could not believe that they would choose something so obvious. Then again, the Clubs all had a tattoo of the club sign. Can't get much more obvious than that. And while he had often gotten annoyed with Cameron's earrings, he had never considered the possibility that Cameron might be connected to the Suit.

He stopped pacing. He frowned. Could it be possible? Could Cameron actually be a Diamond?

Only one way to find out! And if he was wrong...well, hopefully Cameron wouldn't be too offended.

Daniel raced back to the table and grabbed his phone. He had to text Layla. Wherever Layla was, Cameron should be around there somewhere.

He stopped short. Oh boy. Did this mean Layla had a Diamond as a bodyguard? That couldn't be good.

But only if he actually is a Diamond, Daniel thought.

He could practically feel the blood coursing through his veins. He could actually do this! He was on the path to taking out two Suits!

He sent the text: *Where are you??*

Hopefully, she'd respond as soon as she saw it.

He waited. And waited. And waited. Until he was sure his hair was turning grey, and he was going to combust from impatience.

At some point, he decided to lie on the floor. He couldn't figure out why he'd decided that would help the time go by faster, but it seemed to help. At least, time had started to blur, and he was no longer feeling each minute as it ticked by.

Ding! His phone.

He shot up, almost propelling himself to his feet, but he didn't have quite enough momentum. He scrambled for his phone and then wilted in disappointment. The text wasn't from Layla. It was Aunt Jane, giving an update on Karsyn. Which was great, of course, but he needed to hear from Layla.

He was still staring at the screen when another notification popped up. Layla!

She replied: *My apartment…?*

Yes! He jumped up.

Time to figure out where Cameron's loyalties lay. Daniel planned to ask Cameron point-blank, hoping that would catch him off-guard and get an honest answer out of him.

Daniel needed to move quickly—get there as soon as possible. But he didn't want to get caught by anyone trying to make conversation and get delayed. But he knew the fastest way to get caught was to look like you're trying not to get caught. So—

So maybe he was overthinking this.

He grabbed his jacket and wallet and decided on walking casually but with purpose.

That worked well enough. Soon he was on a bus headed for Layla's apartment. He didn't know where Cameron would be, but he would look around for him—making it obvious he was looking for someone—until he either found him or Cameron presented himself.

Daniel got off at Layla's apartment.

The most logical place for Cameron to be, he thought, *is the lobby or somewhere outside where he can see Layla's window.*

Except Layla's apartment did not have a window facing the street. So Daniel went in to check the lobby. He scanned the seats but didn't see Cameron. He looked over at the desk, and there was—

Nathan?

Nathan was waving at him enthusiastically, dressed in a staff uniform.

Daniel wanted to facepalm, but instead he hurried over to get Nathan to stop waving and making things so obvious.

Nathan dropped his hands once Daniel got close. "Hi, Daniel! Don't worry," he dropped his voice and looked around furtively, "I'm incognito."

About as incognito as a flamingo in a paper shop but okay. At least Layla had one person looking out for her who wasn't connected to a Suit.

Unless?

No, no way. If Nathan belonged to a Suit, Daniel had a shot at running for President. Impossible.

"Are you here to visit Layla?" Nathan asked.

"No, actually, I'm here to talk to Cameron."

"Oh." His eyes got big, and he whispered, "Is it about not stopping the mugging?"

"What I have to say to him is between me and him," Daniel said stiffly.

Nathan nodded. "I see," he said seriously, giving way more importance to the situation than was necessary.

"So where is he?" Daniel prompted.

"Oh, right! Somewhere on his rounds—he likes to keep moving, just in case." Then, when Daniel just stared at him, Nathan added, "I can text him."

"Right. That would be helpful."

"He might not answer. He usually doesn't."

Was Nathan...pouting?

"Just tell him I'm here."

After too many moments, Nathan said, "He's walking up the E stairs, floor three—"

And Daniel was gone. Employing his walking casually-but-with-purpose stride that he was beginning to think he'd perfected. When he got into the stairwell, he started hurrying. He looked up but couldn't see Cameron, so he went faster.

Ugh, what is this? Leg day? he thought.

"Daniel, dude, up here!" Cameron called.

Daniel looked up. Cameron had stuck his head over the railing and was looking down at him.

"Give me one second!" Daniel shouted.

He kept up his pace as he continued up. Sure, Cameron could wait now that they'd made contact, but Daniel couldn't. He was eager to find out the truth and wanted to make sure he didn't have time to back out or overthink. He had to find out.

Cameron was standing there, waiting for him, arms crossed.

He started to say, "What's up?" when Daniel blurted out, "Tell me the truth. Are you a Diamond?"

Wait, maybe he should have double-checked that Cameron was wearing the diamond earrings. Daniel's eyes flitted to Cameron's ear. Yep, they were there. All good.

Cameron raised an eyebrow and frowned. Daniel's heart plummeted. Shoot. He didn't look taken aback one bit. Surely there should have been some element of surprise.

"Now, what makes you think that?" Cameron drawled.

At this response, Daniel's spirits lifted but only slightly. He decided to just be honest.

He nodded towards the earrings. "Diamond earrings," he replied. "They're the Diamond's identifier."

Then he held his breath. He had absolutely no idea what was coming next, but it was killing him to wait to find out.

Cameron stared at him for a long time.

Finally, he said, "Maybe I just like them."

This was basically confirmation. If he wasn't a Diamond, he would have already been denying the accusation. Cameron was testing him.

"Look, I have no interest in turning you in," Daniel said. "Yet." He was still a GDRS agent, after all. He just had priorities. "All I want is to meet with the Queen."

This time, Cameron's face flickered. A break in the stoic facade. "My—" He checked himself. "The Queen? Why?"

Daniel crossed his arms. How much honesty was he supposed to allow here? Suppose Cameron really wasn't a Diamond, and he was trying to trap Daniel and get him fired. No—his slip up was too revealing.

"If you must know, I want to make a deal with her. That she'll find a way to turn the Ace of Spades over to us."

Cameron's eyes lit up with a strange light. Daniel couldn't identify what emotion it was, but Cameron was feeling a lot of it.

"You want to..." Cameron breathed out, his words trailing off.

And great, they were back to the staring contest. Daniel wasn't going to speak first. If this was intimidation, it wasn't going to work. If Cameron was thinking, Daniel would stand there till his legs went numb rather than risk saying something that would work against him.

"Give me one good reason I shouldn't kill you right now," Cameron said.

That was not what Daniel had been expecting.

"Not that I'm going to, of course," Cameron added. "But humour me."

Daniel was so thrown off that at first the only thing he could manage was a weak, "Cameras?"

Cameron did a puff-of-air laugh.

"No, uh..." Daniel urged his brain to work faster. He was so close! He took a deep breath. "Because the GDRS will turn a blind eye to the Diamonds' activities for a while should they succeed." Yeah, maybe. Probably not. But he had to say something. "And once we have the Ace of Spades, we can take control of this branch of the Spades." He leaned forward. "Imagine that—being one of two Suits here in Toronto. The Clubs as your only competition."

"Until the GDRS finishes with the Spades and returns their attention to us," Cameron pointed out.

Daniel shrugged. "Can't pretend that isn't our whole aim."

"Fair enough. Just like I despise you to the very core of my being." What?

Cameron started laughing. "You should see your face! Dude!"

But he didn't clarify if he was joking or not. Probably not.

Once Cameron recovered from being amused by himself, he said, "All right. But I can't directly set up a meeting. You have to prove yourself."

"Excuse me, what? I figured out what the identifier for your Suit was. In one day. Haven't I proven myself enough?"

Cameron rolled his eyes. "You partially figured it out, and it was a lucky guess besides."

Daniel wanted to protest, but he stopped short. Partially?

"But I can tell you this: The Jewel of Luck casino, after seven, before midnight, three days from now. Good luck."

He turned to leave.

"No, wait!"

Cameron stopped but didn't bother to turn around. "What?"

"That's all you're gonna tell me?"

"Well, if you've figured out the identifier, and if you're as clever as you seem to think you are, you'll be fine. And even if you aren't," he looked back over his shoulder and smirked, "They'll find you. And then you'd better hope my Queen agrees to your deal, or you might be in trouble."

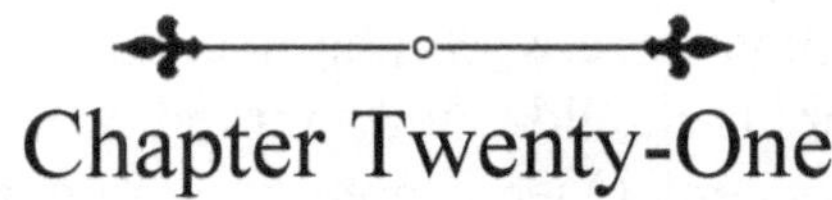

Chapter Twenty-One

Daniel walked through the doors of the Jewel of Luck casino, trying to look like he belonged there and not like it was his first time in this kind of setting. Sure, he had done his research, and plenty of it. He'd picked a few games and learned their rules, terminology, and strategies. He didn't know how long it would take to find the Diamonds (or for them to find him), but he wasn't planning on just standing around and looking like an idiot until then.

But research can only take you so far. And Daniel didn't come here to play, or lose money. Taking stock of the casino would be the best place to start, so he headed to the bar. Plus, he could use a drink. He was already getting nervous.

He took a seat. The bartender headed over. She leaned on the counter and looked Daniel up and down.

"Daniel Zakkar?" she asked.

Daniel froze. How did she know? He couldn't see her ears, her hair was blocking them, but he assumed she had to be a Diamond.

"Yes," he answered cautiously.

She smirked, nodded, then left.

Daniel considered shouting after her, but somehow he knew it wouldn't help. So he waited, looking around and taking in the casino. All the different tables, different games. Bright lights. Alcohol flowing freely. A fight broke out a little farther down the bar, but it was quickly subdued by security.

The atmosphere was chaotic, lawless, and he disliked it instantly.

What idiots they all were to come here. So confident in their skills or luck to think they wouldn't lose, or so confident in their wealth that if they did lose, it would hardly matter. Ridiculous either way. Daniel knew what it was like to be without enough money, and the idea that what some people would carelessly lose tonight could have changed his family's whole future seven years ago was enough to make him sick.

Then again, wasn't Daniel here tonight to do a very similar thing?

Trusting in his luck and skill of persuasion. He was about to make the biggest gamble out of anyone here.

And he hadn't even gotten that drink for his nerves.

"Daniel Zakkar?"

Daniel turned his head to the left. While he'd been looking around the casino, someone had approached him, staying in his blind spot. It bugged Daniel that he hadn't noticed the man at all.

"I heard you wish to meet with my Queen," the man said. He was wearing Diamond earrings, cut just like Cameron's, but his were black. Maybe to match his suit?

"Yes," Daniel answered.

Out of the corner of his eye, Daniel could see the bartender return and come closer.

The Diamond dude crossed his arms. "You sure that's what you want?"

No.

"Yes."

It was too late to back out now. Toronto needed this. Needed Daniel to succeed. And Daniel was pretty sure his life depended on him succeeding too. As if that thought helped his nerves.

"Then follow me," Diamond Dude said. "And pray to whatever gods you think are listening."

Well, wasn't that a nice, dramatically morbid thought?

Steeling himself, Daniel got off the stool and followed.

Toronto is counting on you, he reminded himself. *Every innocent who has been harmed because of the Suits is counting on you.*

He thought of Karsyn, and his heart squeezed. Resolve gave him an iron backbone. Whatever it took, this meeting had to succeed. He needed to be witty, charming but not annoying, intelligent, and determined.

Daniel didn't know where he was going. Diamond Dude cut through the crowds easily. They didn't exactly part for him, but no one ever bumped into him or was in his way. Daniel wasn't so lucky. He almost tripped several times. One man bumped into him on purpose. Probably drunk. When Daniel sent him a glare, he backed away.

Then Daniel realized they were going towards some elevators he hadn't noticed before. He hadn't even known there was a second floor.

Standing on either side of the doors were two security guards. When they saw Diamond Dude, one nodded and pressed her ID badge to a scanner. The doors opened.

Daniel quickly glanced at both of their ears as he passed, but neither were wearing a Diamond earring. But both had their ears pierced. Pierced and empty. Huh. Maybe their identifier *was* more complicated as Cameron had been hinting.

The ride up was silent. It wasn't a long ride, but there would have been plenty of time for second-guessing if Daniel hadn't been doing his best to not think at all.

I've prepared as much as possible, he thought. *This is it. Whether I'm ready or not.*

The doors opened. Diamond Dude stepped out right away. Daniel was experiencing a confusing combination of nausea, eagerness, nerves, and purpose. But he forced his legs to keep on walking.

To his surprise, more tables were set up, sparser than downstairs, but the people playing were different. All calmness, a cool exterior. Indifferent to how the game turned out because they could afford it, whatever happened. They radiated wealth. The elite of the elite.

Daniel definitely looked underdressed in his dress pants and white dress shirt. Too late to change now.

He didn't bother trying to look like he belonged, either. They would see through him in an instant, and he was too busy trying to look confident anyway. But not like a boastful confidence. A quiet, self-assured confidence. He hoped he was nailing it.

Diamond Dude led him to the farthest back corner. Sitting at a small, round table, surrounded by standing Diamonds, was the Queen.

She sat with her back to the wall, her eyes following Daniel. On her face, she wore a teal masquerade mask, adorned with jewels. Her hair was piled on her head in a complicated-looking twist. Her dress was the same colour as her mask, which popped against her black hair and bronze skin.

The rest of the Diamonds wore black, which made the Queen stand out even more. No doubt that was the desired effect.

The Queen was mindlessly shuffling a deck of cards, as if it were second nature,

Daniel swallowed, still unsure whether to feel nervous or elated. Both? This was the turning point. The thought of all that could happen if he succeeded was enough to keep his legs moving. If leaving hadn't been an option earlier, it in no way was now. His choices were to freak out or stay calm. He preferred the latter.

Diamond Dude pulled out the chair opposite the Queen and gestured for Daniel to sit. When he did, the Queen put the cards aside.

"So," she said, drawing the word out. "You wanted to meet with me."

"Yes," Daniel answered cautiously. Then, when it looked like she wasn't going to respond, he said, "I wanted to—"

He fell silent as the Queen lightly lifted one hand.

"So eager to get to business," she said, her voice holding a hint of laughter. "Aren't you going to introduce yourself? We are, after all, strangers."

Right. Like the Queen of Diamonds wanted a nice little chit-chat.

"I know who you are," he said.

The Queen chuckled. "Indeed. But who are you?"

"Daniel Zakkar," Daniel said. "Agent in the GDRS, specifically the Diamond Elimination Unit." Maybe he shouldn't have thrown that in there, but she was starting to annoy him.

She tilted her head to the side. Daniel worried momentarily for the hair amassed on her head, but it seemed stable enough.

"You are dedicated to eliminating the Suits," she said. "Yet here you are, meeting with me. The Diamond Queen. The leader of the Suit you are...actually in the unit for eradicating."

Like that needed elaborating. Could she just let him get to his offer already?

"It was necessary," Daniel said. "I want to form a brief alliance in order to eliminate another Suit."

"Specifically, you want me to eliminate the Ace of Spades," the Queen said bluntly.

Daniel frowned. So Cameron had talked to her, then. He was beginning to think he hadn't, what with all this preamble.

"Yes," he answered. "I do. Kill him, or capture him and give him to us. Whatever's easiest."

"Such a gentleman to allow me to pick."

"And in return," Daniel continued, ignoring the interruption, "The GDRS will turn a blind eye to your activities. For a while. Only a while, you understand."

The Queen considered his proposition. "No money? I'll think less of you if you didn't bring any with you."

Well, he really couldn't care less what she thought of him, as long as those thoughts weren't of his death. Honestly, she had seemed really intimidating before she had opened her mouth, but now...? This would be easy.

"I didn't bring money," Daniel announced.

This statement caused a reaction among the other Diamonds. A few chuckled and shook their heads. He actually heard one say to another, "Well, he tried. Idiot."

The Queen didn't react. She might have lifted her eyebrow, but with the mask, it was hard to tell.

Daniel leaned back in his chair and crossed his arms. "If your Diamonds are as skilled as they're rumoured to be, surely they can take the required payment out of my account themselves."

More stirring among the Diamonds. One nod of approval.

Daniel could hear his heart thumping away as he waited for the Queen to respond. Was it too daring of a move?

The Queen leaned forward. "You have guts," she said at last. "Cameron seemed to think otherwise."

Ouch. But not unexpected.

"I have whatever the situation calls for," he said.

"Indeed." She sat back. "My Diamonds have already emptied your bank account. When you fulfill your end of the bargain, we will return all but our payment."

Daniel was a master at keeping his face blank by now, and it was no problem to do so now, even as his pulse skipped. They really were skilled. Also, no one else in the GDRS knew he was doing this, so could he even keep up his end of the bargain? Was it even necessary to keep up his end? According to Austin, his unit didn't do anything anyway. Unless the Diamonds were planning on doing something big.

All this thinking was useless! It didn't matter. He had to proceed.

Keeping it casual, as if it didn't bother him one bit that all his money was gone, Daniel said, "You're just going to leave me with nothing until then? What if I have to buy groceries?"

The Queen smiled. "Very well. We can return a couple hundred tonight."

How generous.

"You haven't answered me yet," Daniel pointed out. "Can you, or can you not accomplish this?"

"You think that we couldn't? Of course we can. The only reason we haven't yet is because of the strength of the retribution. The Spades would know it was us—the Clubs are incapable of subtlety in any form. The GDRS must *immediately* seize control of the Spades."

"Do you plan to kill or capture the Ace?" he asked.

She leaned her head forward again. "I thought that was my choice to make," she said, as though it was a private joke between the two of them.

Daniel didn't know how he felt about the possibility of her choosing to kill his cousin, but it was too late now.

"It is our job," he said again. "You have my word that the GDRS will work to undo the Spades as soon as possible. As long as it's understood that this is only a temporary alliance."

"As long as you understand that once I kill the Ace, our part to play in this is over. We will not be your pawns to bring down the other Suits, just to have you turn on us once you're done."

Daniel swallowed but nodded. "This will be enough." He did his best to ignore the fact that she'd said "kill" as though that was her definite choice.

"Will you play a game with me before you leave?" she asked. "As a way of securing this temporary alliance?"

"I don't know any casino games."

Lie. But Daniel didn't have any money to gamble with, even if he had wanted to. He had some theories about the Diamond presence in this casino, and they all pointed to the Diamonds being killer at all casino games. No, he did not feel like getting his butt kicked in a game.

"What about...Hearts?" The Queen lingered on the last word. "Surely you know that one."

"I do."

But it was a household game. Not something played in casinos. He didn't even know how you would bet in Hearts. And why did she place such emphasis on the word "Hearts"?

Don't tell me there's another Suit, please, he thought. *I have enough to worry about.*

The Queen flashed a smile. "Fantastic. We'll play that then."

What, he hadn't actually agreed! He just said he knew the game.

Too late. She grabbed the deck and gave it one more quick shuffle, for good measure, then dealt four hands, using all the cards.

"Four?" Daniel asked.

"You didn't think we'd be playing by ourselves, did you?"

At her words, two Diamonds sat at the table. Diamond Dude to Daniel's left and a lady to his right. Daniel felt his chances of playing decently shrinking into non-existence.

The Queen introduced the two as Meera and Arther. Daniel looked for their earrings. He wanted to figure out as much of their identifier system as possible. But he had already seen that Arther's earrings were black, and Meera was wearing a hijab, so he couldn't actually see her ears.

They all inspected their cards and chose which three they were going to give away. Daniel tried to keep his panic from rising as he desperately recited all the rules in his head. It had been a while since he played, and forgetting a rule or getting one wrong would not be helpful in this circumstance.

He gave three high hearts to Arther and received three cards, all different Suits, from Meera. Including the queen of spades. No!

Then Meera played a two of Clubs to start the game.

Daniel knew he did not want to get the lead, whatever happened. Too much pressure that way. Better to stay under the radar. So he played the seven of clubs. Arther played an ace. Oh yeah, you couldn't break hearts in the first round! He should've played his jack. That would've been the smarter move, just this once.

The Queen played a low card as well.

Arther's eyes flickered over to the Queen in momentary surprise. The look was quick, but Daniel caught it. Was that different from how she usually played? What did it mean, if anything?

Aurthur threw down the jack of diamonds to start the next turn.

The game continued on. Daniel grew nervous as several rounds passed and no hearts were broken. Where were they?

They're waiting to give most of them to me, he thought with dread.

He had so far avoided getting the lead. But the queen of spades was his only spade left, and he was afraid he was going to get stuck with it.

Meera played a five of spades. Daniel winced, playing the queen of spades. Arther smirked as he threw in his lower spade. But Meera was watching the Queen cautiously. With an air of resignation, she put down the ace of spades.

If Daniel hadn't been smarter, he would have been elated. That was half the points right there! Instead, he was worried. She could have gotten rid of the card way earlier—why keep it until now?

The Queen looked up and met Daniel's gaze. Her lips barely curved upwards in a smile. Daniel looked down at his hand. He had only one heart, which he hadn't been able to use. He could now, if the Queen played another spade.

She didn't.

She played all her cards: The ace, king, queen, and jack of hearts, saving one.

Meera reluctantly played four hearts. Daniel laid down his one heart and discarded three others. Arther threw down his four hearts in disgust.

The Queen carelessly tossed her last card onto the table. It didn't matter. She had all the points. She had shot the moon, and now the rest of them had twenty-six points.

The Queen didn't bother to hide her delighted smile as she gathered up all the cards. After a quick and skillful shuffle, she distributed them again.

Daniel carefully looked over his cards. He knew he wasn't skilled enough to shoot the moon, as the Queen had. Which, besides needing skill, required a certain hand to pull off. But he could avoid as many points as possible.

So that's what he set out to do. He looked over everything with a critical eye. Analyzed every move. He mentally ticked off cards in his head, so he knew when certain Suits were running low. Through this strategy, he managed to trap Arther into getting stuck with two hearts.

He never knew a simple game of cards could be so mentally draining. It took a lot of brain power to play this well against the three Diamonds.

The round finished, and he didn't win. But he didn't get the most points either. If he stayed to play all night, he suspected he could eventually manage to win...one round. Maybe.

"Would you like to play another?" the Queen asked Daniel as Meera shuffled the deck.

"Are you actually asking me what I want?" he said.

"Would I have used those words if I wasn't?"

Daniel would enjoy bringing down the Diamonds when the time came.

"I have no desire to be beaten again," he said. "Your skills in this game are way better than mine."

She nodded. "Then you may leave. You played better than I

expected. You'd be an excellent poker player."

Well thanks.

Daniel stood up. "When can I expect the Ace to be either gone or in our hands?"

"You have my word—it will be no less than two weeks."

Two weeks? That was an excellent time frame, but could they pull it off? He hoped so. He honestly didn't know what he was supposed to do in the Diamond Unit while he waited.

He nodded and said, "Great." There was nothing else to say, so he just left, half expecting one of them to follow him. Make sure he actually left. But no one did.

Daniel never looked back and made his way straight for the exit. He wasn't sure what to think about the deal he had just made. Not sure if he wanted to think about it. But it was done.

"Soon, very soon," Daniel vowed. "All the Suits will be gone."

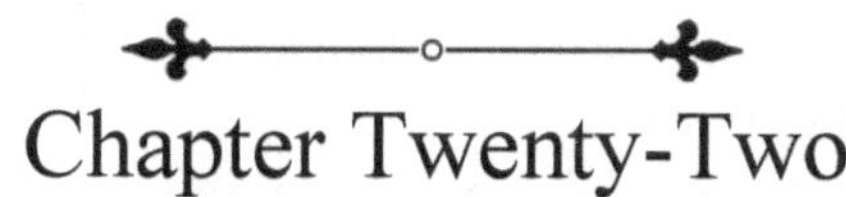

Chapter Twenty-Two

Layla hiked up the strap of her backpack as she walked down the sidewalk. Taking the bus would have been smarter. She was probably going to be late. Not that it mattered much, since Jason wouldn't be mad. And she needed the walk. Too many things crowded her brain, needing attention.

Like how Cameron was apparently a Diamond. He'd waltzed into her apartment yesterday, telling her that now was the time to act. He had given her a packet of some stuff that was supposed to knock Shayne out, and reminded her of what would happen if she didn't. Her choice was between protecting the brother that abandoned her years ago, put her family in danger, and caused Karsyn to be hospitalized; or the cousin that hadn't done anything wrong.

She'd almost cancelled today's lessons. But she needed something to distract her, if only for a little while. If she thought for too much longer, her brain was going to explode. Plus, Jason only had time for a free lesson every so often.

When she reached the studio, she rushed in. Before the receptionist could say anything, she said, "I'm meeting with Jason!"

He might have nodded, but by that point, he was too far in her peripheral vision for her to be sure.

Jason was coming down the hallway.

"Layla!" he exclaimed. "There you are—I mean...uh, you weren't here—were late. I was just...just getting...worried."

"Sorry. I wanted to walk, but that turned out to be a poor idea."

Jason waved his hand. "Don't w—that is, it's fine—you're good."

It wasn't fine. His stutter was worse than usual. Either something in the last session had agitated him, or her being late had done it.

She slung her backpack off her shoulders and held it up. "I'll just go get dressed, and then we can get started!"

He gave her a thumbs up.

She headed into the change room, only to discover she'd forgotten her leggings. She'd taken them out yesterday to wash and never put them back in.

Great. Just what she needed.

When she entered the workout room a few minutes later, Jason looked confused at her attire.

"Forgot to pack leggings," she explained. "It's whatever. These jeans are loose enough. They'll be fine for today."

Jason shrugged. "If you say—I mean..." He sighed. "Okay."

Instead of warming up on the treadmill, Jason took her through some dynamic stretching. Layla was so glad she didn't have to run. Running was bad enough on its own, but to do it in jeans? Yuck.

After that, they moved onto practicing with the dummy, just like last time. Same moves and everything. It didn't do much in terms of taking Layla's mind off things. Pretty soon, her brain was occupied with the same thoughts that had consumed it on the walk over.

Her moves became mechanical and automatic, and she barely registered what Jason was calling out.

"Okay...Layla...maybe...stop?" he said. "Hey—no."

The words didn't register, and she aimed her fist towards the dummy's stomach. Jason put his hand in front of hers, gently stopping her punch.

She blinked and took a step back. She looked at him.

"Sorry, Jason. I'm a bit distracted today."

"I noticed—that is—" He checked himself. "Are you...okay? I know—um...how's Karsyn doing?"

Karsyn. Right. Naturally, Jason would think she was worrying about Karsyn.

"I didn't—wasn't—uh...gonna ask, cause..." Jason rubbed his forehead. "The words aren't wording today—for me," he muttered.

"It's fine, Jason," she said. "Karsyn got hurt, but his condition is stable. And he's not in a ton of pain, cause, you know, medicine, so." She shrugged. "Yeah."

Jason nodded. "Ooookayy," he said slowly. "Then—something else?"

"What makes you say that?" Layla asked, knowing full well she was distracted but having no idea what she was going to cover it up with. She should've just said she was worrying over Karsyn.

Jason hesitated. Scratched the back of his neck.

Layla wanted him to drop the subject but knew he wouldn't. He cared too deeply, and normally, she admired that, but right now, it was causing her some panic.

"Layla...your, um...moves, they're...mechanical. Like, you're doing them right, but—that is, you're not focu—concentrating. Your mind—you're distracted."

Yeah, she knew all that already.

"So..." He seemed to be waiting for her to fill in the blanks, but no way was that happening.

Jason took a deep breath.

"If it's not—you're not...not worrying about Karsyn...what?"

"That's...it's not important," she answered. "Can we just get back to the lesson? I could use some distraction today."

"Maybe you could—need—to talk. Maybe you need to talk. About—that is, whatever's going on."

"No," she said quickly, then cringed. That was probably suspicious. But there was no way she was telling him anything. Besides, she knew what he'd say. Nothing new.

"Layla, something's wrong," he insisted. "If you...just—I can help! You can—that is...you can tell me anything. And I can't...you know, if you're not—I can't teach you if you're not..., you know, paying attention."

"And why should you care so much?" Layla raised her voice and ignored the fact that, as one of her best friends, of course he should care. But she didn't know what to do! "I *was* listening, and I *was* doing what you said! What does it matter if my heart and soul aren't in every move?"

Jason took a step back, surprise and hurt registering on his face. Layla realized this might be the first time she had ever seriously raised her voice at him. And now she felt bad.

"Listen, Jason, I'm sorry. I just...it's been a really crazy couple of weeks."

"Is it Ryden?"

The venom in his voice was like nothing Layla had ever heard come out of his mouth before.

"What?"

"Ryden? Your new—uh, I mean...ever since you—your first date, he... you've been off. He's not...good."

"You don't know a single thing about him to be making that accusation!"

Layla, however, did, and Jason was totally correct. Ryden wasn't anyone worth defending. But now wasn't the time for rational and logical thinking!

"I'm an adult and perfectly capable of choosing who to date!"

Aside from the fact that everything Ryden had said was a lie. Details.

"Yeah...but, it's not like—you don't..." Jason threw his hands down at the ground. "How well can—do you even know him?"

"Why do you care?"

"I just...I want..." He huffed, then stretched out his hand towards her. "I just...just want you to be safe."

Layla stared coldly at him. "Yeah, you and everyone else."

When would the people in her life stop acting like it was their designated duty to protect her?

Jason stared at her. "What's happened to you?" he said quietly.

His words hit Layla like a punch to the gut. She could feel her eyes welling up with tears.

"No...Layla, I'm...I'm sorry, I just—you..." Jason sighed, then took a few steps closer and put his arms around her.

The shock that he would be so bold to actually give her a hug was enough to stop the tears. Then it was comfort. She wanted to stay here, in his arms, forever, and never have to leave to deal with the reality of the Suits. If he could just block the world out—

No. What?

Was she thinking that she wanted him to protect her? No. That was weakness. That was the very thing she disliked most.

She had told Shayne she was going to prove she could take care of herself. And she was! This was not the way to do it. She knew she had to pick her path, now, whatever it was, and not waver from it again.

Shayne's position was hurting them. All of them. Including himself. It would be best for him—for everybody—if he was no longer the Ace.

Layla shook free of Jason's embrace, ignoring how, as soon as she did, she wished she hadn't.

He took a step back. "I'm sorry if—that is, I didn't mean for..."

The look he gave her took her breath away. His eyes held such a deep, intense caring. For her.

She looked away. "I don't want to fight, Jason. But you have to let me make my own choices."

"I don't...either, but...I don't want you to, uh...be hurting. But..."

He hunched his shoulders. "You can, that is, you..." He nodded. "I won't stop you. But...you can always—always—talk. To me."

How she wished she could.

"I should go now," she said.

"I won't stop you," he said again.

But the look in his eyes made it clear that he wanted to.

Layla dumped her backpack on the bench and kicked off her shoes. She hurried into her living room. There he was, waiting on the couch, just like his text said.

He wanted to apologize for the fight, figure things out. He didn't want to be enemies with his own sister.

They weren't enemies. But Layla had to make sure he couldn't cause her or Karsyn to be hurt again. Besides, if she didn't do this, Karsyn's situation would only get worse, and Layla didn't think there was much room for that without things getting fatal. Which made her want to throw up, so she pushed that thought aside.

"You're early," she said.

"So are you," Shayne pointed out. He walked over to her, then frowned in concern. "What's wrong?"

Everything. She was trapped between bad choices with the only way out to pick whatever was the necessary evil. And this was it.

Besides, Cameron had assured her that they wouldn't hurt Shayne. As long as he revealed the headquarters' location.

"Nothing," she said, shaking her head. "It's no big deal."

Shayne raised an eyebrow. Of course he wouldn't believe her. She wouldn't have even believed her.

"Would you like something to drink?" she asked. She pressed her hands to her legs, because she could feel them start to shake.

"Get me something that represents me," Shayne requested.

Really? He couldn't just tell her what liquid and make things easier for her? Whatever.

"Make yourself comfortable," she said, gesturing back to the couch.

She went into the kitchen. Before she did anything, she glanced carefully out to see where Shayne was. He had taken a seat again, and his back was facing her. Perfect. As long as she moved quickly, and he didn't try to come in, everything would go smoothly.

She grabbed milk out of the fridge. She didn't have coffee, and water probably wouldn't be strong enough on its own to mask the taste.

The packet! Where was it?

Her brain froze for a second, but then she remembered. It was also in the fridge, hidden behind a jar of maple syrup.

She grabbed it, ripped it open, and poured it into the milk. The packet went into the trash, and she grabbed a spoon. She stirred the contents so they mixed into the milk.

Then she froze again. Wait, had Cameron told her to only use half the packet? She had been so focussed on going fast she didn't think about their instructions. He had definitely said either "Make sure you use more than half" or "Make sure you don't use more than half." Problem was, she couldn't remember which, and those were opposite instructions.

It would have to do. Hopefully the taste wasn't too strong.

She brought it out and offered the drink to Shayne. It felt like her hand was trembling so hard she was going to spill the milk. But it didn't look like Shayne noticed.

"I think I'm offended," he said as he took the cup from her. "I was hoping for dark coffee. Or just...coffee."

"I don't have coffee. Drink your milk," Layla ordered.

"Yes, ma'am!" Shayne exclaimed with a salute.

Layla watched him. She wanted to cry out for him to stop, but fear for her and Karsyn's lives kept her silent.

He took a sip. Swallowed. His expression turned cautious, and he sniffed the milk. Then he took another sip. Swallowing with difficulty, he grimaced.

No! It was too much.

"What's wrong?" she asked. As if she didn't know.

"I think this milk is spoiled."

"What? Are you sure? Try once more."

He frowned at her. Maybe he was just trying to be extra nice so they wouldn't fight again, because he took one more gulp. This time, he gagged.

"Yeah, NO. You try it if you want." He held the glass out to her. "But I'm not drinking any more."

She took the glass from Shayne and went back into the kitchen.

"Sorry Shayne!" she called out. "Looks like you'll have to drink plain water."

"Hey, no problem," he called back. "I like water. You know, I'm actually honoured that you gave me milk as the beverage to represent me. Shows that you don't think I'm as bad a guy as everyone else does."

Yeah, sure, whatever. Think what you want, Shayne.

Layla was too busy getting mad at herself. She opened the fridge door and grabbed the bag of milk she had used. Making quick calculations, she started pouring the milk out. She had to commit now.

"The entire bag is spoiled. Yuck!" she shouted.

Meanwhile, she was thinking, *If I used the whole packet when I should have used half, and the amount of milk he drank was almost half...will it still be enough to be effective?*

If she failed...if Karsyn had to pay the price...

She kept the glass of milk out, just in case.

"Would you like anything to eat?" she asked. Maybe she could mix some of the milk in his food or something?

"Nah, I ate supper already," he answered. "Panda Express takeout. And something I ate did not agree with me."

Was it working already?

"Just water then," Layla said.

No way could she mix the milk in with water. Resigned to hoping for the best, she filled two cups with water and went back out into the living room. She handed Shayne one cup, then sat down in the armchair.

Shayne looked at Layla for a moment, then said, "What I said a minute ago—that was too soon to say after our fight, wasn't it?"

Layla fiddled with her earring. She didn't want to fight. But she also wanted to be truthful.

"Probably," she admitted.

"Because you do think I'm a bad guy, like everyone else, or just because you're still upset about our fight?"

Wow. He sure knew how to apologize and try to keep the peace.

"What do you want me to say?" she asked. "You are a criminal. You're committing crimes. That's the definition of a criminal." She took a sip of water, then hastened to swallow it so she could add, "But I don't think your heart is bad. Just misplaced. And anyways, I thought you said you didn't want to fight?"

Shayne set his cup down with more force than necessary.

"Misplaced?" He scoffed. "Seriously? You've barely excused me, if that's what you were trying to do. Do you think the King of Clubs is a bad person and deserves to be jailed?"

"Well, yeah," she answered automatically.

Too late, she realized her mistake.

"Then why am I any different?" Shayne demanded.

She looked at him. *Was* he any different?

"I didn't know and love the King of Clubs as my brother before he became anything else," she answered finally. Because, despite everything, Shayne was her brother. She was only doing this to him because she had to. Because others would pay if she didn't.

Shayne gave a short and harsh laugh. "Family connections don't mean anything. That's what I learned."

Layla frowned. "What are you talking about?"

"Haven't you wondered, at least once, why I looked so beat up?"

She had, but what did that have to do with family connections...? Her eyes widened.

"No."

Shayne stood up and walked over to the window. He looked outside. "After Karsyn's car crash, once I heard he was out of surgery, my first instinct was to go to the hospital. I'll admit...I wasn't thinking straight." He casually lifted one shoulder. "I might have been drinking a bit after I heard he got hurt. Some of my bodyguards tried to stop me from leaving. Things got physical." He absent-mindedly touched a spot on his leg. "I was stumbling around in the dark, trying to find the hospital, when...Daniel showed up."

Layla almost told him to stop, sure she wouldn't like what he was going to say next. She set her cup down.

"He said he was going to arrest me." Shayne turned to face Layla. "We fought," he said it as if it was a casual, everyday occurrence. "He threw the first two punches, if that makes you feel any better."

"No, it doesn't!" Layla exclaimed. "What happened next?"

"After the fighting? Oh, well, first he used a knife on me."

Layla's eyes widened. She didn't want to hear this.

"Then he pulled a gun on me. Luckily, one of my Spades made a timely appearance and knocked him out. What, did he never say anything about it to you?" He scoffed. "Probably would have been bragging about it to everyone if he had succeeded. But he failed."

"How'd he even find you?" Layla asked. Not because she

particularly cared about the answer, but because she couldn't think of anything else to say.

Shayne shrugged. "Cameras, probably. Toronto's full of them. One recognized my face or something. But we're taking precautions against that now."

"Wow. Daniel actually...he was gonna use a gun on you?"

"Daniel? Ha! I'm surprised he even had the guts to pull it out. I doubt he would have ever pulled the trigger."

Layla needed more water. She took a few hasty gulps, then asked, "Weren't you worried?"

"Nah. I always beat Daniel."

"Sure, but, this time, it wasn't just him. I mean, he was an extension of the GDRS."

Shayne shook his head, laughing again. "No way. They sent backup for him way too late. We were long gone. You know, we make fun of the Clubs for being the dumbest Suit, but the Hearts really give them a run for their money sometimes."

Hearts? Layla stood up.

"Shayne, what do you mean by Hearts?"

"Oh yeah, you don't know," he said. He stepped closer. In a voice that was letting her in on some sort of private joke, he said, "Want to know what we call the government? Ever wonder why there are only three Suits?" He didn't wait for a response. "Hearts. The government is Hearts. Their job is to help people, protect them, because they're loving." His voice lost its mocking tone and became serious. "But a heart can hate just as easily as it can love."

"But...the GDRS they're—"

Shayne held up a hand. "The good guys, I know."

Not what she had been going to say.

"We covered this last time," he said, tone bitter.

"Speaking of last time, you texted that you wanted to apologize for that?" Her brow furrowed. "Speaking of texting, how'd you have my number?"

Man, she was being really slow on the uptake recently.

"Eh, Ryden gave it to me." This was also said much too casually.

"Okay." She considered this for a second. "Get out. Please."

"Wait, what? All of a sudden you're just kicking me out?"

She nodded. "Yeah. Your text said you wanted to apologize, but your words now are showing me you have no intention of that."

Plus, he needed to be anywhere other than her apartment when he collapsed. Which should be at any moment now.

"Oh, right, cause I need to say sorry for caring about you and trying to protect you. That's not something most people would need an apology for you know."

"You're supposed to apologize for *lying* to me!" Layla exclaimed. "There's a way to care for someone while being respectful!"

Like Jason, her brain added.

Not helpful right now.

She took a deep breath. "I am not in the mood to argue right now. So if you're not in the mood for apologies, I'd like you to go. Please."

Shayne opened his mouth, looking like he wanted to argue. But then he sighed. "Okay."

He went over to the entryway and grabbed a hoodie Layla hadn't noticed earlier. He put it on, flipped the hood up, and pulled out sunglasses. *That* was his precaution against the cameras?

But when he turned back to face Layla, she had to admit it worked. The hood was large enough to cast his whole face in shadow, and with the sunglasses, well, it was hard to tell who he was.

He struggled with something for a couple seconds, then muttered, "For what it's worth, I am sorry."

In the next instant, he was out the door. Leaving Layla alone with her guilt.

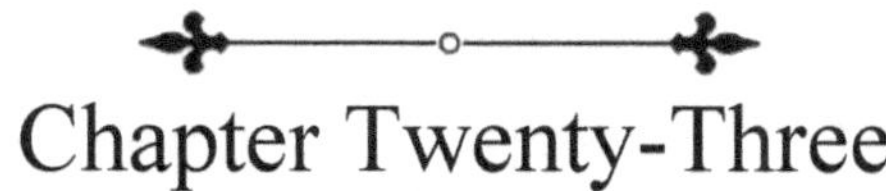

Chapter Twenty-Three

Oh joy of joys, Timothy was waiting for him just outside the door, his arms crossed.

"That went well," Timothy said. His meaning was sarcastic, but his tone was as bland as ever.

Exasperated, Shayne huffed, "Were you listening to the whole thing?"

"What else are these for?" Timothy gestured to his black earpiece.

Shayne wanted to take his out, now that they were together, but he knew what kind of lecture he would get from Timothy if he tried. Stuff about his safety. What if he got lost? Stranger danger. All that stuff that made him feel like a child being babysat. Honestly, there was a difference between being protective and being...overbearing...

He didn't like this realization. It sounded too similar to Layla's complaints and was making him second-guess himself.

"Well," Timothy began, "After that stellar—"

"Oh, just shut up," Shayne said. "I don't need"—gestured at Timothy— "any of this right now." He looked at Layla's door. "She used to always look up to me, no matter what. Now I think she might hate me."

"And you expected otherwise? Did you think joining the Spades was the best way to preserve the family connection?" Before Shayne could object, Timothy added, "You're not the only one who has family problems, your Aceness. Some of us just don't parade that fact around."

Shayne frowned. He didn't know what Timothy was talking about, and frankly, he didn't care.

"Why are you even here?" he said, walking away. "Send the car back without us. I feel like walking."

He knew Timothy had fallen in step behind him, even if he didn't hear him. Shayne headed towards the stairs. He was in the mood for lots of walking. But then he still didn't hear anything behind him. He turned around.

Yep, there was Timothy.

"Didn't you hear—"

"I heard you," Timothy said. "Heard you give an order that was reckless, dangerous, and just overall stupid in nature."

"Well, isn't it great that you don't have to agree with me to still relay the order? I outrank you, Timothy. So give the order."

"Right now, my biggest priority is getting you back to headquarters safely, Ace. That priority outranks you."

Shayne frowned. Well, he had no such priority. He tapped his earpiece twice, then said, "Go back to headquarters without me. I'm going to walk."

Timothy's glare could cut steel. He, too, tapped his earpiece. "Frank, Marco, you're not to leave with the car. You will be walking back with us."

"Don't you think two bodyguards is kinda overkill?"

Timothy didn't say anything, just marched past him and started down the stairs. Shayne grinned. His safety might be the number one priority, but even Timothy couldn't overrule a direct order given by the Ace. As much as he probably wanted to.

Shayne wondered why Timothy didn't go on ahead with the car, so he could spend less time in Shayne's presence. But no. No matter how much Timothy despised him (and Shayne was pretty sure it was off the charts), he was fully committed to the Spades, and keeping the Ace alive and safe was important.

They walked down the stairs in silence, as was usual with Timothy. Maybe Shayne should try to think over what had happened between him and Layla, but the upset shifting of his stomach was increasing. He was starting to regret sending the car away, but he could make it. He'd have to, now. No way would he admit to Timothy that he wished he'd taken the car. All because of a little stomach ache.

Except, as they walked onto the street, the pain grew. Shayne rubbed his stomach, hoping that would help but not sure why it would.

The two bodyguards didn't say anything. They just started walking behind them.

They were halfway back to headquarters. Shayne was beginning to feel confident again. The shiftings had quieted, making him hopeful he would be able to get back without a problem, then he could just take some Pepto Bismol or something.

Then, pain flared unexpectedly. Shayne stumbled, then halted completely, hands clutching at his stomach. What was this? No ordinary stomach ache, that's for sure.

"What's wrong?" Timothy asked. His voice was the closest to concern Shayne had ever heard from him. On his behalf, at least. Timothy put a hand on Shayne's shoulder.

Shayne shook his head, trying to clear it. "I don't know, I—" His knees buckled suddenly, and he almost fell forward, but Timothy latched onto him. "I feel awful."

Understatement of the year. His insides were being melted into pools of lava, twisting and writhing as they did so. All his muscles ached and shook like he'd just run a marathon. What was happening to him?

"You're going pale," Timothy observed.

How helpful, making observations that did nothing. Shayne wanted to yell at him, but he had no such strength. In fact, he worried that if he opened his mouth too wide, he was going to vomit.

"My stomach," Shayne groaned, barely moving his mouth.

His legs shook to the point they were no longer able to support him, and he fell to his knees. He barely felt the pain of them smacking onto the sidewalk. What was that pain when compared to what the rest of him was feeling?

"Carry him," Timothy barked.

Shayne felt someone's arm on his back, and he leaned into them. Next thing he knew, he was being carried in their arms. Must be one of his bodyguards.

As much as Shayne could think around his brains being electrocuted, he was actually glad Timothy had stayed with him.

"We need to get off the streets," Timothy said. Shayne was hearing the words but not doing much to comprehend them.

"Go back to Layla," Shayne mumbled.

"Don't talk—save your strength," Timothy ordered, looking over at him. His eyes held an unreal amount of concern for Shayne, considering they were Timothy's eyes.

Shayne wondered how coherent his sentence had been. He'd understood it just fine, but maybe that's because he already knew what he meant.

"Headquarters is too far away," the bodyguard pointed out.

Oh, it was Marco. Good call. All of Frank's strength was in his legs. He wouldn't be able to carry Shayne. But Marco probably felt nothing.

It was taking all of Shayne's concentration just to keep breathing, so he let his head flop onto Marco's shoulder.

Timothy took a deep breath. "We're drawing attention to ourselves. Is anyone close by?"

Frank answered. "Just one, but she's visiting the Chicago branch right now, so we can't get into her place."

Timothy swore under his breath. He turned in a circle. "There's someone else, but..." He looked at Shayne again. He muttered something else under his breath. It sounded something like "just let you die."

Wasn't that heartening.

Timothy reached out and yanked Shayne's hood so it came down, partly covering his eyes.

"Follow me," he said.

They started running. Shayne could barely make out the sound of Timothy giving commands over his earpiece over the sound of their feet pounding on the sidewalk. Something about a doctor and...victory? Going to victory? No, that couldn't be right.

He couldn't tell where they were going either. But really, he wouldn't have been able to even if his eyes hadn't been obstructed by the hood.

Shayne didn't know if the pain was increasing anymore, or if it was just unchanging in intensity. Whatever the case, he wished he could go unconscious so he could stop feeling it. But then he realized how short of a jump it was from unconsciousness to death, and he was grateful for the pain (for about ten seconds). At least it meant he was still alive.

Then they were inside a building. Pounding up the stairs. Every jolt sent more lightning bolts of pain through Shayne's body.

Timothy was knocking on a door. No, *pounding*. The person inside was yelling a response, then the door was flung open. Silence.

Shayne messily shoved his hood up, somehow bringing down his sunglasses enough to poke himself in the eye. Just what he needed right now.

He looked at the doorway. Hey, he knew that person.

He frowned. Wait, how did he know that person?

"Victoria," Timothy said. "I need your help."

Hey, Timothy and this mystery person looked alike, Shayne noted dully. Victoria. That was Layla's friend!

"I refuse to grant you any help," Victoria said. "I especially refuse it to *him*."

Ouch. She must be referring to him.

"If you won't help him for me—"

"You?" Victoria scoffed. "What do I owe you?"

"M'scuse me?" Shayne said, lifting his head up. It was wobbly. How odd. "This iiis nice." He tried to gesture and almost threw himself out of Marco's arms. "But I hurt."

Victoria's eyes widened. "What...?"

"If you won't help him for me, help him for Layla," Timothy said. "We know *she* still loves her brother."

Victoria flashed a glare at Timothy.

Even in Shayne's addled brain, he could put two and two together.

Timothy and Victoria were siblings.

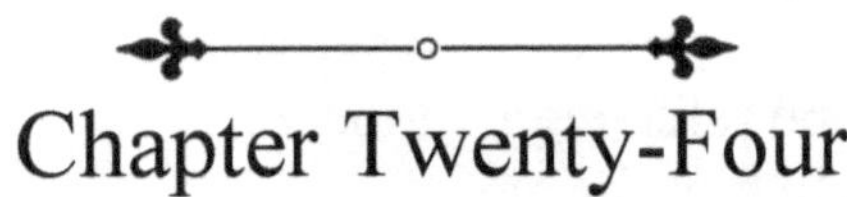

Chapter Twenty-Four

L ayla paced around in her apartment.

What had she done?

Soon, if not already, Shayne would be in the Diamonds' possession. If he didn't cooperate and give them what they wanted, he would surely get hurt.

That doesn't matter, she argued with herself. *There wasn't any other way.*

But no matter how much she kept telling herself that, she was about to choke on her guilt.

Her phone rang. Her pulse skyrocketed. But it was only Victoria.

She answered, trying to keep her voice level. "Hey! What's going on?"

"Layla, you need to come to my apartment right now." Victoria's voice was urgent.

"What's wrong? Are you okay?"

Layla rushed to her entryway to grab her purse and jacket.

"Me? I am well enough, only in the proximity of people I can feel nothing but resentment for. No, Layla, Shayne is here."

Layla froze.

Victoria continued, "And he is very, very sick."

Layla barely managed to shout out "I'm coming!" before hanging up. She grabbed her stuff and raced out the door. Her heart was pounding.

Sick! Why was he sick? He was supposed to be unconscious!

Fear grabbed at her, and she fought to keep her mind blank. Maybe Victoria meant unconscious? But not even a small part of her could believe that.

She would have never believed she had the ability to run straight from her apartment to Victoria's, but she managed it. Took the stairs, even, and before she knew it, was throwing open the door to Victoria's apartment.

Next thing she knew, her purse was taken from her, and her arms pinned behind her back.

"What the heck?!" she cried, looking around.

Victoria was standing next to a man who looked familiar, even though Layla was positive she'd never seen him before. Her eyes flitted between Victoria and the man. No way...

The man rolled his eyes. "Guys, let her go," he said. "That's Layla. The Ace's sister."

Her arms were released, and Layla yanked her bag back. She rushed over to the couch, her mouth dropping when she saw Shayne. He was deathly pale. White as a sheet, as the cliché goes.

"He looks awful," she whispered, her heart sinking. This was not what she had been told would happen.

Shayne's eyes darted over to her. "Layla!" he exclaimed, throwing his arms out wildly.

Layla took a step back. She looked at Victoria. "What's wrong with him?"

It was the man who answered instead. "Now, Layla, don't panic," he said, his tone almost chiding. "We've called our doctor, Lee Abbot, to come and look at him."

"Who are you?" Layla asked.

"Timothy," he answered. "I'm your brother's secretary and common sense."

Layla looked at Victoria, who sighed and nodded confirmation to the unspoken question.

Timothy caught the exchange and sighed himself. "Yes, and I am also Victoria's brother."

Wow. She would process that information later.

There was a knock on the door. One of the Spades opened it, and a man basically jumped into the apartment. "Symptoms?" he asked before anyone could say anything.

A few other Spades (she assumed) filed in behind him.

Layla guessed this must be the doctor, Lee. He was a fairly average-looking man, with hair dyed bright green.

"His stomach hurts, he's really pale, and he's sweating," Timothy answered. "I have no idea what's wrong. He was fine until all of a sudden...this happened."

Lee moved over to the couch, and Layla moved away, going to stand beside Victoria.

Lee put a hand on Shayne's forehead. "You're burning up, Ace," he observed.

"I didn't order you here to tell me I have a fever," Shayne growled.

All calmness, Lee pulled a stethoscope out of his bag and listened to Shayne's heartbeat. "Rapid," he murmured. "Dilated pupils...fever.... Tell me, Ace, how is it to breathe?"

"Work. Hard work."

"Any nausea?"

"I expected to throw up thirty minutes ago, if that's what you mean." Shayne groaned in pain, and his whole body stiffened.

"It hasn't been thirty minutes," Timothy said.

Layla clung to Victoria's arm. Had she just poisoned, genuinely poisoned, her brother? This was all her fault. She wanted to shout and confess it all and demand that the doctor *hurry up*. But she was unable to speak at all.

Lee hummed. "Confusion, nausea. Was his speech slurred at all?"

"Yes," Timothy answered. "Just before you got here, I couldn't understand anything he was saying."

Lee nodded. "He's been poisoned."

Timothy blinked. "Poisoned?"

Layla's heart dropped into her shoes.

"I can't tell for sure, of course. If we were in a hospital, and had that kind of time, I would order a toxicology report."

"Well, we don't have that kind of time. So maybe you should start acting like this is urgent?" Timothy kept his voice calm, which Layla didn't appreciate. Someone needed to goad this doctor into action!

Lee was unphased. "What to do best...?" he mused. "Most of my equipment is back at the lab, of course...but we can't move him. That's silly. My dear," Lee said, turning to Victoria, practically beaming, "How would you feel about letting the Ace throw up in here? Cause I couldn't guarantee it'd end up neatly in a bowl."

Victoria took a step back. She hated even the thought of vomit. If there was ever a possibility of it, she was ten kilometres away from the person. Layla was about to try to speak up in her friend's defence, but Lee changed his mind.

"No." Lee frowned. "No, that's not recommended anymore. Never—" He stopped suddenly, as though he had choked.

He leaned closer to Shayne, who was still writhing in pain on the couch.

"Ace, could you...describe your pain to me?"

Shayne tried, but his speech had become slurred. Layla could only catch a few words, the most prominent being "lava."

When Lee pulled away, he looked worried for the first time.

"We are both lucky and unlucky," he said, his voice grave. He addressed Victoria again. "My dear, I wonder if you could get me a large bowl of warm water and a cloth from your kitchen? Oh, and I'll need another bowl of room-temperature water. A normal cereal bowl."

Layla didn't even think of going to help Victoria, but Timothy followed her into the kitchen. Layla was unable to do anything but stare at Shayne, feeling like if she took her eyes off of him, he would be gone.

Victoria and Timothy returned.

"Thank you very much," Lee said, taking the bowl from Victoria. He placed that one on the ground by his bag.

"Can you heal him?" Timothy asked as he handed over his bowl.

"I can do my best. But that's it, I'm afraid." Dr. Abbott dipped the cloth in the warm water, then placed it on Shayne's forehead. "How could Ace have been poisoned?" He looked at Timothy. "It would probably be orally. Any ideas?"

Timothy frowned. "Uh, he ate Panda Express takeout. Delivered by UberEats. He complained about something he ate not agreeing with him."

Layla remembered him saying that too, but that was only after she had poisoned him.

"I would check to see if any Clubs or Diamonds work in that Panda Express," Lee said seriously. "And the Uber driver as well."

"Why?" Timothy asked.

The doctor produced a vial of clear liquid and a needle.

"Ace, this is a painkiller. It should help the pain."

"Great," Shayne said. "Sho I can...ugh...die painlessly."

"Oh hush," Lee ordered as he drew some of the clear liquid into the needle. "And stay still so I can find a vein."

But it was apparent Shayne was in too much pain to hold completely still, for any amount of time. So Timothy moved around Dr. Abbott and held Shayne's arm down. Then he had to dodge Shayne's other arm, which came flying towards his face in a messy and uncoordinated attempt at a slap.

In spite of the situation, Layla had to stifle a laugh.

Timothy looked at the other Spades.

"Well?" he said.

One started and jumped forward to help. He pinned Shayne's legs down while another held Shayne's shoulder to keep his upper body still.

"Thank you," Lee said.

He found a vein on the arm Timothy was keeping still and expertly administered the drug. Layla could see Shayne start to relax.

"Whas'm tha?" Shayne mumbled.

No one answered.

"Dr. Abbott, the antidote now, please," Timothy said pointedly.

"That is what I'm doing," Lee said mildly.

He was once again rooting around in the bag. Timothy stood up and got out of his way.

Lee pulled out another vial, but this time the liquid inside was purple, of all things. He poured the entire vial into the bowl of water, then mixed it with a spoon that had just appeared in his hand. The water turned into a cute shade of lilac.

Layla felt like she was holding her breath but couldn't actually figure out if she was or not.

To Shayne, he said gently, "Ace, you must sit up." There was an undercurrent of urgency in his voice. "You *must* drink this."

"Can you not use a needle for insertion, just as with the pain medication?" Victoria asked.

"No. Ace, you must sit up."

On limp arms, Shayne attempted to push himself up. He moved maybe one inch.

"Marco, can you...?" Timothy gestured to Ace.

Marco reached under Shayne's arms and pulled him up into a semi-sitting position. Lee held the bowl up to Shayne's lips, allowing him to take small sips.

"Mm, tase yucky." Shayne made a face.

"And yet, it will save your life," Lee said. "Drink it."

Shayne frowned harder but kept drinking.

"In answer to your earlier question, young lady," Lee said, "The antidote must be administered through the digestive system because it was taken through the digestive system. The poison particles latch onto the sides of the esophagus all the way down and then take root in the stomach. Eventually, the throat begins to swell. Ace's probably would have in less than ten minutes—oops, careful."

Shayne had tried to drink too much at once and begun to cough. Lee thumped him on the back and waited for the coughing to stop. Then he raised the bowl to Shayne's mouth again.

"Part of what makes this poison so deadly," Lee continued casually, as if nothing had happened. "is that it blocks the contents of the stomach from leaving the body via the mouth. In other words, you can't throw up, which would help your body get rid of the poison. But the real kicker is that it destroys the stomach lining. Then your stomach floods with acid, it burns a hole in you, you die."

Layla's heart shrivelled within her. "How can one poison do all that?" she asked, her voice hoarse.

"Nam insidias," Lee answered.

"What?"

"That's the name of this particular poison."

Timothy frowned.

Victoria crossed her arms and didn't bother to hide the suspicion in her voice as she said, "And how is it that you know what poison it is?"

Shayne finished drinking. Dr. Abbott set the bowl on the ground. Shayne slumped down and sighed.

The whole room seemed to hold its breath. All eyes were on Shayne. Layla could've sworn the colour was already returning to his face. Shayne gave another sigh, visibly relaxed, then fell asleep.

"Is that a good sign?" Layla asked anxiously.

"The best we could have hoped for," Lee said. "And now, to once again answer your question with a delay, young lady, I know because we created it."

"Hold on—are you saying a Spade did this?" Timothy asked, brow furrowed.

"Not necessarily," Dr. Abbott answered slowly. "Some of our chemists were concerned by the possibility of a break-in recently, but there wasn't enough definitive evidence. We cannot deny the possibility, however."

The Diamonds. Had to have been.

"I remember a report coming in from the lab," Timothy said. "Ace barely skimmed it, then dismissed it as unimportant."

"So, naturally, I know the antidote," Lee continued. "But he will need to drink that same dosage at least thrice more."

He began packing everything he had taken out back into his

medicine bag. "Ace will be safe to carry in about ten minutes." He looked up at Victoria. "You must tolerate us for only a little bit longer. Thank you for your...hospitality." He chose that word carefully.

Victoria smiled, but it was without warmth.

Layla was clutching onto the strap of her purse like it was her lifeline, staring at Shayne. The antidote had to have worked. It *had* to. She couldn't...she couldn't be responsible for...

"He's out of danger, Layla," Timothy said. "It's all rightt."

She thought he might be trying a comforting tone, but it wasn't working very well. She nodded, not trusting her voice at the moment. She felt like she was about to cry. How could they be sure that Shayne was going to be okay?

Then an idea occurred to her, and she turned to Timothy. "Can I come with you?"

"Absolutely not," he said without hesitation.

"Why not?"

"Only three types of people enter our headquarters: Spades, future Spades, and captives. You are none of those."

"I'll go as a captive," Layla said. She held her hands out.

Timothy rolled his eyes. "It doesn't work like that. The answer's still no." When Layla opened her mouth to continue arguing, he held up his hands. "It doesn't matter what you say. Those are the rules, and no one is allowed to break them except under emergency circumstances. Ace is now healed, so it is no longer an emergency situation."

Layla ground her teeth together but didn't argue.

Timothy turned to Marco. "Carry Ace. And let's go."

Layla watched as the Spades packed up and left and then were gone. The only evidence they'd been there was the two bowls of water and the cloth on the floor. That, and the roiling guilt in Layla's stomach.

Victoria gathered up the bowls and cloth to take to the kitchen. Something occurred to Layla, and she followed her.

"You didn't call the police," Layla said. It was both a statement and a question.

Victoria was putting the bowls into her almost fully loaded dishwasher. "No. I figured it would be better accomplished this way" There was hidden amusement in her voice.

Layla frowned. "You didn't call them, right?"

Victoria shook her head. "I did not," she said as she rang the cloth out. "But I shall."

"What?"

What was Victoria hinting at?

Something in her sweater pocket trilled. Two quick high notes and a sharp low note. Layla knew that sound.

She set her purse on the counter. Then, quick as she could, she snatched the tracking device out of Victoria's pocket.

"Hey!" Victoria whirled around. "Return that to me!"

Layla held it out behind her. "You're tracking them?" she asked in disbelief.

"One of Toronto's most wanted criminals enters my apartment. Do you truly believe I would just allow him to leave?"

Layla tilted her head to the side. "Wait, you just happened to have a tracker lying around?"

"I have multiple," Victoria said with a shrug, as if it was no big deal. "Mom gave them to me."

"I forgot she was a police officer," Layla muttered.

Victoria jumped forward, taking advantage of Layla's temporary distraction. Layla scrambled back into the living room.

"You're not going to lead the police to my brother!" she said.

"No, I would be leading the police to the Spades. Through this, they could be shut down."

Layla went behind the couch. They stared at each other. It was dawning on Layla that she wasn't really in the position to take this moral high ground after what she'd just done.

"Fine," she said. "But what if the Spades notice the tracker? They'll be able to figure out who put it there, for sure. And then you'll be in danger!"

"That is a risk," Victoria conceded. "But one worth taking."

Layla pressed her lips together. Now that she had thought about this, she was getting increasingly worried about Victoria. What if the Spades got really mad? They could hurt her.

Victoria raced around the couch while Layla was once again caught up in her thinking, and she lunged for the tracker. She grabbed it, rolled backwards off the couch, and jumped to a standing position. Layla stared at her but didn't make a move to retrieve it.

Layla took a deep breath. "Victoria, if you don't get rid of that tracker, the Spades could come for it! You could get hurt."

"They have not yet stopped," Victoria said with a glance at the tracker. "I find it hard to believe they would have noticed yet. And once they reach headquarters, their main concern will be the Ace. I doubt they will notice before I have a chance to call the police."

"Where did you place that tracker?"

"A safe location."

"Victoria..." Layla's tone was pleading.

"Feel free to leave now," Victoria said, tucking the tracker back in her pocket.

Layla opened her mouth to speak, then closed it when she saw Victoria's determination. Besides, she knew some people who would also be interested in that tracker. They could take it before the Spades had a chance.

"I'll just grab my purse," Layla mumbled.

As she did, she thought of something else that terrified her.

She had failed.

Sure, she didn't wish that Shayne had actually died—not for anything. But the Diamond Queen wouldn't be happy. Thank goodness she did have the tracker to offer. Maybe they would not get so mad at her once they had that.

She said a quick goodbye to Victoria, who just nodded, then Layla rushed out of the apartment. She had to act quickly.

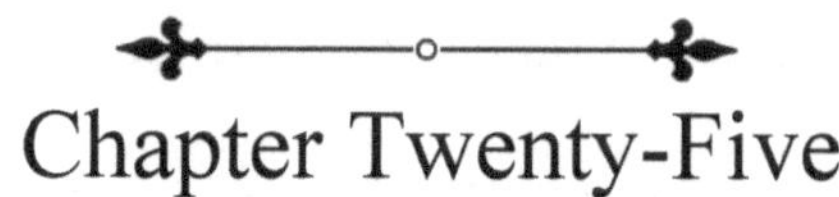

Chapter Twenty-Five

Layla all but stormed out of the apartment complex and over to where Cameron was standing. Her anger grew when she took in his casual stance and unconcerned expression. It flared when he said, "So, he didn't die."

"You told me"—Layla yanked her purse off her shoulder—"it would just knock him out!"

She swung her purse at Cameron. He dodged and then caught it, holding it fast so she couldn't try again. But he looked shocked, so Layla was at least partially satisfied.

Still trembling, she said, "I was told it would ONLY knock him out. Unconscious. Not dead."

Cameron shrugged. "Maybe you put in too much."

Layla froze. Had she? She'd figured afterwards she was probably only supposed to put half in, but was that enough to make the difference between life and death? No, couldn't be. The doctor said the poison was burning a hole in Shayne's stomach! Less just means it would do it slower. Right?

"Or maybe," Cameron added, "You weren't told the whole truth."

"Not telling the whole truth is the same thing as lying!" Layla exclaimed. And it had almost cost Shayne his life.

She shouldn't have done this. She should never have gotten involved with the Diamonds. What was she thinking? Everything she had used to justify her actions now seemed like frail and twisted logic. Except for the nagging feeling that she hadn't had a choice either way.

The Diamonds had just done the same thing she had been getting mad at Shayne for but with far worse intentions. Except the Diamonds had never pretended to care for her, so it wasn't exactly a betrayal. Her fault for trusting criminals in the first place.

"My Queen will not be pleased you failed," Cameron said.

Layla's heart stopped. Said so nonchalantly, yet the implied threat was clear. She stared at Cameron, eyes wide.

To her surprise, Cameron did a double-take, and he almost

looked...guilty? He released her purse. It swung back to her.

Then Layla remembered—the tracker.

"Victoria put a tracker on them," she blurted out.

"What?"

"Victoria hid a tracker on the Spades somewhere," Layla said. "Which means she'll know the location of the Spades' headquarters, provided they don't notice it before then. If you can steal the tracker from her—"

Cameron's eyes gleamed, the guilt gone. "We'll know their location."

"Isn't that so much better than just killing the Ace?" Layla said, cringing as she did so but also hoping desperately that it was better.

Cameron studied her. "Give me a moment."

He walked a short distance from her, just enough so that she couldn't hear him, and brought out his phone. He called someone on it, and they talked for a few minutes.

Layla hugged her purse to her body. This was not how this night was supposed to go. How *stupid* she'd been! But what about Karsyn? What would have happened to him if she'd refused? It wasn't making her feel any better right now though.

"Do you have the keys to her apartment?"

Layla looked at Cameron. "Do I what?"

"Have a pair of spare keys to her apartment? Much more efficient than breaking in." Cameron waited expectantly.

"Yes," Layla admitted.

He held out his hand.

Reluctantly, Layla unzipped her purse and brought out her key ring. "It's this one," she said, pointing.

"Take it off. I just want it."

Layla struggled with the key ring, dropped some keys into her purse, and finally got the right one off. He took it.

"What're you... gonna..." she trailed off, realizing it was a pretty dumb question.

"I'm just going to run in and grab it. You can start walking home. I'll come and return this"—he held up the key—"when I'm done."

Cameron started walking to the apartment complex.

"Wait!" Layla called.

He stopped but didn't turn around.

"Please don't hurt her," Layla mumbled.

Cameron laughed and turned back. "I'm built for speed, not strength. I'm just zipping in there and grabbing the tracker. That's all."

"Thanks."

He studied her for a second. "I like you a lot better than your cousin. Don't worry. I don't get people involved who don't want to be involved. Otherwise people...people get hurt."

Then he walked into the apartment lobby, as if he didn't just say the most confusing thing in the world. Layla watched him go through the entrance doors.

What was that statement all about? She agreed that Daniel was a jerk most of the time but...weird. And what was the rest about people getting hurt? She sighed. Why was he like this?

She started walking home, keeping her phone in her hand and glancing at it as often as she could. If Victoria called and needed help, she would zoom back there right away.

Just before she reached her building, Victoria called.

She fumbled to answer for a second, so anxious to answer as soon as possible that she got in her own way.

"Victoria?" she asked.

Please don't let her have been hurt, she thought.

But, funnily enough, she didn't think Cameron would have hurt her. Why did she believe him? He had just lied to her about the poison.

"You were correct, Layla," Victoria said, with only the slightest of tremors in her voice. "The Spades came. They stole the tracker."

Except it wasn't the Spades, it had been Cameron.

"Are you hurt?" Layla asked. She didn't care about the tracker anymore, she just wanted to make sure Cameron had been honest.

"No," Victoria answered. "Fortunately, I had time to hide myself. They took the tracker, then left, just like that. I never even saw them."

Phew.

"Really? Just like that? Thank goodness! You didn't get hurt. I'm so glad."

What was she even spewing out? She wasn't sure, but she was trying not to seem like she had already known the theft was going to happen.

"And glad that I am no longer in possession of the tracker," Victoria muttered.

Layla frowned. What, she couldn't be concerned for her friend's safety as well? After she had just spent all that time worrying, too!

She was about to reply, but then she heard a sound that made her freeze. Breaking glass.

"What just happened?" she cried.

"I have no idea," Victoria said, sounding more curious than anything.

Layla waited for more of an explanation but dreaded to hear what that might be.

She slowly came to the realization that the call had ended. Victoria had hung up on her. She slowly brought her phone down from her ear. She stared at it, uncomprehending, as her brain tried to register what had just happened.

Oh.

Her stomach plummeted.

The Spades! They must have realized already! It had to be them—the chances of a random break-in happening tonight, not five minutes after Cameron had left, were astronomical.

Worry for Victoria squeezed at her heart, and she continued on to her apartment. She would be able to freak out as much as she wanted there.

She walked through the lobby doors, then stopped and grimaced. Jason was sitting in one of the chairs. No doubt waiting for her.

No. Not now! Not when she was terrified for Victoria's sake and trying to ignore her crushing guilt at the same time. If she talked to him now, she'd end up spilling everything. And then he'd hate her.

For some reason, she couldn't bear the thought of Jason not wanting to be her friend.

It took a struggle, but she turned and hurried towards the elevator.

"Layla!" she heard Jason call.

She went faster and ducked into the elevator. The doors closed.

Something was tickling her cheek. She swiped at it with her finger. A tear.

The elevator doors dinged and opened. Automatically, she walked out. Down the hall. Unlocked her door. Went inside.

Then she couldn't bear the anticipation any longer and called Victoria. Funny, the ringing of the phone had never seemed mocking before, but it was definitely taunting her now.

She went straight to voicemail.

Ignoring the way her head was starting to pound, Layla tried again. No luck.

"No, no, no," she muttered.

She stared at her phone, wanting to try again but not knowing what she'd do if Victoria didn't pick up this time either.

Her door swung open. Cameron marched in, tracker held high.

"See, what'd I tell—" He stopped. "What's wrong?" he asked, managing to sound both concerned and unconcerned at the same time. "Layla, I told you I wouldn't hurt her."

She didn't care at all for his exasperated tone and was going to inform him of that when her phone rang. Victoria.

"Are you okay?" she all but screamed into the phone.

Victoria audibly winced. "Layla..." her voice sounded groggy. "Don't shout."

Obliging, Layla lowered her voice to ask again but kept the same urgency in her tone. It gave her no small sense of alarm to hear Victoria use a contraction.

"What happened? Are you all right?"

"They knocked me out with a dart of some kind."

Layla winced in sympathy. "Ooh, those hurt."

"Then they ransacked my apartment. I don't know if they took anything."

"Who?" Layla asked.

Cameron was standing in front of her now. "What's going on?" he mouthed.

Layla ignored him.

Victoria took a deep breath. "He was a Spade."

Which Layla had already guessed. But she had to act surprised.

"What? A Spade? I thought they already came?"

Cameron raised an eyebrow.

"I thought so as well but apparently not. He was one of the Spades from earlier—one of the bodyguards that stood around, useless. He was shocked to hear that someone else had taken the tracker."

"This is weird...maybe they accidentally sent two groups?" Layla offered.

"No. He called someone over his earpiece to ask the same question. The answer was negative. He asked me who had stolen it. I told him I had no idea."

"But no one else knew!"

"Except you."

Layla froze. But Victoria's tone was of one stating a fact, not making an accusation. So she said, "Yeah, true. But who would I tell?" She considered saying more but decided against it. The more she said, the more likely she would expose herself.

Victoria sighed. "I am extremely frustrated by all this."

"Are you going to call the police?" Layla asked.

"What could they do for me now? I am unhurt, the tracker is gone, and I have no helpful information to give."

"I'm glad you're not hurt," Layla said quietly.

"Me too. Goodnight."

"Goodnight."

Layla looked at Cameron. He once again held the tracker up.

"Got it," he said.

"Yeah, I see that," Layla said.

"Ouch," he said, looking mildly offended. "I went in and out. She didn't even see me. Why're you so upset?"

"It's been a day."

Cameron rolled his eyes. "Yeah, whatever. So, I'm gonna go now, then. I assume your friend was saying the Spades broke in?"

"Yes."

"Ha! Idiots. Too late, once again."

"Except they clearly realized there was a tracker, so doesn't that mean they probably got rid of it? Doesn't that mean the one you're holding probably doesn't show their location anymore?"

Cameron frowned. He peered down at the tracker. Layla could see him processing this. Then he pointed at her.

There was a pause.

"I don't know," he said.

Then he left.

Layla stared at the door, feeling like this sort of leaving had been happening here a lot lately. Didn't anyone know how to politely end the interaction?

Whatever. She was going to bed.

It really had been a day.

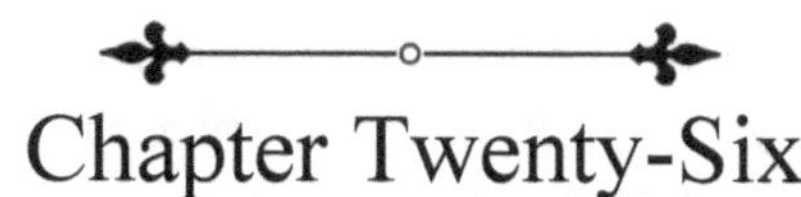

Chapter Twenty-Six

Shayne paced the length of his office. Back and forth. Back and forth. Some paperwork sat on his desk that was probably important, but he didn't care about that right now. Today was the last day he would need to drink the antidote. The final dosage, and then he would be allowed to see Layla.

Timothy had told him how she had reacted to his poisoning, and Shayne wanted to assure her that he was all right. And that they were doing everything possible to find out who poisoned him. That should reassure her.

Of course, Timothy had also warned him against going to see Layla so soon. He'd said that the other Spades already weren't happy with how often he visited, but especially so after all that went down the last time.

Shayne was starting to care less and less about what the other Spades thought.

He also wanted to run a theory by Layla: that Daniel was behind the poisoning.

Did he have any proof of this? No. But he knew that Daniel had been ordered to bring him in and had failed. Since his last encounter with Daniel had ended with Daniel pointing a gun at him, Shayne assumed he wouldn't have any qualms about poisoning him.

"Ace," someone said.

Had to be Timothy. No one else sounded like a worn-out parent when they used his title.

Shayne whirled around. Sure enough, Timothy had entered his office. He was holding a glass cup of lilac liquid.

"Finally!" Shayne said.

He strode over to Timothy, grabbed the glass, and drank it all in one gulp. Which was quite impressive, really, but Timothy didn't look impressed.

"What if that wasn't your medicine?" he asked.

"You know any other drink this colour?"

Shayne tossed the cup at his desk. He missed. It shattered on the ground. Neither of them flinched.

"Whoops," Shayne said. "Thought I could do that without looking."

Sighing, Timothy put a hand on his earpiece and said, "Send a 2 up to Ace's office with a broom and dustpan...No, broken glass...Yep." Then he looked at Shayne with his I'm-completely-and-utterly-exasperated-with-you face, but he'd used it so many times, Shayne was unaffected. "Ace, do you ever think about being just a little more careful?"

Shayne shrugged. "Being a 2 is so boring. They're probably fighting over who gets to take the job."

Timothy just stared at him.

Yes, he should probably change the subject now.

"Did you find anything about the Panda Express?" he asked. "Or the Uber driver?"

"There are no Diamonds, Clubs, or GDRS agents in either employee list."

"And?" Shayne prompted.

"I just said no GDRS agents," Timothy said.

"But..."

Timothy sighed. "Daniel has never been in that building or even anywhere near it. So far as we can find, he's never been served by that particular Uber driver, although he has, of course, used Uber Eats before."

Shayne's expression fell. "Well then...who poisoned me?"

"As of right now, obviously, we don't know. We're still investigating, but until we discover who's behind this, my advice is that you don't leave headquarters."

Shayne scoffed. "Of course you'd say that." He walked over to his desk, avoiding the glass, and flopped down in his seat. "And of course, I'm not going to listen."

"Someone tried to kill you. They almost succeeded. I need you to take this seriously!"

Wow, Timothy was starting to raise his voice. That was a new one.

"Yeah, but we know who it was, so just trail him and make sure he doesn't come after me."

Timothy pinched the bridge of his nose. "Ace...you don't know it was Daniel."

"I'm pretty sure—"

"That's not knowing!" Timothy took a breath and gathered himself. "There are two possibilities you need to consider."

Shayne tilted his head back.

"One," Timothy began, "That the poison was not in your Panda Express food."

Okay, he could accept that. Although that made things even more complicated, because where'd he get it then?

"Two, it could have been a Spade, and there was no break-in."

Shayne leaned back in his chair. He wanted to protest this, but he couldn't deny the possibility.

"I know I'm not the most likable Ace," Shayne said.

Timothy scoffed.

"But surely no Spade here is so unloyal that they'd want to…" Shayne trailed off. Each word had just felt less and less informed. People in positions of power were always under the threat of assassination, even if they were excellent leaders. Sometimes more so then. "Are you also investigating this chance?" he asked.

Timothy nodded. "We're exhausting every possibility."

"Great." Shayne stood up. "So I can go see Layla then?"

"What? No."

"Come on! I'll take five bodyguards if it makes you feel better, and I won't eat or drink anything."

"Daniel…might be headed to Layla's apartment," Timothy said, sounding like he regretted even mentioning it.

Shayne stared down at his desk.

"I see," he said at last.

"We have men tailing him, like you asked. Once he stops, if he doesn't stop at Layla's, I'll let you go over. On the terms you just mentioned."

Timothy would *let* him? That was laughable. Until he remembered the fight he went through to even get out of headquarters the night of Karsyn's accident.

"Agreed," he said.

"I'll let you know where he stops," Timothy said, then left.

Shayne sat back down at his desk. He shuffled around those papers that he really should deal with. The most progress he made with those was putting them in a neater pile and reading about five words. Not consecutively.

He tapped his fingers on his desk. Looked at the ceiling. Spun around in his chair. Looked at the clock. More spinning.

Timothy re-entered his office.

If the chair had had brakes, they would have been squealing with how fast Shayne stopped spinning.

"Where is he?" he exclaimed.

Then he noticed that Timothy's expression was veiled.

"Daniel hasn't stopped yet," Timothy answered.

"What? Then why—"

"We've found out who caused Karsyn's accident."

Shayne shot up. "Who?" he demanded.

Timothy hesitated. "The Clubs."

"I knew it!" Shayne slammed his hands down on his desk.

"A meeting has been called to discuss these developments, but—"

"How dare they?" Shayne seethed, not paying attention. "How *dare* they take revenge on an innocent?"

Timothy crossed his arms. "Because they're the most violent and ruthless Suit. They don't care that Karsyn's innocent. They just figured it was the best way to hurt you."

"What if it wasn't?" Shayne exclaimed. "I haven't seen him in years!"

"I don't think they'd have cared one way or another."

The overwhelming implications of that washed over Shayne. Suddenly, he was feeling the same emotions he had felt the night of Karsyn's accident, right before Daniel had shown up. This—all of this—might have been the wrong choice. He was on the wrong side of people who couldn't care less about if they took someone's life, and if that person was completely innocent.

"Ace—"

Shayne's head shot up. He was just now realizing that Timothy had been using his actual title lately.

"The meeting's already started."

Timothy's expression was a blank slate.

Shayne didn't want to go. He didn't know what to do. But neither of those were options right now.

He drew himself up, then marched out of his office. On the way, he passed the 2 carrying a broom and dustpan. Timothy hadn't told him what room they were meeting in, but he could hear the loud, boisterous conversation as he approached meeting room B.

He took a moment outside the door to compose himself. Then

entered.

Conversation died, and everyone turned to look at Shayne.

He couldn't help but smirk. He loved having this effect.

"Don't stop just because I arrive," he said as he walked to the head of the table. "Let me hear your opinions." He made a point to look at every Spade before he sat down. "Also, stop starting meetings that involve me without me. Seriously."

No one spoke. Ah. Were they afraid to voice their thoughts? Did they think he was going to protest?

"Autumn, what about you?" Shayne said. "You always enjoy giving your opinion."

"Do not retaliate," she answered immediately.

"No retaliation," Shayne repeated, turning the words over in his mind.

A few Spades stirred uneasily.

They expected him to fight back on this. Which normally he would have, if he hadn't already been coming to this conclusion himself. What would be next if he did—them doing something worse to his mom? No, not an option.

"Why should you?" Autumn continued. "They're targeting your family, not us. Your old family. Your strategy backfired. Instead of dissuading them from doing anything else, you only proved that your family was your weak point."

Nick leaned forward, just like he did every time. "Ace, we don't want you proving this is your weak point any more than you already have. We don't want to give them any more reason to exploit it."

He raised good points. If Shayne got the Spades to retaliate, the Clubs would only attack again. Then where would it end? Revenge would be a continuous back and forth until somebody paid for it with their life.

Shayne's eyes scanned the table. All Spades were nodding, except Julia. She was again fidgeting with her hands.

A drop of adrenaline went through him, and his mind flashed back to the last meeting. She had almost suggested he step down before he cut her off; he was sure of it.

"Ace," she said.

He nodded.

"There are some who want you to know..."

That wasn't good, almost the same opening as last time.

"That if it weren't so close to the annual tournament, therefore being the worst time, we would cast a vote on your ability as Ace."

If majority rules on that vote, the Ace has to step down.

The problem was Shayne wasn't sure what he thought about that anymore.

"Is that a threat?" he asked lightly.

"Just a warning," she said, meeting his gaze.

He almost scoffed. A warning was just a threat with more honourable intentions. And he didn't think hers actually were.

"So..." Shayne lightly ran his hand over the table.

"Ace, you cannot still be thinking about revenge!" Autumn exclaimed.

Shayne looked up and raised an eyebrow. "Don't take that tone with me," he said. "I still outrank you."

Autumn straightened in surprise.

Shayne stood up. "The vibe I'm getting from all of you is that we don't want to retaliate. Anyone disagree?"

Silence.

"Great."

He left.

Timothy was waiting for him right outside the conference room.

"Whatever it is, I don't want to hear it," Shayne said.

"Daniel stopped at Layla's apartment."

There was a moment of deadly silence.

"Then I say let's just kill him before he kills me," Shayne said quietly.

Timothy rolled his eyes. "You have no proof that he was behind the poisoning."

And that was Shayne's biggest fear right now. That Daniel wasn't. That it wasn't him or a Club or a Spade. Some unknown assassin who might succeed.

"I'm going," he said, leaving no room for argument.

"Five bodyguards, that was the deal," Timothy said. "And let it be known you went against my approval and the approval of any sane person. Because if something happens, I don't think you can get anyone to come to your aid anymore."

On that cheerful note, Shayne rushed off.

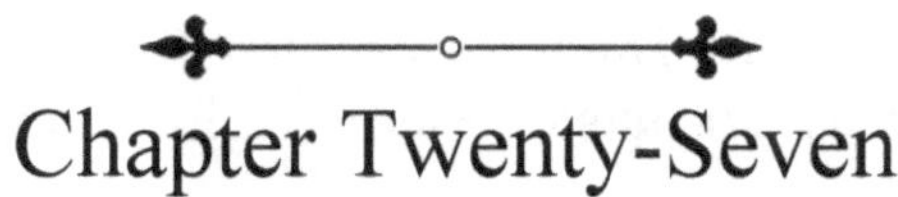

Chapter Twenty-Seven

The car ride took three times longer than usual. Twenty-three minutes stretched into...twenty-three minutes that just felt really long. Every red light taunted Shayne and seemed to purposefully make them wait. Shayne didn't want Daniel to leave before he got there.

The car pulled into the parking lot. Shayne threw the door open and went to jump out, but Marco grabbed his arm and pulled him back in.

"Hey!" Shayne protested.

Marco held Shayne's sunglasses out.

"Oh. Right."

Shayne put them on and grabbed the hoodie sitting next to him. He pulled it on, threw the hood up, and then was allowed to jump out.

"I just need Marco to come in—the rest of you wait out here!" He barely got through shouting that back at the car before he was out of earshot.

He ran into the building and to Layla's apartment. Unlocked, so he threw the door open and rushed inside.

"What?" he heard Layla exclaim.

He ran to the living room, then screeched to a halt. Layla and Daniel froze too, Layla with her eyes wide, and Daniel in the process of getting up out of his chair.

"Shayne?" Layla asked. Then her eyes lit up. "You're okay!"

Daniel stood up and strode forward. He stopped a safe distance from Shayne. "You have a lot of nerve coming here."

"What, so now it's a crime to visit family members?"

"You're a criminal. Everything you do is a crime."

That logic didn't track.

"You gonna to arrest me for having breakfast, then?" Shayne asked. "Because according to standards, that's a serious offence."

Layla hurried over to them just as Daniel started forward. She squeezed in between them, forcing both to back up.

"Guys, please, don't fight," she pleaded. "Can't you just...put some things aside while you're in my apartment?"

She had to know that was impossible.

"I have to arrest him!" Daniel exclaimed at the same time Shayne said, "How about we go outside then? I'll have no problem beating you up then."

"Shayne!" Layla cried in dismay.

He ignored her. The mere sight of Daniel had been enough to make his blood boil. All doubts had left. It was Daniel. He was behind all of it, for sure. And he still had the nerve to stand in Layla's apartment, glowering at Shayne, who had probably visited Layla more times than Daniel ever had.

Why had Layla let Daniel in anyway? He had told her what Daniel had done. But maybe she still didn't believe him.

"Did you tell Layla yet?" he questioned. "I did, but she didn't want to believe me."

"Tell her what?" Daniel spat.

"About our...encounter"—Shayne lingered over the word—"last week."

Layla's eyes flew to Daniel. Shayne knew she knew what he was talking about.

Daniel avoided her eyes. "How much did you tell her?"

"Everything."

For the briefest second, Daniel's eyes widened in panic, and he looked like a cornered animal. Then his facial features smoothed back into anger. But it was too late.

"It is true!" Layla exclaimed in an accusatory manner. "Daniel, how could you?"

"How could I? Why are you acting like I did a bad thing? I work in the GDRS, our whole purpose is to get rid of criminals. Why—"

"By things like poisoning?" Shayne asked.

Layla sucked in a breath.

"What?" Daniel said.

"I know you're behind my poisoning," Shayne said. "Who'd you get to actually do it?"

In Daniel's eyes dawned understanding, and that was all the confirmation Shayne needed. But Daniel scoffed.

"You have no evidence that I had anything to do with that," Daniel said.

Layla's eyebrows were furrowed together, and she kept looking back and forth between the two.

"How about the fact that you pulled a gun on me a week ago?" Shayne said. "That seems like enough evidence to me."

Daniel's face hardened. "You still have no evidence. It's my word against yours."

Layla backed up. "Wait, hold on."

Shayne started to reply, but Layla shouted, "Both of you, stop!"

They both looked at her.

She took a deep breath. "Take a seat," she ordered, gesturing to her couch and doing her best to sound stern.

Shayne jumped around both of them and into the armchair. He lounged back in it, crossing his legs. He would appear at ease, no matter how he felt, because he knew it unnerved and annoyed Daniel.

Daniel glowered at Shayne like *he* had wanted the armchair. Slowly, he sat down on the couch. But while Shayne was all relaxed awareness, Daniel was stiff and unsettled.

Layla stayed standing. "Is it true?" she asked Daniel. "Did you attack Shayne?"

"He did a lot more than that," Shayne muttered.

"I did," Daniel admitted reluctantly. "We fought." He didn't sound sorry.

"You also poisoned me," Shayne added.

"You have no proof!" Daniel shouted, surging to his feet. "And if it was me, so what? That's. My. Job!"

"I almost died!" Refusing to let Daniel tower over him, Shayne also leapt to his feet. "So forgive me for getting in the way, but I value my life more than your precious job."

Then they were shouting at the same time, their words blurring together as they reused the same excuses. Out of the confused mess, Daniel shouted, loud and clear,

"Ace, I'm arresting you right now and taking you in!"

Though he probably meant it to be insulting, there was major irony in Daniel using Shayne's title. Shayne didn't think Daniel realized it though.

"Both of you stop it!" Layla pleaded.

Shayne looked at her, and he could see she was close to tears. He took a deep breath and a step back.

"You will not leave!" Daniel exclaimed, jumping forward. "For the safety of Toronto, I cannot just let you—"

Shayne rolled his eyes, then socked Daniel in the jaw. Daniel stumbled and fell, breaking Layla's coffee table. Layla let out a shriek of surprise.

Daniel stared up at him, momentarily frozen. But then he jumped up, swinging his fist at Shayne. Layla's cries for them to stop were ignored.

This was nothing like the fight they had had the other night. That had been controlled, timed, precise movements. This was chaos. Caged animals fighting over the last piece of meat. Shayne's only thought was to knock Daniel out, but his head was surprisingly resistant.

A picture fell off the wall. Layla shrieked again. The apartment door opened, and then all five bodyguards descended on them. It took all of them to break them apart, and then two to restrain a furious Daniel, and one, for now, to hold Shayne back.

Shayne looked at Layla. She hadn't been hurt, thank goodness, but she had started crying.

Daniel fought, but he was no match for the combined strength of the Spades.

"Are you going to kill me?" he spat.

"I should!" Shayne exclaimed. That's what he had wanted for the past hour. Then his eyes strayed to Layla. "But I won't."

His bodyguards gaped at him, but Shayne didn't care.

Daniel laughed. "Of course. When it comes down to it, you're a coward."

"A coward?" Shayne said quietly, dangerously.

"You'd better kill me now, Ace. We both know you don't have the skill to best me alone. You need your Spades to get you out of it."

One of the Spades kicked the back of Daniel's knees, making him fall to the ground.

"You should be more respectful," he hissed.

Shayne turned to Layla. He hesitated. So many things he wanted to say, but how to say them? Giving up, he nodded to Daniel. "You'll be okay with him? Because I'm more than willing to take him and prop him up against another bus stop."

"*I'll* be okay," she muttered.

Shayne didn't miss her emphasis but decided it wasn't worth commenting on. "I'm sorry," he said.

She smiled shakily. "And that's your exit line, right?"

He walked over and hugged her. Fiercely, tightly, for just a few seconds. Then he pulled back and said again, "I really am sorry."

Then, he had to leave. He was angry at himself in so many ways that he couldn't name.

This was not how I wanted tonight to go, he thought.

The two Spades released Daniel, and in the next instant, they were gone too.

It was just Layla and Daniel, once again.

The apartment had sustained some physical damage in the fight, and Daniel had a bruise blooming on his cheekbone. That, and the silence that settled over them like a blanket, was the only evidence of what had happened.

Funny. Layla had always thought Daniel and Shayne were polar opposites. But they were both power-hungry idiots, apparently.

She swiped at her face, and her hands came away wet. Tears. She hadn't even realized that she'd been crying.

"That's the second time this week," she muttered.

Daniel gingerly got to his feet. He brushed his hands over his bruise and winced. He muttered a few foul things about Shayne and then, when he caught Layla glaring at him, snapped, "Don't you start now too! Why doesn't anyone realize I'm the good guy in all this?" He gestured everywhere.

"At the moment, I'm having a hard time figuring out who the good guy is." Layla sank into the armchair.

Daniel groaned, walked over to the couch, and flopped down, face first.

Layla stared at him. She shouldn't press...but, "Why are you so focussed on the Spades?" she asked. "There are two other Suits."

Daniel raised his face and exclaimed, "Everyone keeps telling me that! I know the number of Suits! I can count."

"That doesn't answer my question. Why the Spades? Why not do one less...personal?"

"That's exactly why!" Daniel lifted himself into a sitting position. "It's personal! Didn't you see that smug smirk Shayne had? He doesn't think I can do it. None of them do! But they'll see. When I succeed, they'll see."

"Wait, hold on. Who doesn't think you can do it?"

Daniel wasn't making sense, but he had just been punched several times.

"Ms. Curts." Daniel frowned. "Giving me that task, just to see if I could but not expecting me to. Do they think I'm weak?" The question, asked to the side, was directed more at himself.

Layla had no idea what to say.

Daniel rubbed his legs, then stood up. He started pacing, and muttered things Layla could only half catch.

"Refusing...Spades assignment...too personal...I'll show them! Who cares...?"

Was she watching the unravelling of her cousin's sanity?

"I could do it...despite personal..." He scoffed.

"You aren't actually assigned to the Spades?" Layla asked. "Is that what you're saying?"

Daniel stopped abruptly and looked at her. "What? Of course I am." He was trying to sound reassuring, but he was too distracted for it to work.

"You said 'refusing Spades assignment,'" Layla said.

"Well...Layla...it's not like..."

Daniel was rarely at a loss for words. Layla stood up.

"Why are you going after Shayne if you're not in the Spades unit?"

"They don't think I can!" Daniel said. "They're wrong! I have to..." He breathed out. "Have to prove them wrong."

Layla stared at him as she tried to fit all the pieces together. "Wait. You're trying to destroy the Spades, jail your cousin, probably risk your position cause you're not doing your actual job—"

"I am doing my actual job!" Daniel protested. "I'm in the Diamond unit. And if they had succeeded, it would have been two birds with one stone."

All the air left Layla's lungs. If the Diamonds...had succeeded?

"What are you talking about?" she asked.

He shrugged. "Nothing, don't worry about it." Then he muttered, "They failed anyways."

Layla's legs couldn't support her anymore, and she fell back into the armchair. She buried her face in her hands.

Had Daniel...made the deal with the Diamond Queen?

When Cameron gave her the poison and told her what to do, he had insinuated that a GDRS agent had made a deal with them, asked them to do this. Layla had thought he'd just been trying to sow distrust in Layla, make her question the GDRS. Sway her loyalty to the Diamonds. Because she'd never thought that an agent would actually make a deal with a Suit.

Daniel had been the one to make the deal.

She had been chosen, been in a perfect position, to carry it out.

How messed up was that?

"Layla? What's wrong now?"

He didn't sound concerned.

"Seriously? Look, there's nothing to do in the Diamond Unit. Even Austin says so. Like fifty times a day. So when they find out I've been working to take down two Suits, once I succeed, well, they'll be grateful."

Layla scoffed and looked up. "Grateful? That you disobeyed your superior's orders, not only by continuing to pursue the Spades when it sounds like they told you to stop but also by meeting with the Diamond Queen?! And what success, Daniel? Your assassination attempt failed!"

"You're supposed to be on my side!" Daniel yelled. "I'm working to end crime in our city! I just need to—" He broke off suddenly and looked at her peculiarly.

Layla's pulse sped up. Oh no! She'd said too much. He was going to figure it out. She had to distract him.

"Plus, what you should be worried about is figuring out who's behind Karsyn's accident," she blurted out.

Daniel's eyes widened. "Karsyn's accident," he murmured. He turned his head to the side.

"He's doing a lot better now," Layla said. "The doctor even said that—"

Daniel held up a hand. He looked at her. "You know...Shayne's always been very protective of you and Karsyn."

Layla huffed and crossed her arms. This was hardly new information.

"The day the Clubs kidnapped you...he got there fast."

"What are you talking about now?"

Daniel clearly wasn't listening to her. "That's why Karsyn got hurt. The Clubs realized what Shayne's weakness is. I should have realized sooner." He'd gone too long without blinking. "He'd rush to save you again."

Layla's blood turned to ice as a cold fear doused her. "What..." He couldn't be suggesting...

Daniel stretched his hand out to Layla. "You have to help me! With you, I can set a trap for Ace! If he thinks you're in danger, he'd come immediately. But you wouldn't actually be in danger, of course. So you have to help me."

All she could say was, "His name is Shayne. Not Ace."

Daniel brushed that aside. "Who cares? What do you say?"

She jumped up. "No! And get out!" Where had her cousin gone? "Why would I *ever* agree to pretend to be kidnapped when it's happened for real? How could you suggest—I can't believe...Hearts. You really are Hearts. I don't—"

Daniel blinked, his face losing its mad edge. "No. No, I'm sorry Lay Lay! I didn't mean it like that, I just...I wasn't thinking straight. But, still—"

"No! Get out!"

He froze. Took one hesitant step back.

"I would never help you. Ever."

He looked hurt. Good.

"I'll just..." he pointed, "I'll just go." He left quickly, not looking back.

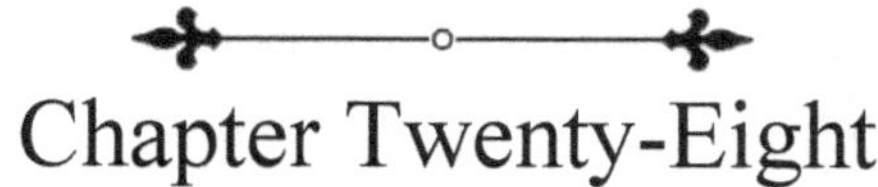

Chapter Twenty-Eight

"You're the last person I want to see right now."

"The feeling's mostly mutual. Can I come in?"

Layla glared at Cameron.

"You don't have a choice, by the way," he added.

"Fine." Layla opened the door wider but just a bit so that he had to squeeze in. "What do you want now?"

She didn't leave the entryway, so neither did he. Whatever Cameron was here for, he was leaving as soon as it was done.

"For you to agree to the plan Daniel mentioned to you last night."

"What, no!"

Cameron rolled his eyes. "Listen, you failed the poisoning, which I realize you're probably happy about. The tracker thing was a bust—"

"A bust?" Layla interrupted. "What do you mean a bust? You stole the tracker."

"Not in time. The Spades found and destroyed the one Victoria planted, so we never got a location."

Layla huffed. "Well, it's not my fault you didn't think to snap a picture or something."

"Be that as it may, you still have to uphold your end of the bargain. Once Ace is in our possession, you can walk away from the Diamonds, if that is what you want. But Ace first. You wanted that to happen, remember? For the safety of your family."

"I don't know what I want anymore," Layla muttered.

Cameron sighed. When he spoke, his voice was surprisingly soft. "That doesn't matter. Rework Daniel's plan to whatever you like. Just make sure the GDRS successfully captures Ace so then we can." He grinned, softness gone. "Kay?"

Not having any other choice, Layla agreed.

Two hours later, and Layla was just getting up the nerve to call Daniel when he called her first.

"Hello?" she said, then cringed. She had sounded way more annoyed than she expected to.

"Lay Lay, I'm calling to apologize," Daniel said.

Layla was instantly suspicious. Daniel, apologizing? In the moment, yes, that was normal. After the fact, when he'd had plenty of time to think and excuse himself from blame? Yeah, no, something was up.

But, "That would be nice," was all she said.

"I got some burgers and junk food delivered, and I thought, you know, it'd be a pretty good apology," he said.

Going to his office? Doubly suspicious, he was definitely going to re-suggest the plan. Which was what she wanted, so...

"Did you buy ice cream?" she asked.

"Yes. I couldn't remember which was your number one favourite, so I bought a tub of chocolate fudge brownie and a tub of chocolate chip cookie dough."

"Ben and Jerry's?"

"Naturally."

Wow, that wasn't a cheap purchase. He was really going all out on this.

"All right. Were you thinking now?"

"Yeah, all the food's already here, so that'd probably be best."

"Then I'm on my way."

"I'll meet you out front."

Roughly half an hour later, Layla was stepping off the bus at the GDRS building, having spent the entire ride mentally prepping. Daniel was waiting out front, as he said. He grinned when he saw her. It was a calculatedly guilty grin.

"Hey," he said. "Hope you're hungry."

"For burgers and ice cream? Always."

But she stayed reserved when she answered. She had to make him think, whenever he brought up the plan, that he made her change her mind. Which shouldn't be difficult, given how highly he thought of himself. But she was worried that if she started out agreeable, not still upset about last night, he would get suspicious.

They walked up to his office with the usual catching-up small talk, neither of them invested in the conversation. When they entered Daniel's office, Layla's eyes were caught by the food.

It was...a lot. No way would they need burgers, four bags of chips, fries, *and* ice cream. It was just the two of them.

As if sensing her thoughts, Daniel said, "We don't have to eat all of this. I just wanted to make sure you got your favourites." He took a deep breath. "Look, before we start eating, I just want to say... I'm sorry. I got so caught up in figuring out how to reach the goal, I...I didn't think of how it would sound to you. For that, I'm sorry."

A carefully crafted apology, which never actually apologized for what he did but for how she received it. Typical.

"Apology mostly accepted," she said.

Daniel's face fell. "Mostly?"

"Once I eat, I think I'll be more inclined to make it completely accepted."

Daniel grinned. "Well, then let's eat!"

The food was great, and Layla couldn't remember the last time she'd enjoyed hanging out with Daniel this much.

She had to remember to save some room for the ice cream. No way would she be able to finish an entire tub, which she usually couldn't anyway, but she'd be able to have some at least. She took the chocolate fudge brownie, and Daniel worked away at the chocolate chip cookie dough.

Too soon, Daniel put down his spoon and took another deep breath.

"What I suggested last night," he said, slowly, carefully.

Oh no, here it comes.

"Even if it was out of line...it would work, wouldn't it?"

"It would," Layla had to admit. "But that's not the point."

"No, that's exactly the point." Daniel put the ice cream aside. He leaned forward. "Layla, think of all the good you can accomplish."

Layla stared down at her ice cream.

"I'm not asking for anything major. Just pretend to be in danger, so that A—Shayne will come to rescue you, and I can trap him."

Layla ate another spoonful.

"Please, Lay Lay...think of all that can come from this."

She already knew what would come from this. All the civilians out of danger. Less fear in the city. Her brother gone. The good, and the bad. Sacrifice her brother to save how many other lives from future damage.

The Diamonds had promised last time that they wouldn't hurt Shayne, but they'd also promised the powder would only knock him out. But what choice did she have? She couldn't pretend like the only reason she was hesitating was because Shayne was her brother. Was that enough to excuse all the bad he caused, crimes he committed?

"What would...me being in danger look like?" she asked cautiously.

Daniel's eyes lit with excitement, which just as quickly was replaced with a neutral look. How unnerving. "That depends," he answered.

"Depends on what?" Layla asked.

"How we're gonna get his attention. Any thoughts?"

Layla mentally debated, then revealed, "I have his phone number."

Daniel lit up again, but this time he didn't try to hide it. "Perfect! We can send him a picture."

"Of what, though?"

"Picture of you, uh, you tied to a chair or something."

Layla shuddered.

"Or," Daniel added hastily, "you could just pretend to be knocked out."

Layla mulled this over. "All right. I'll do it." The words were heavy on her tongue, but she forced them out.

"Yes!" Daniel jumped up. "I have everything else arranged and even got a few volunteers to help out."

"Wait. You recruited people before I agreed?"

"Oh. Well...I was going to do something at least. Probably wouldn't have worked as well, but, you know. Duty calls."

They just looked at each other for a few seconds.

Then Daniel said, "Well, c'mon!"

"What, now?"

"Yes. The longer we wait, the more damage the Spades can do."

Which was logical, she had to admit.

Layla took a deep breath, steeled herself, then said, "Then let's go."

"I never knew that we had a basement," Wyatt whispered into the darkness.

"The bodyguard unit uses it for training," Daniel explained.

Mason clicked on the light switches. The lights went on one by one, which Layla thought was unnecessary.

"No duh," he said.

Roped-off training areas, mats, dumbbells, weights, and punching bags filled the basement. There were change rooms and benches off to the side.

"Looks like a boxing training area," Wyatt said, still whispering.

"Stop whispering," Mason said.

They all filed into the room. Daniel, Layla, and seven other agents Daniel had introduced her to earlier. They had all congratulated and thanked her for being brave enough to do this for their city and for their country. Apparently, none of them minded that Daniel didn't have permission for this.

"Where is the bodyguard unit then?" one agent asked. Layla couldn't remember his name.

"Today and tomorrow they're at another training facility," Daniel said. "Mandatory skills assessment."

What perfect timing.

"I thought he was in the bodyguard unit," the same agent said, pointing at Cameron.

Yeah, Cameron was one of the agents. Great.

He crossed his arms. "Yeah, why wouldn't we *all* just abandon the people we're watching and leave them to the hands of the people we're supposed to be protecting them from? I go tomorrow so that someone can take my place."

"Okay!" Daniel interrupted. "Layla, you have two options. We can tie you to a chair, or you can just...lie down in the boxing ring, I guess. Pretend you're knocked out."

She was starting to wish she *was* unconscious. She wasn't sure if she just wanted to get this over with as fast as possible or back out entirely. But with Cameron here, that wasn't an option. This was happening.

"I'll lie down in the boxing ring," she answered.

"Okay, go ahead." Daniel gestured to it.

Feeling self-conscious, Layla headed to the ring. She ducked in between the ropes.

Why is it even called a boxing ring? she wondered. *It's a square.*

"You're good. Just go ahead and lie down," Daniel called. He had her phone out.

Everyone was staring at her.

Layla lay down, trying to make it look like she was authentically knocked out. Not that she had any idea what that would look like.

"Perfect," Daniel said. "Close your eyes."

Layla obliged.

This might possibly be the weirdest thing I've ever done, she thought. *I wonder if Shayne'll come.*

Part of her wished he didn't, but another part would be extremely offended if he didn't.

"Okay, you can sit up now," Daniel said.

Great. She opened her eyes and sat up.

Daniel was typing on her phone—probably the text.

The other agents were situating themselves into hiding positions. Except Carly and...that other girl. She had been introduced to six new people at once, she couldn't be expected to remember all of them.

"I expect the Ace to come immediately and alone," Daniel announced. His back was to Layla as he addressed all the agents. "But we are prepared in case he has other Spades. Be alert. Do *not* engage until I give the order. He is attentive and likely to spot some of you. If you attack before I have time to distract him, he could see and run before we have a chance to get him. Agents Carly and Annalise will be waiting in a supply closet by the bottom of the stairs in case this happens, but it's a risk I am not willing to take. Do you understand?"

They all nodded. Several brought out their guns.

"Hide."

They disappeared.

Daniel sat down on the edge of the ring and leaned against the ropes. He looked at Layla and grinned. "This is it."

Layla felt her heart sink. Yep. This was it.

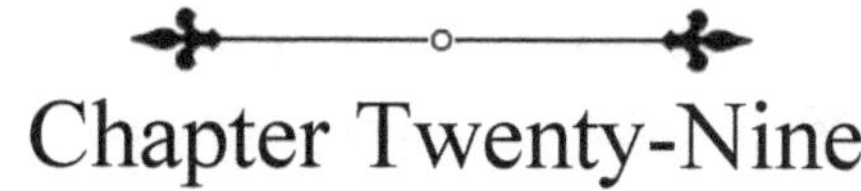

Chapter Twenty-Nine

Shayne didn't know why he'd ended up in the hospital, sitting next to a sleeping Karsyn. He'd had to wait a bit for his mom to leave, and the whole time he tried to convince himself to turn around. Go back to headquarters. What could be accomplished by a visit? Potentially an arrest, which was the last thing he wanted.

But despite the risks—which he increased by removing his sunglasses without knowing if Karsyn's room had security cameras or not—he had to see Karsyn. Had to.

Karsyn had so many bandages, and Shayne's heart ached to see them. All the Clubs doing. Nothing on Karsyn's part had warranted such pain. He just had the unfortunate luck of being related to Shayne.

Shayne almost hadn't even recognized him but not because of the bandages or bruises. How many years had it been since Shayne had seen Karsyn in person? Now here he was, almost an adult. No longer a chubby toddler, running happily around the apartment while they all did their best to make sure he never realized the severity of their situation.

Looking at Karsyn was too much. Sighing, Shayne lowered his head into his hands.

"Why did I choose this path, Karsyn?" he said aloud. "It seemed like my only option at the time, but I'm not so sure about that now. Maybe it would have all turned out better if I hadn't done what I did that day. But that's the worst part, almost. I think if I had a second chance, I'd still do the exact same thing. Every time." He laughed bitterly. "What does it matter now, anyways? I chose a bad time to get philosophical."

"Dude, the worst time," a voice said.

Shayne cautiously lowered his hands and gazed at Karsyn, who was staring back.

"You couldn't have thought of any of that before this happened? I can't play basketball now. For, like, ages, the doctor said." Karsyn's words were serious, but his tone was somehow light.

"You know who I am?" Shayne wasn't sure why he whispered.

"Yeah. You look like Layla," Karsyn said. "But with my hair." He squinted. "Actually, yours is a lot darker. But I've seen pictures of you before. When you were young. You mostly look the same but more muscley."

"I was a pretty gangly teen. That's true." How could they be talking so casually? "Are you going to kick me out?"

"Nah. Not right away, at least." Karsyn adjusted his blanket. "Why're you here?"

"Because you're hurt. And it's my fault." And nothing he did could ever make up for that.

"Yeah, Layla said that too."

Fair.

"I'm so sorry, Karsyn," Shayne said.

Karsyn's eyes narrowed slightly. "Sorry for being a criminal in the first place or only that I got hurt as a result?"

Dang, what a direct question.

Shayne hesitated, even though he knew the answer. Sometimes he wished his morals were better. Most times, he didn't care.

"That you got hurt," he admitted quietly. "But I'd give up everything if it meant it had never happened."

"So why don't you?" Karsyn's eyes pierced him. He still had such big brown eyes. "Turn yourself in."

"Well, I mean, I can't just—that's a lot of jail time! Plus, you know—" He didn't want to.

Karsyn sighed. "Then you don't really care."

"No, I do!" Shayne scooted his chair closer. "Listen, I am so sorry that you have to have a criminal for a cousin, but—"

Karsyn put his hand up. "I'm gonna stop you right there. I don't care that you're the Ace of Spades. It's pretty lit, actually."

What. How could he say that after getting hurt because of Shayne's position?

"But would it kill you to actually act like my cousin? Layla told me you've visited her a few times. Why haven't you tried to see me?"

Again, what? None of this was going remotely in the direction Shayne thought it would.

"I didn't know what Mom would do," Shayne said. He'd wanted to try, sure, but fear had held him back. What if all his mom looked at him with was contempt? Disgust for a son that had chosen a criminal path? He didn't think he'd be able to recover from that.

"You still could've called or something," Karsyn mumbled.

"Are you *pouting*?" Shayne said in disbelief.

"No." Karsyn pouted further.

"You totally are!" Shayne exclaimed. "Stop it! You're, what, sixteen? Good grief."

"Seventeen," Karsyn corrected, bringing his lip back into its normal position. "Whatever."

Shayne couldn't help but grin. Some things hadn't changed.

"All right," he said, "I promise to do my best to keep in touch with you. Starting now."

"Can you really keep that promise?" Karsyn asked, his voice tinged with doubt.

"I'll do my best. I'll even give you my phone number."

He brought out his phone. Oh, a text from Layla? Odd, she'd never written him before.

But when he looked at the message and the picture accompanying it, it was clear they weren't from Layla. His blood ran cold. "I have to go," he managed to get out.

"What? Why?" Karsyn's voice was an inch from whiny. He'd already grabbed his phone.

"Layla—it's...she..."

Shayne didn't understand. He hadn't retaliated. Why would they do this?

Understanding dawned on Karsyn's face. "Dude, don't just sit there! Go!"

Shayne ran from the room, phone tightly clutched in his hand. *I'm coming, Layla,* he thought.

Chapter Thirty

Daniel tapped his foot. It had only been fifteen minutes according to his watch, but he was already growing impatient. He could see that Shayne had read the text. Shayne would undoubtedly come as fast as he could, but depending on where he was in Toronto, it could be up to two hours.

Ugh. He hoped it wouldn't take that long.

Daniel let his head fall against the corner post of the boxing ring. He wasn't able to wait like this for two hours, alert, adrenaline simmering. The longer Shayne took, the bigger the risk that their plan would be discovered. Daniel shuddered to think what Ms. Curts's reaction would be. She'd never understand, no matter how he explained it.

But wait. Footsteps!

Daniel perked up. But two minutes passed, and no one entered. Daniel frowned. He must have imagined it.

Oof, that wasn't a good sign.

He looked around, trying to clear his mind. He couldn't see any of the agents. Hopefully Shayne wouldn't be able to either.

Layla was lying down in the ring, eyes shut. He'd explained to her the necessity of staying perfectly still no matter how long it took for Shayne to come. If she was sitting when Shayne entered, the whole thing could be ruined. She had agreed, albeit reluctantly. Like a champ, she hadn't moved a bit. Daniel almost wondered if she had actually fallen asleep.

Daniel's ears twitched. He heard something, but it took five more seconds for his brain to register what it was. Footsteps, pounding down the stairs.

Shayne, for sure.

Daniel arranged himself into a Shayne-like position. A relaxed, careless arrogance.

The door was pulled out, and Shayne walked in. He took in the scene. He noticed Layla, and his eyes widened.

"Daniel!" he shouted. He was shaking with barely constrained rage.

Excellent. Let that cloud his judgement. He would be easier to take down.

"So, you finally decided to show up," Daniel said casually.

"Did you do this?" Shayne demanded.

"Are you alone?" Daniel asked.

Of course he was alone. But Daniel wanted to draw this moment out. Savour it.

Shayne strode forward suddenly and aggressively. Unbidden, Daniel flinched, then hated that he had.

That's not happening again, he vowed.

"If you hurt her, I'll kill you," Shayne announced.

A laughable thought. Daniel almost wanted to see him try.

"Relax, I only knocked her out," he lied. "She won't even have a headache when she wakes up."

"How could you?" Shayne shouted.

Daniel had never seen him filled with such rage. Ever.

"How could you drug your own cousin?"

Daniel shrugged and stood up. "The end result is worth it."

"No, it's not."

"You in jail? The Spades taken down?" Daniel stepped off the edge of the boxing ring. "Safety of everyone in Toronto increased? Who cares if I drug her for an hour to accomplish this?"

Shayne laughed. "Just because it's the lesser of two evils doesn't mean it becomes acceptable." Shaking his head, he added, "I thought you were supposed to be the moral one."

Anger coursed through Daniel. Who was Shayne to talk down to him like this? To talk about morals? Shayne had abandoned them and left Daniel to shoulder the workload!

"I'm protecting her—"

"Protecting?" Shayne scoffed.

"This will get rid of all the Suits," Daniel said, remaining outwardly calm. "When they're all gone, when she's no longer in danger—because of you—then she will be safe."

"You're insane! You could have set any number of traps for me. Why drag Layla into this? The only thing you and I ever agreed on was that we would always protect her. And Karsyn."

Shayne didn't deserve an answer to that. Instead, Daniel said, "Oh, you realize this is a trap then? Good."

"I should've known when I realized this was the GDRS building," Shayne muttered.

Yeah, he really should've. He needed to be more analytical.

Shayne continued. "But I hope you realize that even if it is a trap, I'm going to fight with everything I've got until Layla is free."

It was Daniel's turn to laugh, and it felt good. "Till she's *free*?" He repeated. "Are you aware of how foolish you sound right now? Once we have you, I'm going to let her go. Fighting is pointless."

Shayne shrugged and stuck his hands in his pockets. "Then I suppose I should turn around and walk out. Right now."

Yeah, right.

"Except you wouldn't leave Layla," Daniel said.

"I might, if you're just going to let her go anyways," Shayne countered. "What would be the point?"

Panic surged through Daniel, but he just as quickly clamped it down. "I half-believed you," he said with a scoff-laugh. "But you couldn't just leave. You hate me too much."

Daniel could practically feel the anger rolling off of Shayne in waves.

"Which makes me want to leave all the more, actually. Just to spite you. Because, funny enough, I don't feel like going to jail today, thank you." Shayne did a short, shallow bow.

How could Shayne still sound unconcerned and cocky? Daniel had the upper hand! There was no way Shayne was escaping.

Well, Daniel could match his tone.

With leisurely motions, as if he had all the time in the world, Daniel pulled out his gun. He brought it up and aimed at Shayne. "Then I'll just have to shoot you before you can leave."

He didn't miss the way Shayne shifted uneasily. Shayne brought his hands out of his pockets.

"No!" Layla cried from behind him. "Daniel, you couldn't!"

Shayne took a step back, eyes wide.

Daniel cursed under his breath. This complicated things.

What was going on?

Shayne couldn't wrap his head around this new development. Daniel had announced his intention of shooting Shayne, which didn't worry him for a second—like Daniel had the guts. But all of a sudden, Layla was on her feet. When she yelled her protests, her voice wasn't groggy or anything.

It was dawning too slowly on Shayne that she'd never been unconscious at all.

"What? You...you were—" He gaped, too thrown off-guard to be annoyed at his lost composure.

Daniel laughed, and it was the most unhinged he'd sounded yet. "What's the matter, Ace," he taunted. "Cat got your tongue?"

Layla, at least, seemed guilty. "I'm sorry, Shayne," she said.

Just like that, confirming his worst fears. She had been a part of this plan to trap him. She had agreed to it.

"Please believe me when I say I had no choice," she said, her voice shaky.

And just like that, Shayne's anger at her evaporated and was redirected towards the person who actually deserved it. Daniel. What lies did he tell? What threats did he utter to get Layla to agree to this? And while he might not have actually drugged her, Shayne fully believed he would have if Layla had said no.

Just like he was starting to believe him fully capable of pulling the trigger this time.

Right. Better refocus on the little problem of Daniel pointing a gun at him.

"You can't win this one, Ace. Just give up." Daniel's eyes glinted.

Shayne's brain kicked into high gear. How to get out? He wasn't dumb. He knew there were agents hiding in this room somewhere. So why hadn't they already...of course. Daniel wanted all the glory for himself. Hopefully he threatened them into waiting for his signal, and they were cowardly enough to listen.

Shayne would make sure Daniel never had time to give that order.

But it was too risky to shoot him. Layla was behind him, and if he missed...

"I'm never giving up," Shayne said.

In one fluid motion, he pulled his own gun out and shot Daniel's foot. Daniel shouted in shock and anger and probably pain. He was so startled, he dropped his gun.

Shayne sprang, like a giant cat. He latched onto Daniel, and they went crashing to the floor. Luckily, Daniel mostly cushioned Shayne's fall.

Daniel tried to scramble for his gun. Shayne blocked him and punched him in the jaw.

Layla was shouting something, but Shayne's brain wasn't computing the words.

Shayne managed to wrap his hands around Daniel's throat.

"I'll kill you," he seethed.

Daniel tried to speak, but he couldn't get enough air. The words came out a weak rasp. He struggled and thrashed but to no avail. Then Shayne heard the door bang open.

Someone started shouting, "Everyone freeze! Ms. Curts—oh!"

This was enough distraction that Daniel managed to wrench Shayne's hands from his throat and wiggle free of his grasp.

"Attack!" he shouted weakly, massaging his throat.

The agents burst forth from their hiding places.

Shayne sprung back up to his feet. Was this all? What, seven agents, one of them a middle-aged woman, who, judging from her outfit, would not be fighting.

He grinned and rolled his shoulders. He could take six. Especially if he could get back to his gun.

They all swarmed him at once. Adrenaline coursed through his veins as he threw punches, swept legs, kicked knees, and ducked. He took a few hits, but he hardly felt them. He hadn't felt this alive since they robbed the Clubs.

He was only fighting three now. Two had withdrawn, clutching their injuries. The girl who had been shouting hadn't joined, for some reason. This was almost too easy.

Until more agents started pouring into the room.

Shayne did a double-take that cost him a hard blow to the stomach. He was still trying to regain his breath when the new agents jumped into the fight.

He was vaguely aware of a stern voice saying, "Don't shoot him! Subdue him."

Faster than he would have liked, Shayne was brought to his knees. He struggled against the agents holding him down, but it was no use. He realized, heart sinking, that he wasn't going anywhere.

Daniel limped into his line of vision, his expression triumphant.

"You see, Ace! No escape!"

"Daniel Edward Zakkar!" thundered the older lady still standing by the doorway.

Despite the situation, Shayne couldn't help but be amused. She knew Daniel's middle name?

"Would you care to explain what is going on?"

"We have caught the Ace of Spades!" Daniel exclaimed. He gestured grandly, which Shayne thought was a little much. "And we can use him to take down the Suits, one by one." His eyes were focussed on Shayne, still savouring the victory, apparently.

The woman's expression turned so fierce that Shayne almost felt afraid for Daniel. Almost.

All the agents visibly tensed. The atmosphere became charged. An explosion was about to happen, and Daniel was the target.

Yes. Shayne couldn't wait to see this lady start yelling at Daniel.

But in that moment of silence, Shayne heard a thud from behind him.

Oh. Layla had fainted.

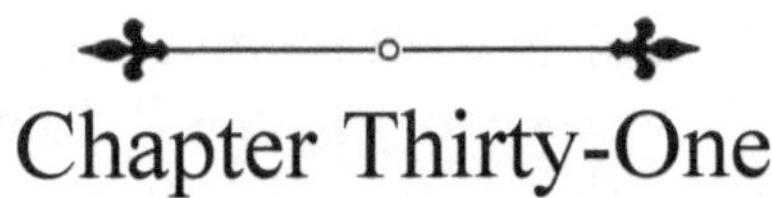

Chapter Thirty-One

Layla was regaining consciousness faster than she liked, being drawn into a state of awareness by whoever was yelling. From the sounds of it, they were yelling at Daniel. Good. He deserved it.

Memories of the way Shayne had looked when she stood up came flooding back to her, and she groaned. It had physically hurt her to see the betrayal in his eyes.

She pried her eyes open to see...Cameron. Cameron was right there in her direct line of vision. What the heck?

As soon as her eyes were fully open, Cameron leaned over. He spoke quietly and urgently.

"Cry," he said. "Cry. You're emotionally unstable. Daniel lied to you. You're just generally upset."

Layla didn't know what he was talking about, but she nodded anyway so she wouldn't have to hear his voice anymore.

Cameron helped her sit up, and she was able to take stock of the scene. She was in some sort of nurses' office, laying on a cot with the crinkly paper. Daniel was sitting on a cot opposite her, and a nurse was bandaging his foot. Ms. Curts was giving Daniel a loud and stern piece of her mind. Daniel occasionally shouted back, but he never got far.

The nurse winced every time he shouted. Whenever he moved, she would mumble, "Please stay still."

He didn't seem to hear her.

Layla had half a mind to join Ms. Curts. She had a few things to say herself, and she would've, if she had the energy. But every lie she got told was harder and harder to recover from. Daniel had been going to kill Shayne! Shayne had actually shot Daniel.

"And you are now fired," Ms. Curts said. "From the entire GDRS. Permanently."

Daniel's mouth hung open. "What?—you can't," he sputtered. "I just captured the ACE OF SPADES! Why am I getting punished?!"

Quite calm now, Ms. Curts said, "You disobeyed my direct orders. I didn't assign you to the Spades for a reason. And if you cannot follow my commands now, you never will. Did you meet with the Diamond Queen, too?"

Daniel's silence was confirmation.

"Double the reason then." Her voice was steel, and Layla flinched, even though Ms. Curts wasn't addressing her.

Daniel tried to protest. "I don't get—"

"If you still don't understand now, then nothing I say will change that." Ms. Curts looked at the nurse. "You are finished now." It was supposed to be a question, but it was said like an order.

The nurse nodded.

"Then put him in a wheelchair and wheel him out of my building."

"I can walk," Daniel said.

"You have a bullet in your foot. You cannot."

"Oh, what about—" The nurse had noticed Layla was awake.

"She's fine," Ms. Curts said. "Go."

So the nurse wheeled a protesting Daniel from the room.

Ms. Curts turned to Layla. "So..." she said. Then she didn't say anything for a long time.

Layla resisted the urge to squirm under her gaze.

"Did you know that you were agreeing to help him do something that wasn't yet approved?" Ms. Curts asked.

Cameron's elbow was already resting against hers because of the way they were sitting on the small cot. But when Ms. Curts asked that, Layla felt him press it closer, ever so slightly. What he had said earlier suddenly made sense now.

"No, I had no idea," Layla said. "Why would I have ever suspected that he didn't?"

"Why indeed?"

Ms. Curts seemed to stare straight into Layla's soul, which was worrying. If Layla knew anything, it's that she never wanted to get on Ms. Curts's bad side.

"So why did you agree to his plan?" she asked.

Layla let her head drop, so she was looking at her lap. "Karsyn got hurt because of Shayne," she mumbled. "Daniel convinced me that if Shayne was no longer the Ace, our family wouldn't be at risk anymore."

Cameron's elbow pressure increased.

"And I was afraid of how he might react if I disagreed," she added.

"Hmmm." Ms. Curts's eyes narrowed. "Of course you would be afraid. He has shown himself increasingly unstable. Cameron, could I please have a moment alone with Layla?" Cameron must have looked like he was going to protest because Ms. Curts added, "You are only her bodyguard, and these are sensitive matters."

Cameron nodded and said, "Of course," so neutrally, Layla almost believed him.

Ms. Curts went with him to the door, then pointed out somewhere he could sit. She watched him go until, presumably, he sat down. Then she closed the door and came back over.

"Now, Layla, I want you to be completely honest with me. Can you do that?"

No. Cameron had given her earrings earlier, just before she met with Daniel, that had little microphones in them. Anything she said, the Diamonds could hear. And if she said anything about them to Ms. Curts, she doubted they'd still feel inclined to just let her walk away.

"Yes," she said. After a second's hesitation, she also shook her head "no."

Her heart constricted. What would Ms. Curts's response be? She was pretty sure the microphones were able to pick up whatever Ms. Curts said too. So if she revealed anything, Layla was sunk.

But Ms. Curts didn't even appear fazed. "Great. Is there anything else about this whole business that is important for me to know?"

"No." She nodded. "I can't think of anything."

Ms. Curts walked over and sat next to Layla. "Now," she said, "I understand that today has been a lot for you..."

Layla realized that Ms. Curts had pulled out her phone and was typing something, even as she continued to talk. She handed Layla the phone. Layla read:

If you are able to use this medium, tell me whatever it is that you cannot say out loud.

Layla wanted to. She was done getting involved in these sorts of things. All people did was lie to her, use her, betray her. She couldn't take anymore. But to tell the head of the GDRS that she'd participated in Suit criminal activity?

"And there's no judgement," Ms. Curts said pointedly, then continued. "If you are feeling tired..."

Layla started typing. She wrote out:

I made some bad choices. The Diamonds approached me a while ago. I got involved with them. My involvement is supposed to end as soon as I help them break Shayne out of here. But I'm worried they'll threaten me to keep helping them.

She handed Ms. Curts the phone. Oh, wait, should she have said something about the bugged earrings? Too late now.

Ms. Curts said, "Well, now that I've talked your ear off, do you understand what I've been telling you? Any questions?"

As she started to read, Layla said, "I understand. I just—" she sighed. "It's so frustrating!"

"Of course it is," Ms. Curts said.

Woah, she was a fast reader.

"And you are completely allowed to feel frustrated. But I have something that might help. These"—she held out her hand, which now held what looked like a Bluetooth earbuds case—"instructions." *Trackers*, she mouthed.

Layla's heart flooded with gratitude. She took the case, which was flatter than the average earbuds' case.

"Go home, and rest," Ms. Curts said.

Layla opened the case. Two small, dark grey circles. Like a sphere that was cut in half. The back looked like a magnet.

"Take as much time for yourself as you need," Ms. Curts continued. "Those are my instructions."

"Thank you!" Layla said. This was more than she could have hoped for. Her mind whirled with the possibilities, the ways she could use the trackers.

"Of course." Ms. Curts stood up. "I'll let you go home now. Please, rest. You need it."

Layla nodded. "I will."

She wished she could. But that wasn't an option. Not yet. She had a brother to break out, and trackers to place.

This was all going to be over soon. And she couldn't wait.

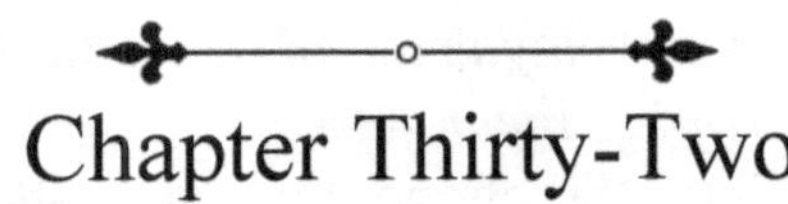

Chapter Thirty-Two

"**L**ayla?"

Ryden sounded confused, as well he should be. Layla hadn't wanted to call him, but she had no other way to tell the Spades about Shayne. She hadn't seen him since the night of Karsyn's accident, and he hadn't tried to contact her. She assumed Shayne told him she had figured out he was a Spade.

She let her voice be shaky. "Ryden, it's Shayne. The GDRS they—they have him."

"What? Are you sure?" Ryden exclaimed.

"One hundred percent."

Ryden went quiet. "I'll have to tell the rest of the Spades," he said. "But they won't believe just me. You'll have to...if there's any hope of convincing them to rescue Ace, you'll have to come to headquarters and explain."

"Why would they need convincing?" Layla asked.

"Not everyone likes your brother," Ryden said grimly. "Myself excluded. But we should be able to convince the rest." He didn't sound sure. "But are you okay with that?"

"Of course. It's my brother we're talking about."

And the sooner she was taken to their headquarters, the sooner she could place the tracker.

She had it all figured out. One tracker at the Spade headquarters, one at the Diamond headquarters. Such a simple thing, placing a tracker, but the results...significant, if everything went right. And too many things had the potential to go wrong.

She also appreciated the irony of trying to do the exact thing she had gotten mad at Victoria for doing.

"All right, I'll be there as fast as I can," Ryden said.

As fast as he could turned out to be twelve minutes later, when he knocked on her door. When she opened the door, a flood of emotions almost knocked her off her feet. Just by looking at him. She was almost annoyed with herself. Nope, scratch that, she was.

"All right, you ready?" he asked.

"Nope." She held a finger up. "First, I'd really appreciate an apology from you."

This would delay them a bit, but it was important to her.

Ryden drew his head back, looking surprised and guilty at the same time.

"Of course, I'm sorry, Layla, but we have urgent things to do."

She stared at him.

He sighed, and his gaze softened.

"I truly am sorry, Layla. I really did like you—"

Ha. Whatever.

"And I never wanted to lie to you."

And yet he did anyway.

"Ace isn't good at thinking long term. He wasn't considering all the ways my act could go wrong in the future. Also, it's not like I really had a choice, since he's my boss. But I am sorry. I understand if you can never forgive me for what I did."

She had no intention to. She'd experienced how well he could lie and been completely deceived by it. How much of this (subpar) apology could she believe?

Didn't matter. She had heard what she wanted to hear. And now she could let it go. Part of her couldn't believe she'd managed to be so assertive and asked for an apology.

Mentally smiling, she nodded and said, "Okay. Let's go."

As they walked down to the car, Ryden said, "Just so you're prepared, once we're in the car, you're going to be blindfolded so you can't see where we're going. Security reasons, obviously."

Obviously. Not that in this case it would help them.

"Once we're there," he continued, "we're gonna be scanned for active trackers."

Oh. That was inconvenient.

"Active trackers?" Layla echoed.

"There was a tracker incident recently, as you're probably aware. Can't risk our location falling into the wrong hands."

"Hmmm. Why scan, though? Wouldn't a simple search—"

"Not if the tracker is so tiny it's been sewn into your sock or something."

"Ah."

Layla brought a hand up and fiddled with her earring. Were they trackers as well as audio transmitters? It wouldn't surprise her, but she hoped if they were whichever Diamonds were listening turned the tracker off for the scan. That would not be beneficial if they didn't.

Ryden led her out to the parking lot where their ride awaited them. It was a black limousine. Subtle.

The door opened. Ryden grabbed a blindfold from someone inside.

"I'm sorry," he said.

"It's fine," Layla said.

"I'll be gentle," he promised.

Someone inside coughed.

"She won't be able to see us. Don't worry," Ryden snapped.

He tied the blindfold around her eyes.

"Is that too tight?" he asked.

"No, it's fine."

"Good." Ryden fiddled with it, making sure her eyes were covered. "I'm going to help you into the car now. Is that all right?"

The same person from inside the car groaned and said, "We don't have all day, man, let's speed this thing up."

Ryden didn't say anything. Layla got the sense he was still waiting for her permission, so she nodded. He placed his hands under her forearms, then guided her with verbal instructions into the car. And then buckled her in.

The buckling in part was extra. Layla had to remind herself that he had done nothing but lie to her. That he had never been who he pretended to be.

But on the other hand, she reasoned as the car started moving, *how can I not get butterflies when he acts so dang chivalrous?*

Ugh. Anyway, moving on.

You've got more pressing things to think about right now, she told herself sternly.

Like would the tracker in her pocket get caught by the scanner? No one would notice if they only looked at her. She'd changed into her pants with the biggest pockets, which wasn't really saying much, and put the case in there. The case was small enough and flat enough that it wasn't noticeable.

But what about the scanner? What constitutes an "active tracker"? If it meant they were in the process of actively tracking, then Layla should be fine. If the trackers were in their case, why would they have started tracking. Right?

At least, Layla hoped so. But she was not an expert on trackers, by any means. Hardly knowledgeable, really. She'd just have to keep hoping. Nothing else to do at this point.

"Are you scared?" Ryden asked. "Cause you don't have to be."

"I'm not scared," Layla said, which made the mystery person snort. "But I am nervous."

Going into the Spades' headquarters, she'd consider herself silly if she wasn't nervous. Nervous because she had to succeed. But there was an element of excitement, also. She felt like a spy on a mission that was finally being led by the good guys.

But a spy in charge of her own destiny, because Ms. Curts had never told her how she had to use the trackers. Only given them to help her. Layla was choosing to use them to do the right thing. She had made some mistakes, but they had placed her in the perfect position to benefit the city of Toronto.

The car started slowing, and Layla's heart started beating faster. The car felt like it pulled into a parking spot. Then it stopped.

Ryden assisted her out of the car, then started undoing the blindfold.

"C'mon, wait," the mystery person said,

"What's there to see?" Ryden snapped again.

He took the blindfold off, and Layla could see again. There really *wasn't* much to see though.

They were in a standard underground parking lot, filled with assorted black vehicles. They had gotten out right next to the elevator.

"I'm telling Mom you snapped at me again," Mystery Dude muttered.

"Grow up," Ryden said.

Layla looked over and had to stop herself from laughing. It was an older Ryden, if Ryden's hair was naturally unkempt and he had terrible fashion sense. It was the brother whose pictures they'd mocked on their first date.

"Shall we?" Ryden gestured towards the elevator, and they moved towards it.

Not-Ryden pressed the button for the 18th floor.

"When we get out, someone will be waiting with the scanner," Ryden explained as they went up. "They'll scan all of us, then we'll go to Meeting Room F, where all the 10s should be gathered."

Layla's heart skipped a beat, but she nodded. This was the first gate. Either she got through it, or she didn't.

The elevator glided to a stop, and the doors opened silently.

Two Spades were waiting for them. One had a scanner, which looked like a normal, handheld, metal-detector wand that security guards have. The other Spade had way more muscles than necessary.

Ryden exited the elevator first, and Layla followed. She was hesitant to get scanned, but Ryden also did that first. The Spade waved the tracker-detector in front of him, going head to feet. A nice sounding beep emitted from it.

"Clear," the Spade said.

Ryden moved out of the way.

Layla's heart was definitely beating fast now. She tried to take some calming deep breaths, but that's hard when you're trying not to look like you're taking deep breaths.

Not-Ryden went next and was clear.

Layla decided 'forget it' and took a deep breath. Ah, oxygen.

Then she stepped forward.

It seemed to take twice as long for the Spade to wave the detector in front of her, and an eternity of thumping heart beats for the detector to reach its decision. Which was a nice beep interrupted by a cranky beep.

The Spade frowned and raised the device. Stared at it.

"What does that mean?" Ryden asked.

"I don't know. I've never heard that sound before."

Layla desperately wanted more oxygen for her now out-of-control heart, but a deep breath would be doubly suspicious now. Could it sense the trackers? Would they search her?

"Maybe it's my earrings," she blurted out. She started taking them off.

"Why would it be your earrings?" Ryden asked.

She went over and deposited them in his hands. If the situation wasn't so dire, she would have laughed about how confused he looked. She returned to where she had been standing.

"Okay, try again?"

Looking confused as well, the Spade once again waved the detector in front of her. The verdict was the happy beep, uninterrupted this time.

If it was possible, Ryden looked even more confused. He inspected the earrings. "Uh, Layla, why did these half trigger the alarm?"

Layla shrugged and did her best to look innocent. "I don't know.

They were a gift." Which was technically true.

Realizing what her words then implied, she gasped and said, "Does that mean they're trackers?"

Ryden looked at the detector Spade, who said, "It could. If they're trackers but not currently activated, they could have confused the system."

"Who gave them to you?" Not-Ryden asked with such heavy suspicion Layla was surprised he didn't choke on it.

She hadn't thought that far ahead. But they might think it suspicious that she happened to be wearing them today, so, "Daniel," she answered. "He gave me the earrings today, actually. As an apology. That's why I'm wearing them now."

They accepted this story and decided to leave the earrings there. She could pick them up on her way out.

"Even if Daniel turns the tracker on," Ryden reasoned. "There's no way he would know this is our headquarters."

Just like that, it felt like, they were walking down a dimly lit hallway. Layla saw no reason more lights couldn't be turned on. It was unnerving. But then, perhaps that was the desired effect.

The few Spades that passed them openly gawked at Layla.

"You just look so much like Shayne," Ryden said.

"It's like we're related or something," Layla muttered.

Not-Ryden laughed.

Too soon, they reached the meeting room.

"Enjoy," Not-Ryden said. Then he melted away.

"There're probably going to be about twelve Spades in there," Ryden said. "Don't be alarmed. They just want the facts, then I'll take you right back home. You ready?"

No.

"Yes."

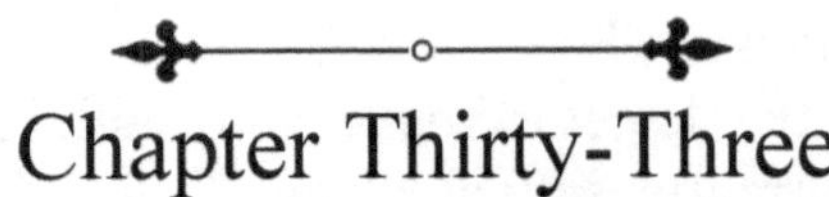

Chapter Thirty-Three

Ryden opened the door, and they entered the room. All the Spades turned to stare at them. Definitely more than twelve. Way more.

The room was so quiet Layla was suffocating.

"This is Layla Zakkar," Ryden announced. "The Ace's sister."

This brought on a few dark mutterings that made Layla involuntarily move closer to Ryden. Their gazes pinned her to where she stood.

Any excitement and anticipation Layla had felt earlier vanished. How could she sway any of their minds? How had she ever thought she could?

Ryden nudged her, and she started walking, although she wasn't sure to where. She did her best to avoid meeting any of their eyes, which meant she mostly stared at the floor.

A charade of bravery or defiance was unnecessary. They would see right through that.

Ryden got in front of her and led her to the head of the table. He moved the chair off to the side, then gestured for Layla to stand there. She did but kept some distance between herself and the table.

Timothy, who was sitting directly to her right, stood up. He addressed the rest of the Spades. "This meeting is to hear Layla's account of what has happened to our Ace. I want no interruptions. When she's done, we will discuss in an orderly manner. First, to ask her any questions, then to come to a decision. Any opposition to this?"

No one said anything.

"Great." Timothy sat down. "Layla, you may begin."

For the third time this month, Layla started explaining to others how an event had happened. This was the largest group she'd had to talk in front of, though. Slightly terrifying, especially given they were all criminals, but she tried to focus on getting the story right.

She'd figured out earlier how exactly she would tell the story. Obviously she couldn't mention any of the Diamonds' involvement.

She didn't want to mention that she chose, however reluctantly, to cooperate either. No doubt the Spades would not take kindly to that fact.

So she gave them a version that omitted the Diamonds, presented her as an unwilling accomplice, but still retained the basic fact that Shayne was now being held in the GDRS building.

At a few points, some Spades made noises like they were going to start speaking—or worse, shouting. But Timothy would clear his throat, and they'd settle back down.

She finished and mentally made a sigh of relief that she'd gotten through it without any major slip-ups.

"Well..." she said, when no one spoke. She spread her hands out. "That's it."

Timothy sighed and pinched the bridge of his nose. He muttered something about Shayne under his breath. It didn't sound complimentary.

He stood up. "We have heard her story. Any questions?"

A Spade not far down the table said, "Yes, I have a question." She stood up, which Layla thought was unnecessary. Flipping her very red hair behind her shoulder, she glared at Layla and said, "Why should we trust your story? What evidence do you have that this isn't just a ploy by the GDRS to capture more of us if we go to rescue our Ace?"

A few Spades murmured in agreement.

Layla involuntarily snorted.

The redhead's eyes shot sparks.

"Uh, sorry," Layla said hastily. "It's just...what purpose could that possibly serve? That the GDRS would maybe have a few Spades in custody. How would that help them?" Layla wanted to elaborate better, but the Spade's glare was too intimidating, and her brain wasn't working properly.

Timothy spoke up. "She's right. Plus, we have already demonstrated how easily we can break into their building and rescue those in their custody. I do not think this is a ploy, Autumn."

Autumn crossed her arms. "I don't care. I want proof before we take needless risks."

"I can show you the picture Daniel sent to Shayne," Layla said. "He used my phone."

Timothy held out his hand.

Layla dug her phone out of her pocket, which was not the same one she'd put the tracker in. She knew better than that. She brought the texts up and handed it to Timothy.

He studied them, then nodded. He passed the phone to the next Spade, and they all took turns looking at the photo. Then Timothy took her phone back and put it on the table.

"I'm just going to keep this for now," he told her.

She nodded. Fair enough. She was surprised they had allowed her to keep it this long.

"I also have a question I would like to ask if that is all right," said a quiet voice from the very end of the table.

"Yes, Julia, proceed," Timothy said.

"I was only wondering if you could, perhaps, explain why you would choose to call Ryden after these events transpired," she said.

Well wasn't that a lot of extra words.

"Shayne's my brother," Layla answered, "And I don't want him to be in jail."

Julia fiddled with her hands. "You are saying, if I understand correctly, that you would rather he be free and participating in criminal activities, which I'm assuming you disapprove of, than have him be in the custody of the people you deem, again, I assume, in the right in terms of good and bad?"

What?

Layla stared at her as her brain short-circuited, trying to find what Julia had actually said.

In an undertone, Timothy said, "You'd rather Shayne be free and committing crimes than in the hands of the 'good guys'?"

"Oh. Oh, I mean—yes. Although, admittedly, neither option is...great. But," Layla sighed, "he came to my rescue. So I owe it to him to go to his."

Autumn scoffed and rolled her eyes. Why was she still standing?

"Any more questions?" Timothy asked the table.

"Why should we rescue your brother?" an older man asked. He adjusted his glasses and leaned forward. "You want us to. That is clear. But why should we?"

Layla frowned. "What?...You...he's your Ace! Why wouldn't you guys want to rescue him?"

A lot of shifting up and down the table.

The man adjusted his glasses again. "He was not always competent, and there has already been discussion of replacing him. This would be a rather painless way to do it."

Layla did her best to make herself look like she was panicking. She widened her eyes, took short, shallow breaths, and looked around. In reality, when Ryden had given her the warning, she'd taken the time to think of an argument. But they didn't need to know that.

"Well, you...All right, so even if you guys don't care about him anymore, you still need to rescue him."

"Why? For you?" Autumn asked, her tone dripping with hostility.

Wow, she was just mean.

"No—yes. That is..." Layla took a deep breath. "Shayne would know how you all feel about him, given how openly hostile some of you are." She made it a point to look anywhere besides Autumn. "So he probably wouldn't conceal anything from the GDRS if they start questioning him. If he no longer has any loyalty to the Spades,...what's to stop him from giving away this location?"

Autumn's eyes widened, as did many others. "He wouldn't dare..." she trailed off.

"He would too! He's been a thorn in our side for years, and now he's going to turn on us!" someone shouted.

"We made our intentions clear," another said. "And now we're going to pay for it. He won't withhold information."

More and more Spades started speaking, and clear words were lost in the din.

Timothy rolled his eyes and said something in Ryden's ear. Ryden nodded, then took Layla's arm.

"Let's go wait outside," he said.

Five minutes later, and they were still waiting outside, which, in Layla's opinion, was far too long. But she still needed to plant the bug somewhere, without Ryden noticing. But she would never be allowed to leave him. Unless...

"Ryden?"

He looked over.

"Is there a bathroom I can use?

He hesitated. "It's not that there isn't. It's just...well, I'm not supposed to let you out of my sight. They're already mad enough that I let you in here."

Doing her best to infuse her voice with a carefree lightness, Layla said, "C'mon, what mischief could I possibly get into? They've already searched me. I don't have my phone on me."

Ryden scratched the back of his head. "It's the other Spades that

I'm worried about, really. Oh, but there's a single bathroom somewhere on this floor."

Layla slowly let out the breath she had been holding. She could place the tracker there. No one would ever think to look there. Of course, no one should be looking for a tracker at all.

Ryden led her down the hallway, and after a few left turns, one right, they were at the bathroom.

"I'll just, uh, be waiting out here," he said.

Layla entered the bathroom and shut the door. She paused. No, there wouldn't be security cameras in the bathroom. That would just be wrong. No. She just had to figure out where to place the tracker. And quickly, because Ryden was waiting.

She scanned the room. A typical bathroom. The back of the tracker was magnetic, but were any surfaces in this bathroom magnetic? She didn't have enough time for trial and error. Her heart was pounding in her chest, and she was convinced any moment Ryden would knock on the door and ask what was taking her so long.

Her eyes landed on the trash can. Of course! Who's going to look in the trash can—for anything? Hands shaking, she pulled the tracker case out of her pocket. She pulled one out, activated it, and dropped it into the trash can.

That was done. The GDRS had a way to get to the Spades' headquarters.

She flushed the toilet, then washed and dried her hands, just in case Ryden was close enough to hear. Then she left.

"Thanks," she said, then dropped her gaze. She couldn't look him in the eye for long. Somehow she felt her eyes would betray what she did.

Twenty minutes later, and they were *still* waiting outside. Layla had gotten tired of standing and was sitting against a wall, thumping her head against it. Neither of them were in a conversational mood, so there was nothing to do. Except dwell on all the bad possibilities. Because that was helpful.

"They're going to rescue him," Ryden said. "They have to. You made some great points." He sounded like he was trying to convince himself as well.

The door opened, and Layla scrambled to her feet. Timothy stepped out. He closed the door.

"We're going to rescue him," he said.

Layla let out a breath. Good. She just hoped the hardest part was over, but she had a feeling this whole ordeal was going to be hard.

"What's the plan?" Ryden asked. "Who's going in?"

"You," Timothy said.

Ryden nodded, looking resigned.

"Mai and J as well," Timothy continued. "They wanted the whole team that broke into the Club headquarters with Ace, but Ash refused, point blank."

"Doesn't surprise me," Ryden muttered.

Timothy looked at Layla. "And you're going in too."

"What? Why?"

"With you, we can get him easier and much more efficiently. You are going to ask to see Shayne. We'll put a tracker on you so we can find out his exact location. Then you just have to let everyone else do their part."

More trackers. Great. So technically she was about to break into the GDRS. Huh.

It's for the greater good, she reminded herself. Not that that made her feel a ton better, but once again, what choice did she have?

Then something occurred to her that did make her feel better. This was how she was going to get the Diamonds' location! If she was with Shayne when he was rescued, and then the Diamonds did...something to get Shayne. They'd take them all to their headquarters.

Layla grinned. "Excellent," she said. "Then what are we waiting for?"

Ryden raised his eyebrow. "You sure?"

She nodded. "Absolutely."

She'd never been surer.

In a few hours, this was all going to be over. Her life could return to normal.

Personally, she couldn't wait till her biggest worry was her job at Staples and trying to explain to customers that no, they couldn't just take a display laptop home for a few days to "try it out."

"Let's do this," she said.

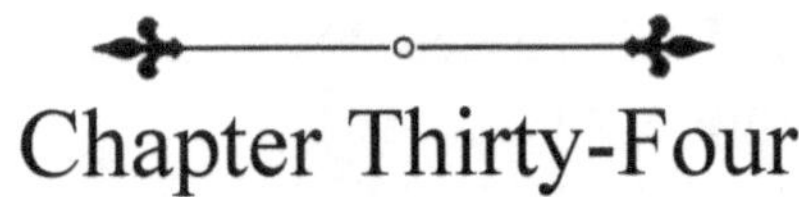

Chapter Thirty-Four

The black SUV that looked completely normal, and so far sounded completely normal, but Ryden swore had a souped-up engine, pulled into the GDRS parking lot. Ryden parked it.

"You ready?" Ryden asked Layla.

"You ready" was starting to be the new "Are you okay" in her life, and Layla wasn't enjoying it.

"I'm about to break into the GDRS and break out a major criminal," Layla said. "Why on earth would I be ready for that?"

Ryden frowned. "I recommend a slight attitude adjustment. If we're gonna succeed with this, you need to be confident."

"Surely false confidence is worse than legitimate trepidation?" Layla asked.

Ryden put an arm up on the wheel and turned to look at her. "What?"

"Just something Victoria likes to say," Layla muttered. "I'm ready, let's do this."

"Good luck. I'll be waiting right here."

Layla opened the car door.

"Good luck!" Mai whisper-shouted from the backseat.

"Yeah, you're gonna kill it," J said.

Layla got out. She took a deep breath, fiddled with the earpiece she'd received, and then started walking towards the main entrance.

There was only so much anticipatory anxiety one person can feel, and Layla had reached her limit. Either this worked, or it didn't. If it didn't, that would not be great for her, but—her stomach swooped. She had to stop walking and take a few calming breaths.

Apparently she hadn't reached her limit.

This is no small thing, she told herself. *So it's okay to feel anxious. But I've got to do it. So the Diamonds can be shut down.*

The Diamonds who'd lied to her, tricked her, and used her. She was going to bring them down.

Her earpiece crackled and Ryden's voice came through.

"Layla, are you okay? Why did you stop?"

"I'm...fine. Just...some anxiety, but I'm good now." She started walking again. "I'm good now."

She entered the building.

All right, first step done. So far so good. Now to find someone who knew where Shayne was and would allow her to visit him. Layla wanted that to be Ms. Curts, as she would understand there was something bigger going on. Ms. Curts would let her.

"Layla," a voice said.

She turned.

Mr. Greer was walking towards her. Maybe he would allow her to visit Shayne?

He reached her. He frowned. "I know why you're here," he said.

Layla's adrenaline spiked.

"You can't fool me," Mr. Greer added.

How could he know? Did Ms. Curts tell him? He was going to spoil the whole thing!

"I wouldn't try to fool you," she managed to get out. It seemed like a good choice to say.

Mr. Greer sighed and shook his head. "Sibling sentiment. You must understand I can't possibly let you."

Layla didn't know what to say to that. She was too worried that he would reveal what was going on. She had two Suits listening in, as she'd gotten her earrings back. If either one of them found out the truth, the whole plan was ruined.

"Shayne is a criminal, Layla," Mr. Greer said firmly. "And visiting him now will only make this harder. On both of you."

Visiting?

Did...did he not know...?

Cautiously, Layla said, "I know, but please. Just five minutes."

Mr. Greer was shaking his head.

"He came to rescue me. I feel guilty, and—"

"Then why did you agree to bait him in the first place?" Mr. Greer asked.

Layla's heart stopped, and her eyes widened. No, no, no.

"Layla?" Ryden's voice came through the earpiece. "You agreed to Daniel's plan? You told us he drugged you!"

"I didn't have a choice," she said, more firmly than she'd meant to. "I never would have gone through with it if I had a choice."

Ryden didn't say anything.

Mr. Greer frowned. "Regardless, I cannot allow you to see him."

"No, please, you have to—"

"Layla!"

Ms. Curts! Yes!

She walked over, all business. She frowned. "What are you doing back here? I thought I told you to go home and rest."

Before Layla could answer, Mr. Greer said, "She wishes to visit Shayne."

"Only natural, I should think."

"Yes, but we cannot let her. The security issues involved..."

Mr. Greer wasn't looking at her, so Layla pleaded with Ms. Curts with her eyes.

"I don't see why she can't have a few minutes with her brother," Ms. Curts said.

Layla breathed a sigh of relief.

Mr. Greer motioned with his head, and Ms. Curts followed him a few feet away. Layla could just make out their voices but not the words. Mr. Greer was definitely protesting.

"Layla..."

Ryden. Again.

"What?" She tried to move her lips as little as possible. More difficult than she thought it'd be.

A pause. Then, "Did you really have no choice? Because if you choose, I will abort this mission right now. We will try again without you, because if you can't be trusted—"

"Ryden," Layla said. "I promise. I didn't have a choice."

And they definitely shouldn't trust her.

"I trust her," Mai's quiet voice came through. "She has a good heart."

Layla was oddly touched by Mai's comment. It almost sounded like Mai was...excusing Layla for the fact that, technically, she was about to betray them. Even though they were the criminals in this equation, Layla couldn't help but feel bad. Who knows what circumstances brought them to where they were, and if they hadn't had a choice either?

Ms. Curts came back, without Mr. Greer. "It took some persuading," she said, "But I can give you five minutes."

"Thank you," Layla said. "It means more to me than you know."

"Don't make her suspicious," Ryden hissed.

If Ryden didn't stop talking, she wasn't going to be able to focus.

"Ryden, chill dude," J said. "You keep distracting her, she's gonna mess up."

Thank you.

Layla guessed that Mai and J were on the move already, otherwise J wouldn't have needed to use the earpieces to say that.

"Follow me," Ms. Curts said.

Ms. Curts led her to the elevator, which they took down to the basement level.

"He's being held in the training area?" Layla asked.

She wasn't eager to see that again.

"No," Ms. Curts said. "There's another section to the basement where we keep any Suits until they can be transferred to a more secure facility."

Seems like they could just send them to the regular prison, but what did Layla know?

The elevator came to a stop. They exited it and right away, boom, two security guards.

"Badge?" one asked, which Layla thought a bit extra. Even the head of the GDRS needed to show her badge? They couldn't just...recognize her?

Ms. Curts showed her badge, vouched for Layla, and they were allowed to continue. They hadn't walked very far before they reached a set of doors that required a scan of Ms. Curts's ID. She scanned. The doors beeped and opened.

"Wow, high security," Layla remarked. She was growing nervous about their chances of breaking Shayne out.

"We don't want to take any risks," Ms. Curts said. "Especially with the possibility of break-ins." She gave Layla a knowing look.

But that's what needed to happen! How could Layla communicate that to Ms. Curts?

As it turned out, she didn't need to.

Ms. Curts held out a hand for Layla to stop, and put her finger in front of her mouth. She held out her phone, where she had once again written something. When, Layla had no idea.

It read: *You may have my ID badge if you need it, but I must warn you, I am trusting you, but your actions are your own. I have no knowledge of your plan, so I can neither condone nor disapprove.*

That seemed fair.

Every risk you take, you take on your own. Or, you can tell us all the details, and we can put you under protection, if necessary. Your choice.

Layla looked up at Ms. Curts, then back down. She hesitated.

She could. The tracker for the Spades was placed already. Did they really need the Diamonds too? They didn't seem to do anything, and Layla really was taking risks here. There was no telling if she'd even succeed in placing the second tracker, or if she'd even get the chance.

If she didn't, Shayne would be left in the hands of the Diamonds, and there's no telling what they'd do...

But no. This could be the GDRS's only chance at the Diamonds for *years*. And Layla wanted to stop being involved in all of it. Snitching now would only ensure she spent the rest of her life living in fear. The Diamonds would hold a grudge, she knew that much. They'd bide their time and wait.

No, Layla didn't plan on living her life out like that. She was ending the Suits. Today.

Well, that was a bit of a stretch. She was...kick-starting the process of shutting down two of the Suits. Yeah.

She handed back the phone, shaking her head.

Ms. Curts nodded. She didn't look pleased. It was more of an acceptance. She gestured, and they resumed walking. As they did, Ms. Curts slipped her ID into Layla's pocket.

They rounded a corner, and Layla's insides shrivelled. Too many agents. Security guards. Whatever.

There were two standing on either side of their doors. She counted...eight. Yeah, that was eight too many.

Ms. Curts led her to the first door on the right and informed the agents that she was allowing Layla five minutes to speak to her brother. In private.

Layla was inspecting the door. Some thick steel, with a tiny window at the top that didn't have glass. It had bars.

One of the agents pressed their ID badge to a scanner on the left on the door. It beeped, and Layla was allowed to enter.

"I hope you accomplish what you wanted," Ms. Curts said.

But Layla wasn't listening. Shayne was staring at her, his expression dark. The door was shut behind her.

"Why could you possibly have wanted to come here?" Shayne

asked.

The room seemed to hold little security itself. Shayne was leaning against a wall. One of his wrists and one of his ankles were handcuffed to a chain attached to the wall, allowing him some movement. Layla couldn't tell if there was a security camera in the room itself.

"Well," Shayne prompted.

"I'm here to rescue you," Layla said.

Shayne laughed. "Seriously? You're the entire reason I'm in here right now—you know Daniel couldn't have pulled off his plan without you. So, what, you suddenly had a change of heart?"

Layla sighed. "Can't you believe that I had no choice?"

It hurt that he would suddenly think so little of her.

"You know, I did. But after stewing in here, alone, for a few hours, I don't think I can anymore."

Honestly...fair enough. Layla could respect that, given she'd absolutely helped trap and jail him, and that was the only piece of the puzzle he had.

"You know, I just can't understand why," Shayne said. "How could you do this to me, Layla? Your own brother? You would jail your own brother?"

Normally, Layla would have felt guilty. But now, she just stared at him. So done. She was so emotionally done with this.

"You may be blood-related, yes," she said. "But that doesn't excuse you—"

"Excuse me?" Shayne repeated, spluttering. "Last time I checked, I didn't need your—"

Layla huffed and turned around, no longer listening. "Ryden, I need you to give me some instructions here, otherwise I might punch someone."

"We're gonna have to move fast," Ryden said. "Our people still haven't managed to hack into the security cameras. They've patched the holes from the last time. Can you get Mai and J in there?"

"Yes."

"Then head back now. Mai, J, move in. Then, Layla, just follow them."

"Will do." Layla turned back to Shayne, who had gone silent, eyes wide.

"What...?"

"Just be ready to move," Layla said.

She knocked on the door, and one of the guards opened it. Layla froze for a second, wondering if they had been able to hear any of that. But neither gave her a passing glance as she walked out.

The set of doors didn't need ID when you were going out, so she passed through those easily. Then she reached the elevator. As she waited for it to descend and tried not to meet either of these agent's eyes, she wondered about Ms. Curts. Was she going to do anything to help them? To make sure they would succeed?

Layla doubted it. Ms. Curts had made her uninvolvement clear.

The elevator door opened, and there was J.

"Badge, ple—"

The agent didn't even get to finish. J had both of them knocked out faster than Layla's eyes could register.

"How...?"

He grinned. "Years of practice. C'mon, let's go."

"Where's Mai?" Layla asked as she followed after him.

"Turns out, this section"—he waved his hand around—"has its own security room, with cameras and everything. Mai's gone to deal with that. The old-fashioned way."

Which Layla assumed meant more knocking out.

"Hey." J frowned.

They had reached the doors.

"These need ID, man."

"What?" Ryden exclaimed. "Layla, you didn't—"

"Stay calm." Layla grabbed Ms. Curts's badge out of her pocket. "I have ID."

"You stole that?" J asked admiringly. "Niiice."

The scanner beeped, and the doors opened. Layla didn't bother to correct him as they continued down the hallway.

"It's just around this corner," Layla whispered. "What now?"

"Put this over your mouth and nose," J said, handing her a little...gas mask thing?

It had a triangle part that felt like a mix between rubber and plastic, which fit over her mouth and nose area perfectly. It stuck to her face in a way that was tight but not uncomfortable. The triangle had a tube that connected to a small oxygen tank. Like, small. Layla hoped she wouldn't need it to breathe for too long, whatever J's plan was.

J put one on his face as well. As Layla watched, he rolled a small steel ball around the corner. It had lines etched in its surface, like grooves.

Layla heard a hiss. If she had to guess, it sounded like some sort of gas. From the ball? Hopefully just knockout stuff. She didn't want to be responsible for a bunch of deaths!

"It only takes thirty seconds to knock them out," Ryden said, as if he had heard her thoughts. Bodies were starting to thud to the floor. "Then all the gas will be sucked back in, and you'll be clear."

The sound changed. Now it sounded like someone sucking in their breath through their teeth. Then, silence.

J held up a hand. He glanced around the corner, then nodded and removed his mask. "All good."

Layla handed him her mask. "Did all that fit into your pockets??"

"Yeah," J said casually, looking at her like he didn't understand why it would be a big deal.

He went around the corner.

"That's so unfair," Layla mumbled, following.

J also grabbed the gas-ball device and pocketed it too.

"Which one's Ace?" he asked.

Layla pointed to it. All the guards were on the floor, unconscious. J stepped over the bodies and inspected the door. Just as Layla was about to say that he probably needed one of the guard's IDs, J swooped down and grabbed one. He pressed it to the scanner.

Beep!

It unlocked, and J pushed the door open.

"It's about time," Layla heard Shayne drawl.

"Man," J said with a chuckle. "You should just be happy we're here at all. Thank your sister for that one."

"Really?"

Layla reached down and grabbed the key for Shayne's handcuffs off of the female agent's belt. She hoped it was the right one, anyway. She didn't see any other option.

"Yeah, she's the one who convinced the Spades to still rescue you. But you're no longer the Ace, man. Not a chance."

Layla straightened and handed J the key. "Try this."

"And *speed*, guys!" Ryden said. "Anyone remember me saying that?"

J went and unlocked Shayne's handcuffs. Shayne was watching Layla with an expression she couldn't decipher, and honestly, she didn't care to.

Once he was free, Shayne rubbed his wrist and rolled his ankle.

Sounding like an exasperated parent, Ryden said, "If none of you are on the move yet, you have five seconds to do so, or I stop helping you."

Layla thought he was kidding, but judging from the way J and Shayne sprang into action, he must've been serious.

They took off down the hallway, leaving Layla in their metaphorical dust. She had not been prepared to start running, at all. Her body protested as she scrambled after them. A calf muscle flared with pain. Layla must have pulled something with that sudden start.

By the time she reached the elevator, they were already standing there, waiting for it to descend.

She came to a halt, gasping for air. Maybe she should consider doing more running when all this was over. Her stamina was embarrassingly low.

She was vaguely aware of Ryden giving some instructions but didn't bother to try to hear them. Shayne and J were probably listening.

The elevator arrived, and they hurried inside. J pressed the button for the fourth floor.

"What? Why not the ground floor?" Layla asked, massaging the back of her calf.

"Wha—did you seriously miss everything I just said?" Ryden spluttered. "Why do I even bother!"

"It's super quiet where this elevator comes out on the fourth floor," J explained. "Not a high traffic area, really close to a back stairwell. Better this way."

"Ah, got it."

Layla noticed Shayne was now wearing J's hoodie, with the hood flipped up.

"Mai's already out," J continued. "And there's gonna be cameras once we step out."

Ryden took over. "Which, as I said, means move with purpose. Fast but not rushing. They can't be looking everywhere at once, and this is not a high-priority area. But if they realize Ace's missing too soon, we might be done for. I'll tell you when to start running."

Not more running. And down stairs? Sure, stair chases were super dramatic in movies but not super realistic in real life. At least they'd only have to run down four floors, at the maximum. That was doable, right?

The elevator stopped, and Layla held her breath. If an agent was on the other side when the doors opened...

Nope, all clear.

They strode out, following J. He led them to their left, where sure enough, stairs.

Even with Ryden's instructions, Layla itched to go faster. If it was likely no one was watching these cameras, why couldn't they just run? Not that she wanted to, but she wanted to be out of here as fast as possible. She couldn't stop fiddling with her earrings and accidentally popped one out.

"Don't go back for it," Shayne said under his breath.

She didn't plan on it. Instead of risking losing the other one, she put her arms around her stomach. Like a self-hug.

An alarm blared throughout the building, echoing through the stairwell and making Layla jump.

"Run, run, run!" Ryden exclaimed.

J took off, somehow managing to take the stairs two at a time. Layla tried to go as fast as she could but running down stairs is just an awkward thing, and now she was certain she'd pulled something in her calf, which also didn't help her speed. Her heart was pounding in her chest, along with their footsteps on the stairs.

Shouts, now, also echoing up and down the stairwell. She couldn't tell if they were coming from above them or below.

"Whatever happens, don't stop!" Ryden yelled.

Layla flinched. People speaking into earpieces should never yell.

They were about to pass the door connecting to the second floor when agents burst through it into the stairwell. J leapt at them, limbs outstretched, taking all four down. One hit and their heads were on the ground with a nasty thud.

Shayne and Layla continued on.

"What about J?" Layla asked.

"Don't stop, just go!" Shayne said.

Layla gripped the railing for support, so she could go faster without worrying about face planting.

If they got caught now, the GDRS would never get the Diamonds. Layla didn't know if she would ever be able to explain the situation properly. They couldn't get caught!

Layla heard footsteps behind them and risked looking over her shoulder. Phew, just J.

Then she hit something solid, headfirst. Pain burst in her head, and she saw stars. Shayne grabbed her arm.

"Watch where you're going!"

She was disoriented but had to continue running. It took her a full minute to realize she'd run into the wall where the stairs turned. Ow. She could already feel it bruising.

Shayne kept a hand on her arm to steady her.

They reached the ground floor, and there was the exit!

Agents shouted behind them, their voices, footsteps, and alarms mixing and reverberating in a way that made Layla's head ache even more.

The door opened, and they were outside!

Layla skidded to a stop.

No! More agents!

Shayne somersaulted forward and knocked two of them over, like a human bowling ball. Interesting strategy but effective. J jumped forward, punching the gun out of one agent's hand and kicking it out of another.

Layla was frozen in place, watching with awe as the two of them fought the five agents. It was like watching blurs.

A car horn honked, and Layla saw their getaway car.

She scrambled around the fight and jumped into the backseat. Mai was sitting there, grinning.

"Excellent job, Layla!" Ryden said encouragingly, not taking his eyes off the fight. "Even if you didn't listen to me once."

"We're not out yet," Mai reminded them, sounding far too cheerful.

The agents were on the ground. Not all were knocked out, but it was enough of a pause for J and Shayne to jump in. Shayne in the front with Ryden, of course.

"Nice to see you all in one piece," Ryden said. "Hang on!"

The car shot forward, going from zero to one hundred in what felt like two seconds. This was definitely no regular SUV. Tires squealed as Ryden drove out of the parking lot and into the street. He dodged around cars and squeezed through an intersection a mere second before the light turned red.

This was not safe. At all.

"Please tell me everyone's wearing seatbelts!" Layla exclaimed.

"We've got more pressing matters!" Shayne said.

"Your seatbelt isn't on?" J exclaimed.

Huffing, Shayne pulled his seatbelt down and clicked it in. "Happy now?"

Layla practically fell onto Mai as Ryden made a sharp right turn.

"Where to?" Ryden asked. "Can't go back to headquarters yet. It's too risky that they'll follow us."

"Just get out of the city," Shayne ordered. "The fastest route. We'll regroup there."

Ryden moved through traffic, absolutely speeding, but with zero fear. This was Toronto, so Layla fully expected they'd crash before they made it to safety.

Mai was keeping watch out the back window and would periodically report that they were still good, no one was following them.

Ryden was like a ghost. No car touched them, and in way less time than Layla would have ever guessed, they were in the suburbs. Next thing she knew, they were out of the city completely on some small back road.

J whooped. Layla could see Shayne settle back in his chair, tension going out of his shoulders.

Ryden slowed down a bit, as they were now on a much smaller, less travelled road. But still going faster than Layla would have liked.

Ryden went to turn around the corner, and the car spun out of control. He fought the steering wheel, but they crashed into the ditch.

Layla wasn't surprised but was just thankful that it wasn't any worse. Her head didn't appreciate the impact or being tossed about like that, but they were all still alive.

"What happened?" Mai exclaimed.

"Anybody hurt?" Shayne asked, turning around to look at them.

"Naw, we're good," J said casually, as if he was used to cars suddenly spinning out of control and crashing. "You crashed, Ryden. What's up with that?"

"One second." Ryden climbed out of the car. He bent down and inspected the tires. "Flat!" he exclaimed. "Blown out by a...dart." He stood up and scanned their surroundings. "Someone did this on purpo—"

He stopped, stumbled, then slumped to the ground. A small dart with a red feather on it stuck out of his neck. It was then that Layla noticed two red cars driving towards them from opposite directions.

Oh! The Diamonds.

In all the chaos, Layla had almost forgotten that there was more to be done.

Ugh, all she wanted to do was ice her head and sleep! But no, she had to stay alert. Place the tracker.

"What is this?" Shayne said.

Before any of them had time to do more than register what was happening, their car was surrounded. Guns were out, pointed at the car. Blood-red diamond earrings in every ear.

"Come out!" one man shouted.

"Oh. That's not good." Once again, Mai did not sound like she was fully appreciating the gravity of the situation.

Shayne took a deep breath, then got out, hands raised. No fear showed on his face.

The man smirked. "Ace. How nice of you to join us."

He pulled the trigger on his gun, which shot out a dart into Shayne's chest. Shayne crumpled to the ground.

Layla swallowed.

"What are the rest of you waiting for?" he yelled at them.

A lady opened the backseat and smiled mockingly. Neylan!

"Come out. Come out and join the party."

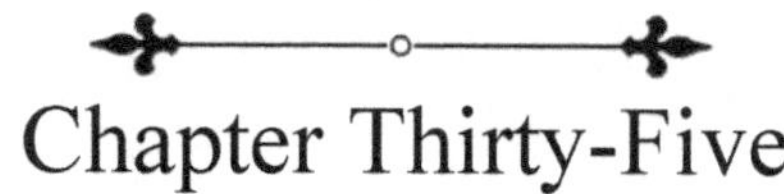

Chapter Thirty-Five

"I am thoroughly unimpressed by the way things have turned out."

"Really, Mai? Unimpressed? Why? Surely ending up in the Diamonds' jail was part of the plan!"

Layla groaned in pain as she woke up fully, and missed Mai's response.

As more of her senses returned, she was able to take stock of the situation. She was lying on a hardwood floor that was, woah, really good quality. But her whole body ached as if she'd just run a marathon. Her head, especially, hurt. If she didn't get some painkillers in her, she was going to pass out again from the pain.

Unsteadily, she pushed herself up into a sitting position. She didn't trust herself to stand.

The cells themselves were surprisingly nice. Nothing like what she'd picture if someone said "jail." They were clean, a comfortable temperature, and the benches (one per cell) were cushioned. Except for the wall of the room, the cells themselves had only bars for walls, meaning she could see Ryden in the cell next to her.

Shayne was pacing like a caged animal in the cell across from hers. J, in the cell to Shayne's right, was lying on the bench, unbothered. Mai (to Shayne's left) was sitting on the floor, holding J's hoodie against her leg. The material was too dark to tell, but Layla hoped she wasn't bleeding.

"Hey, you're awake," Ryden said. "How're you feeling?"

"My head hurts."

"Yeah, headaches are a common side-effect from these kinds of darts," he said.

J snorted. He sat up. "No, man, she ran into a wall. That's why her head hurts."

Ryden stared at her. "You ran into a *wall*?"

She half-shrugged. "Well...there was a lot going on," she mumbled. He shook his head.

Layla looked over at Shayne. His eyes had been on her, but as soon as she looked, he went back to staring at the floor. Still pacing.

Should she apologize to them now? Let them know...But what good could that do?

The trackers!

The thought bolted through her, and her eyes widened.

Had they searched her? If they had...if they discovered the tracker...

That thought was not helping with the rising nausea she was already trying to fight off.

J lay back down. Ryden asked Mai how her leg was doing, and they started talking. Everyone was distracted.

Casually, Layla put her hand in her pocket. Her heart dropped, and she shivered. Empty. Maybe it was the other pocket?

The only thing in that pocket was Ms. Curts ID, which they must not have thought important.

The GDRS tracker was gone.

Layla brought her knees up and buried her face in them. She wanted to cry, but that would only make her head hurt worse.

To come all this way and fail. How was any of that fair?

Ms. Curts had put faith in Layla, but now...

The GDRS wouldn't get to capture the Diamonds.

She'd just made them lose the Ace of Spades.

What would happen to her?

If the Diamonds realized what she had been trying to do, what would happen to Karsyn? Or her mom?

She felt guilty, scared, and frustrated all at once.

"Layla..." Ryden said softly. "Are you okay?"

She lifted her head. "No." Those were definitely tears sliding down her face.

He reached through the bar and put a hand on her knee. He opened his mouth, as if he was going to say something comforting. Then he closed it.

Good. She didn't really deserve his comfort anyway.

The door at the far end of the room burst open, and a Diamond stormed in. He stopped in front of Layla's cell and glared at her with an unreasonable amount of anger, considering they'd never met. Cameron strolled in after him.

The Diamond, who had on a blindingly yellow (of all colours) tie, slammed his hand against the bar. Everyone flinched. "Where is your other earring?" he seethed.

What?

"You're missing one of the earrings we gave you," Cameron explained. "Where is it?"

The room's temperature seemed to drop from "comfortable" to "frigid." Shayne froze. J sat up. All eyes were on her.

"Layla," Cameron prompted.

"I was fiddling with it, just out of habit, and it fell," she answered.

Yellow-Tie Guy threw back his head and laughed. "Yeah, and I'm supposed to believe this is a habit of yours—WHERE IS IT?"

Layla hugged her legs closer to her. "In the GDRS! Why?"

Yellow-Tie Guy took a step back. Then his face got close to her cell. "This could ruin us," he hissed. Then he stormed from the room.

"Don't mind him," Cameron said. "He's...always like that."

"What?"

"Well, the earrings are also trackers. Duh."

Yeah, she'd figured that.

"So, Francis was worried that if someone got a hold of the other earring, they could do some MacGyver stuff to figure out where you were."

"Is that...possible?" Layla asked.

"Yeah, in the show *MacGyver*, maybe. Real life, I'm thinking not so much. But they're already not happy with you after discovering the tracker in your pocket. What's up with that, Layla?"

She shrank in on herself.

Cameron shook his head. "You really could have just walked away, Layla, and you would have been fine. I'm sorry you thought you had to do that. It's still unactivated. No one's coming for you."

She closed her eyes. How stupid had she been to even try? Now everything was going to be so much worse.

Her cell door opened. She opened her eyes. Cameron was helping her up.

"C'mon, let's get you medical attention for your head," he said.

They were walking out when Shayne said, his voice deadly, "Stop."

Layla automatically stopped. Cameron did too, albeit reluctantly. She turned to face Shayne.

He was staring at the ground, not meeting her gaze. "The Diamonds gave you earrings...that are trackers. You conspired with the Diamonds?"

Layla stared. How could she explain? How could she explain that they threatened to hurt Karsyn? That she had believed them when they said Shayne wouldn't get hurt? That she had thought she could be a hero?

"How dare you," he said. "I'm your brother."

He was. It was true. But...

"You left us," she said.

Shayne's head shot up.

"We were struggling, and you left Daniel and Mom and me and Karsyn. We were in an awful situation, and you ducked out of it and all the responsibility you had, making it *so* much worse for the rest of us." Her voice was rising. "Then you thought you could just jump back into my life as a brother once we'd made it out of that? No. You've been a criminal apart from our family for more time than you spent being my brother. Because of you, I got kidnapped by the Clubs. Because of you, Karsyn was in a car accident. Because of you, the Diamonds approached me and threatened me. I owe you *nothing*."

"Damn!" Cameron whispered.

Shayne swallowed. He nodded and turned aside.

Cameron led Layla out.

"That was awesome," he said.

It didn't feel awesome. But it did feel...therapeutic, in a way, to finally voice those feelings.

"Just in here," Cameron said, turning into a much smaller room. "Sit there."

She sat on a bench that looked the same as the one in her cell. Comfy. But it was also the only thing in the room.

Cameron shut the door.

"What's going on...?" Layla asked. "There're no medical supplies in here."

"No, I..." Cameron seemed to struggle with himself for a second, then held out his hand.

In his palm was the tracker.

"I—you—what?"

"Take it."

Hastily, Layla scooped it up. "Why are you giving this to me?"

"I didn't know I was going to till now," he muttered.

Huh?

"Don't get me wrong," Cameron said. "I am leaving this building once I escort you back to your cell. Last thing I'm doing is getting caught by the GDRS. But you, you're just a kid who got roped into something much bigger than yourself."

Something more was going on here.

"This isn't a trick, is it?" she asked.

He shook his head. "It's payment of a debt I owe someone. Someone who...I can't repay anymore. Plus, hearing the way the Diamonds were talking about you"—he shrugged—"None of this could have happened without you, yet they're talking about you like you're just a tool for them to use and dispose of. They don't deserve a victory. Neither does the GDRS, honestly, so I'm still hoping there's mutual destruction and no one really comes out on top, but...as long as you make it out."

She reminded him of someone.

"Thank you."

"Please don't thank me. I don't want to think I've done something right here."

She grinned in spite of herself and activated the tracker.

No one was talking to her. Icy silence was all that greeted her when Cameron brought her back to her cell, which was just fine with her. Not only had he not gotten her medical attention, he'd given her way more to think about.

Mostly grey areas. Grey, grey areas. Grey people. Grey actions.

She sighed and rubbed her forehead. She was in too much pain to try to figure anything out right now. This whole ordeal was gonna take time. Lots of time. And probably therapy.

How long would it take for the GDRS to get here? And how fast would they find her once that happened? She had no idea what time it was, and there was no way she was trusting herself to make an accurate estimation.

An alarm blared in the distance. They all jumped and turned towards the noise, as if there was something to see. Layla could faintly make out gunshots and shouting.

The GDRS! It had to be!

"What's going on?" Ryden asked the room at large.

Layla grinned.

"Uh, Layla, you know what's happening?" J asked.

"If it's what I think it is...it's the GDRS," she answered.

J threw up his hands. "I'm so confused, man. Someone update me when this is all done as to who's on whose side."

Mai laughed to herself. "Layla temporarily sided with the Diamonds and the Spades at the same time to bring down both. She brought the GDRS here."

Layla had to nod. How had Mai figured all that out?

"You did all that?" J asked.

"Not by choice, really," Layla had to admit.

"Stuff of legends," J said.

Shayne scoffed. "What, you're happy about that?"

"I'd rather be in the GDRS's prison than the Diamonds. So yeah, I'm happy about it."

The door burst open once again.

Please don't be Yellow-Tie Guy, Layla thought.

It was.

C'mon!

He headed straight for Layla. He was calm this time, which terrified her more than if he'd been his angry self.

"So...you still brought them here?" he said. "How?"

"Blame Cameron," Layla said. She hoped he'd made good on his promise to be far from here, otherwise she'd just sold out the guy who'd helped her.

Yellow-Tie Guy snorted. "Of course. Cameron, who's conveniently gone missing." He opened the cell door.

Layla jumped up and scrambled to the back.

He brought his gun out and pointed it at her. "You're gonna come with me."

"Leave her alone!" Mai shouted.

Layla appreciated the support, but she knew she didn't have a choice. She had to force her legs, but she walked out. "Where are we going?"

"Just keep walking. You're gonna be my ticket out of here."

Layla exited the prison room. She went straight.

"Left here," Yellow-Tie Guy instructed. "Take the stairs."

Layla's mind was racing. How was she supposed to escape this situation unscathed? No doubt he meant to use her as a human shield. Classic move. The only problem was she fully believed he could get away with it. Yeah, that was not happening. Not when she was so close to being free.

They emerged at the top of the stairs, and it was chaos. Agents fighting Diamonds in hand-to-hand combat. Guns firing. Layla's eyes were going everywhere. She didn't even have time to fully appreciate the lushness of the headquarters. Honestly, the decor looked like it was more at home in a casino or something, not a criminal headquarters.

Yellow-Tie Guy harshly grabbed her arm. "Stay close to the wall, and let's go," he said.

"What are you doing?" a female voice asked. It was Neylan again. "Nice to see you, Layla," she said.

"Could've been better circumstances, though," Layla said.

Neylan gave a tight grin, then said to Yellow-Tie Guy, "Why is she out here?"

"I'm getting outta here before the cops have a chance to grab me," he snarled.

Her eyes glittered. "You're abandoning your Suit?"

"We're all gonna get jailed!"

"Not if we all fight. But if poor-excuses for Diamonds like you are bailing, then we will."

Woah. Layla was wondering if her chances of getting killed by a stray bullet were becoming higher than Yellow-Tie Guy making it out.

This room had cleared out except for one duo fighting in the corner, but the sounds of fighting were everywhere.

Neylan and Yellow-Tie Guy were staring each other down, Layla in the middle. Layla was desperately trying to recall any self-defense tips Jason had taught her but couldn't think of any that would work when her back was to her opponent. All she could think of from movies was smacking her head back into his, and that was a "no-way" move on a normal day. But with her head hurting the way it did? No! Way!

Neylan took one calculated step forward, and Layla was yanked back, closer to Yellow-Tie Guy. She could feel his gun come to rest against her head.

Everything inside her screamed to get away from the situation, and without thinking, she dropped. Just went limp. Yellow-Tie Guy wasn't prepared to suddenly be the only thing trying to keep her up, and he dropped her. She hit the ground hard, scraping her knees.

Crawl, crawl, crawl! her brain yelled.

She scrambled on all fours for a second, then once she thought she was far enough away, jumped to her feet. She didn't dare look back, but nothing happened to her. Neylan must have started throwing punches once Layla was out of the way. She was rounding the corner just as a searing pain ripped through her leg.

Layla stumbled and went down. The already broken skin on her knees broke further, pain blossoming, but it was nothing compared to her leg. A bullet. She instinctively knew nothing else could cause this pain. But more Diamonds and agents were in this room, and neither knew whose side she was on. She had to get to safety.

It was too painful to try to stand, so she crawled. Not much better, but it was her only option. She tried not to look at the bodies she passed littered on the floor.

Then it occurred to her that she had no idea where she was going. She pressed herself into the nearest corner to try to think. Approach an agent? Wait it out? Keep going and hope for the best?

A Diamond saw her and ran towards her. She screamed and kicked up her foot, catching the Diamond in the stomach. Her leg was on fire now, and between her head and the bullet wound, she was in serious danger of fainting.

She swept her not wounded leg into the Diamond's, and down they went. Layla didn't bother trying to stay to knock them out. She forced herself to her feet and did a limp-run thing to get away.

I'm not worth it, don't come after me, she thought.

Someone barrelled into her side. She hit the ground hard, her head banging on the floor.

Her body couldn't handle anymore. It shut down.

As the darkness engulfed her, she could only think, *Please be a GDRS agent.*

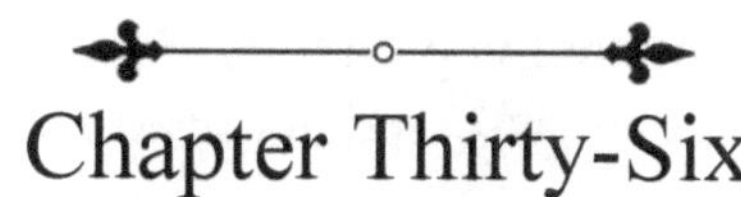

Chapter Thirty-Six

Once again, Layla regained consciousness lying on the floor. She couldn't even gather the strength to audibly express her pain. Everything hurt.

She needed to stop making a habit out of this. It was, what, the third time she had been knocked out in some way in one day? That *couldn't* be healthy.

As she lay there longer, she came to realize, actually, the pain was localized in two major spots: her head and her leg. She'd be lucky if she didn't have a concussion by now.

Arms shaking, she pushed herself up.

She was the only one conscious in a room with several other bodies on the floor. She was still in the Diamond headquarters, and it looked like the same room she'd been tackled in. It must have been a Diamond who moved on once she was unconscious.

"She's in here," she heard someone say.

Footsteps were coming closer to the room.

No! If they were Diamonds, she was doomed. She struggled to her feet but only managed to stand just as a bunch of people entered. She sank back down to the floor, relief flooding her. It was the GDRS.

Mr. Greer stepped forward, frowning. "Young lady," he said, his voice stern, "What are you doing here?"

Layla held her hands up. "I can explain."

"Please do." Ms. Curts stepped forward out of the crowd. "I would like to know how much of what I allowed goes against my ethics."

"Honestly...a lot."

Ms. Curts, being incredibly intelligent, as Layla had come to appreciate, saw right away that she was injured. She called for a medic to attend to Layla first.

"But you will be telling us today," she said. Then she smiled. "Good job."

"Will someone tell me what is going on?" Mr. Greer said.

The medics put Layla on a stretcher and carried her out to an ambulance. She'd never been in one before and almost enjoyed the ride. But the siren was killing her head.

She didn't have to endure the pain long. The doctors gave her some effective painkillers as they assessed her head and treated her leg. She only threw up twice.

The time went by in a blur. It could have been thirty minutes or three hours for all Layla knew. Diagnosis was definitely a concussion, and the bullet to the thigh, with time and physiotherapy, would heal up just fine.

Once she was finished being treated, Ms. Curts and Mr. Greer came into her hospital room. Layla was relieved to finally be able to tell the honest story, but it was also exhausting.

Mr. Greer was fighting between approval and disapproval. Layla got the sense he wanted to say more on the subject but that Ms. Curts had given him a strict warning not to. He made a lot of "hmming" noises and frowned through most of her story.

Ms. Curts just kept nodding, her face that of an attentive listener.

When Layla was finished, Mr. Greer said, "Well..." He looked at Ms. Curts, who shook her head. He sighed. "I've got agents to tend to." Then he left.

Ms. Curts gathered her breath. "Layla...I definitely disapprove of many of your choices, but you were put in difficult spots. I would never have done it that way. Once you start making deals with criminals, your bar for what is acceptable in the name of justice gets lower and lower. But I am grateful to you. You took the situation you were in and managed to turn it around, so to speak. I will have some follow-up questions, but, for now, go home. Rest." She stood up. "Your mother hasn't been called. It's been a chaotic day, what with the raid on both the Spades and the Diamonds. But I can get you a phone to call her if you wish."

Layla just nodded.

A few minutes later, an agent ran in, handed Layla an unlocked phone, then ran back out. Layla was now holding a stranger's phone. Well.

Layla called her mom, who was actually in the hospital already, with Karsyn. They had been wondering what all the commotion was about. Layla was able to get wheeled down to Karsyn's room.

She dreaded having to explain it all again, but then Ms. Curts just showed up and did it for her. Except she gave much fewer details and made Layla out to be more of a hero than she really was. Layla could not have been more grateful.

"She's had a rough week," Ms. Curts ended with. "So I suggest you don't ask her any questions for now and just let her rest."

Layla's mom was understanding, and once Ms. Curts had left, and Layla assured her mom she was okay, she fell asleep.

The next two days were blurs, and when Layla fully came to on the third day, she barely remembered what had happened since Cameron gave her back the tracker in the headquarters. Funny how she could have spent so long looking forward to the moment of victory, and when it came, it was over so fast.

Her mom was being exceedingly nice to her. Layla figured she suspected more than she was letting on, and Layla fully planned to tell her what had actually happened. Some day. Karsyn thought she was the coolest thing since sliced bread. She had already given him more details one night when her mom had gone back home to shower and change clothes.

She was sitting there in the hospital bed, wishing she could be back home, when she remembered—Jason! The last time she'd seen him, they'd argued. No, wait, the last time had been when he was waiting in the lobby, and she'd avoided him.

He deserved a full apology and explanation.

She used her mom's phone to call him (her phone was who knows where), and Jason agreed to go to her old house that afternoon so they could talk.

Layla was so nervous. Almost more nervous than when she was breaking into the GDRS, which was ridiculous, but that was how she was feeling. And guilty. She'd yelled at Jason when pretty much everything he had been saying was right. She hoped their friendship wasn't destroyed.

They went home at noon, and Layla had never been so happy to see her old house. She didn't want to stay for too long, but right now, she had no thoughts of returning to her apartment within the week.

She was sitting on her bed, clutching her Iron Man plushie, when someone knocked on her door. Layla straightened.

"I can't do this," she whispered to her plushie. "Come in!" she said loudly, stomach churning.

Jason entered, shoulders up by his ears, awkward.

Good to know she wasn't the only one who was nervous.

"Hey," he said quietly.

Layla patted the bed in front of her.

He sat.

"I'm sorry," she said, looking down at Iron Man. "I, uh, said a lot of hurtful things to you, and none of them were true. But everything you were saying was...and I—" She took a deep breath. Dared to look up.

Jason's eyes were full of forgiveness and caring, and it caught Layla totally off guard.

"It was—that is, you were going through...a lot," he said. "I understand."

"How do you...?"

"Have you, uh, seen...the news? Your story"—he gestured with his hands—"All over."

"Not the full story," Layla muttered. "And it doesn't excuse my behaviour."

Jason thought for a second, and Layla waited nervously to hear what he was going to say.

"You...you yelled," he said. "But—that is, you were...stressed. Suits, poison, it—you were in over your head."

Layla fiddled with the plushie. "Can I...can I tell you what happened?" she asked.

Jason smiled encouragingly. "Only if you...you want to."

For the strangest reason, she did.

It took way longer than telling Ms. Curts, because she threw a lot of her feelings into this retelling. Rants, frustrations, all spilled out. Jason listened, never breaking away, never interrupting unless she invited him to. His reactions were few and far between, but they were all genuine.

Layla had been dreading this moment when he knew all the bad choices she had made (who poisons their brother??), but for some reason, she felt lighter. A weight was lifted off her shoulders. Her stomach settled. She felt better than she had in weeks.

"I'm sorry you—I mean, that's a—so much!" Jason said. "Are you..." he hesitated. "Are you okay?"

Layla couldn't believe how little aversion she had to the question this time. She was so happy to be back around people who actually cared about her as a person.

"I will be," she said. "Thank you. Can you forgive me for what I said to you?"

"Of course." He grinned. "We're still, you know...still friends. If you were scared—that is, worrying. About that."

Layla looked at him, and all she could see was someone genuine. Totally different from Ryden.

"Thanks," she said. "Have I ever told you you're the best?"

Jason shrugged. "I try my best. Maybe—that is...therapy? For you? This"—he gestured with his finger—"It was...a lot."

"Oh, definitely," Layla said. "But before even that...there's something else I need to do."

Layla knocked on Victoria's door. The churning feeling in her stomach had returned. Jason's hand holding hers was the only thing keeping her steady right now. She hadn't walked this much yet, and her leg wound was burning. But she had to do this. Now.

The waiting was awful. She didn't know if she could handle telling everything again.

Victoria opened the door.

Jason squeezed her hand.

Before she could back out, Layla blurted, "There's something I need to tell you!"

Victoria raised her eyebrows. "I am listening."

Layla tried to take a deep breath, but her lungs weren't working properly. She fiddled with her earring. "I have to—" She tried to take a breath again. It worked this time. "I have to ask if you can forgive me for some mistakes—"

"Yes," Victoria interrupted.

Layla blinked. "What?"

"Forgiveness granted," Victoria said.

Layla looked at Jason, baffled, then back to Victoria. Just like that? "But you haven't even heard what I did yet."

Victoria shrugged. "I have my suspicions, but it truly does not matter to me. You clearly regret those mistakes. Jason has clearly forgiven you for them already." Her tone was light and teasing.

Layla blushed. Jason did too.

"And I trust his judgement," Victoria continued. "Additionally..." She smiled. "I value our friendship more than I am worried about you being a perfect human—such a thing does not exist."

Layla nearly wilted with relief. It felt like a heavy yoke had been lifted off her shoulders. Both her friends had forgiven her, just like that. She didn't deserve them, and it filled her with a determination to be a great friend back.

"Would you feel better if you did tell me?" Victoria asked.

Layla considered this. "Maybe some day. But not now."

Victoria nodded. "Then I am so glad to have you back, Layla. We have not been together as much as we usually have this past month. I have missed you."

Jason sniffled.

"Are you crying?" Victoria asked in disbelief.

"No—I mean, well...yes! Obviously."

Layla had to grin. It was such a normal exchange for the two of them, and yet it felt like ages since she'd heard one. Shoot, maybe she was tearing up too.

"Group hug!" Jason exclaimed, raising his arms.

He went over to Victoria, and since they were still holding hands, Layla went too.

Victoria sighed but allowed it, hugging them both tight. Layla had never felt safer.

"So," Victoria said, as they were still hugging. "Are you two a thing now?"

"Victoria!"

"Not yet!"

"What, you are holding hands! That is suspicious!"

Chapter Thirty-Seven

Layla frowned as she stared at the puzzle she was working on. There was an empty spot where there was water, yet there were literally no pieces left with blue on them. Either a piece was missing, or she was terrible at puzzles. It was definitely the latter. But the doctors had ordered a long period of rest, both physically and mentally, and one way her mom was enforcing that was by making her do puzzles.

"Aha," her mom said, fitting a piece into the empty spot.

"How?" Layla asked in disbelief.

"Practice," her mom said, grinning.

"Meaning you've done this puzzle like ten times already?"

"Perhaps."

Layla grinned too and started working on the next section.

It had been a week since she'd told Jason everything. The headquarters of all three Suits had been raided, since J had given the GDRS the location of the Clubs. Not every member of every Suit had been caught, naturally, but the majority were now in GDRS custody. The city of Toronto was safer than it had been in years. And Layla was being given a lot of the credit. Which she not only felt was too generous, but she didn't want it at all.

She had only gotten involved because of Shayne, and because she had been blackmailed by the Diamonds. She felt she deserved praise for neither.

Her mom had tried to correct her several times, saying the praise was for how she handled the situation. Turned it around. Been brave.

But Layla still felt like she'd done too many wrong things. She couldn't yet feel like they could cancel out the good that had happened, even though the elimination of the Suits was an extraordinary feat.

She had told her mom everything. There had been lots of tears.

Victoria and Jason had been most understanding. Giving her space when needed, coming over and distracting her when that was needed.

Karsyn was on the mend and was already back to painting with the hand that wasn't broken.

As for Shayne...he was also in the custody of the GDRS. Her mom had tried to see him, but he hadn't wanted to talk to her. Layla wasn't sure yet what her feelings concerning him were. They also didn't know what his future held. He had been the Ace, and he refused to cooperate with the GDRS.

Layla didn't know what her future held either. But it was steadily getting better.

About the Author

Helen Lawrence grew up in a small town in Northern Ontario, on a 60-acre property, and has wanted to be an author ever since she could write. She loves daydreaming about her scenes and then forgetting what she thought up. She is never short of ideas, just short of time. Currently, Helen goes to university for English and Piano, and procrastinates her assignments by writing her books.